what it's
like in
words

what it's like in words

A NOVEL

ELIZA MOSS

HENRY HOLT AND COMPANY   NEW YORK

Henry Holt and Company
Publishers since 1866
120 Broadway
New York, New York 10271
www.henryholt.com

Henry Holt® and Ⓗ® are registered trademarks of
Macmillan Publishing Group, LLC.

Distributed in Canada by Raincoast Book Distribution
Limited

Library of Congress Cataloging-in-Publication Data

Names: Moss, Eliza, author.
Title: What it's like in words : a novel / Eliza Moss.
Other titles: What it is like in words
Description: First edition. | New York : Henry Holt and
    Company, 2024.
Identifiers: LCCN 2024011655 | ISBN 9781250355058
    (hardcover) | ISBN 9781250355065 (ebook)
Subjects: LCGFT: Novels.
Classification: LCC PR6113.O874 W47 2024 |
    DDC 823/.92—dc23/eng/20240329
LC record available at https://lccn.loc.gov/2024011655

Our books may be purchased in bulk for promotional,
educational, or business use. Please contact your local
bookseller or the Macmillan Corporate and Premium
Sales Department at (800) 221-7945, extension 5442, or
by e-mail at MacmillanSpecialMarkets@macmillan.com.

First Edition 2024

Designed by Meryl Sussman Levavi

Printed in the United States of America

10 9 8 7 6 5 4 3 2 1

For my parents

Now, to pry into roots, to finger slime,

To stare, big-eyed Narcissus, into some spring

Is beneath all adult dignity. I rhyme

To see myself, to set the darkness echoing.

—Seamus Heaney, "Personal Helicon"

what it's like in words

When I was six weeks old, Mum left me in a playpen for three minutes, and returned to find a boy standing in the pen, holding me, his teeth clamped around my pink head. I don't know where the boy is now but I still have the marks on my skull.

CHAPTER 1

DAYLIGHT HAS DRAINED FROM THE ROOM, AND THE LIGHTS HAVE turned on in the skyscrapers. Circles. Rectangles. Fluorescent verte-brates across the ceilings. I imagine them humming like machines that zap insects.

My cracked phone is a memento from the tube station last night, and there is another on my collarbone, below the trim of my *Mario Kart* T-shirt, like a club stamp from a night out: a bruise the size of a thumbprint.

Count to three and then stand up.

One.

Two.

Three—

I turn on the main light, and my bedroom is familiar. Desk with laptop; bed between two windows; table with a notepad by the Pixar lamp; bookshelf holding color-arranged books; wardrobe, with last night's clothes crumpled at its foot like a chalk outline from a crime scene.

THIS IS WHAT A FEMINIST LOOKS LIKE.

Ruth bought me that shirt for Pride, but now the arms are broken and the spine is snapped. Ruth and I never used to argue before him. When we broke up a year ago, she told me that my first impression was the right one. But how can I separate the first impression from the last one?

Converse over the yellow line. White threads in the rip in his jacket. The murmur of the train.

The quiet Monday of the pub, two years, one month, and three days ago.

When I met him.

IT WAS OUR BIMONTHLY writers meetup, and Amy, Chris, Hugo, and I were sat in a pub in Broadway Market with splayed crisp packets and printouts on the wooden table. It was my turn to bring a chapter to discuss, but it wasn't finished. When I told the group that, they made the same noise at the same time and told me to just bring *something* for the next meeting.

Before we started, we ordered drinks and chatted. Chris remarked on how the pub had Halloween decorations up already. Hugo said that he was going to Torture Garden's annual Halloween ball in a couple of weeks. Amy immediately changed the subject by telling us about the renovations that she and her fiancé, David, were making to their Stoke Newington home.

Can you believe I've only just discovered Farrow & Ball?

I asked her what Farrow & Ball was, and she looked at me like I had ruined the story. She continued explaining the differences between décor in our early twenties and décor in our late twenties (less color) when he arrived.

A tall stranger in a bleached denim jacket with a rip in the shoulder flicked his chin in vague greeting and reclined in the chair next to mine, resting large feet in old Converse next to my Malbec. Hugo and Chris exchanged a glance, I moved my glass, and Amy continued her anecdote, with the irritation of someone who just had a fly land in their drink.

. . . and I've turned all the books around in the bookshelf so they match the walls, she concluded. Then, as if she hadn't been the one speaking, she asked if we could begin, *please*.

Chris kicked us off: Right. Yeah, so for *me*, Amy, the protagonist's desire for retribution was a tad reductive. You don't want her to fall into an offensive trope.

But as the group discussed Amy's novel, I was drawn to the stranger in my periphery. Downturned mouth, grayish-brown hair, deep lines framing unsymmetrical features, pen between his lips like a cigar. There was something grotesque about him. I glanced down at his arms, muscular, with a mole on his forearm like a planet.

Amy's rebuttal was a skimming stone: Chris, how exactly is it an offensive trope? A male protagonist can do anything he wants as many times as he wants, but a female protagonist has to justify why she is or isn't a trope?

I kept watching him: his face didn't move; it was hard to tell if he was listening.

Amy wore a mohair jumper cinched with a belt. Her favorite shows were filmed before a studio audience, and she wrote crime fiction. Hugo wore a ponytail with a suit jacket and wrote erotic science fiction. Chris wrote about the "male experience." He had a female cat called Humphrey and commitment issues. I knew what they might say and how they might say it; when Chris would be offended and when Amy would pretend to be. But I couldn't work the stranger out. His age? His sexuality? Was he a good writer? Although, somehow, I already knew that he was.

Enola, how about you?

Is that a coffee stain on his T-shirt?

Amy tapped her paper with her pen. She was always impatient to hear feedback. It was one of the reasons that the others found her grating, that and the fact that they were jealous; her first book was being published next year. But, as always, her writing was brilliant and listening to her words increased my relief at not having brought my own.

It didn't feel like a trope to me. I loved how you subverted the mystery convention, I said.

Thank you, Amy responded, with a look to Chris.

Hugo called me diplomatic, using the third person.

No, said Amy, whippet-quick, she just got it.

When we paused for more drinks, the stranger jumped up first, like he couldn't wait to leave the table, and Amy immediately tapped my arm and gestured to where he stood, wallet on the bar like a coin on a pool table. Why was I so *aware* of him?

Mat texted that he might bring a mate, she said.

Mat was the final member of the writing group. He wrote historical fiction, and ironed his jeans.

But then Mat got food poisoning, Amy continued. *Typical.* And this friend came anyway. I mean, he's not quite the vibe for our group, is he? He doesn't *look* like a writer.

Skimming over Amy's thinking food poisoning was "typical," I asked her what a writer looked like, and she said: Clean?

I laughed, but I wasn't in a position to judge. I felt more and more like writing was something I'd stumbled into and couldn't find my way out of, like those hikers who die in caves. I said it was weird that no one had introduced him, and Amy's coral lips puckered.

He should have introduced himself, Enola.

The stranger returned sipping a fresh pint of beer or cider. I might have imagined it but it seemed like he shuffled his chair closer to mine.

Shall we carry on, Amy said without the question mark.

Cider. I can smell it on his thick lips.

He wiped his mouth with his thumb, and I wondered how dirty his thumb was, or why he hadn't repaired the rip in his jacket. His face reminded me of one of those papier-mâché dummies from art classes at school.

Chris's novel was up next, and, adjusting his roll-neck, he asked for our thoughts. Before anyone else could speak, the stranger removed the pen from his mouth and said: I thought your protagonist was a cunt. Then he leaned back and watched the damage. There was a stunned silence before the group launched into platitudes: No, no, he's not a cunt, Chris. He's just nuanced! Yeah, there's only a *slight* dusting of misogyny. But Chris's protagonist was a cunt. I stifled a laugh, and the stranger grinned at me like we had robbed a bank.

And just like that I was invited in.

The difference a smile made to skin was paper being folded and unfolded. The deep lines lifted as if by fishing line and he had, at once, the warmest face I had ever seen. His eyes were green and his smile was suggestive but kind. I wanted to play with him. I wanted to look after him. I wanted to slap him. I wanted to fuck him. I snapped my head down to the stain on his gray T-shirt, but, wait—

HE CAN'T BE WEARING that gray T-shirt? This was two years ago and his stepmother, Karen, only bought it for him last Christmas. How can I be objective when my memory has him wearing a T-shirt not yet woven into significance? Anyway—

WHEN THE BELL RANG for last orders, we were ready to leave. I went to the toilet, and when I returned, he was gone, pub door swinging as though he had just passed through. I put on my coat and left feeling disappointed and then confused as to why. I didn't want to see him again, and yet I had put on lipstick in the bathroom.

I wanted to walk home, but it was raining, so I went to the bus stop. I thought about how it felt when he smiled at me, or rather, how it felt to be the person he had chosen to smile at. I tried to think of something else—my novel or what snack I might make—but it was like there was nothing to look forward to, just a novel I had no desire to write and a morning shift I had no desire to do.

A bus approached, and it wasn't my number, but people embarked, and that's when I saw him. Leaning against the glass. Rip in his jacket. Cigarette where the pen had been.

My heart started.

We pretended not to notice each other. Or I did. I wasn't sure if he was pretending. Then he looked over and said, saturnine: Hi, do you come here often? I tried to hide my smile, but he moved closer. He remarked that everyone had been pretty pissed. Do you always meet in a pub? I told him that Amy believed alcohol softened criticism. I'm not sure about that, he replied. The guy in the jumper wanted to punch me.

You did call his character a cunt.

He grinned, and I turned away—eye contact was too much.

We were quiet until he reached over his head and yanked it to one side. I didn't mean to squeal, but the crack was so loud. He looked pleased to have shocked me. I told him it would be embarrassing if he died breaking his own neck, and he said that wasn't how he was going to die. He told me that the last hours of his life would be dedicated to watching *Friends*.

Why?

I've never seen it.

You've never seen *Friends*?

Are you calling me a liar?

I couldn't tell if he was joking. It was such a stupid thing to joke about. But every word he had said so far sounded like it could mean something else.

Well, you'll have to die slowly, then. There are about seven hundred seasons.

He looked at me like I had said the right thing, and so I smiled. He smiled too. Perhaps he thought my smile was nice?

You have red wine on your teeth, he said.

Oh god.

I rubbed my teeth. He said that he was joking, and I lightly hit his arm—his muscle was hard beneath his jacket. He rolled his eyes to demonstrate that it didn't hurt and it felt, in that moment, like I knew him. Just then, a crack of thunder. The sky was thick with dark cloud.

He groaned. Fucking *England*.

I felt a stabbing in my breastbone. Rainstorms always made me think about camping with Dad.

He asked which bus I was getting, and when I answered, he said he was getting the same one, quipping: We're neighbors. I made a joke about borrowing sugar, and he returned one about a quick shag. My eyes drifted to his hands: long fingers, rough palms. I asked whereabouts he lived. He looked amused, like I had asked for his number.

Between Shadwell and Whitechapel. You?

Between Whitechapel and Aldgate.

Nice area, he said, eyebrows raised. What's the rent like? My stomach dropped the way it always did when I had to answer that question. It was bought when I was twenty-one, so the area wasn't as *nice* six years ago, I said.

He whistled. I got a watch for my twenty-first, but a flat would've been fine too.

I laughed to make the moment less awkward, and he asked if I had a cigarette. That was my last, he said, looking to the wet stub on the tarmac. I told him that I didn't smoke, but, on seeing his disappointment, I wished I did. Then he frowned and said: I feel like a prick, but I cannot remember your name.

There were only four of us at the pub. How could he not remember my name? But there was that look again, as if perhaps he did remember but was trying to achieve something.

It's Enola.

. . . as in Gay?

There was a beat while I came to understand the reference, and then he laughed. I wasn't sure if he was laughing at his joke or my slowness to register it. But it was such an incongruous sound, rising and falling like music, that I laughed along at my own expense. Then he finished with a hum and asked if I fancied a drink. The sentence dropped at the end, as if he was nervous. But he knew what he was doing. His self-deprecation was a performance, for effect—to make me laugh, to unsettle me? But still I answered: Yes, let's get a drink.

I know a place that'll be open.

Now? Oh no, I can't now.

Jeez. Pull the rug out, why don't you?

I wasn't wearing the right clothes. I hadn't shaved. I needed to speak to Ruth. The same way that I needed to call her before I wore my new school shoes with the thick heel for the first time. I explained that I was working in the morning, and he gave me this look that knew me, that sprouted from one side of his face and stripped me.

Stumbling over the consonants, I said that we had the bus journey to chat. He muttered something. I asked what he said. He pretended he hadn't said anything. I thought what he'd said was that a bus journey wouldn't be sufficient for what he had in mind, but I couldn't have been sure. Then, with a nod, as if he had summoned it, the bus splashed the curb.

WE SAT AT THE top of the bus, and condensation covered the windows. His skin was damp with rain; the cigarette smoke faded to leave aftershave, woody, with a hint of citrus. I undid the top two buttons of my shirt.

So . . . where are you from? he asked in a mock perfunctory style, like he was afraid of sounding sincere. My answer was rehearsed: I was born in the Midlands, where my mum is from, but we moved to Kenya when I was four. We were only there for a few years, though. Mum and I moved back to the Midlands when I was nine, for school. Long story short, I've been in London since uni.

So . . . the Midlands, then.

He was looking at me like I had made a simple thing complicated, so I agreed to be from the Midlands. Not that it was a lie, but it wasn't the truth either. Kenya felt like home, though I'd never been back. Dad's sister, Louise, lived there now. She had visited and fallen in love with a man from the coast. But Mum didn't let me speak to her.

Poor you, he said. Why were you in Africa?

Dad worked for the foreign office.

What does he do now?

What do you mean?

You used the past tense.

I changed the subject and asked him what his novel was about. His face lifted like it had done in the pub. He said that it was a political satire, or at least it would be when it was finished. I asked what he did for work, and he told me that he was doing a bit of freelance writing.

You know the drill, he said conspiratorially. But I did not know the drill. I told him how impressive it was that he was a full-time writer, and he laughed, a short, explosive sound, and told me that he had given me the highlights.

So, there are lowlights?

He leaned in and told me that there were shadows.

Very good.

And that's why Woking's Free Fish Company pay me the average bucks, Gay.

He relaxed back, and his knee grazed mine. I thought about moving my leg but that would tell him that I wasn't interested. I thought about letting my leg fully relax against his but that would tell him that I was. Tension formed in my thigh from keeping my leg *almost* touching his.

So, where do *you* day job? he asked, as if asking where I summered. I told him that I worked in a café at a hedge fund with my best friend. I thought about getting something permanent, but Ruth—

That's your friend?

My best friend. Her family moved to Kenya the same year and left the same year too. Nobody knows me like she does.

I nodded.

Ruth said that I'd never finish my novel if I did. So I've given myself until I'm thirty to finish it, and if that doesn't happen, then I'll look at getting something more—

Grown-up?

I nodded again.

He told me that, from someone who had turned thirty a few years ago, I shouldn't put a time limit on things. And you might even get sick of making sandwiches for posh wankers before then. How old are you? I blushed, and he rolled his eyes again: Come *on*. I replied that I was twenty-eight next month, and he hummed and said: I take it back, that *is* old, you probably should get a grown-up job.

We make quiche too, I said.

The light behind his eyes clicked on: I had surprised him. Oh, well, that's different, he said warmly, and the desire to please him bloomed like an addiction.

We sat listening to the road and the rain and the world blurring.

When there was a big rainstorm on safari, we would wait in the car until the ground was dry enough to put up the tents. The windows would steam up, and our skin would turn sticky. Mum hated camping, so she would sulk in the front seat, but Dad would start a game: *I went to the market and bought—*

All right, Enola, he said, enunciating my name like it was fictional. If this bus journey is a drink, tell me: favorite book, TV show, and food?

Erm, I'm not sure. *Ulysses*, *Grey's Anatomy*, and kiwis?

He made a face and told me that he was allergic to kiwis. I blow up like an acid attack victim.

I clamped my hand over my mouth.

And *Ulysses*? Christ. Come on . . .

He asked me what my *real* favorite book was, muttering that I was honest about *Grey's Anatomy* at least. I asked him what his favorite book was, then, and without missing a beat, he said: Gary Neville's autobiography.

Just past the mosque, I reached for the red button in a way that caused my collar to hover below his nose. He cleared his throat to let me know that he had noticed. Then, in the knowledge that our stop was next, we allowed our knees to touch until the bus juddered and we disembarked, him first and me behind.

We stood with the rain ricocheting around us. He was tall, and my eyes reached the triangle of his collarbone. I lifted my chin and met his gaze. I felt a pulse between my legs and a less pleasant sensation in my stomach.

Well, this is me, I said in the tone the cliché demanded. This is me too, he replied in the same way. I gestured to my right. He to his left. Opposite directions, then. My trainers were soaked and rain was dripping off his nose, but neither of us moved. I didn't know what he was thinking, but then he inhaled and said: Well, goodbye then.

Oh god. Is he just waiting for me to leave?

I quickly said goodbye and walked away. I got three paces before hearing his voice, building like a sneeze: Maybe we could have our own writing club soon or just that drink . . . ? I turned back and he was grinning. But, he added, I already know your pretend favorite book and you already know how to murder me and make it look like an accident, so I suggest skipping to date three.

He handed me his phone. I took it, and the warmth of it felt like my hand in his pocket. I typed my number under where he had already typed "Enola, the" and waited for him to drop call me. But he didn't.

Okay, I said. Bye.

Bye.

I went to leave but then stopped and asked him if he knew that Chris had based his protagonist on himself. He grinned like I had given him a compliment. I mean, it was fucking obvious. Besides, they *were* a bunch of cunts, weren't they? I opened my mouth but expelled only air as he walked away, clutching his jacket to his chin.

A shop alarm cut through the night, or, wait—

My buzzer is going! Someone's downstairs! It can't be, can it? It's only ten past four. I'm not dressed. It's the afternoon, and I'm still wearing the pajama T-shirt he gave me. I reach the receiver, and the noise stops. Wrong number. *Thank god.* I lean against the door and pick us back up like a book.

By the time I got home, the wind was howling through the gaps in the windows. I opened my laptop and picked at the words on the page. I imagined Amy, Chris, and Hugo typing manically while I alternated between making a vase red or blue, deciding that it was just a vase. I put a pen to my lips the way that he had held one to his. Apparently only two percent of the population has green eyes. When would he text? *Would* he text? Did I even want him to text? His face confused me. It was like his teeth were too big for his mouth. And he didn't even seem nice. And I couldn't date a smoker. And what was that kiwi thing? Fuck. Why did I tell him my favorite show was *Grey's Anatomy*? I liked the show, but it wasn't my favorite. I didn't know what my favorite show was. Ruth would have said something that no one had heard of yet but that everyone was about to. I should have told him that my favorite show was something political or funny or—

SHIT! A KNOCK SOUNDS behind my head. Could it be Ruth? No, of course not. She's in Bath. She has a key. And we're not speaking. Was I lucid enough to have locked the door last night? Then a familiar voice:

"Enola, it's me, are you in?"

Fuck.

CHAPTER 2

I FOUND HIM ON THE SOFA BY THE WINDOWS: THE NAIROBI SUNSET sliced him in half like a magician's trick. He put down *Ulysses* and stood to greet me. His skin was warm like he had been lying in the garden.

You're reading *Ulysses* again?

Honey, you know it's my favorite book.

I told him that I was going to make risotto, and he made a sharp sibilant sound. I hit his arm, and he drew me closer. He smelled like the house, comforting and warm. Come on, he said, I'll make the risotto. He led me to the kitchen, where he pulled out the chopping board that Ruth got us as a wedding present with *Enola & Ruth* scorched into the wood. My dad was on his way over with a pack of Tusker and we were going to watch the sun set from the porch. *You must always take time for a sundowner.*

He pulled a kiwi from the shopping and started eating it.

There was a knock at the door.

Are you going to get that?

Then the sound of a train like a wave.

Enola, are you going to get that?

The dusty warm air.

Enola!

It's getting closer.

I looked back at him, but his face was bloodied and swollen.

For fuck's sake. Enola, answer the door! Why are you such a cunt?

* * *

"Enola?"

Please go away, just go away.

"Enola? Are you in?"

Why is he here?

"I'm on late lunch. I texted you. Enola?"

A demonstrative exhale. I'm not sure whose benefit he thinks the sound is for.

"Yeah, okay, you're not in."

Making sure he is actually gone and not hiding somewhere, I wait for the ding of the lift, the clap of the doors, and the whirring in the walls before opening the door. There is a plastic bag on the welcome mat.

The many-worlds interpretation of quantum mechanics proposes that every time we have a choice to make with more than one possible outcome, all of the outcomes occur, splitting us into unlimited parallel timelines. So, in this second of staring at the plastic bag, I have both brought it inside and left it outside. Does that mean nothing matters or everything matters?

I bring it inside.

The strip light shudders on with a horror movie crackle, crudely illuminating my kitchen: forest-green walls, kettle on the stove, mugs hanging above the counter, small table, and on the window ledge, a row of recipe books. I lay the contents of the plastic bag onto the table: peanut butter, scented candle, bath oil, and a postcard with a picture of an otter in a bubble bath. In neat, rounded letters, the underside reads:

Just a few things to say that I miss you and that I'm still quietly confident . . . —Virinder

There is nothing quiet about Virinder's confidence. I unscrew the lid and scoop some peanut butter out. As I turn my finger, the peanut butter sags but doesn't fall. Like the transitory paste, I am stuck between where I am and where I want to be: back at the start, where a vase can be red, blue, and just a vase all at once.

RUTH AND I WERE sat in an art gallery in Shoreditch. Oil paintings on the walls, cocktails by our feet, and a naked man with straight black pubic hair who was stretched over sheets in the center of the circle. He looked like he owned a whippet and was called Simon, or perhaps the whippet was. My drawing was terrible: half an arm, misshapen eyes, hands without fingers. Ruth had sketched the man without genitals, his penis, large and unattached, was floating above his head in a thought bubble.

I put down my pencil and picked up my cocktail.

Ruth was always thinking of fun activities: new brunch spots or pop-ups or crazes like morning raves or Drag Bingo. Tonight, it was figure drawing and cocktails.

Roo, do you think I'm boring? I lowered my voice because the man with the perm who ran the gallery was staring. Don't be ridiculous, she said without looking up.

I watched the right side of her face, three piercings in her lobe, curls black and cascading, brown skin with a smattering of freckles over the bridge of her nose and up her cheekbones like she was a Disney cartoon. She would put her picture in the bin as soon as she got home but she was taking such care over it now.

Enola, stop staring. You're making me self-conscious.

You don't get self-conscious.

Self-*aware*, then.

I told her that the other day Amy asked if I was asexual because there were no sex scenes in my book. Ruth laughed, and the man with the perm looked over again. She nodded to the model, stretching his hamstrings, and said that not everyone was comfortable putting it out there. I said that the other side of the circle were getting more for their money.

I told her that he had asked me out for tomorrow. He wants to play Scrabble.

Your favorite!

And did I tell you that he writes full-time? I'm worried I'm still going to be working in the café when I'm thirty.

I hope I still am, Ruth said subversively.

Ruth lived as a property guardian in a warehouse in North London. She currently had pages folded in ten books and changed her hair more often than she changed her bedding. She interviewed for jobs she didn't want but inevitably got, ending up back at the café two weeks later. Ruth found comfort in instability. For her, being still meant being trapped.

But you know what I mean, I said.

She turned to me. He's really got under your skin, hasn't he?

We picked up our drinks and leaned on our knees. Go on. What's he like?

I told her that he was hard to describe. Tall. Brownish hair, green eyes. And funny. Really funny—in a crude, dry way. Unapologetic. Mega-confident. But I don't feel relaxed around him.

You've only met him once?

Yes, at the writing thing. He came in with this *energy*. Put his feet up on the table. Didn't say a word but then called Chris's character a cunt.

He sounds like a twat, if I'm honest.

He was, I mean, he is.

Right . . .

I can't explain it. But we've been texting. Every time I get a message, I panic. You know like when you eat a sour sweet? How you immediately want another one? That's weird, right? It's probably a bad sign that it doesn't feel . . . effortless?

Loads of life-changing things aren't effortless. Jumping out of a plane, or rock climbing, or—

Camping with lions?

Swimming with hippos?

Don't exaggerate. The hippos were on the other side of the lake. But I feel butterflies, you know?

Ruth sipped her drink and said: I read this thing that said but-terflies are our body's fight-or-flight. We think they mean love or attraction or whatever, but they actually mean danger. It's your body warning you to run.

Roo!

But, she added, danger isn't always bad.

She explained that it was in my nature to hold back, because I liked things neat. I reminded her that I was trying to be a writer. Can you think of a more chaotic career than that? She said that I was also the person who double-cleaned the coffee machine. I protested that no one cleaned it properly, and she laughed and said that I was both chaos and order.

Ruth always made words sound like they should be printed on cushions.

Well, I think you should go for it, she said turning back to her drawing. But please focus on what you think of him? You're great. Is *he* good enough? Then one side of her mouth lifted into a smile and she added: Jump out that plane, Laa.

AFTERWARD, WE WENT TO Ruth's parents' home in Islington. The house was warm, and there was a selection of miniature pumpkins next to a witch made of twigs in the entrance. Jon, her dad, was already in bed, but Catherine greeted us affectionately in her faded flower-print dressing gown.

Once, I was staying with Ruth and we were making peanut but-ter cookies. Catherine had come in and kissed Ruth as we were shaping the dough. It was such a normal moment for them, but I cried myself to sleep in the spare room. Catherine always kept the spare room for me, but she didn't like when I called it spare. *It's your room, Enola.*

We showed Catherine our drawings, and she pinned them on the fridge next to the scan of Emily's new baby and a photo of us from last Christmas. I'm not sure why I had chosen a cream dress; you couldn't tell where the fabric ended and my skin began. Ruth, as if preparing to be stuck on a fridge, was making a face like a disruptive toddler, and Emily was smiling nicely.

How is Emily?

Oh, you know. Working up until the wire, Catherine answered proudly.

Ruth made a noise and then pretended that she hadn't.

Part of the reason that Ruth lived like she was being chased was because her sister, Emily, didn't. A doctor in Maidenhead. Her husband, Samson, worked in finance. All her appliances matched. Her walls were shades of beige.

There's some food on the stove for you girls.

Catherine looked to me. Enola, please do not let Ruth go at it with a spoon. It needs to be heated. She said that our rooms were made up, and I knew there would be a book on my bedside table—a poetry book or something obscure and Russian or a contemporary prizewinner that she would pretend not to have bought new.

She kissed us both, tightened her dressing gown, and left, calling: Lights off when you're done. I turned back, and Ruth was perched by the stove, swinging her legs and eating out of the pot with a spoon. Texted him yet? she asked, mouth full.

WHEN I ARRIVED OUTSIDE the tube, he was already there, and he made a joke about lateness. He walked ahead but didn't seem to think that was rude. When I questioned it, he said it was so that he could smoke. I trotted behind, dress riding up and a sheen appearing above my lip.

I had been anxious all day remembering his arrogant gait, his lined face, his unpredictable smile. I had also changed my outfit five times. *You clearly want to be there*, Ruth pointed out. *Fight or flight.* I had asked her if there was a third option. She said: *Fuck?*

Entering the pub, I relaxed, because nineties music was playing. I commented that the song reminded me of school discos, and he remarked, dryly, that it reminded him of Freshers Week. I tried to think of a witty retort, but the moment passed.

He sat us next to a bookshelf of board games and went to the bar. I checked my phone to give myself a task. There was a message from Ruth:

Need rescuing?

I looked to where he was waiting to order. There were people on either side of him who were there first but he was taller and his elbows were splayed, as though being served were a competition.

I replied that I wasn't sure, and Ruth said that she was having dinner at the warehouse. She suggested that I join later if I wasn't otherwise engaged, and then sent the plane emoji.

He returned, placing down two old-fashioneds.

Oh, I—

Was it stranger that I hadn't told him what I wanted or that he hadn't asked?

I hated whiskey. My mum used to drink it on the holidays. She might have drunk it other times, but after she moved to France, I only saw her on the holidays, so that was when she drank it. Christmas. Easter. The occasional week in the summer.

We clinked our glasses and I thanked him for the drink. Sláinte, he said.

Are you Irish?

No, he answered.

He took a sip and sighed. Perfect, he said, referring to the drink. Then: I fucking hate dates. He said that he couldn't think of anything worse than meeting a boring person in a boring pub to hear about their boring hobbies. I looked around the pub to make a point, and he said: Ah, but *this* pub is a *good* pub. Settled, his face was cantankerous, angry even, and I remembered Ruth's words: *What do you think about him?*

Flight.

Ruth had all sorts of ways of ending a date. The main one was just being honest and leaving. But there was something about how his hands gripped the glass.

Fight?

I took a large sip of the drink I hated and tried not to be boring.

But is a date even a date if no one talks about hobbies? I asked.

It's much like the tree in the wood, he replied.

FUCK.

He laughed, and it was as unruly and brilliant as I remembered. He was two very different, equally disarming things. He removed his denim jacket to reveal a black wool shirt with the sleeves rolled up. I wanted to touch the mole on his forearm.

Shall we?

He set up the Scrabble board. I arranged seven tiles on my rack so that they almost made a word, and we began. He placed down the first word: "NOW." I added an "S" to make "SNOW." Before I could take a replacement tile, he spelled "WHISTLE" on a triple letter score.

Wolf or tin?

That's not the game, Enola.

We played, and I watched him study the board like it mattered more that he won than what I thought of him. It was sexy, his confidence, his ability to exist in every moment.

Jump out that plane, Laa.

You know, I'm actually glad that tonight isn't a date, I said.

He looked up. Oh?

I nodded. I'm not wearing date underwear.

His face reddened, and it was thrilling. I knew then that I wanted him to win. I asked why he had come to our writing group last week.

Fuck knows, he said. Maybe I wanted my ego stroked, maybe Mat said he would fucking be there.

Are you and Mat close?

Not really. We did a three-month writing thing and he was the only person I didn't want to punch.

Because his entrance into my life had been a truck crashing into a house, it felt more like he had been compelled to our writing group by forces of the universe—the way that I always felt Ruth and I had been brought together for those same four years in Nairobi. It seemed impossible that he had just entered my life on a whim.

I said that he had missed a window to say something smooth. He asked me for an example. Like . . . you were hoping to meet me? I said, and immediately cringed. I had hoped to sound sexy, like with the underwear comment, but this felt wrong.

His eyes didn't light up, but he chuckled, slightly.

I'm not smooth, he said.

No?

Apart from my body, which feels like a baby seal.

I noticed the dark hair where his shirt met his chest; there was nothing smooth about his body. I can't comment on the seal thing but I think you're smooth, I said, because it felt like a good thing to say. And it must have been, because he made a face, like the one my dad used to make when I did something silly.

He replied that he was glad he had fooled me, but that I looked like someone who was easily fooled. I asked why he thought that and he asked if that was another window. It was my turn to ask him for an example, and he said that I was blushing. I said that I wasn't, but he pointed to my face, which instantly warmed under scrutiny, and said: See.

That's not a window, that's a trap.

We spent the rest of the evening debating every choice. You can't use slang. That's not slang. It's absolutely slang. *You're* slang. When the board was full and he had won, we ordered two more drinks that we didn't need. The conversation slowed, and I realized the whiskey had gone to my head. He was staring at me like he was scrutinizing my face, and so I asked a stupid question about how many times an old-fashioned needed stirring, and he leaned across the table, placed his hand on my cheek, and kissed me.

Everything stopped.

The anxiety. The pressure. The world.

It all stopped.

Pulling away, he whispered: There, now that's taken care of.

IN THE BATHROOM, I pressed my lips to my hand to re-create the sensation of kissing him. I wondered what it had felt like for him. I texted Ruth:

> Sorry for lateness. Won't come by. Got a bit drunk. Kissed him and it was the best kiss of my life. Don't make fun of me for saying that.

My mouth tasted stale from the whiskey. (Was it stale when he kissed me?) I put some gum in my mouth. Ruth replied:

> You gonna stay with him tonight . . . ?

Did I want to sleep with him tonight? (I had lied about the underwear; I was wearing a black lace set.) My mum's voice, uninvited: *Enola, women wear underwear for themselves, not for a man.* Did she wear nice underwear in France for Paul? Did she wear it for my dad? But it was only date one, and something about him made me uneasy. And it wasn't just his large frame or the gray in his hair, it was him, how he spoke, how he placed the tiles on the board like he knew what I was going to do next.

I came back out, and he was leaning by the door with his arms folded, like that photograph of James Dean. You ever played two truths and a lie? He wound my hair around his finger. One: I have an enormous bed. Two: I have a bottle of champagne in my room. Three: I have no interest in you coming over tonight.

I'm not coming over tonight, I said decisively.

Come on, let me see those granny pants. Or are you a date-three girl?

I pushed his chest, but he wrapped my hands around his waist.

The texture of his jacket. The warmth of his face. I wanted him to kiss me again. I wanted it more than food or sleep or water.

So, this *was* a date?

Semantics. Come *on*, he repeated. Don't you want to see how big my bed is?

I told him that I had to write, and he said that he was taking a break from his novel because he was stuck in a writing k-hole. I asked him what a k-hole was, and he said that it was when you took too much ketamine and wandered around in a circle. I told him that I had only taken ketamine once: Ruth gave me a corner at a festival and we were mermaids. He pulled me closer and whispered: What sort of creature are you?

The sort that's *not* easily fooled . . .

He shook his head. Gay, yours is a face that a con man would target.

It's not!

You look like someone who plays Candy Crush.

It's good for mindfulness!

I bet your favorite ice cream flavor is vanilla.

Stop!

I pressed my hand over his grin. Fine. I'll bite. How big *is* your bed? He pressed his lower body into mine. That pulse between my legs. That spice in my blood. *Kiss me.* Fuck it. I lifted onto my toes and kissed him.

You'll just have to wait and see.

CHAPTER 3

I SCREW THE LID BACK ON THE PEANUT BUTTER AND RETURN THE jar to the lineup. It's barely four-thirty but completely dark. I turn on the side lights until the room marinates. When I first moved in, Ruth and I passed a bottle of prosecco back and forth because I didn't have glasses. I didn't have a bed either, and so that night we slept in sleeping bags like we were camping. Everything here is mine. The beaded cushions on the sofa. The vase on the table. The color-coded books in the bookshelf. I chose them. I paid for them. I placed them. This was my space. My *home*. But then he made fun of my cushions, he bought me flowers for that vase, he teased me about the books in the bookshelf. Now everything mine has become his, and I'm not sure when or how that happened. Amy's house is full of photographs of her and David, but I don't have any photographs of us, so our memories are in the items. I thought that made the relationship more intimate, but Ruth said it was because he never viewed it as a real relationship. And yet, if the police dusted, they would find his prints everywhere.

I open the balcony doors and feel the sting of cold. The sky is streaked like a watercolor, and the buildings have darkened to the same shade of gray. I can see the photographs we never took as clearly as I can see him standing on the platform edge last night.

I close my eyes and breathe in what feels like fresh air but I know isn't.

* * *

We were stood outside his front door for the first time. He kissed me, and his hands pushed inside my coat. I told him to stop. Your neighbors might see! He told me to fucking come in.

We had gone for a drink in London Bridge, and the plan was tapas in Borough Market, but we never made it. It was date three. I had an overnight bag. He offered us gum.

Inside, the lights were on and I could smell food. He put his finger on his lips and indicated the kitchen. I won't introduce you to my housemate because he's a twat. I asked if there was anyone who he didn't think was a twat and he smiled at me.

We took off our shoes, leaving them in the pile by the door, and he showed me into his room. It looked more like the room of a student than of a thirty-five-year-old man. Popcorn ceiling. Exposed bulb over the bed. Wardrobe doors ajar; trainers, sleeve, corner of a laundry basket. A bookshelf with a dead spider plant, crispy babies hanging from the tips. Washing over a radiator: comic book socks, stripy boxer shorts, single black glove. Chair pulled from a desk like he had just stood up from it. Atop, a spread-eagled crossword, laptop, and *Family Guy* mug.

I asked if the bed was a double. He said that it was one of those small doubles that landlords loved.

So, that was the lie?

I don't have champagne either. This isn't the Ritz.

He put on a song with no words and turned the main light off. I removed my coat and jumper so I was just wearing a black dress with buttons up the front. I wasn't wearing tights, and my legs were covered in goose bumps.

Hey, he said, with a childish lilt.

He ran his hand up the side of my body. He didn't kiss me, but I could feel his breath. He lowered his hand to my leg.

You must be freezing, Gay.

His fingers grazed the lace of my knickers, and he made a noise to let me know that he approved. I unbuttoned my dress. He reached to unhook my bra but couldn't work the clasp. I reassured him that everyone struggled, and he joked: You've had other men? I pulled up his T-shirt. Dark hair on defined muscles. Heady smell of aftershave. The whole scene was soundtracked by drums that matched my heartbeat, or maybe my heartbeat was directing the tinny blue speaker but—

AND I'VE DONE IT again. Like the gray T-shirt. This isn't what happened. I wasn't wearing a dress, because I struggled to get my jeans off and he commented that there was a reason skinny jeans were out of fashion. And then when he touched me, he said: *I'm relieved you have a nice one of these, it could have been a dog's dinner.* I had felt insecure and asked if we should wait, but he said it was just a joke. It was like the first time I had sex. I hadn't wanted it, but I told everyone that it was passionate and spontaneous and that this boy whose name I didn't remember was the right person for me to open my legs against a garage door for. But it doesn't matter whether I remember only the good or only the bad or if I get as close to objectivity as it is possible to get, because the truth is: I wanted him.

Really think about it, Laa, about how he makes you feel.

SHALL WE WAIT?

Enola, it was just a joke . . .

I know. Sorry. Forget it.

He shuffled out of his boxers and threw his socks to opposite corners of the room. His cock was bobbing. I had guessed he would be large. Ruth told me to look at the index. I told her that was an old wives' tale. She said that expression was sexist. He kissed me with an aggressive tongue, and I responded with my nails on his back like I was a woman in a film who sleeps with a man and then murders him. When he pushed inside, it hurt, and I pressed my face into the pillow where the smell of his sleep lingered. Was he enjoying this? Was I? His joints moved. His muscles flexed. I thought of those images of the human body from biology class, red stripy muscles stretching under the skin. I wanted him to overpower me. To take what he wanted. I wanted to be useful. He moved more fervently. Everything became hot and wet. I grabbed his hips, pulling him harder, faster, deeper in until he came and I pretended to.

Fuck.

Fuck.

He withdrew and collapsed, ribs jerking. Then he reached for his vape, holding his breath before releasing.

Wow, he said. We came at the same time.

That almost never happens to me, I said.

The words were true; the context was a lie.

Same, he said, like I was special.

My heart skipped, and feeling as special as he'd said I was, I relaxed onto the hard mattress. I was glad that the first time was over. Now it could get better. I wondered what he was thinking. Then he spoke: I thought you'd make that harder on me. He whistled air. I mean, date three . . . ?

Oh god.

Don't be upset. I'm thrilled you're a slut.

His eyes stayed deadpan while mine widened. Then he grinned. I called him a prick.

Jokes aside, he said, I was glad that you made the first move.

Excuse me? You were the one who said you weren't hungry.

Then you charged up the bridge like a dog in heat.

I said that wasn't exactly how it happened, but he forced my head onto his chest. Shh, Enola, shh. That's *exaaaactly* how it happened. The joke was over, but neither of us moved my head. We lay in silence until he clucked and asked about my hobbies. I burst out laughing and told him that it was too late to ask me those questions. We had seen each other naked. He chuckled—the noise twisted and curved as a roller coaster. I propped myself up on my elbow. My hair fell forward, and he tucked it behind my ear. I told him that his laugh was *insane*, and he said that his friend Pat said he sounded like a husky trying to talk.

The smell of garlic drifted from the kitchen, and I remembered Dad cooking on Sundays. I also remembered Aunt Louise commenting: *Your mum should be the one cooking. It's his only day off! My brother was always going to end up in politics. He just has one of those minds.*

Are you hungry now?

He raised an eyebrow: Are you?

We did skip food.

We did, he repeated, stressing the "did" as if it had been my fault.

I asked if he liked cooking, and he scoffed like it was a stupid question. *And he can cook?* Affection built in my abdomen. I knew that I wanted these moments: the time he cooked for me; the time he stayed at mine; the time we met each other's friends.

Pizza?

Pizza.

He kissed me. His hand on my face. The heat between our bodies, the duvet lowering, and—

Or we could just skip the pizza . . .

So, how was the big third date last night?

Ruth had me on speaker, and I could hear her getting dressed for Halloween. I told her that it was good. She said that meant it was either really good or really bad. Well, it wasn't really *bad*, I said.

So you're not asexual, then? I told her to please forget that I had said that. She asked for more details, and I told her that it was incredible.

On the first time?

She sounded more skeptical than impressed.

I guess that's what happens when you have that much chemistry.

And you communicate? Is he easy to talk to in that way?

The last time I'd had sex was nine months ago. I met Ben (marketing, Gemini, 5'11") speed dating with Ruth—a suggestion following an article she had read over someone's shoulder on the tube. She had chastised me for faking it: *We're not twenty-one anymore. They have to learn, Enola.*

Yes, I said. He's really easy to be open with. He was super focused on me and just really listened.

Good, because I know you put their needs before yours sometimes.

Ruth was right, but I liked not having to decide what I wanted. To have someone make the decisions for me. I would tell him what I wanted over time, and my fake orgasms would seamlessly transform into real ones.

The doorbell sounded. It was only this morning that I was waking up to the light from where his blinds didn't hang flush, and now he was coming over to have takeaway and watch scary movies.

Roo, he's here. I'll call you later.

Okay. Have fun. Remember that I loved you when you cut your own fringe.

We hung up the phone and I quickly scanned the flat. It was the first time he had come over and I had hoovered and dusted and repositioned every trinket, as if it would matter to him that my candle holders were symmetrical, but, like all our interactions over these past three weeks, I needed it to be perfect. I opened the door, and there he was: dark green shirt, silver chain, denim jacket with the rip.

Happy Halloween, Gay.

Long time no see.

We looked at each other for a moment, both thinking, I hoped, how well this was going. Then I told him to come in, and he thanked me like I had suggested something dirty. I wanted to bite his earlobes. He didn't wait for me; he just moved through the flat, peering in each room. There was a spot in the kitchen where you could smell the neighbor's fish curry.

I know, it's annoying, I said as he sniffed and scrunched his face.

But it didn't annoy me. I saw them in the lift sometimes; they were a family and I liked that they ate together.

He moved into the living room and pointed out the buildings from the balcony window as if I hadn't seen them before. I sat on the sofa and saw my home through his eyes: embroidered cushions; double bookshelf; coffee table with a book on succulents, a gilded bowl, and a tray shaped like a monstera leaf. He picked up the tray and blew the dust off it. You should move this to the front door to put keys in, Gay.

He ran his hands across the bookshelf and called me a twat for organizing my books by color. He held up a romance novel. I told him it was a Secret Santa present. I gestured to the Vonnegut section and told him that he was ignoring the books he liked. He picked up a photograph of me and Ruth. The knees were the widest parts of our legs and our smiles had matching gaps. It was a print of the one by her bed. I didn't have any pictures of our childhood because Mum burned them.

Is that Ruth?

Yes.

Where's this taken?

An elephant orphanage.

He sat next to me; his eyes were pale in the light from the window. He leaned back, and his face changed. He pulled a cushion from behind him. What the fuck is this? You'd slice an artery on those sequins. I took the cushion and told him to thank me for saving his life.

The tortured doesn't thank the torturer, he said.

They do in Torture Garden, I said, recalling how tonight Hugo would be donning a leather harness and dog collar.

He laughed and pulled me close.

You want to go to Torture Garden, honey?

Honey.

I shook my head and rested it on his shoulder. His shirt smelled like it had been left in the washing machine too long. He asked how I'd afforded to buy a flat with my café salary. Are you a poor little rich girl? Don't worry, I won't think less of you. I'll probably like you more. I've always wanted to be a kept man.

I told him that when my grandparents died, they left me money from their house sale. They didn't have loads, but because they were basically my caregivers from—

Where was your mum?

She moved to France to be with her boyfriend.

He made a noise that implied he understood. He didn't get on with Karen, his stepmother. He said that it must be nice to have somewhere to go in France. I told him I hadn't been there in years. When Mum left, she decided that we should speak once a week, and that's the extent of it still now. Five minutes every Wednesday.

Once a week is loads.

Is it?

He nodded. I only speak to mine once a month.

I suppose it's less the amount and more the—you know.

He said that wasn't a sentence then made a face like a sad clown and told me not to feel sorry for myself. He was so *light* that I thought about telling him everything about my child-hood. But perhaps sensing that I might say something serious, he started humming the *William Tell* Overture, and galloped his fingers over the coffee table. I began to copy him, but he told me to stop it. Your horses would be shot for physical deformities, honey.

What?

Your hands look like how children draw hands.

No, they don't!

Like a circle with five sticks.

He leaped his fingers over the monstera tray with a whinny and then tapped my leg. Come on, then. Let's go out.

I thought you wanted to eat here?

Nah, I feel like curry now.

Okay, well, I just need to freshen up.

Be quick, he said, getting his phone out to scroll.

I went to the bathroom and touched up my appearance. Being with him was exhilarating. There were challenging parts; he was blunt and occasionally rude, and he wielded humor both as a weapon and a shield. But I felt happy, in that fizzy way you feel as a child jumping in a lake or seeing snow for the first time.

I came out of the bathroom, and he was in the hall holding my otter soft toy.

And who's this?

Otter.

I see.

We stared at each other until the air turned red, and I handed myself to him like an item. He fucked me, and I felt the soreness from last night and again this morning, but I didn't care because I was flesh and bone and blood and as crucial to the world as an old tree with hard, thick roots, while at the same time like an adult woman from a television show that I would binge-watch and envy, thinking: Her, yes, her, *she* is alive.

He came, and I didn't (which was okay because, I justified, it was only a quickie), and he zipped back up with dexterity. Right, he said. Glad we got that out of the way. No way I'd be up for it after curry. He headed for the door, and I stood naked from the waist down wishing that I had tissues and contemplating moving the monstera tray from the coffee table to the front door.

RUTH ENTERED THE BAR already removing her coat. Sorry I'm late, the interview ran on! I poured her a glass of wine and pushed her the bowl of olives. She put down an envelope and a small purple box on the table. The card is from Mum, she said. The box is from me.

Inside was a selection of Turkish delight.

It's only small, she said.

I thanked her and put the card in my bag to open later. I asked how the interview went, but she said she didn't want to talk about it, which meant it had gone well. Then she asked three questions without waiting for the answers: How was your birthday yesterday? How's it going with *him*? He's coming to the party on Saturday, right?

I laughed and she told me to answer the third one.

I nodded that he was. She said that things were moving quickly. I told her that it was going really well. Roo, I'm obsessed. I can't stop thinking about him. Things he's said. Or thoughts he's expressed. His odd socks and the deodorant stains on his T-shirts.

God, men are gross.

He makes me laugh so much. And he gets angry about small things. He's so passionate. He'll go off on a rant about the publishing industry because he's read this tweet.

And that's good?

It's . . . I don't know, he's just so *present*. And Roo, he is the sexiest man I've ever met.

You're doing other stuff, though, right? You're not just having sex?

Why? Do you think that's bad?

She said that it had been very intense so far and she didn't want to see me get hurt. I reminded her that the last woman she'd been seeing moved in after two weeks.

Yes, and you see how well that worked out?

When the afternoon light faded, the music was turned up and the bass pulsed like a heartbeat. The waitress lit the candle on our table. She had short black hair, and her neck was swanlike. As she cupped the tealight, Ruth mouthed to me that she was beautiful. I told her that she thought everyone was beautiful.

Everyone *is* beautiful! Is he telling you how beautiful you are?

Roo, you're the only person who thinks I'm beautiful.

You're the only person who thinks you're not. But is he being good to you?

I smiled, because earlier he'd said that I looked like someone who would stand for their stop while the train was still moving. But I didn't tell Ruth that because she might not understand the joke. Her instinct was to protect. Even when we were children, if a grown-up told me to smile, she would snap: *Leave Enola alone, she's just thinking.*

The song changed, and she laughed, because we had missed this band at a festival. We had waited for two days to see them, but we were hungover and exhausted and decided to lie down on haystacks, just for a moment, waking only to fireworks above us.

How amazing this summer would be with him now, too.

Ruth put an olive in her mouth and licked the oil from her fingers. She spoke, probing her tongue around her teeth: Speaking of your birthday, Mum is asking if you're free for a dinner next weekend. Em says she can be around, although she might have had the baby. They've got a dog now too! God, my sister is fucking insane.

I thought about Emily and Samson's beautiful beige home, soon to be filled with a new baby and a dog to run into a room and demand love, love that they would give effortlessly. But Catherine was the epitome of Celtic warmth, and Jon had been adopted from Colombia by a Norwegian family, who then returned to adopt his biological brother. Emily and Ruth were born with love in their bones. I couldn't keep a succulent alive.

My phone rang on schedule, and I turned it straight over. Ruth asked whether I was sure I wanted to ignore her. She probably wants to say happy birthday.

She sent a card.

But didn't you miss last week's call too?

The device vibrated twice more before stopping. See, Roo, she doesn't want to speak to me either.

We drank our wine quietly, and then Ruth said: So, a week Sunday for dinner?

Sounds good. I love Catherine's birthday dinners!

That's because you're the favorite. I got leftovers. Speaking of, she said. Noodles? There's a new place round the corner that's meant to be epic.

As we stood to leave, a man knocked into us and his hand lingered on Ruth's shoulder. She lurched back. Do you mind? He laughed it off, and I smiled at him in apology. Her eyes flicked to me. Why did you do that? I didn't know what to say; it had been an impulse.

Ruth's figure drawing came to mind; the model's severed penis hovering like a rain cloud. Ruth smiled to let me know that she wasn't cross, and as we walked to the noodle place, talking about films and restaurants and people, my feminist guilt sunk to the place where I kept the other hidden things.

CHAPTER 4

NINE O'CLOCK AND AMY ARRIVED IMMACULATE AND LOUD.

He had been the first to arrive. I had opened the door to find him holding a chocolate cake that he had baked himself. It was the first time I had seen him look nervous.

Twenty-eight! Happy birthday, darling girl!

Thanks, Ames.

David can't come, she said with a saccharine tone. He really wanted to but he's hell for leathered at work. I told her that she wasn't using that expression correctly. She waved her hands and then pulled me in for a kiss. Coats?

On the bed.

I led Amy through the flat, where my friends were spaced around the living room and kitchen. I handed her a plastic flute, at which she looked confused and said: I suppose it saves on washing up. She forced eye contact before clinking my glass. Bad sex for seven years, remember! Then, noticing him, she lowered her voice: I cannot believe you're dating him! He's so . . . and you're so . . . She couldn't find the words for him but concluded that I was "quiet," "reserved," and "intelligent." I told her that those were adjectives people used to describe serial killers.

Do be careful, though, babe, she said. I've always said that about your writing. It lacks an identity. I don't mean that as a criticism, but, well, it does, and he—from what I can tell—is someone who has such a strong identity. Do you remember when he just waltzed into the pub?

He didn't waltz, Mat invited—

And he didn't say a word and just shoved his feet on the table.

I know but—

And then he called Chris a cunt.

Chris's character.

Same difference.

I smiled: So you're saying you agreed with him?

Her mouth fell slack, and she conceded. Fine, we all know that Chris can be a "See You Next Tuesday," but he didn't need to say it!

I wasn't offended by Amy's thoughts. I would rather that people had an opinion than think he was just *nice*. I worried that people thought that about me, because it took me longer to reveal the colors of myself, which he and Ruth and even Amy offered confidently. I was still curating pieces for him. The "funny" piece. The "sexy" piece. The "sweet" piece.

I pointed to the cake on the table and said that he had made it for me. Amy looked confused and replied that perhaps he wasn't as hostile as he seemed. I replied that he was exactly as hostile as he seemed, and she looked even more confused.

Well, she said, sipping her prosecco, I'm just happy you're seeing someone. You do know that if you don't have sex for more than six months, your vagina seals back up? Oh my god, there's Floo! *Floo!* Amy opened her arms to our friend Fiona, prosecco swishing from her glass, and I returned to him.

For the first fifteen minutes of the party, he had awkwardly flipped through the recipe books on the window ledge and I had realized, as he muttered things like *Thirty minutes, my arse*, that he cared about tonight.

He pressed his lips to my hair, then took a swig of beer. Why is she here? he asked, nodding to Amy. She's like a Stepford wife.

She's a friend, you know that.

Yeah, but like, a *writing* friend?

Amy and I were at university together.

You were?

I told you that!

You didn't.

And she's not a Stepford wife. What even is a Stepford wife? She's really talented.

Just what the world needs, he said, taking another swig of beer.

I told him that for someone who didn't care what anyone thought of him he was surprisingly critical of others.

(the "no-nonsense" piece)

He told me that was because he was always right. Then he pointed to my blinds and said that I had moths. I told him that I knew. He asked why I wasn't getting rid of them. I said that I didn't want to bother them.

(the "adorable" piece)

He furrowed his brow. They're *moths*, honey, he said, his voice beer-drenched and delicious.

I felt a deep happiness thinking about how at the end of the evening everyone would leave but he would stay. We hadn't used words to define our relationship, but his directness was a comfort; he wasn't the sort of person to be anywhere he didn't want to be. If he didn't want to be at the party, he would leave; if he didn't want to be with me, he would leave me. But still, the words would be nice.

So . . . this is nice . . . you being here, meeting my friends . . .

Okay . . .

Some would say that's a big step.

Some?

Not me, obviously.

(the "cool" piece)

He rolled his eyes, but I could see that he was fighting a smile. A feeling of warmth rose in me like when I saw a baby otter.

The doorbell went.

It's Ruth!

She's late.

* * *

RUTH ARRIVED IN AN eighties' waistcoat, high-waisted jeans, and a selection of gold necklaces. I was wearing a black dungaree dress and a white shirt. She looked like she was in a fashion campaign and I looked like a Victorian ghost.

I went to the kitchen to make her a cocktail and watched them: him on the sofa arm, holding his beer, arm muscles flexed; her, gesticulating, bracelets sliding down her arm. Ruth didn't curate pieces of herself. I remembered my therapist at school telling me to separate my emotions from myself. Ruth had always been able to do that; her core was fixed.

I joined them and handed her a passion fruit martini. I'm sorry, I used too much syrup!

He raised his eyebrows, and Ruth nudged my arm. Where's my beer? he asked. Ruth told him to get it himself. I loved how comfortable they were with each other already. He asked if he could change the music. Ruth, have you noticed how crap Enola's taste in music is considering otherwise she pretends to be cool? And she can't cook for herself, he said, and laughed. How do you survive, honey? You're like a baby deer in the wild.

She's fine, said Ruth. And it's cooler to like the music you like as opposed to the music that everyone else likes.

He made a face at me. I made a face back. Ruth sipped her martini and told me that it was delicious. He said that it wasn't kind to lie. I laughed and he laughed.

I wanted him more every day. I was addicted to the details: what his skin smelled like, how big his cock was, the songs he hummed in the shower. I even loved the smell of his cigarettes. Sometimes, when he smoked, I asked for a drag. I never inhaled, but I held the smoke in my mouth and blew it out, imagining a smoke ring.

I pressed my head to his, and it was perfect. He was perfect.

HANG ON—

I can hear my phone ringing. Fuck. I'm expecting a knock at the door, but what if it's a phone call? Could it be Ruth calling to tell me how the team-building exercises are going? *They asked me for an interesting fact about myself and I told them about the guy I killed in Vegas.*

I slide shut the balcony doors and return to the warmth. In the bedroom, my T-shirt is a bad joke by the wardrobe and my phone is still smashed but sentient. It's not Ruth, but I'm relieved when I see the name on the screen.

"Hi, sweetheart." Ruth's mum's voice is deep and warm.

"Hi, Catherine." I'm surprised to find that mine is trembling—I realize this is the first time I've spoken today.

"Oh, sweetheart," she says, "how are you doing?"

"Oh yes, I'm fine, I just . . . I just have a sore throat," I lie, coughing. "That's better!" My voice comes out stronger. "How are you?"

"Can't complain . . . Have you heard from Ruth yet?"

Catherine doesn't know that we're fighting. I answer that I haven't, and she pauses, then: "I just hope she gives this job a real chance."

"She went to Bath for the training day, which is a good sign!"

She tells me that I know her daughter better than she does. "And listen, I wanted to check in with you about Christmas. Are you going to be coming to us? It'll be a quieter one this year, as Emily and the girls are at Samson's."

Will Ruth want me there this Christmas?

"I'll let you know in the next couple of days, if that's okay?"

I sit on the edge of the bed, and the photo that Catherine gave me last Christmas stares at me from the wardrobe mirror. Dad's sloping nose, weak jawline, and protruding ears are mine now. But my eyes still belong to Mum. Pale brown, almost amber, with a dark ring framing the iris. They are reptilian. Mum's beauty is the first thing people comment on if they meet her, with a note of surprise, like they weren't expecting her to be. My mum was an actress before she met my dad. She made people admire her for a living. I am not my mother's daughter.

"Oh, of course. There's no rush. You know me, I'm just getting organized," Catherine says.

"Thank you."

"Your room is always here."

I remember the first time she said that to me: *Don't call it the spare room, Enola, it's your room.*

I smile. "I know it is."

But I am not Catherine's daughter either.

"Are you sure you're all right, sweetheart? You sound a little down. Do you want to come over for dinner? I'm making that fish dish you like."

I really want to say yes. I want to be wrapped in that house. The blankets on the sofa. The books in the toilet. The photos by the stairs. When Catherine calls dinner she makes an effort to say my name: *Emily, Ruth, Enola . . . food's ready!*

"Maybe when Ruth gets back?"

"Have you got something on?"

"I'm just waiting for something."

"A delivery? Anything nice?"

I lie again. "Yes, something nice."

"That's good, sweetheart, you should treat yourself. And have you heard anything about your book yet?"

"Not yet."

"Well, try not to worry too much. And call if you change your mind about tonight?"

"I will."

"And did you manage to speak to your mum yesterday?"

"Yes."

Catherine knows I am lying. She knows me in a different way to Ruth, but she sees through me in the same way.

"Oh, sorry, Catherine, there's someone at the door. I think it's my delivery?" One final lie.

She sighs. Ruth inherited the same noise. We say goodbye, and I immediately miss her voice.

I check my messages. Two unread ones from Virinder. His "online" status flickers like a broken lightbulb. There is still nothing from Ruth. I should have realized at my party just how much she didn't like him, but it's easier to believe the reality you want.

THE PARTY ENDED WITH Amy being the first to leave, declaring how much fun she had in a tone that implied she hadn't expected to have any, and Ruth the last to leave. Any other year, Ruth would have stayed over, but this time he was here.

Ruth zipped up her raincoat and gathered me in. She smelled like passion fruit and Chanel. She told me that she had shifts on Monday and Tuesday. I told her that I wasn't in until Thursday because I needed to write. She asked me if I was getting much writing done.

Not really. He's a little . . . distracting.

She asked if it was nice having him here tonight and if I had met his friends yet. I shook my head, and she then said that he seemed guarded, as if she was agreeing with me, but that wasn't what I had meant.

Don't you like him, Roo?

She adjusted the hood of her coat. Look, she began. It's always weird meeting someone's best friend, and maybe he was awkward or keen to make, like, a good impression or something. But I'm never going to love hearing someone put you down.

When did he put me down?

What do you mean? The music, the cooking?

I leaned backward to check that he wasn't listening, but he was on the balcony smoking and the music was still playing. I told Ruth that he was only teasing. You didn't think he was funny? Ruth said that he was confident and magnetic, but that he didn't have a nice word to say. I reminded her that he had made me a cake, and she said that he also made sure everyone knew he had made it. I told Ruth that she was being harsh. I like the banter. I hate all that heavy stuff. It's nice that it's chilled! She said that banter was good, but it seemed like the jokes were his and not mine. And chilled is good if that's what you want? But it seems like you really like him, Enola.

Ruth, if you don't like him, just say you don't like him.

It doesn't matter what I think.

It matters to me.

I stepped back and folded my arms. He made me laugh at myself. He took me out of my head. He made everything exciting. My blood was pumping for the first time in years. How could she not see that?

Ruth reached for my arm. I'm sorry, she said. I like him as long as he makes you happy, but if he hurts you, I will kill him. If anyone deserves happiness, Enola . . .

I told her that I was happy, and she said that she was happy too, then. Both of us were slurring our words. I told her to text when she was home, and she said that she was meeting a date. I told her to be careful. She told me not to worry. Claire is a primary school teacher who cross-stitches. I told her that those were the ones to watch out for.

They're not, actually, Laa.

I closed the door wishing that Ruth knew me just a little bit less.

IN THE LIVING ROOM, I surveyed the detritus: leftover cake, torn streamers, and half-drunk drinks. The balcony doors opened and closed, and he was in my arms, crisp and cold.

Did you like Ruth?

Yeah, he said. She seems cool.

I wanted more details, but he handed me a badly wrapped present from the inside pocket of his denim jacket. Happy birthday. I looked down at the gift and then up at him. I told him that he had already made me a cake and that this was too much. I wanted to cry, I managed not to, but still, noticing my sincerity, he told me not to be dramatic.

Besides, Steph helped with the cake.

Steph was a name I heard as much as he heard Ruth's. Patrick—Pat—and Steph were his closest friends. Steph was an actor, and Patrick was an illustrator.

Steph could have come tonight, you know.

She had plans.

Okay, but she *could* have, if you wanted her to. I'm just saying that I'd love to meet your friends, if you—

Just open the present, Enola.

I hated that Ruth was getting in my head. We hadn't even been dating a month. I would meet his friends when he was ready.

I tore open the cheap paper to find a CD that he had made. In the sleeve was a piece of lined paper on which he had written a list of the songs. The last song on the list was by Kate Bush and he had quoted:

Keep us close to your heart, so if the skies turn dark, we may live on in comets and stars.

It was the most beautiful, thoughtful gift, and I told him that I would make him one in return. He said that if he wanted to listen to the *Dawson's Creek* soundtrack, he would buy it. Then he went to the kitchen, got a bin bag from the second drawer, and began clearing the rubbish.

His affection was there in scrawled black Biro, in a homemade cake, in the fact that he knew where my bin bags were kept. I imagined the party where he and Ruth met and loved each other. That version was so close to this one that it didn't matter. And it didn't matter that I didn't know his exact feelings yet, because mine were weaving over the hole in my chest. I wanted to tell him how much I adored him, but I didn't; I went to the kitchen and interlaced my fingers with his so that they dangled down by his crotch. He dropped the bin bag and kissed me. The perfect punctuation mark of a kiss, a beat lingering like someone had pressed the sustain peddle on a piano. Then he pulled back and shook his head. Well, this is going pretty well, isn't it?

CHAPTER 5

His foot nudged mine from the other side of my sofa. How's it going? I tucked my feet under myself and groaned. Not well. He smiled as if he had expected me to react like that.

We had been spending regular nights like this at mine, with our laptops and a bottle of wine. We didn't go out much anymore, but it was nice, I reasoned; we had skipped to the part where we were a proper couple at home. Only, as Ruth pointed out, we still hadn't defined the relationship and we didn't live together.

He typed rapidly, with reading glasses and deep concentration lines, but I couldn't write with him—not that I could write without him, but having him here dominated my thoughts. I was always on high alert, like I was afraid to concentrate on something that wasn't him. Last week, I had read him a section of my novel, and he had listened and nodded and told me to just keep writing. *You can't call yourself a writer when all you do is stare at a blank page, Enola.* I joked that the blank page was my favorite, and he had said that made me a fantasist, not a writer.

When did you know you wanted to be a writer?

After I read *Catch-22*, he answered without thinking.

He didn't ask for my answer, but when I was seven, Dad bought me a book of ghost stories. One story was about a girl who found her room full of dust. She cleaned, but the next morning it returned, thicker. This happened again and again until, finally, she left. The first morning that she wasn't there, a truck plowed through the wall and smashed where she would have been sleeping to pieces. The dust had been a warning. I asked Dad who put the dust there, and he shrugged and said: *The writer?* That was the part of the answer I wouldn't have shared. The fact that it was about control. The school therapist had encouraged me to write whenever I felt powerless. If she had suggested I pick up the bassoon, maybe I'd still be pursuing that.

Are you insisting on a prologue? he asked.

After I had read him a section of mine, he had read me a section of his, and it was everything I knew it would be. Sardonic and intelligent and warm. Every word belonged to him. He wasn't trying to be a writer. He was one. And I was just writing to stop a truck from smashing through my bedroom wall.

I nodded, and he looked up. Why? he said. You're not writing a thriller. I answered that there were thriller elements, and his face crinkled. What does that mean, thriller *elements*? It's pretentious. Focus on the story.

I explained that I wanted to write something with a dark female voice, and he stretched his neck as if he was preparing for a fight. Honey, why do you talk like your gender is separate? You *are* female; anything you write will have a female voice. You have to be honest, or the reader will see through you.

I asked if he meant that people should only write about things they have personally experienced.

I didn't say *truthful*, I said *honest*.

Is there a difference?

Yes.

I sighed, and he softened. Enola, he said, you're a good writer, much better than Amy or Chris. You could write something great. But it has to come from you. You're wasting time. And I say that as someone who spent their twenties wasting time.

Didn't those experiences help your writing?

Sure, but I'm thirty-five and there are people making debuts at twenty-two.

It bothered me that he insulted people from the group. I hadn't been back since we met, partly because I was afraid that he would make fun of me.

You know, you can compliment me without insulting my friends, I said.

I could, but what's a compliment without relativity?

He continued typing like he was writing the next great master-piece, and I pressed "Control-A" and changed my font to Garamond.

There, he said, holding up his laptop like a trophy. Fuck, I get so much work done at yours, honey.

I looked at my work, unchanged apart from the font.

I keep hearing of all this crap being published and I *know* that my book will have an impact. I mean, all those guys from your writing group, none of those books will get published, let alone get agents—

Well, Amy's is.

Is what?

Amy's first book, I'm sure I told you? The one about the detective and the serial killer that turn out to be twins? It's getting published next year. She has a deal—a big one. You didn't know? It's the 2015 lead debut for—

His face clouded over. Why are you telling me that now?

I don't know. Because it's true.

No, it's because I pissed you off and rather than tell me I pissed you off you're being passive-aggressive.

He removed his reading glasses and started rubbing his eyes.

I told him that I hadn't meant anything by it, but that he shouldn't feel threatened. Amy was just further along. She has an agent and has been on submission before.

He slammed his laptop down. You know why? Because of her—how did you put it?—*dark female voice.* I opened my mouth, but he pounced: Don't defend her, Enola. She's written about a female killer and a female detective. It's the "thing" at the moment. What's it called?

I don't remember . . .

Enola, come on. What's the book called?

It's called *The Dark Side of the Coin*.

Fuck off.

He reached for his glass, but it was empty, so he finished the wine in mine and then left. I assumed that he'd gone to the bathroom, but then the front door opened and closed. Minutes passed, and I started to feel uneasy, like I might never see him again.

Why *had* I told him about Amy? Because I wanted to hurt him? Because it was a normal thing to tell someone? Because I wanted him to know everything that I knew: my favorite color, Ruth's middle name, how I liked my tea?

I went to the front door. My keys were gone from the monstera tray, which meant that he was coming back. I waited until the handle was pushed down and then ran back to the sofa like I had never moved.

He started explaining straight away: Look, I've just been working on this book for fucking ages, and when I finish it, I'm going to be told by every agent that it's great but it's not what they're looking for. And then I'll watch while every Gen-Z with a laptop gets handed a six-figure deal. Celebrity memoirs. *Fuck*, don't get me started on celebrity memoirs.

Gary Neville? I joked softly.

He smiled at my joke and rested his head on my shoulder; his hair smelled like cigarettes and rain. Enola, he said. I know I can be a fucking nightmare. You wouldn't be the first girl to say that. But you don't understand how stressful it is. He lifted his face and his eyes looked heavy. I didn't know anything about the other girls he had been with, but I wanted to be different. If they found him a nightmare, then I would understand him.

Listen to me, I said. You are the most amazing, talented, funny, honest man I've ever met. Agents are going to jump to sign you when you're ready to query.

He told me that I hadn't read his book. I told him that I had read enough. He told me that I hadn't even read three chapters. I told him that I knew *him*. Then he asked me to hold out my hand and placed a chocolate egg in my palm. Let's go on holiday after Christmas, he said.

I looked down at the egg and then up at him.

I really need a fucking holiday. And look, I know it's early days but I'm pretty confident I'll still want you to be my girlfriend. If you still want me?

Girlfriend.

The word ran through my body. I wanted to squeal and kiss him and tell him how happy I was to be his girlfriend. I wanted to call him my boyfriend and tease him about being too old for that word. But I couldn't let him think that mattered, so I hummed to tease, to lighten, to minimize that which I felt profoundly, and said: I'll still want you to be my *boyfriend*. The word tumbled awkwardly off my tongue, but he smiled when he caught it. He kissed my cheeks, my neck, my lips, and I was coming up from a drug.

Later, we had sex like a couple who just had their first fight: without foreplay. After, I asked him what he was thinking, and he said that he wasn't thinking anything, he was just happy. I told him that I was happy too. And I was. But it was a different kind of happiness, the kind that made me question if I had ever been happy before. And it meant more, I thought, that we were people to whom happiness didn't come easily.

CHAPTER 6

IT WAS A MONTH INTO THE NEW YEAR. I HAD SPENT CHRISTMAS with Ruth's family. Emily had her new baby. Ruth was an aunt again. (*And so are you, Enola*, Catherine said.) Ruth had a brief hiatus as an admin assistant for a gym company, but she was now back at the café. My novel was the same length as it was before the bells rang in 2015, and when they did, Ruth and I had celebrated in the warehouse. He had celebrated with Steph and Pat, whom I still hadn't met. But we were still together, and we were still planning a holiday.

We lay in my bed as the thumping of someone else's Saturday night bled through the walls. He was scrolling social media, and I was picking at my novel. His eyes drifted to my screen.

Try Wingdings, honey.

I pushed his face, and his smile curled. He was adorable and endearing and frustrating and I couldn't focus on anything.

What? he said, sensing my thoughts.

Nothing . . .

We continued with our separate activities, and then he picked up Otter.

No! Leave her alone!

I tried to grab her, but he hid her behind his back and said that otters were pieces of shit.

They are not! They collect rocks!

I hate to break it to you, but otters are violent rapists who bite the females' noses to stop them from escaping and hold their children hostage. They are fucking pieces of shit.

That can't be true! And anyway, Otter is female.

I seized her back, and he grabbed my hand. Why are your nails so bitten, honey? What is wrong with you? You're like a child . . .

No, I'm not. I just don't like them long.

Like a grubby little child.

I'm not!

So, you bite them down? Like a monkey?

I told him that I used nail clippers. He told me that I must be the only woman he knew who used nail clippers. I told him that was sexist and that he only knew one woman. What are Steph's nails like? I asked (hoping that her name might prompt an introduction). But he put my finger in his mouth. I told him that we should stop getting distracted. We still haven't booked a holiday!

Fine. He took my laptop—Hey! I protested—and started typing in destinations: Mexico, Tokyo, Jamaica. I told him I was thinking of somewhere closer but he wanted sun. When is the last time you had a proper holiday?

Good question, I thought. Ruth and I went to Lisbon, two, three years ago? Thinking of Ruth, I made a mental note to text her back. She had asked if I wanted to see all three Lord of the Rings films and have a shot each time it looked like Legolas forgot a line. We had been seeing less and less of each other lately.

I told him that I hadn't had a proper holiday since I was a child. Ruth was always in between jobs, and it was hard to find time and money. He told me that I didn't always have to go with Ruth. It would do *you* good to go on holiday by yourself, honey.

The way he said that bothered me. I didn't want him to think that I was boring or unadventurous or codependent or any of the things that I worried about, so I began talking about Kenya. But as soon as the words came out, I realized how much I wanted to say them. We knew so little about each other outside of these few months, and the more time we spent together, the odder that felt. Like forgetting someone's name and it becoming too late to ask.

He stared as I rambled about camping trips to the Maasai Mara. He told me that my childhood sounded like Animal Planet. I asked him what his family used to do for holidays. Caravan park, he said with a lilt to make me laugh. Didn't you ever just lie on a beach?

We used to go to the coast.

What coast?

Watamu. Turtle Bay. The airport is Malindi, I think.

He started typing. I asked him what he was doing, and he said that he was seeing how much flights to Malindi were. My throat turned dry. I told him that it had been nearly twenty years since I had been there. He said that he was confident the Indian Ocean hadn't changed. I told him that it would be really hot. He said that hot was perfect. I told him that it would take ages, you'd have to fly to Nairobi and change. He said it would be an adventure. I said that it would be expensive, but then the prices appeared. That's doable, he said. Where did you stay? I scratched the back of my head, which was suddenly itching.

This beach house by the sea. I think a friend of Dad's owned it? I wouldn't know where to begin now. Although my aunt might. She moved to Kilifi, I think. But I'm not sure if she's even there anymore. I haven't seen her since, well, since I was eight or nine. Aunt Louise was pretty eccentric.

He shut the laptop. Honey . . .

He was looking at me as if I had something that could make him happy, so I agreed to contact her. He asked why I looked terrified, and I made a noise that wasn't quite a laugh and did an action that wasn't quite a shrug. He told me that I was a strange creature.

You're all ice queen by day and sparrow by night.

I didn't recognize myself, but I still felt seen.

I LIFT UP FROM the bed; a man and a woman are shouting in the alley on the street below. Sometimes they smoke crack in the stairwell. They are harmless, I think. At least to me, not to themselves. Their faces are scabbed and their bodies are thin. I can't hear what they are shouting, but the noises are the same, recognizable ones, shocking, like when you first hear foxes, but then you realize what the sound is.

I don't know whose idea it was to go on holiday to Kenya. I don't remember if I wanted it or if I just wanted to make him happy. I feel like he pushed me into it, but he said that I had gone on about how much I wanted to go and so he had no choice. And if he was right about that, then what else was I wrong about?

I touch the bruise on my collarbone.

THE BAR WAS PINK and red, and the music was early 2000s pop. Amy was standing in front of a semicircle of women all drinking prosecco rosé through penis straws. She had a BRIDE TO BE sash over her white playsuit and wore a veil decorated with pictures of David's face. I had stopped drinking after the wreath-making workshop, because I was working in the morning. Being sober made listening to Amy describe her favorite sexual position in front of her mother even more uncomfortable.

I hadn't been able to stop thinking about him all day. It had been nearly three months since he first called me his girlfriend, but it still felt new. Being anywhere that he wasn't was exhausting. These other women had probably met their partner's friends and told each other that they loved each other. But I felt sorry for them, because they didn't have what I had.

And I have to lift one leg up like this so that he can then—

Amy continued like she was reading the instructions for a microwave.

Oh yes, your dad likes that, said Amy's mother, and Amy flung her head forward so that David's faces turned inside out. *Mum!* she squealed as everyone laughed.

I waited until the game was over and then went outside to call him. He didn't answer, and so I called Ruth. Ruth always answered, and I always felt honored, because when I was with her and someone called, she ignored them.

Hey, Laa, what's up?

I asked her what she was doing, and she said that she was eating edibles and listening to records. I told her that she was so cool. She laughed and said that her face was covered in Sudocrem. How's Amy's hen?

I just find hen dos so weird.

Oh god, me too. Still up for coffee in the morning?

I am. I'm going to leave soon so I can get more than five hours' sleep. Fuck, it's fucking freezing.

I wrapped my arms around myself and pressed my legs together.

I bet you can't wait to be in Mexico, Ruth said.

I still hadn't told her the truth about where we were going. I had been afraid that she would talk me out of it. But now it was booked and now I was lying.

Just then, my phone beeped.

Oh, Roo, he's calling me. Can I call you later?

I barely said hello before he started talking about his book. I waited until he finished and then told him that I wanted to come over. He said that he thought I had work in the morning. I told him that I did but that I wanted to see him. It's all this talk of sex, you see . . .

Oh yeah? he said with a suggestive inflection.

Yeah, I said, biting my lip as if he could see me.

He told me not to be long.

Inside, everyone was dancing to Beyoncé. I congratulated Amy and said that I couldn't wait for the wedding. She asked me if he was going to come.

Sorry he can't come for the whole day, but it's costing us one hundred pounds per head, and honestly, babe, I really don't know him.

I said that I hadn't mentioned it to him yet, and she told me to hurry up. She kept her hands above her head and her hips moving as she spoke. I reassured her that I would ask him soon. And I would. I wasn't sure why I was nervous. Going on holiday was a bigger step than going to a wedding.

If he won't go to a wedding with you . . .

He will! I promise I'll ask him soon.

I danced to three songs, and an hour later I was in his bed.

THEY HAVE TO LEARN, *Enola.* I thought about how openly Amy's friends had discussed their orgasms, and so when he moved between my thighs, I asked if he could touch me first.

Oh, he said. Okay. Sure.

He paused and then started, mechanically, like he was demonstrating that he had been asked to do it. It was awkward, and so I told him to forget it. I'm ready. I want you. I licked my hand and positioned him. Persevering, I directed him to go deeper and faster or slower, but when I opened my eyes, he looked frustrated.

Are you okay?

Yes, he said. Just . . .

Am I telling you what to do too much?

He said that the instructions made him feel like he was doing everything wrong. So I let him do what he wanted—or rather, I let him think that I wanted what he wanted. Maybe he knew the truth, but regardless, when he finished, I felt a similar release to him (information I wouldn't have shared with a pack of women drinking from penis straws). Before he rolled over, he said that we were going on holiday in a week. He squeezed the soft flesh above my hip and said: You feeling beach ready?

SORRY I'M LATE! RUTH breezed into the room the way she breezed into every room. I pushed a flat white across the table and asked her how her weekend at Emily's was. She said that Evie made her watch an awful thing about a pig but that the new baby was cute. My stomach was churning. There was a couple in the corner of the coffee shop having an argument. The woman's fringe was dyed in rainbow stripes. I wondered if *she* had a distinctive writing voice—lots of one-word sentences? *I bet she knows how to ask for what she wants in bed.*

Ruth was staring. Enola, what's wrong? Is it him? You know you can talk to me about him, right?

I took a deep breath. So, you know how we are going on holiday?

Ruth tipped her head as if to tell me to continue.

We're not going to Mexico. We're going to Kenya. To Watamu.

Ruth's lips parted, but before she could speak, I told her that I had contacted Aunt Louise and rented her friend's beach house. Ruth looked down into her coffee. She was silent for a long time. I told her to say something. Fine. She asked me why I lied to her. I told her that I wasn't sure. I thought she was going to get angry, but she reached for my hand and asked if he understood what the trip meant. I didn't know why, but her kindness frustrated me. I told her not to be histrionic. It's just a holiday! I said in the same tone as when something is *just a joke*. Ruth blew air and said that she didn't know where to begin. I picked up my coffee. Well, don't, then. Just be happy for me. She asked if I had told my mum. I told her that my mum wouldn't care.

But don't you think you should tell her? I assume you're going to be seeing Louise?

Shit. I hadn't thought about that. All I had thought about was him on the beach in his swimming trunks. Even when we got vaccinations and malaria tablets, nothing had felt real until this conversation.

Roo. Stop, okay? It's just going to be a fun holiday!

Ruth held her hands in front of her chest. Her nails were painted yellow, apart from her right thumb, which was black. Okay. Don't have a go at me. I'm just worried, Enola. You've spent a long time getting your life to a place that you're happy with and to go back to Kenya after nearly twenty years with someone you barely know?

I told her that I did know him. And that I didn't think my life had been in a place that I was happy with. Ruth asked if that was true. Do you really think you've not been happy, Laa?

I told her that I wasn't sure, but that I was definitely happy now.

Ruth lifted an eyebrow. I asked her why that was so hard to believe. She ran her tongue over her gums, and I knew that she was going to say something that I didn't want to hear.

For one, she began, you keep saying that he's straightforward and easy to talk to, but if that was true, you'd literally be going anywhere else! Think about it. You're so keen to please him.

I told her to stop getting in my head. She told me that I was different at the moment. I rebutted that she was different when she met someone. How? she challenged. I told her that when she was with Elle, she watched lots of German films, and with Kris, she started bouldering. Ruth dropped her chin and said that was taking an interest in their hobbies. Does he take an interest in yours? I told her that we wrote together. She said that writing wasn't a hobby, it was my career.

It's a *hobby*, Ruth.

And is that from him?

No! But sitting watching him type just reaffirms that I have absolutely no hope in being a professional writer.

She said that she hated that I was doubting my writing. I told her that I had been doubting my writing for years. She said that this was different. And if that's the case, why not spark something up, write something new, do a course—don't just sit there watching him type!

I'm not just watching him—

Ruth interrupted. We're going off topic. At the end of the day, I'm concerned that this trip is going to hurt you. And that you're not protecting yourself enough with this guy.

I told her that I was fine. But then the coffee shop became louder and brighter, like a video game, and I had to blink to settle it. Ruth asked me if I had eaten enough. She had on an expression like we had this conversation all the time, but we hadn't had it for years. I said that the real issue was that she didn't like him. She said that was irrelevant. Did you like the last guy that I went out with, Enola? I reminded her that the last time she went on a date with a man was fifteen years ago and he paid for his own dinner with supermarket vouchers. At that we laughed, and I was relieved until her eyes glossed and she said that she always thought we would go back to Kenya together.

Oh, Roo.

I plunged my hand into hers and told her how sorry I was. I'm so selfish. I didn't think. She told me not to worry.

I'm so sorry, Roo.

She waved her hand like it was nothing before condensing her feelings into pithy advice: Just make sure you pack the Jungle Formula.

The conversation was over. Ruth checked her plastic strawberry watch and finished her coffee; then, singing a thank-you to the waiter, she opened the door and stepped aside to let me go through first. With us the air was cleared as easily as it was filled.

CHAPTER 7

THERE WAS A CURRENT RUNNING THROUGH ME, AND I COULDN'T sleep, so I watched a television show where people showed doctors the parts of their bodies they were embarrassed by. I wasn't sure if there was power in revealing your flaws publicly, in close up, under indiscriminate white lighting, or whether these people were masochists. I hid the parts of myself that I didn't like and sometimes I wondered how much of me was left visible after that. But *he* liked me, he wanted me, he was happy with me. Ruth was wrong. This is what happiness looked like: a week's worth of day and night outfits rolled up in a suitcase that had been packed for two weeks. When he saw it, he had teased: *Jesus. How many clothes do you need, honey?*

After the show finished, I watched a movie about a tsunami and when there was nothing left to distract me, I texted my mother:

I'm going on holiday tomorrow, so I'll miss Wednesday's chat.

I would tell her that we were going to Kenya if she asked, which she wouldn't.

Ruth wasn't the only person who tried to repair the relationship between me and my mother. My grandparents used to drop hints in the same unsubtle way as Amy, who had recently started attempting to set me up with David's friends. We would be eating cheese, and Gran would say something like: *You know, Enola, they have great cheese in*

France! But I hated it the most when Catherine did it because it made me worry that she just wanted her spare room back.

I went onto the balcony and looked out over the cold, sharp city. Now that the trip was real, the daydream of us on the beach, him in his trunks, both of us happy and golden, had been replaced by something violent and awful: a plane dropping out of the sky, a car crashing into a tree, a wave washing our happiness away. I shut my eyes and fantasized about being killed in a tsunami. He survived and, finding my name on a list of the dead, collapsed, weeping about how much he loved me. Then I went to bed and masturbated to a video he'd sent of him making bread from scratch.

TIREDNESS HOVERED IN THE terminal. Teenagers slept on backpacks by the windows, and couples in bejeweled tracksuits had their children riding suitcases like ponies. He was in old jeans with a hole in the crotch, because he said that they were comfortable for the flight. I was in a loose blue playsuit for the same reason. I wanted to smell the perfumes in duty free, but he pointed to the champagne bar: Come on!

We sat on high stools at the black marble bar in our raggedy clothes, while the only other patrons looked like oligarchs. I commented on how one woman was wearing fur, and he laughed. Fuck it, I'm on holiday. Two glasses of the cheapest champagne were handed over by an unsmiling Polish woman. We clinked our glasses, and he looked happy. I touched his smile lines, and he didn't stop me. Then he said: You know, I've never been on holiday with a partner before.

This was the first time that he had spoken about his past relationships, and I wanted more information. I knew the answers to the questions that writers were supposed to ask about their characters: What does he have for breakfast? (*Whatever he made for dinner.*) What is his favorite color? (*He always wears blue or black.*) What items does he carry in his pocket? (*Gum, cigarettes, keys.*) But I didn't have the answers to any of the big questions.

What about your ex—what was her name? I asked, scrolling on my phone so that he didn't think I was *too* interested.

Jessica.

And you guys never went away together?

He curled his lip and told me that she wanted to. But she worked a nine-to-five, so the concept of freelance was alien. I asked what Jessica did. He drank half his champagne in one gulp and ignored the question. To be honest, Enola, it got to the point where it was too difficult. She was a lovely girl, but in the end, she just needed help that I couldn't give her. Steph always says I have crap taste in women, he added with a wry laugh.

I didn't like the way he said that, but who was I to judge? He was so straightforward. Perhaps she *was* challenging.

I asked when they broke up, and he said two years ago. It occurred to me that he might have easily said "the day before I met you." I asked whether he had dated much since, and he said he had been on a few but that he always lost interest after date five.

What were you looking for?

Someone to blow me away.

He grinned, and I was unsure whether he was trying to appear as if he was joking to cover up the fact that he was serious or trying to appear serious when he was only joking. Either way, I was relieved to have made it past date five and into an airport.

I waited for him to ask me about my exes, but he didn't. I was keeping mental lists of the things that he told me in an effort to know him. Pinning snippets on a wall in my head, clues linked with red thread on a true-crime-podcast murder board. But was he doing the same? It wouldn't have been a long answer: Adam at university; Ben, who was here on a temporary visa; and Thomas, who ghosted me after three months. I hadn't been on holiday with any of them, apart from a long weekend in Amsterdam with Adam wherein I realized I was more interested in the museums than in Adam.

Oh, I said. That reminds me. You're invited to Amy's wedding.

Why? he asked, frowning.

I told him that it was just for the evening do. He said that Amy didn't really want him at her wedding. I told him that *I* did, keeping my tone nimble so that if I needed to, I could tell him that I was only joking.

I hate weddings, honey . . .

Me too! I said, because I didn't want him to think that I was trying to get him to a wedding so that we could organize our own.

I told him there was an open bar, and he said that I should have led with that. I pictured him in a suit. Me in a dress that I hadn't bought yet. Both of us at the bar, laughing about how much we hated weddings, but then there would be a moment, during the first dance, maybe, where we both just *knew.*

I told him that we'd have to book a hotel, and he put his glass down and wrung his hands like he was going to deliver important information.

You know, honey, something my dad always said, that people need to prioritize themselves in a relationship.

I laughed but his face was flat. But surely if two people always prioritized themselves, then the relationship would be a disaster?

Ah, he said, as if he'd solved a puzzle. But if two people both getting what they want out of a relationship is a disaster, then I would argue those two people aren't compatible.

So, you're saying . . .

I'm not coming to Amy's wedding.

All right, we should go, he said, finishing his champagne. I tried to finish mine, but it fizzed up and spilled down my chin. I told him that I wasn't a fan of champagne, actually.

Did he repeat that to himself? Enola, not a fan of champagne.

As we walked into the terminal, I started to feel dizzy. An announcement told us to go to the gate, but he searched the board like he needed to see the information himself.

We're boarding. How did we miss that?

The orange letters were blurry. He called me a lightweight. But it was more than that. My heart was racing. I thought about my words to Ruth: *It's just going to be a fun holiday.* For the first time, this felt like a mistake, and more than anything, I wished that Ruth were here. I was going back to Kenya with a man who didn't know that I didn't like whiskey or that I faked more orgasms than I had; who didn't know that I was only pretending to write my novel when he was writing his, and who didn't know the truth: that I was desperately, painfully, consumingly in love with him.

CHAPTER 8

Day 1

WE ARRIVED AT MALINDI AFTER FOURTEEN HOURS OF TRAVELING, and the air was thick with the kind of heat that held your body up. A man handed us keys to a car and told us to text when we wanted to return it. There was no paperwork, and the tank was empty.

He had decided that the holiday would be a good time to quit smoking, and so, driving to Watamu, he swore at the hidden speed bumps and the donkeys and the bicycles and the mkokoteni. I had suggested a taxi, but he said he preferred to be in control.

I lowered the dusty window and watched the world unfold and fall behind the car. It was like reading a book I hadn't read in years only to find that it wasn't exactly as I remembered. The colors were duller. There were more buildings. And the potholes were making me feel sick. Dad used to drive over them at speed and I would giggle while Mum held her stomach, the way that I was now, and accuse him of aiming for them to spite her. But there was an occasional smell of something in the breeze, I didn't know what of, but something so familiar that I had to pinch my arm to stop from crying.

He put on the radio and scanned past the static.

The road became smoother the farther we drove from the airport, but the sickness in my stomach remained. When we reached Gede, we turned toward the ocean and drove through Timboni. The buildings were bright colors, and there were stalls selling vegetables, plastic toys, mitumba clothes, shiny party dresses, and kitchenware. Everything was busier than I remembered. The town looked twice the size. I told him that, and he said, withering, that it had been nearly two decades. The final stretch was quiet until we arrived.

Okay, this should be it, he said, turning in. You have the instructions for the keys, yeah?

WE OPENED THE DOOR to the beach house, and it was instantly familiar, but then it changed and became unfamiliar the way that a word does when you focus on it. It looked like a sketch artist's impression of the house that we used to stay in.

He charged ahead but I remained in the doorway, still gripping the handle. There were little red half moons on my arm from where I had been pinching myself in the car.

Enola, you coming?

Yes, sorry!

I pulled my suitcase over the rugs on the sandy wood floors, past a lamp with frayed tassels and a collection of ornate dogs in a cabinet. There were three bedrooms, and the sofas in the living room had mosquito netting too. The house was meant for a family.

He was standing in front of the window in the master bedroom with his arms outstretched. The house was dark, and I squinted in the early afternoon light. Everything was bleached and endless, vast and endless, endless.

Right. I'm getting in the shower, then spending the day in that fucking sea, he said, pointing to it as if there was another one.

The way he made a space his own. Like everything belonged to him.

Did you see the weird dogs?

I laughed. I did.

He went into the adjoining bathroom, and I stared out the window as he sung cod opera. The waves broke over the sand and in the ocean over the reef, a marine park of fish, turtles, long black urchins with blue lights in the center and small orange dots, and smaller gray urchins with white-tipped spikes, like hedgehogs. I had trodden on one once, and Dad had pulled the spikes out with tweezers. Near the horizon, white fishing boats had flags showing their catches.

I left my suitcase by the side of the bed he hadn't claimed and walked through the living room to the outside. The humid air was full of warm, gentle noise. There was a small circular pool and a stout white wall with a wooden gate that led to a path to the beach. Everything was *almost* familiar. Memories hung like undeveloped photographs, and I closed my eyes to see them properly:

MUM IS CROSS BECAUSE I haven't put my jellies on. *The sand will be hot*, she shouts. But I want to catch Dad, so I run to the gate, to his outstretched hand, and he pulls me down the path to the beach. The sand becomes hotter and hotter, and my feet are burning, and just when I think I'm going to cry from the pain, we make it to the darker, cooler sand and run crashing into the waves.

FUCK, I'M THIRSTY.

I went to the kitchen, but there was no water in the cupboards, and I couldn't remember if the tap water was drinkable. My shoulder bag was by the door still, and there was a small amount of water left in my bottle. I drank the warm dregs and sat on the sofa arm with my head between my legs. Everything was happening so fast. I wanted to press pause, to be alone somewhere dark and timeless.

Bloody hell, it's humid.

I looked up to see him holding a blue towel with an orange fish. He was wearing black shorts and sunglasses that I could see my reflection in.

Come on, honey. Let's get you in one of those slutty bikinis I saw you pack. We'll go to the shops and get beers. *But . . .*

He charged at me and lifted me like I weighed nothing. He carried me to the bedroom and dropped me on the bed.

Wait, I smell like plane!

I don't care, he said, pushing my arms aside my head.

No, no, I can't.

Why?

Because I feel like I will burst into tears if you touch me. Just my stomach, I said, from the drive.

It was only a half lie, but I hated saying no to him. He said it was okay because he didn't want me to shit myself. Then he went to the bathroom and I lay on the bed and tried to regulate my breathing. There were cracks in the yellow ceiling and a picture of a goat in a gold frame above a chest of drawers. I hadn't unpacked, but his belongings already covered the room. Covered *our* room. Clothes and shoes. Wallet, keys, and notepad. Inhaler for his hay fever. Three books. The air smelled like his aftershave.

The toilet flushed, and he shouted that it was time to go. I put on my black bikini, white T-shirt, denim shorts, and a wide-brimmed hat that I found in a cupboard next to some playing cards. He said that I looked like someone from a television show I hadn't seen.

I'm just going to brush my teeth.

Okay but hurry up, yeah, I didn't come all this way to stay indoors!

The mirror was steamed up from his shower. How could he have a hot shower? I could smell cigarette smoke in the steam. I brushed my teeth and remembered my mum's face behind my own in a mirror. It wasn't a specific memory but a feeling in the bottom of my stomach.

WHEN WE GOT BACK from the shops, I told him that I wanted to shower before the beach but what I really wanted was to call Ruth. I wasn't sure if it was the stress of hiding my feelings or the feelings themselves, but the morning had felt endless.

I turned on the water and then crouched between the wall and the sink so that my voice wouldn't carry. I'm working, Ruth answered in a whisper. Are you okay? My hands went to my face, and my eyes filled with tears. She told me to hang on. There were muffled voices, then footsteps, and then she spoke louder. She was in the break room. I could picture the lockers and the clock on the wall.

Roo, I'm so sorry for calling you.

Don't be. Is everything okay?

I told her that I was at the beach house, and it was amazing, but that I felt sick or claustrophobic or something. I keep having these half memories. And it's stupid because I only came to this beach, what? Four times in total? And it was nineteen years ago!

Ruth told me that it wasn't stupid. She asked if I had told him how I was feeling. I said that I was afraid of ruining the holiday, because this was his first holiday with a girlfriend. She sighed and sounded, for a second, like Catherine. Enola, if explaining your pain ruins the holiday, then something is wrong.

Ruth already didn't like him, so I told her that I was probably being paranoid.

She paused before replying: Okay, so, talk to him. You don't have to tell him everything. You just need to let him know that being back there is hard—

I didn't say it was hard.

Fine, not *hard* hard, just . . .

Strange.

Strange, then, she agreed. And, Enola, please, *please* know that telling him this isn't ruining anything. It should make you *both* feel better.

Ruth said that she had to go back to work but to please text her with updates. Is the weather at least glorious?

Already thirty degrees. What's it like there?

It's sleeting.

We laughed and then said that we loved each other.

I turned off the shower and looked in the mirror. Nineteen years. That was the length of a whole person. When I was nineteen, I drove and had sex and knew to walk on the road instead of the pavement when navigating Oxford Circus. Every cell in my body had been replaced twice. I thought of my old therapist: *You are not your pain; you are not your sadness.*

I came out of the bathroom, and he was waiting to come in. He started past, but I stopped him. My heart was pounding. Listen, there's something I wanted to talk to you about.

Okay . . . he said slowly.

I picked at a bump on my arm.

Just say it, Enola.

It's just that when I was little, we left here very suddenly. And I guess I didn't think I'd find it this strange being back . . .

Right, he said, clasping his hands. He had the same expression on his face as when I asked him to touch me in bed. Like he was waiting for a catch.

But it is. Strange, I mean.

He shifted his weight and asked what I meant by "strange." I told him that everything looked different, and it was discombobulating. I wasn't sure why I had chosen that word. His face changed, and he laughed. He said that he was relieved that I hadn't said something worse and that I would feel "bobulated" after some time in the sun.

Just don't focus on it. Leave for the beach in ten?

THE BEACH WAS QUIET. Seaweed that had been pushed up by the tide crisped and curled in the sun. I could see Turtle Rock in the ocean and, farther away, Whale Rock. There was another rock on the sand that we used to walk to after breakfast sometimes.

He said that the turtle looked more like a walkie-talkie and the whale looked more like a cat. I asked what he thought the one on the sand looked like, and he said: A scrotum.

All right, honey. Let's get in the water!

I had a blue-and-green-striped kikoi tied to my bikini straps that I was nervous to take off. He had only seen me naked in the half light, and in the bleached day, he would see every dimple and stretch mark and scar. It's not like he could leave if he didn't like what he saw—we were here for the week—but, still, I didn't want him to really *see* me. We left our towels on the sand, and I let him walk in front of me to the water. We waded in until we could float. I gasped as the water kissed my stomach, but the sensation didn't faze him. He pulled me to him, and I wrapped my legs around his waist. He asked me if there were jellyfish. I told him that there were Portuguese men-of-war, and his whole body tightened.

Not this time of year, though . . .

I pressed my mouth to his shoulder; his skin tasted like sun cream. There were new bars and hotels on the shoreline. Turtle Bay must have been less developed in the nineties. Or maybe that was just how I remembered it; the way that those four years existed in my mind a private, unedited paradise.

Just don't focus on it.

I asked if he fancied that local restaurant that Louise had suggested in her email. I wanted him to try maharagwe and mchicha. And apparently the coastal lot all eat this boiled soupy fish with sima? He made a face and said it sounded vile. I bit his neck, and he laughed.

He told me that I didn't seem like someone who had grown up abroad. I asked what someone who had grown up abroad should seem like, and he said: Ruth?

Ruth's different. She's a proper international kid.

Army?

The opposite! Her parents are artists. Her dad's a photographer and her mum's a painter. Ruth spent the first ten years of her life in different countries. Her dad is Norwegian—

Ruth's Norwegian?

I nodded. Colombian heritage—her dad was adopted. But Ruth was born in Norway. Her mum is half Scottish, so they lived in Glasgow for a while. And Canada for a year when her dad was doing a feature on indigenous communities.

Jesus.

Yeah. She's been everywhere, but Kenya always felt like home to me.

How very colonial of you.

Talking about Ruth made me feel better. I could breathe easier with her name on my tongue. Then he asked about my dad's work, but I didn't know much about it. He asked what our life was like. I told him we were in Muthaiga and that we had a security man on the gate and a driver.

Did you have, like, a cook and staff?

We had an mpishi and yaya. That's a cook and a nanny. And a house girl.

He made a noise like he wanted to continue the conversation, but it felt as if he was asking questions as research for a book and I didn't want to think of my life like that. I dropped back and skimmed my arms over the water like I was making a snow angel. I just needed to connect . . . to find my breath . . . to be present. But he unhooked my legs, plunging me backward. The salt burned my nose. Stripped my throat.

You just waterboarded me!

I dived and yanked his trunks. He splashed me. I splashed him. And I was, to anyone watching from the new, unfamiliar buildings on the coastline, happy.

All right, I want a beer.

After swimming until our feet were pale and bloated, we heaved onto the sand as if coming off a moving walkway. As we walked to our towels, beads of water glistened on his calves. He had a triangle of hair on his lower back, and his shoulder blades were already tinged pink. I thought back to our first meeting; I never could have predicted who we would be to each other.

Oi, I said. Watch those trunks . . .

He turned to look over his shoulder, glanced left and right like a child crossing the street, and pulled down his trunks. I screamed, but he swung his hips so that his penis slapped against his thighs.

This may have been the place where I had my last family holiday, but it was also the place where we were having our first. Amy said that a holiday was a great test for a couple. I would take the trip how

I took the relationship, moment by moment, fight by flight. It was only day one; it would get easier. Like having an old dream, unsettling at first, but then you realize that all it is, all it was, was a dream.

DAY 2

I woke not knowing where I was, and then I heard the waves. The breeze driving them blew through the window, and we inhaled seawater from our bed. He was sprawled, one leg under and one leg over the sheet. His face was crumpled, lips crushed on the cotton. I slipped through the netting so as not to wake him, and went through to the living room where the glass table still had on it our wineglasses and Scrabble board from after the restaurant. Already the holiday was starting to feel like it belonged to us and not to the past. I put the kettle on and walked onto the patio. I fished some insects from the pool and watched the boats on the horizon. My stomach felt full from last night's spinach and grains, but it was settling, *I* was settling.

Why didn't you wake me?

I turned and he was by the house, stretching his arms above his head. He had my lime-green kikoi around his waist, and I could see the mound of his penis.

I've only been up for a few minutes.

He came to me, and I ran my hands through his soft, ruffled hair. He told me he was hungover. I told him he would survive. We have nothing to do today, I said, moving my hands down to the lines on either side of his hips. For the first time I felt the impact of that statement: no pressure to write and no guilt when I didn't and no shifts at the café with bankers asking me if I was "doing this to put myself through university."

After a breakfast of papaya scored like a chessboard and peanut butter on toast (he told me that he loved the Kenyan peanut butter, which made me happy, because it felt like he was saying something that he loved about me), I showered, singing because the acoustics were excellent. When I came out, he was standing with his fingers in his ears. At least you're good at other things, he said.

The mischief in his green eyes and how my skin hummed from the sun made me get down on my knees. *Something I bet your ex never did.*

I should insult you more often, he said as I took him in my mouth.

Go on, then . . .

You're a shit cook.

Don't stop . . .

You're probably a terrible barista.

Oh yeah, that's the stuff . . .

You'll never be a writer.

WE DECIDED TO SWIM to the little island before lunch. He took a drag on his inhaler. We shared a madafu; then walked down the path to the beach and looked out at the blue.

Are you sure you're a strong enough swimmer?

He frowned. Are *you*, Enola?

I explained that Dad and I had swum to this island when I was little. Plus, I swim once a month at the pool in Hackney.

He whistled. Well, watch out . . . erm . . .

I folded my arms provocatively. You can't think of a single professional swimmer?

Gary Neville?

We laughed as we waded, then, as the water deepened, began to swim. We swam next to each other at first, but then we stopped talking, and the distance between us grew.

Good job you did all that training, honey! he shouted back.

My arms and legs were out of sync, and I kept swallowing seawater. The island wasn't getting any closer, and I thought of that man who pushed the boulder up the hill in hell. *How on earth did I manage this when I was a child?* It felt dangerous. A boat sent a wave toward us, and I dived under, but when I came back up, he was even farther away. Oh god. What if I couldn't do this? Worse than the notion of drowning was what he would think of me if I drowned.

I switched to a front crawl and concentrated on my movements until I found my stride, so much so that I began to catch him or he began to slow down.

All right, Gary Neville, I called.

He looked over his shoulder, and I thought he might slow to meet me, but he sped up. I felt a spark and kicked harder. He was barely a meter away. I reached to grab his foot, but then I stopped myself. My instincts told me to stay behind him. I would rather him tease me for being a bad swimmer than put him in a mood because he felt like *he* was one. I switched back to breaststroke and let him get to the island first.

When he neared the bank, I shouted to him not to put his feet down.

What?

Your feet.

Huh?

Sea urchins.

I was so focused on communicating to him not to put his feet down that I forgot about my own. He helped me out of the water, and I collapsed onto my knotted back. My ears were ringing, and there were stars where the clouds should be. He told me I was a mess and wiped the hair from my face. He was just as breathless, but I told him he was a good swimmer, and he said, proudly, that he used to go wild swimming. I felt a sting on the side of my foot. Three gray splinters with white tips.

Fuck! The word hooked in my chest, and I coughed.

He laughed, his eyes turquoise in the sun. Okay, honey. Come on. Placing my foot onto his thigh, he pressed his mouth to the skin and sucked. There, he said, presenting the tiny spikes to me. Now, what are you not going to do on the way back?

Put my feet down . . .

He leaned back against a tree, and I slotted between his shins, smoothing the hair into neat lines. A breeze skimmed the ocean, and the sun dried the water on our skin to salt. The moment was perfect. I would have cut my own arm so that he could heal the wound.

Day 3

We had perfected the morning routine. I put breakfast together while he showered, and then he did the washing up while I showered. We had the same things: papaya, peanut butter on toast, coffee, and mango juice. That morning we took one of the yellow boats to the marine park and went snorkeling. He was stroppy because we didn't see any turtles, and we teased each other about how we looked in goggles. After lunch we went to the market and bought a kikoi each. His had blue stripes and mine had pink. I made a joke about gender stereotypes. We found pétanque in the cupboard and played on the sand once the sun had lowered. Now it was sunset, and we were sat on the white wall with Tusker beers. My dad used to say: *You must always take time for a sundowner.* We watched the sun cast pink light, then turn red, shrivel, and sink into the ocean. When the world was lilac, we went inside, lit a citronella candle, and read our books on separate sofas, a bottle of red wine and a bowl of fried coconut on the glass table.

He was in a white T-shirt; his skin had a red-brown tinge, and his reading glasses had slipped down his nose. He gasped and then hummed as if something in his book had surprised him. A murder, perhaps, or a shocking twist. I had read the same paragraph multiple times because I couldn't stop looking at him. I wanted to sink into his body as if it were a favorite chair. Earlier Ruth had messaged asking if things were better, and I had replied:

Soooo much better. Total transformation. I never want to leave.

I couldn't imagine going back to seeing him once or twice a week. I loved knowing that he was with me when I went to bed and here when I woke up. I loved our morning routine and our silly little discussions about which activity we were going to do that day. I loved how confident I now felt in a bikini, without makeup, myself.

You want more wine?

I smiled and stretched.

I'll take that as a yes?

He topped up our glasses until the bottle was empty. He asked what we should do tomorrow, and I suggested lunch at Ocean Sports. He said that he wanted to finish his book before lunch. *A silly little discussion.* We drank and listened to more music, and, when the world was black, he looked at me, dizzying, and told me I was beautiful.

Yes, Ruth, he tells me that I'm beautiful all the time!

I told him to stop, but he looked emboldened. He said that I was funny and cute and he loved the freckles on my nose. I told him that he was drunk, and he said: Abso-fucking-lutely. He stood from the sofa. My heart started pounding. He walked over and sat next to me. *The smell of him.* He lifted my glass, and put it to my lips. Catch up. He pressed his thumb to my lips, catching the drops of wine before they stained my kikoi. And you're fucking sexy, he said. I had never felt sexy before, but I believed him because, at this point, I was what he told me.

DAY 4

The moon was full, and the ocean moved like a Newton's cradle. Crabs scuttled sideways as we lay on the grassy bank. I pointed out the constellations I knew. There's the Big Dipper. And there's the Plow. He told me that they were the same constellation.

One's American. It's like chips and crisps.

Dad and I used to sit on the car and watch the stars on safari. But we had different routines on the beach: walking to the rock after breakfast, staying in the shade over lunch, playing a card game after dinner. When I thought about the last time that I was here, there was a sepia grade over the memory. I had cried at the Malindi airport, as if I knew what was going to happen a few months later. I couldn't have known, but that was what retrospect did to memory: warped it and turned it sepia.

He started speaking as though narrating a nature program: There is the one that looks like a cock. And over there is the other one that looks like a cock. And, finally, there's one more that looks like—you guessed it—a cock. I asked him why the Milky Way looked so far away if we were a part of it. He told me to stop pretending to be stupid. It is mad that they're dead, though, he said. Properly mad. Just then a shooting star darted across the sky.

That one's not, I said.

He chuckled into his beer, then sighed contemplatively. I asked what he was thinking, and he said we needed more beers. Why do you always ask what I'm thinking? I shrugged. We were silent and then in a mock cute tone he said: Why, what are *you* thinking about?

We hadn't spoken about this since the first day, but I felt healthier now, so I answered honestly: I was thinking about how the last time I was here was the last holiday I had with my parents. He didn't seem to register the comment, he just replied that the last holiday *he* had with *his* parents was watching them scream over karaoke about his dad's secret girlfriend, Karen, who moved in a week later.

Keen for more clues for my murder board, I asked when his parents got divorced.

When I was twel—

Do you want kids?

I hadn't meant to interrupt and so my question was given unintended emphasis and he looked at me like I had asked him to impregnate me. But before he could speak, there was a motorcycle whine past my ear. I asked for the mosquito spray, and he gave me a look. Honey, you already smell like a meth lab. I told him that I was allergic to mosquitoes.

Honey, everyone is allergic. That's literally what a bite is.

He swigged a mouthful of beer and said that he couldn't believe we were going home in a few days. I hated hearing that. He was telling me something that I already knew, but it felt like he was saying that *we* would be over in a few days. Our relationship felt bound to this holiday somehow.

You know, we could always come back here next year. Go camping?

He gave me a withering look and reminded me that he wasn't keen on the whole safari thing. *Although,* he added, I have always wanted to see a zebra.

And that was all I needed to hear. It wasn't enough now just to be his girlfriend. I wanted more. I wanted the house in Stoke Newington. I wanted the matching publishing deals and our cover art framed side by side on walls that we painted ourselves. I wanted the hen do where I joked about his favorite sexual position in front of his elderly relatives. I wanted everything. He wasn't saying it in words, but he was saying it in something like them: he wanted that too.

What about a flebra? I asked.

There was a pregnant pause, and then, monotone, he said: Enola, would that be a cross between a flamingo and a zebra by any chance?

I stifled a giggle. Why, yes. What's the problem?

He took a sip of his drink. No problem, he said calmly. I just thought they were called zamingos.

No, that's an Italian in Clapham.

He gave in and laughed first—a symphony of water gurgling from a tap. Our happiness was such a giddy drunk that I almost forgot what was happening tomorrow.

Day 5

I didn't want to go, but I couldn't come all this way, ask her recommendations for restaurants, live in her friend's house, without meeting Louise for coffee. I wasn't sure what to wear. The last dress she had seen me in was a black one. There was only one outfit that I hadn't worn yet: a vintage sage slip that Ruth made me buy. He would like me in it. He would rub my hip bones, and I would feel delicate and lovable.

I came outside, and he was by the pool having a smoke. He didn't notice my dress. Don't, he said, referring to his cigarette. He was looking at me as if I was the one who asked him to quit, and it felt like I had inherited one of his ex-girlfriend's arguments. I told him that I wasn't going to say anything, and he asked me why I was moody. I told him that we needed to leave in twenty (a statement that answered his question but that he thought was a subject change). He stubbed out his cigarette in his coffee mug and asked where we were going.

Aunt Louise. Remember?

And you want me to go to that?

I just assumed you were?

I can if you want, he said, not even trying to match his face to his words. He was already in his trunks. I told him not to worry, but between that, the cigarette comment, and the fact that he hadn't noticed my dress, I was annoyed.

He sighed. What? Why do you look like that?

I just . . . I really don't want to go.

Look, he said. I think you're making too much of this. Just get it over with, thank her for the great house, and come back. I told him that it wasn't that simple. I hadn't seen Louise since I was a child, and my mum didn't know that we were here. He looked at me like I was being dramatic. Who cares if your mum and your aunt don't get on? I feel like you might be making a bigger deal out of this. It's just lunch. You'll be fine.

You don't want to come with me?

Not really.

He lit another cigarette.

Just like that?

Enola, be reasonable. I don't really see the point in meeting some random aunt that I'll never see again and that you have described more than once as mad.

No, it's my mum that describes her as mad, which probably means she's lovely.

I was disappointed, because I wanted him next to me. I wanted to feel his hand on my knee under the table and to see his eyes smiling.

But he wasn't "that kind of boyfriend," as he pointed out when I asked for a photo in the golden hour and he went into a tirade about social media. Perhaps it was for the best. I didn't know what Louise was going to bring up.

Fine, I said, more upset about the memory of the sunset photo.

This is my holiday too, Enola, he said, sharp.

Shit. I moved to him and told him that I was sorry. I pressed my face into his tank top; it was the same one he slept in and it smelled like our bed. He rested his arms on my shoulders and exhaled cigarette smoke over my head. He told me to just get it over with. And don't stress, honey. We only have a couple days left. I really want us to have fun, yeah? I smiled and told him that I wanted that too, and his hands moved down to my hip bones.

Honey, he said. You've lost weight.

I HADN'T SEEN LOUISE—AUNTY Lulu—since I was a child. She would kiss me on the mouth and wipe the lipstick with her thumb. I scanned the bar, and a voice reverberated: Oh, my goodness gracious! My sweet girl! I turned to see a woman with curly gray hair, red hoop earrings, and lips to match.

Aunty Louise?

Lulu, darling. Lulu.

She was wearing cargo shorts and a Tusker T-shirt. When she hugged me, her fingers dug between my ribs, and she smelled overwhelmingly of vanilla. Let me look at you! Gosh, you are the spitting image of your dad. I saw you and thought, that's Kit's and that's Kit's *and* that's Kit's too. She pointed to parts of my body with a long, ring-covered finger.

Kit. I hadn't heard his name in so long. Everyone just referred to him—if they ever did—as "*your* dad." Like he belonged only to me.

I am?

She nodded, clutching my hands so tight that my finger bones hurt. You are, my sweet girl. But not your hair, my darling, your hair is mine. Look how curly it is!

I told her it was only because of the sun and the salt, and she looked at me like I was hiding something. She asked me how old I was now. I answered that I was twenty-eight, and she said she thought I was older. It's because you're such a slip of a thing. Sophisticated. It makes you seem older. Small bones.

She sat, gesturing to the empty chair. Come and sit. She clicked at the waiter, then pointed to me. I smiled in apology and asked for a latte. Louise asked for the same as before and the waiter looked confused. I realized that he was probably a different man, so I asked what she was drinking so that he could hear the answer.

English breakfast, my angel.

As the drinks arrived, I watched her sip. The liquid rattled into her mouth. Her skin was covered in brown patches and deep lines cut her forehead. Her eyes, curved slightly, gave her an expression of sadness. When she smiled, her teeth were yellow and her lips pushed up to show her gums. She dabbed her brow with a handkerchief.

So, my lovely girl, tell me about yourself.

I opened my mouth to respond, but she continued: I was so pleased to hear from you, sweet girl. When I think about how long it's been . . . But I know that will have been your mother's doing. I know that. Don't you worry about that. There are no hard feelings about that. Anyway, I only have this one morning with you—Sam, that's my new man, is fishing, and I told him that we had to take a detour to meet my sophisticated niece. He asked me how old you were, and I almost said: She's six years old. My goodness, you must think I'm an old lady now!

I think you look wonderful, Louise—I mean, Lulu.

Oh, aren't you sweet? It's yoga. I'm doing yoga. So anyway, I have a little place in Kilifi, but my friend Kim, whose house you're staying in—

Yes, thank you so much for—

—rents it on the Airbnb and gets a *fortune*. You two have a very good deal this week. A *very* good deal. I'm thinking about doing that myself. Ours isn't a beachfront, but still, you and your gorgeous man can stay whenever you want. Now, darling girl. Who is he?

I put down my coffee and told her his name. That was all I said, but she gushed that he sounded lovely and then proceeded to say that her psychic had told her that she would meet someone from her past.

Now, tell me. You miss Kenya, don't you, darling?

I told her that I didn't really think of it much anymore. I've been in England for . . . gosh, nearly twenty years now, I said, looking to the ceiling as if the dates were printed on it.

Nineteen years and four months. I had just turned nine when Mum and I arrived at my grandparents' house in the Midlands lit up in Christmas lights.

Louise put her tea down. Your mother really did hate him, didn't she? I shifted in my chair and said that everyone had a different impression of things, but Louise snapped that there was only one impression of things.

Well— I started, but Louise interrupted.

Your *mother*—she said this like it was alleged—hated him. She was unhappy, you know, depressed. And I had to come out every few months to take care of you! She just wasn't made to be a mother. I'm sorry but that's true. She missed being an actress, not that she was very good at it. My brother used to tell me that and we'd laugh— I'd help him to laugh at that. And, of course, she took it all out on him. And he would tell me that he could handle it. Lulu, I can handle her, he would say. But I'm not sure that he could, not really, not in the end.

I couldn't deal with this. I felt myself detaching and watching the scene like a stranger from across the room. Once, when I was eleven, a girl had said something about my dad in hockey practice and I had hit her with my stick. I hadn't remembered doing it. Dissociation, the therapist had called it, but I think I had just been really fucking angry.

But as Louise continued her assassination, I felt an alien desire to come to my mother's defense or perhaps just to stop Louise from talking. But, Lulu, I said, England was home. Dad's work was demanding and, I mean, maybe Mum was just homesick?

Louise shook her head, red earrings swinging, and said that was neither here nor there. England was his home too! He didn't get to feel homesick? His feelings didn't count? And his job. The pressure he was under. No. She can give all the excuses she likes but she was cruel to him. *Cruel.* He was my family. He was my *brother.* You know our parents died young? Well, he never recovered from that. You never do, not really. And your mother never understood him. And that's a hard thing. It's a hard thing not to be understood. You do know that I speak to him? Well, I do. And he is still angry with her.

Had Louise been drinking? Her perfume was strong, and her eyes were red. She was talking in hyperbole, asking the same from me as from her psychic: affirmation.

She dabbed her eyes with her handkerchief and added a sachet to her tea. But I promised that I wouldn't put this on you. Tell me about *you,* my sweet girl. My goodness, that dress is lovely.

Relieved for the subject change, I told her that I worked in a hedge fund café with Ruth. Do you remember her?

My goodness! That beautiful Kenyan girl?

I nodded and immediately shook my head. No, Louise, Ruth isn't Kenyan—

But Louise continued: Gosh, she was a spitfire. The pair of you tearing around the garden. How lovely. And a hedge fund? Is that how you met your gentleman—is he in finance? I nodded because it seemed easier, and Louise talked about her ex-boyfriend who was a millionaire.

I stared into my coffee and wished that he was here. I wondered what he was doing: having a nap or reading, or maybe he'd gone to the shop.

Anyway, I've got Sam now, Louise continued, before making me promise to come back to Kenya. When I asked her if she would ever return to England, she said that part of her life was over. I can't believe that your mother isn't even there after all that. She's living in France with a man, you say?

Did I tell her that?

Louise was staring like it was my turn to speak, so I swallowed and said: I guess it was hard for Mum too?

Her features tightened, and she sunk back in her chair. You know, you have her eyes, she said.

I WALKED BACK ALONG the beach thinking about anything I could to distract myself from Louise. *His laugh. The twinkle in his eye. The way he moans when I run my fingers through his hair.*

I found him in the pool with his book. How was the mad aunt? he asked without looking up. Ignoring an urge to run over and beg him to never leave me, I said that she was fine, because he didn't want to know and I didn't want to tell him.

Shall we eat out tonight?

Sounds good.

He suggested it so effortlessly, and I responded the same way, like normal people in a normal relationship. I wanted to capture the moment: him in the pool with my severed heart in a thought bubble above his head.

Enola, why are you staring at me?

Because I love you and because being with you is like carrying something fragile.

You just look handsome, I said.

Okay, well, stop it, it's annoying.

Because no one could leave the woman who wanted to have sex all the time, I peeled off the straps of my dress. He watched it fall like water and then placed his book on the side. I stepped out of my underwear. He removed his reading glasses. I lowered myself into the water and removed him from his shorts. His fingers pressed between my ribs as if he might tear the flesh from the bone. I looked up and closed my eyes. Pink and white flowers opened behind my eyelids, and I imagined fireworks. Or not fireworks. A meteor shower. Stars were burning the earth. An ache behind my left eye grew and grew until—

Family is who you choose.

AFTERWARD, HE WENT INSIDE, and I remained in the pool, watching the moon appear, first like crepe paper, then settling white. In the silence, it was impossible not to think about it: the past. And it was worse now because it wasn't just in my head. It was sitting across a table with red swinging earrings and an ambivalent stare.

Your mother never understood him.

I hated my mum for what she did to Dad. None of what Louise said had been new information—when I was eleven, she had called my grandparents' house and we talked for a few weeks until Mum put a stop to it. Louise wanted answers and I did too once, but I had learned to stop asking questions. I picked at my arm and noticed then how many little red marks were darkening brown from the sun.

Honey, come inside. You'll be bitten to shit!

I turned to see him standing with his hands on his hips. Then I noticed the mosquitoes around the pool lights. *Fuck!* I climbed out and sprinted past him into the house. I could hear him laughing behind me. I stopped in the bedroom like I had forgotten where to go, and he appeared with my sage dress and underwear.

Come on now, honey. A towel was wrapped around me. Let's get you dry. I couldn't remember the last time that someone wrapped a towel around me and, at his gentleness, the pressure released, and I started sobbing. He lurched away, and I grabbed the towel before it fell. Are you okay?

Yeeess, he answered, adding a diphthong where it didn't belong. I'm just getting the spray. His body was as rigid as when I told him there were Portuguese men-of-war in the ocean. He handed me the bottle, and I quickly wiped my eyes and smiled like my tears had been as normal a thing as a sneeze.

Thank you for looking after me.

He said that it was just insect repellent; then he clapped his hands above his head. Gotcha! He showed me a dot of blood on his palm and said: This one already got you.

He went to leave and I asked if he still wanted to go for dinner. He paused at the door.

Why, don't you?

Yes. I was just checking because it's later than we planned.

He frowned as if I had made everything complicated.

I noticed then a small rip in the mosquito net over the bed, a tiny wound that would get bigger and bigger if I wasn't careful.

Day 6

I woke up covered in bites, which swelled and hardened as the day went on. Now it was night, and the itching was making me feverish. I couldn't control my thoughts. I wanted to scratch my back raw.

All I could find under the sink was this?

He held up a bottle of calamine lotion with the label rubbed off.

Nothing with antihistamine?

If I had found something with antihistamine, I would have brought something with antihistamine.

I asked if he could do it for me, and he sighed.

Don't worry, then, I'll do it.

I didn't say I wouldn't do it!

I sat on the bed in my pajama shorts and bra, and he dabbed the lotion on my back with tissue. I could hear his smile creaking behind me as he counted. That makes twenty-seven. You're not allergic, but you are really attractive to them.

It's not funny. They're really burning.

You're taking malaria tablets. You'll be fine.

Ouch! I said as he pressed too hard.

Right. That's it, he said, and he put the lotion away. He hadn't finished; he was just annoyed. All day I had been too much or too little, but I didn't know how to get back to the person I was at the start of the holiday.

I asked how it was possible that he hadn't been bitten. He pointed to a tiny bump on his ankle and when I didn't laugh, he snorted. Come on, let's get a drink. I told him I didn't want a drink but to go without me. He sighed again. No, it's okay. Let's just go to bed. We lay down in the dark, but there was static in the silence.

I was genuinely happy for you to go without me.

Yes, thank you. I don't need permission.

I asked him what was wrong. He said that there was nothing wrong but he was lying. I hated that he was angry, that I was *making* him angry. But I couldn't stop. The more frustrated he grew, the more frustrating I became. The heat wasn't helping.

Why is it so fucking hot?

It's the same as it's been all week, honey.

That, I thought. I loved when he called me "honey," but today the word sounded different, like it wasn't being used to show affection but merely as a replacement for my name. Or worse, to show his annoyance. I wondered then when he had stopped calling me "Gay."

I told him to please just go to the bar, but he said that he didn't want to go. I said that he clearly did, and I didn't want him to be unhappy because of me. I reached for my water glass, but it was empty.

Fuck! I'm so fucking thirsty!

He told me to calm down. I told him that I was calm. He told me that I had been a nightmare all day. I didn't realize that when you said you were allergic to mosquito bites that meant you turned into a fucking psycho! I told him not to be angry, and his face contorted.

Don't put this on me, Enola. You're the one who's having a fucking meltdown. I told you I've never been someone who tolerates this stuff.

What stuff? I shouted as he jumped out of bed and left the room. *What stuff?*

I tried to digest what had just happened, but it was as if someone had shuffled my insides like a deck of cards. I took off my shorts and bra and lay like a starfish. When the gate creaked, I knew that he had gone to the bar. I got my phone to call him and there was a message waiting from Ruth:

> *How was the meeting with Louise? Let me know if you need to talk x*

Ruth wasn't here, but she could still read my thoughts.

I put the phone down.

The other night I was beautiful and special, and now I was a nightmare. Why was I ruining this? And why, when he left a room, did it still feel like I might never see him again? My eyes were burning; I squeezed them shut and—

MUM IS GATHERING UP everything that belongs to Dad. Books. Glasses. Blue cord slippers. Louise is chasing her, grabbing things that fall from her arms. *Go to your room, Enola,* she shouts.

Come on, Louise says. Come with me, darling girl.

Don't you dare talk to her, don't you dare say anything to her—

OH MY GOD. I couldn't breathe. My fingers were tingling, and my head felt light. I stumbled to the bathroom, turned on the shower, and crouched under the cool water. I counted and breathed and pinched my arm until the room stopped dappling, then I went back to bed and waited for him.

I must have drifted off, because the next thing felt like a dream. He was leaning in the doorframe, tall and perfect. I told him that I had a panic attack, and he told me not to be silly. He walked to the bed, climbed inside the netting, and folded me into his arms. He handed me an ice-cold bottle of water. I told him that I was so sorry for being a psycho. Are you angry? Do you forgive me?

No, Enola, I'm not angry.

Do you hate me?

I asked him to please say the words. No, Enola, he said with a sigh. I don't hate you. I told him that I didn't know why, but that the bites had made me crazy, but he said that he didn't want to rehash everything. His eyes drifted as he realized I was naked.

Honey . . .

He kissed me, and his tongue was rum. I didn't want this. I wanted him to hold me and tell me that everything was going to be okay, but he lowered himself between my thighs. I tried to relax, because he rarely went down on me, but he was drunk and his movements were unpredictable. Eventually he ran out of energy and moved back up my body, flaccid.

You're really not into this, are you?

I . . . I am, I just—

Yeah, don't worry about it.

He zipped up his shorts and slept on the sofa to give me the space that I didn't want.

Day 7

He had been distant at breakfast. I had asked if he was all right, and he'd said he was fine in a tone that warned me not to ask again. The day continued like that: me determined to make our last day special and him determined not to make it "a thing." We read our books separately, and when he wanted lunch, he went inside and made his own. He laughed at a text message, and I asked him what was funny, and he said: Nothing. When the sun started to go down, he got himself a beer (Oh, *did you want one?*) and sat on the white wall to watch the sunset alone.

I still felt unsettled from my meeting with Louise, and my bites were still vexatious, but I had a stronger objective than my own sanity: to prove that I was still *beautiful* and *funny* and *cute* and *sexy*. I put on my raciest underwear, an uncomfortable pink-and-orange set from Victoria's Secret, and some lip gloss to match, then went into the kitchen, cracked a beer, and draped myself against the cabinet of dog ornaments like a mermaid. Then I shouted for him. He didn't answer, so I shouted again. He called back, *What?*

Do you want another beer?

There was a pause during which, I imagined, he finished his current beer. Then he shouted back: *Yeah!*

Come and get it, then!

What?

I have it here.

Can you just bring it?

I hadn't thought this through. If you offered someone something, normally you would bring it to them. And now he would be pissed off because he'd finished his beer. I held my ground until I heard his feet, and my pulse increased. He appeared from the patio and—

I had watched this scene many times, the woman in lingerie holding a pie or a drink or a feather duster as the man returns from work; his eyes then ping like a cartoon dog's and he carries her to the bedroom. But this didn't happen.

He looked at me, bemused, or worse than that, amused, like he was mentally drafting the scene as a chapter in his book or preparing the anecdote for Steph so that she could tell him, once again, how crap his taste in women was.

I held out his beer and said: Beer? I was going for half sexy and half self-aware, thinking that if he didn't find it sexy, he would at least appreciate the joke.

But he spoke in the same tone as when the waiter in the restaurant had put down his bowl of soupy fish: That looks great, honey. But I'm tired from the sun. Stay in that if you want, but I just want to chill before the bar.

Stay in that if you want? Embarrassment burned my body red and every mortifying thing I had ever done rushed back to me, but I pretended it was fine because I needed it to be.

Sure. When do you want to leave?

Normal time, he said like it was a stupid. Fucking. Question.

Then he took the beer and returned outside to have his sundowner without me.

WHEN THE SUN HAD descended for the last time, I put on my black dress and we went to a bar on the beach with a chemical smell and a bartender singing along to a Lana Del Rey song. I sipped my rum and coke slowly because I hadn't been able to eat much. His pupils dilated after his first whiskey, and after his third, he was drunk. He asked me how my drink was, but I didn't hear him and so he repeated "drink" like I had committed a larger crime. I asked him again if everything was okay, and he told me again to stop asking. Are *you* okay, Enola?

I told him that I was a little sad to be leaving tomorrow. Perhaps we could do a mini break in the summer?

He put his drink down. A mini break to *Kenya*?

I said that Amy and David had gone to a winery in England last year and he looked offended. He told me that he needed to write and earn money when we got back. Doesn't David work in the city? We can't go to a *winery*. He turned to the bar and continued drinking. I felt like he was telling me that it was my fault we were spending money and not writing. I looked at my phone and there was a new message from Ruth:

Enola, just let me know that ur okay please?

She would know that something was wrong, so I replied:

Hey, Roo, everything's great! Having the best last day. See you when I'm back xx

Am I boring you?

I looked up and he was staring at me. I told him that *he* had been on *his* phone all day. He said that if I was pissed off about him being on his phone then I should've said so. I told him that I wasn't, and he huffed. He was still annoyed with me about yesterday.

Look, I'm really sorry again about last night—

He slammed his drink down. For fuck's sake!

And I'm really sorry if I've been weird today. And I'm sorry for suggesting a mini break. We really don't have to do that. We don't have to do anything. We can literally live off toast and cereal for the next few months.

He breathed in and held the breath before releasing it. I thought he might say something kind. *We*, he said with a slanted smile. You do realize that *we* have only been dating for a few months?

I felt a pinching sensation in my chest, remembering what he had said about losing interest after five dates. *Just stay fun.*

I smiled brightly, and told him that I wasn't trying to rush anything. We've just had such a great time here and I thought it would be nice to have something to look forward to.

Come on, Enola. *This* is you having a great time?

He took a clumsy sip of his drink. I asked him what he meant by that. Have you had a terrible time?

His eyes narrowed. Don't do that.

Do what?

Twist my words.

I felt an itch on my back and scratched without thinking. The skin split. *Fuck.* I told him that I wasn't trying to twist his words, my voice coming out more frustrated because my back was burning.

He slammed his drink again. Right, I'm—

Stop doing that, I said, referring to the drink.

I'm getting annoyed now. Enola, this is my only holiday—

I know that, it's mine too. I—

All I wanted was a fun, relaxing holiday.

That's all I wanted too!

Fuck, can you stop interrupting me? *Christ.*

The bartender stopped singing.

I asked him to stop shouting. He said this wasn't him shouting. You don't want to hear me shouting, Enola.

This wasn't working. I was losing control. I would have to tell him what was on my mind. I had never told him the real reason why we left Kenya when we did. Perhaps, if he knew, he would understand. Perhaps he would wrap a warm towel around my shoulders again.

Look, I began, finding the words. I know that I've been a little up and down. The other day with Louise . . . I told you that it was hard being back and I'm just feeling very . . .

My words scattered. I tried again.

There is a lot about my childhood that I don't like to think about, and being back here has just, I guess, brought some of that back up.

He frowned, and the pinching sensation spread to my arms and legs. He asked me why we came if it was going to upset me. I said that I didn't know that it was. He told me that he understood but that it was selfish of me to have made this his problem. I'm not your therapist, Enola. Do you understand that when I get back, I'm going to have to pick up shifts in my cousin's bar? I've not done bar work since my twenties. I've been so stressed with writing and . . . *This* is why I don't go away with partners.

I'm really sorry, I said, unable to stop my voice from shaking.

Oh, just stop that, Enola. It's manipulative.

I reached for his arm, but he shook me off. Look, this clearly hasn't been our day. Why don't you just go back?

Are you serious? But it's our last night!

Precisely.

He drained his drink and signaled for another. I didn't want to leave, but everything I had done to try to fix things had made them worse. Okay, I said. I'll see you back at the house? I finished my drink and walked down the dark beach.

BACK AT THE BEACH house, on the bed that we didn't have sex on, I waited once again for him to come back. The rum that I had drank on an empty stomach went to my head and I pinched my skin as hard as I could to stop the room spinning.

We had argued before but never like that. He wasn't just annoyed; he was angry. I realized then the tightrope I was walking; it felt as if any moment that wasn't fun for him could make him angry. And yet I couldn't feel anything but disappointment that I had let him down. I needed to see that spark in his eye. I needed him to smile at me like we had robbed a bank. I didn't want us to get on the plane without fixing this. I couldn't lose him. I couldn't lose another thing that I loved. Not here, not in this place.

I heaved up from the bed, ready to return to the bar and make him listen to my apology, but when I got outside, he was standing by the gate. The ocean moon made him a silhouette, and the song from the bar spun in my head as if on a record player.

It's you, it's you, it's all for you.

We stared at each other, and then he walked toward me like the soft pad of a synth. I couldn't see his face.

Everything I do. I tell you all the time.

He pulled me to him, and I was relieved to find that his eyes were twinkling. He didn't say it, but he was sorry. I started to cry.

Shit. I'm sorry for crying. I'm so sorry.

But this time he was kind, and he wiped a tear from my cheek. His breath smelled like whiskey. I gripped his black T-shirt. He said my name: Enola—

The sentence remained unformed. Something pivotal was happening; I could feel it. *He's going to tell me that he loves me.* But he didn't finish his thought. Or perhaps he did, but he chose not to share it. He just pulled me closer and broke my body into pieces that floated up to join the Milky Way.

DAY 8

We woke as we had done all holiday to the hush of the waves. I nestled into his curve and reached back. He moaned, awake, pushing into my hand. I smelled his breath, foul for a moment: his unedited morning.

I want you . . .

He dropped foreplay like a cigarette, and as he fucked me, I said *I love you too* over and over in my head. I didn't think about my pleasure because it wasn't my pleasure I was addicted to.

AT BREAKFAST WE USED up what was in the fridge, and I asked if he had meant what he said about the holiday being crap. He said that he was just angry and that there had been some really lovely bits. I asked him which bits, and he told me not to push. We packed, and I wondered if I would ever be back here. He said that he was ready to go home. I said that I was ready to go home but I wasn't ready to leave. He said that didn't make sense.

ON THE DRIVE, I started getting a headache. We didn't have any pain-killers, and he didn't want to stop. He told me to drink more water. I watched from the window again as he swore at the roads, and I realized that the experience now had erased the experience then. I couldn't remember what the roads and buildings used to look like.

IN THE CAR PARK, I struggled to lift my suitcase from the boot, and he made a joke about feminism. On the corner of the building a mirror was mounted like a satellite. I remembered seeing a giant spider there when I was eight. He told me to see if it reappeared while he met the man with the keys. I sat on my suitcase as the dust turned dark between my toes and waited for the world's oldest spider.

IN THE TERMINAL, I wanted him to talk to me, but he put on his headphones and moved seats to stretch out. My head was really hurting now. I thought about our long layover in Nairobi and furled and unfurled my hands. He removed his headphones. Why do you keep doing that?

Sorry, I said. I'm just going to go to the toilet.

The bathroom was hot and small. Insects buzzed on the wrong side of the window, and the mirror wasn't real glass. I examined the marks on my arm and put a hair band around my wrist. I snapped it, and the sting helped a little. I'd get an elastic band when I got home.

I stayed for a moment, trying to remember the version of myself that he liked, then came back out.

Do you fancy a drink at Wilton's tomorrow?

He said that he was going to his dad's for a bit.

You are? You didn't tell me?

He asked me why that mattered. I told him that it didn't and that I was happy for him. He frowned and said that he couldn't wait to see the newest member of Karen's china doll collection.

Our flight was announced on time, but he swore like it was hours behind schedule. He flung his bag over his shoulder and said: *Finally,* time to go home.

I paused. What did you say?

H-O-M-E, he repeated, mouth curled around the letters like a snake around a mouse.

CHAPTER 9

WE STOOD OUTSIDE WHITECHAPEL TUBE STATION UNDER THE starless sky. Everything was cold and dark and loud. We were postponing the goodbye. Me, because I didn't want to say it, but I wasn't sure about him. I wanted to believe that he was feeling the same way, that he hated that we weren't still on the beach, in each other's arms, listening to the cicadas.

He looked at his phone and chuckled. He had been doing that all the way from the airport. I asked him what was funny, hoping that he would tell me something that we could laugh at together. He said that it was just Steph. I asked what she'd said, and he asked why I wanted to know. I told him that I didn't really. He made an expression that I couldn't decipher. I asked him if everything was okay, but he said that he was going to get pissed off if I kept asking.

He put his phone away, and I reached for his arm. At first he resisted, but then he unfolded it and handed it to me so that it sat in my palm like something I had picked up off a supermarket shelf. I asked if he was sure that he didn't want to stay at mine, and he said that we had just spent the last week together.

Look, I know the last couple days were—

Let's not do this now, Enola. I'm really tired. It's been a long day.

I know, I had the same one, I thought.

I really do have to go, honey.

He was twisting his lips like I was holding him up. I hated that. I would rather he just leave instead of demonstrating that he wanted to. I told him that I wasn't keeping him, and he shuffled forward and kissed me. I forced a smile and told him to have a brilliant time with Karen's doll collection. Then we picked up our suitcases and he went one way and I went the other, the words "I love you" still unspoken.

OPENING THE DOOR, THE flat stirred as if someone had just run around the corner. Everything looked unfamiliar, like I had been away for years and years and nothing was mine anymore. I undressed and curled into bed. My muscles grew heavy and my brain peeled like an apple until I was at the beach house and—

HE IS WALKING TOWARD me. He wipes the tears from my cheeks. He opens his mouth but then changes his mind.
What? What were you going to say?
The sound of the train.
I scream at him to stop.
The train gets louder.
Please stop it. Please!
But piece by piece he vanishes, and I'm left clutching the dark with cartoon hands.

I WOKE TO FIND the bed cold and damp with sweat. I reached for my phone, hoping for an *I miss you* or *The bed seems empty without you* or *I don't want to go to Norwich in the morning*. But there was nothing. I went to my suitcase and inhaled the smell of the beach on my clothes. It was a familiar feeling, an emptiness, like thirst: *homesickness*. And now he was a part of that. Now when I pictured the places of my childhood, he was there too, like he had been all along. I stood in my bedroom not knowing what to do or where to go, but then my eyes rested on my laptop.

I sat at my desk and opened the latest version of my novel. I looked at the careful words. The adjectives and nouns in perfect small font. Writing never used to be meticulous. When we moved back to England, and the therapist told me to write, I would sit up every night, surrounded by the safari wallpaper my grandparents chose to help me "feel at home," and scribble frantically until my wrist ached and the pad of my thumb was black. And then it hit me: writing was never about control, it was about *losing* it. That was why I hadn't been able to finish anything. I had been terrified of feeling as powerless as I felt back then. So I arranged sentences and placed words and changed fonts the way that I layered my makeup and color-coded my books. Because I wanted to make it flawless and perfect and correct. But to write, you couldn't curate pieces of yourself—you had to bleed, you had to show the ugly parts, the parts scarred and darkened by the sun. Editing might be order, but writing had to be chaos.

Jump out that plane, Laa.

I started a new document. That beautiful blank page. But this time I wanted to fill it; I had to fill it. I hadn't felt this in such a long time. This *mania*. I started writing and I couldn't stop. I typed how Ruth ate a meal, as if she were scared the food would leave her plate, and memories of camping trips flowed like tears: lions roaring in the night; a pink sea of flamingos on a white shore; a mother cheetah nursing under a bush; wildebeest with avalanche chests, chewing grass like cowboys chewing tobacco, ready to spit it with a ping into a dirty bar glass. It was fiction, but it came from a real place, a place that I thought was destroyed when Mum destroyed the photographs. *Honest* but not *truthful*.

The sun rose and I stopped to look at my dust-covered bedroom and the truck that had crashed through the wall. My eyes were stinging; I had written all night.

CHAPTER 10

I CHECK MY PHONE. THERE ARE NO NEW MESSAGES, BUT A PIECE OF glass splinters from the screen like a crystal of sugar. It's nearly six o'clock. Time to get dressed. I lift my *Mario Kart* T-shirt and, glimpsing myself in the wardrobe mirror, recall once overhearing a man on a bus describe a woman as "one of those fat skinny girls."

When I was fifteen and had just gone on the pill, my grandma told me that I was chubby, but that same week Catherine told me that I needed feeding. I've always been neither one thing nor the other. My hair is neither blond nor brown, my height neither tall nor short, my appearance neither attractive nor unattractive. And my writing? I couldn't write before him, I couldn't write with him, and yet somewhere in between those states, like Schrödinger's cat, in the liminal, I started to write. Perhaps I've always existed in the space between spaces, the crack down the side of a radiator.

I open the wardrobe and avoid myself.

Jesus. How many clothes do you need, honey?

But my wardrobe is a diary; the clothes are words. On those dungarees is paint from when Ruth and I decorated my flat. In that sliver of sage is the feel of swimming pool tiles on my knees. By my feet, like a cairn, my THIS IS WHAT A FEMINIST LOOKS LIKE T-shirt smells like his aftershave.

I put on a white tank top, blue jeans, and a checked shirt, no bra or socks, nothing restrictive—Dad used to say that the sole purpose of a sock was to go in a shoe—then I lie back on the bed and continue our story like it's a restored black-and-white film. It's one that I've seen before, but because the Technicolor is new, I'm hoping that it will end differently.

AMY CLEARED HER THROAT. All right, loves, because this is my last session, I wanted to let you know how much your feedback has meant. You will all be cited in the acknowledgments. And I'm sorry to have to bow out for a bit, but with all the publicity for book one and now edits for book two . . . I know it's cliché but debut year really is a whirlwind. Anyway—

She looked to me.

I raised my glass: To Amy!

All right, Mat said. Enola, you're up.

The last time I'd brought my work to the group was nearly a year ago, and the reaction had been tepid. Amy said that she didn't feel safe with my writing; she didn't trust that I knew where the book was going. This story felt completely different to anything I had written before, but I was nervous. I remembered the expression on Chris's face when his protagonist was called a cunt.

I swallowed, and Amy squeezed my knee. I've actually brought something new this week, I said. Chris muttered that at least I had brought *something*.

I had this idea for a YA book and—

A children's book? Hugo asked, judgmentally tightening his ponytail.

Young adult, Amy corrected.

Clever move. It's a growing market, said Chris.

As I read my chapter, I knew there were words to change and sentences to rearrange, but when I finished there was a hush. If Hugo liked something he hummed. If Chris was jealous he went quiet. Mat was always kind, but if Amy didn't like it she spoke in a way that made you feel as bad as it did good: *I just didn't think it was worthy of you, hon.*

Hugo hummed, and I exhaled.

At the bar, Amy told me that she loved my chapter. I waited for the sting, but there wasn't one. Honestly, sweetheart, I just really loved it. It was so different from your usual stuff—

Sting.

My friend Diana, who is my agent's assistant, is building her own list and I'll mention you when I next email.

Gosh, Amy, that's so nice, but you don't need to do that!

Amy looked confused and cross. Diana's looking for a book like yours. It's not a *favor*, Enola. Then she stared like she was trying to understand me and told me to advocate for myself. I apologized and thanked her. That wasn't so hard, was it? she asked. It had been, actually, but I wasn't sure why.

Mat turned with a fresh pint. It had been nice to think about something other than *him* this evening, but they were friends and so his name was bound to come up. Mat said that he enjoyed my chapter, and I asked how his book was. Mat answered that he was rewriting it in the past tense. I sympathized and said that *he* was rewriting *his* in the present tense. He's just gone back to his dad's, actually, to work on it. We've just had a week in Kenya, so I think he just wanted a place without distractions, you know?

Mat looked confused and then slapped his forehead. I'm sorry. I forgot that you guys had met!

Mat doesn't know we're a couple?

The bartender asked what I wanted. I answered that I had changed my mind, but Amy ordered a white wine. As I moved to leave, she asked me if he had decided about the wedding yet. I said that I would ask him soon. I didn't tell her that he had already said no, because I had been secretly hoping to change his mind.

Please hurry, Enola. I have other people I can invite.

Amy started telling Mat about her house extension. He threw small noises like grenades to show that he was listening, but it was making her lose her rhythm.

I went to the bathroom to collect my thoughts.

Him and Mat weren't that close, but still, what if none of his friends had heard about me? He could vanish from my life with no one to explain my absence to. *What if he already has?* We had gone from waking up next to each other every day to me sending a video in the morning of an otter washing its face and hoping that he might reply *ha* before midnight. I hadn't even told him about my new book yet. I wanted him to come back and for us to write together like we used to, this time with me actually writing.

I snapped the elastic band around my wrist. Everything would be okay. Tomorrow I was seeing Ruth, and the world would make sense again.

SASHA, RUTH'S FLATMATE, WAS DJing in Dalston. Melodyless music thumped from black speakers, and groups of friends defended their dance circles like they were in bumper cars.

Air? mouthed Ruth.

On the terrace our voices emerged quietly as our ears adjusted. Ruth asked whether tonight was too full-on, and I told her it was better than moping at home with the post-holiday blues. She looked concerned. You've barely spoken about it, Laa. And you're looking really skinny.

I'm really not.

You are. You've lost weight very quickly.

Ruth asked when he was back from Norwich. I tried to sound casual: It was meant to be a week, but it might be longer because he's writing. Then I changed the subject, because I wasn't ready to tell Ruth how bad things were. When is your job interview?

Monday, but I don't want to talk about it.

There we were, two hiding places: her, the threat of a stable career; me, how empty London was now. The wind changed, and a couple's cigarette smoke blew over. I looked to them: a slim, matching pair with bleached hair and torn leather. I wondered what their sex life was like.

Do you have gum? Ruth asked, palm on her chest.

Juicy Fruit.

Taking a piece, she screwed up her face and said: Great, now I taste like the nineties.

We leaned against the wall, bricks damp from rain, and as the dance floor left our bodies, the air grew colder. Ruth asked if my new book was going well. I said that it was, and I meant it. She shook my shoulders: That's the spirit! I'm so excited about this. I'm so excited for *you*. I told her that it was scary, but that I was excited too. She told me that she was proud of me, and I moved closer into her warmth.

I wonder how his writing is going.

She asked if I was enjoying Sasha's set. I answered that he was great. She corrected the pronoun. Sorry, *they're* great, I said.

She told me that I didn't have to lie. I know your music taste, Enola!

Is my music taste the reason he isn't calling me back?

I asked Ruth what was wrong with my music taste, and she said there was nothing wrong with it. You just like songs with words. Don't let him get in your head, Laa.

I'm not!

I wonder if his tan has faded.

I needed to stop thinking about him. I told Ruth that I might need another drink, and, catching something in my eye, she lifted a silver hip flask with a pagan symbol from her leather bum bag.

Is it . . . ?

She nodded. Dark rum with an MDMA bomb. Do you want to?

Did I want to? I wasn't working tomorrow and getting high might help me take my mind off him. *Fuck it.* I took the flask and drank. The rum was sweet, but there was that familiar chemical bitterness. Ruth took my hand and led me back inside.

Ruth came up first. Her eyes became wide and black, and her arms shot above her head. She told me that she loved me. I was so worried about you going to Kenya, you know?

I know.

And you barely messaged when you were there, so I was worried that you were having a bad time. Because I love you so much and you're my best friend and you deserve to be happy and, like, if he makes you happy then I'm happy for you, you know?

I know.

But *does* he make you happy?

I drew back and looked at her face shining under the lights. Sasha played a remix of "Summertime Sadness," and the beat rose in my chest. Ruth knew that something was wrong, but she would wait for me to come to her like a wounded animal.

Is there any left?

She grinned and handed me the flask. Come on, she said, voice sailing, and she moved my arms to the music. By the time the song changed, tingles were shooting up my limbs, but the high never came. Sasha joined us on the dance floor, and Ruth kissed them on the lips. Your set was *great*, she said. As we danced, someone touched my waist. A dark-haired man was smiling, shimmering pink on his cheekbones.

I signed to Ruth that I was going to the toilet.

The lock was broken, so I leaned against the door. Toilet paper was strewn on the dirty floor, and there was urine spattered on the seat. Someone was vomiting in the next-door cubicle. I called him again. I didn't think that he would answer but he did.

Hey, honey.

His voice.

Hi, I said, sinking into the word like it was a pillow. He asked me if I was drunk in a tone that made me feel adorable. I told him that I was dancing with Ruth and teased that we were surrounded by men.

God, yeah, it must be a nightmare going out with Ruth.

And instantly I wasn't adorable; I was plain and invisible. That was the real reason he was losing interest. He had looked at me under bright beach lighting. He had seen through me like an X-ray.

The door hit my back. One minute!

I asked how he was, and he said that he was fine. I asked him how writing was going, and he answered the same. I asked if his tan had faded, and he said it had. I asked when he was coming back, and he said that he wasn't sure. He left small beats before each answer, and his cadence was a typewriter's.

The door hit me again. *One minute!*

I asked if everything was okay, and he answered this question so quickly that the end was shaved off: What do you mean?

I swallowed, then swallowed again.

Between us?

He said that everything was fine and suggested that we talk tomorrow. I dug my nails into my fingertips. But *will* we talk tomorrow? He asked what that was supposed to mean, and I said that we had barely spoken. You would tell me if there was something wrong?

There was a pause. I wondered whether he had hung up, but then he said: Honey, I was at dinner when you called yesterday. And this morning I was out, and, look, I'm not going to list my activities for you. Go have a glass of water.

We hung up the phone. Or he did.

On the wall, graffiti from someone else's bad night read: *Bitch, he doesn't want you.*

I took the elastic band from my bag, put it around my wrist, and snapped it twice.

At the sinks, I washed my hands between two women. One, an ice blonde with laminated eyebrows, was telling her drunk friend that she was fighting her fiancé for a videographer. They're, like, three thousand pounds but totally worth it, she chirped, eyebrows high.

He's being a right dick, said the friend, swaying.

Here, look! A phone with a photo of a wedding dress was passed across me.

Sorry, she said, giggling.

No worries—nice dress, I said.

The dress looked like everyone else's. Sort of a fishtail. Sort of white. Sort of beaded. Sort of lace. *Vintage* lace, she said in a way that made me think she didn't know what the word meant.

Excuse me. I turned on the hand dryer. The water resisted blowing off my hands like it was trying to grip the skin. When the noise stopped, the woman was talking about how her "frenemy" Suze said it would be sexist to be given away.

Like, I get it, I'm not property, but at the same time I think feminism ruins things for women.

Her friend made a noise that didn't satisfy her need for a response, so she grabbed my arm and said: Would *your* dad walk *you* down the aisle?

No, I said, but my dad's dead.

CHAPTER 11

WE SAT AT A LONG WHITE TABLE IN THE GARDEN. HE ARCHED HIS eyebrow at a gravy stain on my linen napkin. That would have been your dress, honey. He touched the lace.

It's *vintage* lace, I said. He whispered that he didn't give a fuck what it was, he'd be ripping it off me later.

A glass was tapped, and my dad stood.

Happy wedding day, darling daughter. I remember when you were six years old, running around in this garden. It's hard to believe that we're all here now, in the exact same place, to celebrate your marriage to a man that I'm proud to call my son. When you announced that you were moving here, to the house that we lived in all those years ago, I didn't know what to think. And then Ruth decided to move here too!

The room laughed, and Ruth toasted herself.

Dad concluded: What a strange and misunderstood thing time is. Please be upstanding for—Enola, are you taking his name?

There's the sound of the train again.

I turned to him, but there was just a bright light and loud noise and everyone was waiting for my answer. I told Dad that I was still thinking about it.

It's getting louder.

Don't worry too much, my girl. What's for you won't go by you. From far away in space, all of this has already happened.

Meaning?

You didn't have a choice.

He reached for a kiwi and threw it to me.

MY HEAD IS THROBBING. I can hear Ruth saying, *Eat something, Laa.* It's gone six and all I've had is an apple. I go to the kitchen and pour a bowl of cereal but the flakes are stale, and I imagine them in my stomach like dead leaves in a puddle. I leave the bowl and go back to the bedroom where I find my painkillers in the drawer and take two. There is a modicum of relief in knowing that I've solved one problem, until, at the back of the drawer by an unopened packet of condoms, I notice the CD he made me for my twenty-eighth birthday.

I always assumed I'd have my life figured out by the time I was thirty. I thought I would have a stable job. I thought I would be in a real relationship. I thought I would know how to work the oven timer. The generation below evaluate us the way that we evaluate our parents. They talk like we're a completed, finished thing: millennials. But I'm not finished, I'm incomplete, I'm temporized, with a bruise on my collarbone darkening like fruit.

Well, this is going pretty well, isn't it?

HE HAD BEEN IN Norwich for ten days and I was crouched like a goblin between my bookshelf and wardrobe. We hadn't spoken since I'd called from the club, and there were three unread messages on his phone from me. On mine, one from Amy:

> Enola, I need to know if he's coming to the evening do. Please let me know by tonight!! x

I was hoping to bring up the subject of Amy's wedding again when he was back, but I still didn't know when that would be, and at this point, I had to admit the loss.

> Hey, Ames, sorry but no he can't. Thanks so much though! x

I remembered his arms as the sun went down, the Tusker on his breath, our laughter in snorkeling goggles. How had we gone from that to this? Was he even going to tell me that he loved me that night? Or had he got to Norwich and realized that it was just too much work?

The buzzer went, and I rushed to the intercom and waited.

Oh dear, Ruth said when she saw me.

I sunk back down in the corner while Ruth raised the blinds. That's better, she said, injecting morning into the room. Then she made the bed, positioning cushions haphazardly and pulling the duvet too high (Ruth never made her own bed). She sat cross-legged on the floor and took my hand. They said you called in sick. What happened?

I shrugged. I just feel sad.

Ruth paused while she thought about how to say what she wanted to. Enola, I know that you don't want to talk about it, but I really think you should. Going back to Kenya must have triggered—

Don't use that word. It was a holiday, not Vietnam.

Ruth dropped her chin and smiled. Laa, there is a sliding scale from drama queen to war veteran.

I told her that the trip had been hard on occasion, but that I wasn't *triggered*. She traced my palm and asked if I had eaten. I shook my head. She asked if I had spoken to my mum yet, and I shook my head again. Ruth looked down. I know that you loved your dad, but I think maybe you should— Her eyes drifted to my arms, to the little marks. I snatched my hand back.

Enola, when did—

I don't want to talk about it!

Okay, but—

Roo, stop! You're looking me like I'm . . . Yes, I'm picking, and yes, I appreciate that it's anxious behavior, but I'm not taking a knife to my skin. I just scar easily, okay? The sun turned them brown. That's all.

I lowered my other sleeve so that she didn't see the elastic band. It felt sometimes like Ruth could see through me and it was impossible to breathe around her.

She ran her tongue over her teeth. Fine, she said, voice deeper, we don't have to talk about that. But let's talk about *him*. What has he done?

I wanted to defend him like I always did, but this time I couldn't. The warnings were unavoidable: cartoon signs predicting danger ahead; red traffic lights refusing to turn green; a toothless man selling pies, warbling *Turn back*. And so I told her everything and saw the relief on her face at my confession. I said that he had been wonderful at first, but then things changed, or I had changed—I wasn't sure which. I told her that when I told him that I was struggling, he got angry.

Ruth made a noise under her breath, and so I quickly explained that, in his defense, I had been a complete nightmare.

But were you actually a nightmare or did he just tell you that you were?

I ignored her and said that now nothing was the same between us, and I didn't know how to fix it. And if I keep messaging then I'll keep pushing him away, but I miss him. Like, I really miss him. And before you tell me how pathetic I am, I know. I'm completely pathetic. All I can think about is him, wondering when he'll message, if he'll message, if *I'm* allowed to message. And, look, you were right. You and I should have gone there together. We should have walked along the beach to the rock and eaten papaya and, like, I don't know what I'm doing, Roo. I just—

My words dissolved, and Ruth put her arms around me. She hushed me as I cried. But then my phone vibrated. I could see from the shape of the letters that it was him. I sprung from her arms and read the message like I was drinking cold water on a hot day.

Oh my god.

I dropped my head back against the wall. Ruth cleared her throat, but before she could speak, I said that I was just hormonal. It's probably just a delayed suicide Monday from the drugs.

Don't do that, Enola! This feels like an honest conversation for once.

What do you mean "for once"?

You just sat here telling me that something is wrong and—

Okay, but I didn't actually know if anything *was* wrong. I knew there was a chance that I was just being insecure and crazy.

Has he called you crazy?

No, *I'm* calling me crazy.

But you're not crazy! You had a difficult holiday and he wasn't there for you and—

I didn't say that!

You did! You just said it was a mistake!

I told her that wasn't what I meant; I *meant* that we should have gone there together like she wanted. She said that she wasn't upset about that. Yes, I wanted us to go back together, Enola, but that's not why I didn't want you to go with him! I don't like how he treats you and how you treat yourself when you're with him. You were just telling me how upset you are and now you've flipped because he's texted you back?

I told her that she couldn't hold everything I said when I was upset against me. Roo, if I held you to every time you said you wanted a new job, you'd still be standing on people in the name of medical research. Please just forget it, Roo. Please? *Please.*

Ruth squeezed her hands and then stood up. She said that she was putting the kettle on. If you're not going to eat, then you have to at least drink something. She went to the kitchen, and I read the message again and again and again, trying to recapture the feeling of when I first saw his name on the screen.

I'm back this Friday. Drink? Xxx

CHAPTER 12

WE SAT ON GUNMETAL STOOLS IN A TIGHT CORNER OF THE SPEAK-easy. The air smelled like burnt orange, and fifties music played from a laptop on the reclaimed wood bar. I was drinking something short with moonshine, and he was drinking something long with tequila. Our kiss on the street had been quick, but now that he was back, things would settle. My grandma used to say that about houses: *They just have to settle.*

I started by talking about my new book, and he said that it sounded great but then added: Just don't let it take away from your *actual* writing. I told him that it felt different, and that he was right when he had called my last book pretentious. He said that he didn't remember saying that. I told him that I hadn't taken it in a bad way. I asked if he wanted to read some, and he said that he would read it when it was finished. Then he added: I'm not trying to be disparaging. I just want to see you finish something, honey. You've never expressed an interest in writing for children before.

Honey.

He took a sip of his traffic light–striped drink. I asked if it was nice, and he nodded, then asked how mine was. I said that mine was nice too. I felt a swell of relief at the normality and leaned over the table to kiss him. I'm so glad you're back. If I had known you would have been gone for that long, I would've—

Enola. It's been two weeks. I was in Norwich, I didn't go to war.

The waitress asked if we wanted more drinks. Tracing a finger down the menu, he stopped at: Weapon of the Gods? She looked to me, and I asked for the same again, but I thought I saw his chest fall, so I changed my order to a pistachio martini. That sounds fucking disgusting, he said.

The waitress left, and the conversation stalled. I asked how Norwich was, but he said that he didn't want to talk about it; he and his dad had been arguing about his career again. I looked around for inspiration: there was a picture of a bison constellation on the wall. Oh, I wanted to talk to you about Patrick!

He frowned. *My* Patrick? Why?

Amy says it's better to have illustrations—

What's Amy got to do with anything?

Her agent's assistant specializes in YA and, apparently, I should look at submitting illustrations when—

Wait, is the book for *kids* kids?

No, but I wanted illustrations. The protagonist is doing this art therapy and—

He was looking at me like I was insane, so I quickly explained that I thought Patrick might like to do them. He finished his drink with a rattle and said that Pat illustrated high-end stuff. I raised my glass to my lips, but it was empty. I took a fake sip. No worries, it was just an idea, I said, pretending to swallow. I asked how his writing was going, but he tensed up and said that he didn't want to talk about it. Before I could decide whether or not to push, his phone vibrated. He mouthed the words as he read them, then expressed relief; he'd left his wallet at Steph's last night and she had just found it.

Didn't you get back today?

He said that he was meant to, but then Steph organized last-minute birthday drinks and it was late so he just crashed with her afterward.

My brain struggled to process: *He came back yesterday, he went to a party, he slept with Steph?*

Where did you crash?

With. Steph.

But in her bed?

He put his phone on the table with the screen facing down and told me that it was no different to me crashing with Ruth. That was probably true. But I asked him why he didn't tell me that he was back early. His brow creased. Why would I tell you that I was back early when I already had plans? That doesn't make the sense you think it does.

He made a good point. Or did he? Because I had been desperate to see him, but he clearly didn't feel the same if he chose Steph's bed over mine. Something was wrong. There was still tension. We hadn't seen each other for two weeks; the conversation should be electric.

I'm sorry, but—

But what? he interrupted wearingly.

I feel like . . .

Yes?

What I wanted to say was: *Why have we barely spoken? What's changed? Do you love me?* But instead, tiptoeing, I asked why he hadn't invited me to the party. I could have gone with you. I mean, it's been months and I've still not met your friends.

He nodded like he was a detective solving a case. And *that's* it, isn't it? Asking Pat to do your illustrations? Come on, Enola. If and when you're at the illustration stage of your book—because, let's be clear, you actually have to *finish* it first—you could approach anyone to do the art, so why don't you try being honest about what you're attempting to do? He placed his palms behind his head and sighed. There was a rise in my chest, then a drop: the last time he moved like that, he was sunbathing.

What? I asked, nervous about what he was going to say and relieved that I hadn't said everything I was feeling.

It's just—

What?

Boring.

What is?

All this! I've been in a relationship like this before and I won't do it again.

Like magic, my anger and frustration vanished, and all that was left was incapacitating fear. *Please don't leave me, please don't leave me, please don't leave me.* I pinged my elastic band under the table, once but hard.

Look, honey, I'm not trying to be a dick . . .

My hands turned ice-cold.

But I know myself, and I've never been someone who responds well to pressure. I don't know. Maybe going away together was a mistake.

I tried to stop the shake in my voice. No, it wasn't a mistake. Look, I'm really sorry. I don't care about you crashing with Steph, okay?

He said it wasn't just that. He said that some of the situations in Kenya were challenging. Honey, the bites? You completely overreacted. And then it just seemed like everything was a bit *intense*. You know I'm not a fan of the drama.

But I had asked you multiple times if everything was okay and you said—

He hit his hand to his forehead as if he had just remembered something. Yes! he said. *That* was the other thing. The constant asking if I was okay. If you want me to be okay then you have to let me *be* okay, honey.

I promised him that I would do better. I didn't mean to put any pressure on you. I really don't want to break up, I said, putting my head in my hands.

He made a noise like a balloon deflating. Okay, honey. Come on. I never suggested *that*. I looked up and he was grinning and we were back in the beach house and he was pouring wine into my mouth. I told him that I had just missed him. He told me not to be silly. We can spend a couple of weeks apart. That doesn't have to be a big deal, does it? We smiled at each other, and then he began galloping his fingers over the table. I started humming the *William Tell* Overture, but

he told me I was humming "Ride of the Valkyries." Warmth returned
to my hands as the waiter returned with our cocktails.

We stayed for one more, and then I asked if he wanted to come
back to mine. I was nervous about what he might say, but then he
showed me his toothbrush.

So, I'm still your girlfriend . . . ?

What do you think?

We watched an episode of a television show in bed on my laptop,
and then I moved in toward his body. He turned his face and kissed
me properly for the first time since the beach. We had sex, and I
focused on him. I needed him to remember how much we wanted
each other, to remember that no woman understood him like I did.
Afterward, he fell asleep, but adrenaline hammered in my chest. He
was back, he was here, he was mine. I couldn't sleep. I couldn't miss
a moment.

CHAPTER 13

ROO, I DON'T KNOW WHAT I WAS WORRIED ABOUT. IT'S ALL FINE!
Things are back to how they were at the beginning. Just dating and
having fun and not worrying about the future.

Is that what you want?

To have fun? Of course!

Okay. I'm really pleased.

Ruth didn't sound pleased. How many cups?

Two, I said. He's being very different now. Ruth cut a knob of
butter, then licked the knife. She asked me what had changed and I
said that there had just been a shift. The stove clicked and settled.
The smell of melting butter and cocoa permeated.

Did he explain why he was a dick?

I said that I overreacted to some of the situations in Kenya. I've
been a bit intense about the relationship and it freaked him out.

Ruth paused. Intense?

I explained that he hated drama.

Ruth paused again. Drama?

I poured the melted butter into the bowl. Ruth, please stop repeat-
ing words.

Grabbing a wooden spoon, she said: But you're not *drama* or
intense—you're *you*.

I know, I'm explaining it wrong.

Okay, Laa.

Ruth handed me the spoon and told me what was on the schedule for bad-movie night. Once a month we made cocktails and watched a movie just to make fun of it. Normally a romantic comedy. The more popular the better. It always resulted in us pressing pause repeatedly, in peals of laughter. Ruth was always steadfast in her sarcasm but I fought not to get drawn into the romance. *It's the soundtrack that always gets you*, she would say.

Ruth scooped peanut butter into a measuring cup, and I used the spoon to scrape it into the mixing bowl. She hovered her head over it.

Don't eat it yet, Roo.

I asked how her new job was, and she said that she was assigned a desk next to a man who claimed to have invented putting googly eyes above cats' tails to make them look like elephants' trunks. I asked her how long she expected to stay there, and she put a spoonful of the mixture into her mouth, tilted her head, and grinned.

We put handfuls of the batter onto a tray and slid it into the oven. As we washed our hands, Ruth asked if I wanted to come to bingo next weekend. Unless you're doing something with him? I threw the dishcloth to her and said that I was only seeing him once a week.

Did I tell you that he's working at a bar now? He's struggling because he's not worked in a bar since his twenties.

Ruth didn't say anything, she just reached for the cocktail shaker.

Roo, I know you're judging me but I'm really trying not to fuck this up.

She asked where the ice was.

Freezer.

Cointreau, vodka, cranberry juice?

Fridge.

Ruth began mixing cosmopolitans. Listen, she said over the sound of the ice, I'm genuinely happy that things are going well, but I wish that it wasn't *you* doing all the trying. I don't want you prioritizing his happiness over yours. Happiness is so precarious, you know?

Ruth was choosing each word carefully and handing them to me like they were glass, like they could shatter if she was too forceful. I told her that I was meeting Steph and Patrick on Monday. Ruth stopped shaking. Really? Well, that's something.

It *was* something. Patrick would tell him that he approved of "this one," and Steph and I would become friends, which he would pretend to hate but secretly love. Later, he would tell me that he loved me because his friends did.

I got the martini glasses, and Ruth poured. I sat on the sofa, and Ruth turned off the kitchen strip light. She joined me, and I handed her the remote but she didn't take it. Change of plan, she said. We're dancing.

Oh no, I really don't feel like going out, Roo.

Who said we were going out?

Ruth connected her phone to my speaker and dragged the coffee table to one side. Come on, she said, holding out her arms.

In the holidays, we would do this when I was struggling. My grandparents never knew what to do, but Ruth would put on MTV. Catherine had a chest of clothes that belonged to her mother, and we would wear them, with hats and scarves from thrift shops.

Ruth, I really am okay.

I know. Dance with me anyway.

And so I took her hand, and we began to dance, movements that built with each song until we were kicking and flailing like garage tube men on a gusty day to a "Sounds of the Sixties" playlist. Fifteen minutes later, we collapsed, breathless and purged of all our fragile words. Ruth said that *now* it was time to watch the movies. Ready for a night of *ironic fabulousness*, she said in an undecipherable accent. I asked if it was fair to still call it ironic when we did it once a month.

Like how I used to say "lol" ironically and now I just say it?

I don't even like cosmopolitans!

Ruth rested her legs over mine, picked up the remote, and said: Lol.

I saw him walk into the pub, but I looked up at the last minute to seem nonchalant. I was wearing a new "girl-next-door" polka dot tea dress, and my hair was in a fishtail plait. I was excited because it felt like forward momentum for the first time since the holiday. But then he said hello, and my excitement vanished. He didn't kiss me; he just waved his hand in front of his chest and let Steph introduce herself as if I was someone he had met a party whose name he couldn't remember.

Enola! I was starting to think that he had made you up!

Steph's black hair was cut into a bob with a sharp fringe, her eyes were green, and her lips were red. Her nose was small and curved, and her eyes distinctively round. She was wearing a leather skirt and a bleached denim jacket like his, without the rip. Her shirt was a mesh material, and the black triangles of her bra were visible. She looked so *cool*.

They sat on one side of the table, and I sat on the other, like I was interviewing for a job. Steph tucked her hair behind her ear, and I counted six piercings: three flesh, three cartilage.

Where's Patrick? I asked.

Pat couldn't make it, he answered, avoiding eye contact.

Steph turned to me. So, you're a writer? B swore he'd never date another writer!

B? Who the fuck is B?

His eyes darted around the pub as if he were looking for assistance. I replied that I was trying to be and asked what she did. I already knew, but it seemed like the right thing to ask.

She turned her head and dropped her mouth. Excuse me. Why haven't you told your current girlfriend what your best friend does? She poked him in the ribs, and when he poked her back, his fingers grazed her bra.

Current girlfriend?

Steph reaffirmed that she was an actor. I asked her if that was fun, and she said that she loved the après-ski part. I said that I had never been skiing, and she clarified that she was just "in it for the drinks."

Speaking of drinks. He turned to me and asked what I would like. I told him a white wine. He didn't check with Steph. Presumably he already knew what she wanted.

I felt nervous being alone with her; something in the way she was looking at him? Or the way that he wasn't looking at me? Her eyes stalked him to the bar, then narrowed on me like a follow spot. Enola, how is writing going for you? I know B finds it hard sometimes. But he's such a fucking genius.

I agreed and answered that writing was going well, but, hearing myself describe my book, it sounded childish and silly. I remembered his words: *Don't let it take away from your actual writing.* Did he think my book sounded childish and silly? Did Steph? She was making monosyllabic sounds to demonstrate that she was listening, but it didn't feel like she was. I trailed off like a singer running out of breath, and she told me not to give up on my dreams because if she had given up then she wouldn't be at the Donmar now.

Just say something, you idiot. Ask her what the Donmar is.

Before I could think of something to say, she asked why we had chosen Kenya for a holiday. When I told her that I used to live there, she looked surprised and said that "B" had never mentioned that. I explained that we were only there for four years because Dad worked for the foreign office. How exciting, she said. My uncle is in the House of Lords. Is your dad still in politics?

No, I replied. He died when I was nine.

Most people never knew what to say when I told them; it was like they thought the death of a parent might be contagious. But Steph asked me how he died. I wanted to tell her that it was none of her business, but I lied: Heart attack. Then, changing the subject, I told her that my mum used to be an actress. Steph's round eyes expanded.

You're kidding! Is she still working?

I told her that she stopped acting when we moved to Kenya, and Steph looked more offended at this than she had at the heart attack. She commented on how hard it must have been for my mum to give up her career. I lied again and said that she just wanted to be a mum, but instantly regretted it when Steph's smile fell.

Well, if *I* decide to have children, I'd like to think that I could have both.

Absolutely! Do you want children?

Steph shrugged and looked to the bar like she was checking her watch. I quickly asked how they met, and Steph said that they met in Bristol when he was at university and she was at drama school. Her smile returned as she recounted what was clearly a favorite story: He was working in this pub we frequented when I was at the Old Vic. And even though we were a *terrible* couple, we stayed mates.

My body went rigid. *They dated?*

He returned, putting a Guinness and a whiskey chaser by Steph. Sorry, that took fucking ages. He said he ordered a platter. Steph slammed her hand on the table like a drunk pirate and said: We'll have to get through it without Enola—she'll just pick like a bird by the looks of her! Where did you get that dress, darl? It's *gorge*.

They dated.

Enola, Steph asked you where your dress was from.

What?

Your. Dress.

Oh, M and S, I think.

Breathe. He must have had his reasons for not telling me.

The evening went on and left me behind. I ate too much of the platter because I was fed up of skinny people telling me that I was too skinny, while he and Steph howled about places I had never been invited to and people I had never met. All I could think was: *Steph helped me with the cake; I crashed with Steph; Steph tells me I have crap taste in women.*

I bet she fucking does.

When Steph went to the bathroom, he folded his arms and asked what was wrong. He reminded me that I had pushed for tonight. The least you could do is make an effort, Enola!

I told him that I was trying to but— I had a gulp of my wine.

But what?

But why didn't you tell me about you and Steph?

The righteousness fell from his face. Glancing to the bathroom, he asked what she had said.

Just that you dated.

He curled his lips and said that he didn't realize he needed my permission to date people *in the past*. Should I run all my ex-girlfriends by you? I lost my virginity to Pippa Macdonald. She lives in Boston now but I can find her online if you'd like?

I explained that I had felt ambushed. Why *didn't* you tell me?

Oh, I don't know. Perhaps because I knew you would react like this?

I was so angry that he would invite me to meet Steph without telling me their history—and now to make it my fault that I didn't know? I recalled every moment in Kenya when he checked his phone and put it on the table with the screen facing down; how he smiled with his mouth but not his eyes, like he was trying to tell me that there was someone in his life who was a threat to me while, at the same time, getting ready to attack me when I felt insecure about it.

Steph returned, tucking her shirt into her leather skirt as if she didn't have time to do it in the bathroom. She announced that she needed to stop spending money. But we could go back to mine, have a couple lines?

He said that he was keen but that I was working in the morning. Awesome, she said, and like she was concerned I might contradict him, lifted me into an immediate goodbye, silver rings digging into my arms. I hope we see you again soon, Enola!

I tried not to scream at her use of the collective pronoun.

He put on his jacket, and I willed him to return my gaze, but he wouldn't. I wanted to finish the conversation, but Steph was on his arm. I said goodbye, and he mumbled that he would text me later. I tried to kiss his lips, but he gave me his cheek. Steph pretended not to notice, but she did, of course.

I GOT HOME AT midnight, drunk from three glasses of bad wine. The flat smelled like blocked drains, and as the light clicked on, dust was visible in the corners. There was always so much to do. I couldn't remember the last time that I cleaned the oven.

How could the evening have gone so badly? My evaluation probably started the instant they left the pub. *B, she's sweet but she's just not right for you.* Or perhaps she just looked at him pointedly and he shook his head and said *Steph, don't start.* Or maybe they didn't mention me? Maybe they just restarted the night like I had never been there? Did I even care? That thought stopped me as I removed my left boot. *Did* I care? Because he should have told me that they used to date! Or should he have if there was nothing going on between them now? But if there was nothing going on between them now, then why was the evening so uncomfortable? Was that the real reason he didn't want us to meet? Although I hadn't met Patrick either, and they had never dated. Or had they? I still only had a handful of clues on my murder board, all of them fought for, nails bloody.

I slid down the wall and rang him. He didn't answer, and so I rang again and again like I was picking a scab. The more obsessive he thought I was, the more obsessive I became. I pictured him turning the phone over, shooting a glance to Steph, having another line. *God, she's a little intense isn't she, B?* Fuck. I hated her. I hated her! But that wasn't fair. It was me. I was the problem.

Fuck, why isn't he calling me back?

I slammed my palm into the floor and, feeling a twinge in the base of my wrist, did it again, harder, until I clutched my hand to my chest. In the pain, I saw a girl crying until her nose bled over her suitcase. Screaming for her dad, screaming for her mum, screaming not to leave her home. I didn't want to be that girl. I wanted to be a woman who didn't wait by her phone at midnight with one boot on and one boot off, and who knew how to clean the oven. I wanted to thrive, to feel about my relationship the way that I felt about my book when I was alone with it, not childish and silly, but like anything was possible. But I was becoming smaller and smaller. All the choices, all the words, were his. Ruth was right: happiness was precarious. And I couldn't keep giving him the keys to mine. I removed my other boot and put my phone inside so that I wouldn't be tempted to use it.

I got into bed at one, but I was still resolved to wake up and write before my shift. Even through my white-wine emotions, I knew everything would be okay as long as I had my book. That was one story I had control over. I went to set my alarm but remembering that my phone was still in my boot, went back to the hall to retrieve it. I turned on the screen and burst into tears. A message sent fifteen minutes ago:

Sorry for being a dick tonight. Wish you were here. xx

CHAPTER 14

TODAY, SPRING SMELLED LIKE SUMMER. I WAS CROUCHED IN THE break room next to a box of disinfectant and the trainers of someone who cycled to work, with my laptop on my thighs.

I paused typing and leaned against the wall.

What should I wear tonight? It was Amy's book launch, and he had agreed to come with me. Because he was at the bar in the evening and I was at the café in the day, we didn't see each other as much. But he was making more of an effort to text, and I was making more of an effort not to care when he didn't. We had talked about Steph, and he explained that he hadn't said anything because his ex, Jessica, had been irrationally jealous. But he told me that he knew I wasn't like her, and so I told him that I understood, partly because I did and partly to prove that he was right.

Perhaps my black dress and brown boots?

I noticed the time, put my laptop away, and headed back out. Ruth's replacement, Stefan, left a half-made coffee on the machine and timed an exhale as we crossed paths to indicate that my break had overrun.

At the counter, a man was waiting. Gap between his front teeth, brown eyes, dark hair with flecks of caramel, muscles visible through a sleek white shirt. He was neat and clean, and his clothes were not only ironed, but they looked pressed.

I think that's my latte? he said, gesturing to the coffee with a long, slim finger.

Sorry, I'll make you a new one if you can wait.

Sure, it's just work, he replied with a fake huff.

I refilled the grounds, and he asked my name. Enola, I said, placing a clean cup beneath the nozzle. He told me that his name was Virinder. The machine whirred as espresso dripped. I was used to men talking to me at work. There were two types. The first liked to demonstrate that they were the sort of person who spoke to the barista. The second flirted. I wasn't sure which this man was.

I poured the milk into a flower shape, and Virinder asked if I had worked here long. I asked what he was insinuating by that. It was a joke, but he answered genuinely: I haven't seen you here before. I told him that I was referring to my coffee art, and he laughed. The two suits in the queue shuffled their brogues.

If you have to explain it, then it's a great joke, I said, and he laughed again, louder. He asked if this was my full-time job. Normally, that question made me bristle, but Virinder asked questions like he simply wanted to know the answers, and so I replied with confidence that I was writing a book.

Virinder stepped back: Wow, that's exciting!

I dismissed Virinder with a noise, but, as I did, I realized how frequently I minimized my writing so as not to antagonize *him*. He didn't want to write together anymore. He didn't even want to talk about writing. I had stopped asking how his book was going, hoping he would volunteer the information when he was ready. But so far, he hadn't, and the list of things that we didn't talk about was growing longer.

Virinder said that he had thought about a writing a book. An exposé of the life of a city lawyer. I smiled to be polite, and he lifted his coffee as if to demonstrate that he had it. Better jet, Enola. But I'm here on secondment, so you'll see me again. I watched him walk away with a skip in his step, like he was enjoying walking.

Sorry, I said to the impatient brogues. What can I get you?

* * *

I ARRIVED FIVE MINUTES early so that I didn't keep him waiting. I had told him that the dress code was smart, but he was wearing his denim jacket and Converse. He greeted me in a tone that signaled his discomfort. I reassured him that we didn't have to stay long. Thank fuck. He popped gum into his mouth.

Don't I get a kiss? I tried to sound flippant but it came out the opposite because although he kissed me, his mouth remained closed.

Inside, books provided color against otherwise white walls. Servers circulated trays to women with colorful scarves and men with visible socks. He stepped through the door and said that he was getting a drink. I asked if he could get me a sparkling water, and he flicked his hand over his shoulder. Amy appeared in a flurry of cashmere and lime-and-basil hair mist.

Congratulations, I said. I'm so happy for—

But she hushed me and said that her agent's assistant, Diana, was here.

My stomach dropped. But I've not got anything ready, I—

I sent her your first three chapters and she loved them.

You sent them? But they aren't ready!

Enola, if things were left to you they would never happen.

He returned with drinks, and, on seeing Amy, his face dropped. He mustered a congratulations and apologized that he wasn't going to make it to her wedding. Then he handed me my drink and said he was going for a cigarette. I whispered that we had only just arrived, and he whispered that he hated these things. Amy pretended not to hear, but when he left, she told me about David's friend Noah, who worked in television.

Enola, he has just broken up with his girlfriend of five years and he's utterly miserable. I told him about you, and he was super interested.

He sounds like a catch, Ames.

He lives in Leyton in a ground floor with a garden.

Why do you make every man sound like a real estate ad?

I'm just saying, Noah would make an excellent date to a wedding . . .

I thought you filled the space?

We did. But you get my point.

I took a sticky sausage from a tray and was about to put it in my mouth when Amy caught someone's eye like a ball had been thrown from across the room. She turned back to me, excited, and told me that Diana was coming over.

Enola, put the sausage down.

There was no table near, and so I wrapped it in a napkin and held it.

Diana, this is Enola, Amy said, with an instructive widening of her eyes to me. Enola is the writer of the enchanting chapters I emailed.

I shook her hand firmly with my non-sausage hand. Diana said that she had read my chapters, and I apologized. She laughed melodiously and said that Amy warned her I might do that.

Honestly, they were in much better shape than you might think. And I loved the premise. Often, a strong concept makes a bestseller. It doesn't always matter about the writing. But luckily your writing is strong.

Are you sur—

Amy nudged me.

I mean, *thank you.*

She said that she loved the way I had used the animals, explaining that many teenagers retreated into fantasy to cope with adult situations.

It was strange talking about my story with an agent; Diana was speaking about a world that I'd created in my bedroom like it was real. She was the sort of woman who grew up in a two-parent household, had regular meals, went to Durham. She had clear skin, natural highlights, and a diamond on her finger. She made enough eye contact that I knew that she was listening but not too much that I felt uncomfortable. I liked her very much.

She said that she had to run. I have so much work to do, but I just wanted to stop by the party to say congratulations. She scrunched her lips at Amy, who scrunched hers in return. Before she left, she asked me to please send her the full manuscript.

Oh my god.

Amy waited until Diana was a distance away and then said: See, I told you it was good. I said that I didn't know how to thank her. Don't be silly, she replied, already stretching her arms out to the next person. This is all you, Enola. Own it for once!

I watched Amy move through the room with conviction and felt overwhelming gratitude that she was my friend. Then I ate the sticky sausage still crumpled in my hand.

He hadn't returned, so I scanned the room for him and as I did, my eyes landed on Scott, an American comedy agent I had met once before. He bowed his head and strolled over, grabbing a glass of prosecco from a floating tray. He asked who I was looking for, and when I answered, he replied: So not me, then? From anyone else, it might have been sleazy, but Scott had a way about him. His accent was a coffee or an aftershave commercial. He navigated the conversation like he did the party: as if he had learned the choreography. We talked lightly. His client had a book out. A memoir for the socially inept. I smiled and said that was the title of my book too. When we parted, he gave me his card and said: In case you don't find your boyfriend.

What is happening tonight? My head was light, and my chest was fluttering with excitement rather than anxiety. I wanted to stay at the party and be the person these people thought I was. But my heart pulled me outside to where he was still smoking. It was drizzling and cold. His hair was slicked back, and his Converse had holes where the rubber had ripped from the fabric. The bags beneath his eyes were globular, and his mouth was catfish-like. There were two cigarette stubs on the pavement by his feet.

Are you okay?

I can't be at a book thing right now.

Is everything all right?

No, it's not *all right*, Enola.

I looked down at my freshly polished boots. I'd made an effort tonight, but he couldn't even put on a blazer? But then I felt guilty and apologized for the thought that he didn't know I'd had. He told me that it was okay. Then he inhaled deeply and said: It's just that I fucking hate this industry! It's all marketing. And who you know. *And* everyone is either a columnist or a podcaster or went to Oxbridge! What am I meant to say to people in there? "Hi, I'm nearly forty and I work in a fucking bar"?

You are not *nearly forty*, and there is nothing wrong with working in a bar.

Enola, please. I'm not looking for you to fix this, okay?

I wasn't trying to fix anything. I was *trying* to say that your book is amazing and—

I don't need a cheerleader either.

I hadn't been able to say the right words to comfort him in a long time. I didn't know whether Steph managed, but from me, every word I said about his book or his career or his life was an attack. I apologized for asking him to come, and he shook his head like he was disappointed that he had agreed to it. I thought about what he'd said in the airport about prioritizing himself in a relationship. Come on, I said. I'll make us some food.

He whistled and made a face.

Fine, I'll get us a pizza.

His eyes shone, and instantly I was better than the person I was at the party because he wanted me again.

He held my hand, and when I smiled, he told me to calm down. It's a hand hold, not a proposal. I told him that I couldn't wait to get him out of his wet clothes. Honey, he said. Do you mind if we don't? I really don't feel sexy. Can we just eat pizza?

We hadn't had sex for weeks, but I just wanted to be close to him, and his hand in mine felt as intimate. We passed the bus stop, and I threw Scott's card in the bin. And Diana?

Please send me your manuscript when it is finished.
I would tell him soon; I would. But not yet.

I WAS CLEANING THE front of the coffee machine, and Ruth was slicing tomatoes. There were seeds covering the counter from where she had missed the chopping board. I told her that I was sorry it didn't work out at her new job, and she replied that she wasn't passionate about it. I asked her what she was passionate about, and she held up a limp, wet slice of tomato.

I'm serious, Roo! We only talk about me lately.

That's because you're the main character.

Ruth, look at you. You are clearly the main character.

We were wearing the same uniform but Ruth made it look like an outfit she had designed. Her hair was in a scarf and she was wearing a mood ring on each hand. *Half of me is enthusiastic and half is pensive,* she had said when I pointed out that the stones were different colors.

Ruth told me that she wasn't like me; I had known what I wanted to do since I was seven. I said that wasn't a good thing. She paused her chopping and said that I was on the cusp of something. I can feel it, Enola. I asked if she thought that Diana was only interested in my book because of Amy. She said that an agent wouldn't have time to humor me. Besides, who cares? The important thing is that she reads it.

After the eleven o'clock rush, I went on my break and wrote a few hundred words, some I was proud of, others not, but the choosing was mine. When I returned, Virinder was at the counter talking with Ruth. I watched him. His eyebrows were fixed in surprise, and when he left, he inexplicably ran up the escalator. I put my apron back on, and Ruth told me that he was asking about me. I said that there was something in the air, because this man had hit on me at Amy's book launch too. Ruth said that it wasn't the air; it was because of my book.

How do you figure that?

When a person takes care of one problem area, the other problem areas take care of themselves.

I asked where she heard that. She said that she was told it by a dermatologist about skin care but insisted that it applied to life. Then she asked if I had told him about Diana yet. I replied that I hadn't found the right moment. She said that there shouldn't be a right moment to tell my boyfriend good news. I told her that it was complicated. He's having a hard time at the moment. Ruth hung up her apron and tore off the end of a baguette.

Tell him to buck up, she said. It shouldn't make him feel less to see you thrive. Just tell him, Enola.

I will!

When?

Thrown, I agreed to tell him tomorrow and Ruth went on her break.

Why *was* I nervous about telling him? Things had settled; it had been six weeks without a proper fight. He might be angry if he found out that I had kept it from him. He would say something like: *Do you think I'm that pathetic or jealous or insecure?* Yes, there was every danger that *not* telling him might lead to a bigger argument. I wiped up the tomato seeds and imagined a world where he was proud of me.

CHAPTER 15

BECAUSE I HAD UNLOCKED THE DOOR AND PUT MUSIC ON, I FELT his hands before hearing his voice. He kissed my cheek. There was cider on his breath. He must have had a productive day, because he was in a good mood. I felt my unease release; when he was happy, we were happy. I told him that I was making risotto. My friend Fiona, who came third on *MasterChef*, gave me the recipe. He sniffed and asked what she had said to put in it.

Sage, leeks, celery.

Don't put sage in that.

He watched me chop. Make sure they're all the same size. And is that the pan you're using? I asked if that was wrong, and he laughed. It was a valiant effort but I'll make it. He hooked a finger in my belt loop and steered me to the sofa like I was a shopping trolley.

I listened to him chop everything apart from the sage, and the weight of my own thoughts and feelings lifted. The sun was setting through the glass, and he was moving around my kitchen, singing to the music and proffering cooking advice: You have to salt them before you fry them, honey. This was what I wanted: our bad bits gone. The sizzling of onions. Laptops left on the table at night. I remembered how Dad would cut the bruises off pieces of fruit before handing them to me.

By the time we started eating, the sun had set and he was telling me about an idea he had for a column to accompany his book. He told me that it came to him during a shift at the bar as he listened to one of the regulars opine about last week's paper. Do you get it? he said with momentum. The author will be Charlie.

The journalist?

No, Enola, he said sarcastically, the ballet dancer. Then he interrupted himself: Fuck, this risotto is good! Your mate might have *won MasterChef* if she had done this.

It was now or never. There wouldn't be a better time to tell him. I put my fork down and told him that I had some news. He made a noise but didn't look up from his plate.

You know that agent that Amy put me in touch with?

He froze.

She's asked for my full manuscript.

He choked on a mouthful of risotto and took a sip of water. That's great, honey, he said, thumping his chest. I thought that he was going to speak once the mouthful cleared, but he didn't.

Yay! I said like a child at a birthday party that none of her friends had turned up to. He continued eating, and I flashed back to standing by the cabinet of ornate dogs in my underwear.

I offered seconds, but he said he was full. I asked a question about his column, but he said that he might not do it after all. I went to the bathroom, and when I returned, the table was cleared as if the evening had never happened.

I DIDN'T SEE HIM for the rest of the week, and his messages were sporadic and short. I hoped that he might apologize, but he didn't. (*Are you surprised?* asked Ruth.) I felt like I was back in those two weeks after our holiday, and I struggled to write or muster excitement about sending my book to Diana. I suggested meeting twice; the first time he was working and the second he had plans with Steph. But then on Sunday he messaged:

I can come over after my shift if you like.

I opened the door and he instantly made a point of saying that it had been a long one—a warning to me. We watched television like we were waiting for the episode to finish and then got undressed the same way. I put on my flowered nighty that he enjoyed teasing me about. When I first wore it he joked that I belonged in a nursing home and gave me a *Mario Kart* T-shirt to wear instead. *About time you wore something sexy, honey.* But tonight he didn't say anything, and I felt like the punch line of the same joke.

We got into bed, and he checked his phone and smiled. The light was on as if he was waiting for something, so I kissed him, but his lips were pursed. I made a comment about how it had been a while, and he asked me what that meant. I told him that I missed being with him. I wasn't sure what else it could mean. He put his phone down. You know I'm just depressed right now—don't take it personally, Enola. But it was hard not to take it personally when every time Steph messaged, he smiled. I knew that I had to talk to him, but I also knew that might mean an argument, so I geared myself up to speak like I was preparing to jump off something. But I mistimed it, and we spoke at the same time.

Are you going to turn that light off? / Is everything okay?

I wanted to take my question back, but it was out there, half-cooked. He asked what I was accusing him of now. *Here we go.* I told him that it was just a question. He snorted like that was a technicality. I wrung my nighty tightly. He hated when I second-guessed him, but I knew that something was wrong, just as I had known that something was wrong in Kenya. I kept my tone gentle and my posture unconfrontational. I said that things had felt tense.

What are you talking about?

Since I told you about Diana.

Who's Diana?

He knew who Diana was. I wasn't sure whether he was pretending that everything was okay or trying to undermine me, but I explained again. Okay, and sorry, what's the issue there? he asked, like he was poised to write down my answer. I unraveled the nighty and said that he hadn't seemed happy for me.

If you want to talk about anything or if you're feeling—

He interrupted me with a breath. Do you really think I'm that insecure?

No!

You think I'm that pathetic?

Of course not!

Then you must think I'm jealous or something.

I—

Because I think that the problem isn't whether or not I'm happy for you—which I am—the *problem* is that I didn't show my happiness in the exact way that you wanted.

I could feel my heart now, and it was harder to keep my tone soft.

So, everything's okay?

Yes! I've just had a busy week!

I told him that I appreciated him saying that he was happy for me, but something in my tone provoked him because he continued, livelier: I *am* happy, I'm thrilled that Amy thought of someone other than herself.

I told him that Amy had been nothing but supportive. And it's not a competition. There's room for everyone! He snorted and called me naïve.

The rain was coming down outside, and the wind rattled the windows. His rucksack was against the wardrobe, with his manuscript protruding from the top, marked with red scribbles. He was struggling. I had to be patient. I needed to *understand*.

I touched his chest and told him that as soon as he sent the book off, his life would change, but he pulled the duvet up and told me not to patronize him. I'm a "privileged straight white man," as everyone is so keen to remind me. No one cares how good my book is when my voice is worthless.

I didn't mean to laugh, but it seemed absurd. Come on, you can't think that your voice is worthless. Your voice is dominant! Look at the world right now. I mean, Donald Trump is running for president!

He said that I was deliberately missing the point. I asked what the point was, and he said that diversity shouldn't be a genre. I said that it shouldn't be a scapegoat either. He turned his body to me. A scapegoat for what?

My pulse increased.

My failure?

No! You're not a failure! You're not *failing*. Your writing is brilliant.

His eyes flashed, and the fight that had been floating in the shallows surfaced. He was angry now, shirtless and broad with dark coarse hairs, and I was a child in a pensioner's nightgown. You're lucky, he said, sarcasm like an undercurrent. You don't have to worry about being brilliant when you have Amy.

So that's why he's not happy for me. I dug my nail into my thumb. I asked him if that was why he didn't want Patrick doing the illustrations. You don't think the book is going to be good? He asked me how many weeks I had been hanging on to *that* for. I told him that he hadn't even read it. He said that he didn't recall my asking him to read it. I told him to stop doing that. Please just *talk* to me.

What do you think I'm doing?

Trying to win an argument!

And you're not trying to win the argument? Let's recap. So far, you've attacked me for not throwing you a party about your news, which, considering the headspace I'm in, is pretty fucking selfish, and now *you're* lecturing *me* about privilege?

What do you mean by that?

I mean, Enola, that it's easy to drift around working in a coffee shop when you had a flat bought for you in central London.

I put my palms over my eyes and stared into the red-black. When I had spoken to Ruth, my argument was logical, but now his argument sounded logical too. And yet he had been distant all week. I hadn't made that up. But what if that distance was never about

Diana? He didn't have the time to see me, but he had seen Steph. He always had time for Steph. I dropped my hands and asked him what was happening.

We're having an argument, Enola.

Yes, but why?

He smiled. Just say it.

I raised my eyebrow meaningfully. He punched the bed. I pinched my skin and held the pressure.

You see, this is what you do. We're talking about one thing and you blow it into another. I will not argue about Steph. You are insane when it comes to her, Enola.

I hated that he thought that, like I was no better than *Jessica*. But I didn't feel insane; I felt right. I told him that he texted Steph all the time, but I was lucky if I got a reply from him. He told me that I sounded like a child. I said that I was just asking a question. He asked what the question was, but I couldn't remember. He told me that I was waiting for something to go wrong. Asking me if I'm okay. Looking at me with doe eyes. You want something to be wrong because you're happier being miserable for some fucking reason.

That's not fair, that's—

He threw his head back. Fine, that's not *fair*, whatever. But there is always *something*. I told you, Enola, I'm not your fucking therapist!

I told him that I didn't want him to be my therapist; I wanted him to be my partner. He said that he was trying to be, but that it was fucking hard sometimes. *Oh god.* My throat felt like something was squeezed around it. I curled into myself to be alone. What *had* my question been? When I felt the warmth of his hand on my back, I lifted back up.

Honey, you've never been in a long-term relationship before, have you? Have you considered that being in a relationship might not be for you? He lifted his hands like I had a gun pointed at him. Don't take that the wrong way, relationships aren't for everyone. Then he turned and fluffed his pillow.

Panic rose hot and dark. I hated him I hated him I hated him, but I couldn't let him finish fixing the bedding. I asked him to listen. He said that he didn't need this right now. He had a million things to do. *That's enough, Enola.* He lay back and closed his eyes, but the silence was active. How could he turn off a fight like a light switch?

Can we please finish this? I said. You can't let the sun go down on your anger.

He popped up like a jack-in-the-box. Because if you heard it in a song then it must be true?

Fuck you, I thought. *Fuck you.* And I started shouting. I hadn't shouted at him before, and it was a downpour. I shouted that his reaction to my news was upsetting. I shouted that I hated how he went from hot to cold. I shouted that I didn't know how to talk to him. I shouted that I knew that Steph had feelings for him. I heard my high, strained voice and knew that I should shut up; I was in a hole and every word made the hole deeper and darker but I kept hopelessly searching for the right word to close the hole up.

He waited until I ran out of words, and then he said: You're being a fucking cunt.

I slapped him.

He held my gaze and then slapped me with a force that propelled my face onto the bed. Everything slowed the way the tide pulls back before a wave. The rhythm of my cheek. The smell of my orchid laundry detergent. And then it came: the panic.

What have I done? Oh god, what have I done.

I straightened up, and he was dressing. Stop it, please, I said.

He looked at me, growled: Do you know how pathetic you look? Stop clutching your face! *Grow up.* He pulled his jeans up, and his boxers bunched. No, stop it! He put his T-shirt on back to front. Take it off. His trainers. *Take them off.* Pressure built around my head like a helmet. The air was thick and wet. He charged to the door, but I threw myself in front of it. You can't leave. You can't leave me. My nighty slipped off my shoulder.

I'm warning you, Enola, get off me right now. His face was purple. He shoved me into the door.

I'm sorry. I don't know what's wrong with me. Please don't leave me. I'm so sorry.

Fuck! He flung his hands over his head then, from his rucksack, retrieved his inhaler, sat on the edge of the bed, and inhaled twice. But I couldn't breathe. Gaps appeared. The room was dark. An echo told me to sit on the bed.

I am on the bed.

Here, drink this.

There is a glass of water in my hand.

Come on, drink.

I can't grip the glass with my invisible hands.

You need some water, Enola. You won't get your breath back if you don't stop crying. Relax, honey. Relax. He took a sip and lay me back. He pressed his mouth to mine and released the water. He did it three more times, touching my skin like it was tracing paper. I thanked him for feeding me like a bird. He smiled and told me that I was welcome.

OUR BODIES STAYED ENTWINED until the light shone through the blinds. I felt suction when we separated. Holding the duvet over his mouth to hide his breath, he asked if he could buy me breakfast.

I got dressed and thought about telling Ruth what happened but I didn't want her to think that he was abusive, the same way that I didn't want him to think that I was making myself the victim. It wasn't like he hit me; it was a flat palm and I had slapped him first. He was only guilty of being a man.

Ready?

He was stood in the doorway in his olive-green shirt, silver chain, denim jacket, and black jeans. The same outfit he wore when he came to my flat for the first time.

The sun was shining, and we walked to the café chatting about things we could see: a new restaurant, graffiti on a wall, a cute dog.

But then he stopped us in the middle of the pavement, looked into my eyes, and kissed me. I knew then that everything would be okay. He took my hand and we continued walking in silence.

He got us a table while I went downstairs to the bathroom. The cubicles smelled of sandalwood and jazz played from individual speakers in the ceiling. When I returned, he would show me a video that he had found while waiting. Otters in a lake perhaps, or someone falling down. The latter I would shake my head at, and he would roll his eyes affectionately. *Affectionately.* How differently the same action could impact. I looked in the mirror and—

I AM STANDING IN front of the mirror in the beach house. Mum is putting calamine lotion on my back. I am crying, and she tells me to stay still. But the itching is too bad. *Stop it, Enola, just stop it.* She smacks me, and I hit my forehead on the corner of the cabinet. The next day she sees the bruise and asks me how it happened. I tell her that I fell in the pool.

THE MEMORY FINISHED WITH the whirring of a hand dryer in the next-door cubicle. My childhood self was a saboteur presenting a rose-tinted reality the shade of a petal, the kind that she picked from the garden and scrunched into water to make perfume for her mother. I looked at my reflection now, but there was no bruise. I lifted my hand and brought it to my cheek, hitting myself again and again as a saxophone wailed above the toilet. *Here you go, Mum, look what I made you.*

CHAPTER 16

IT'S BEEN THIRTY MINUTES, BUT THE PAINKILLERS HAVEN'T KICKED in. My head still hurts, and my stomach is unsteady. I check my smashed phone, but there are no new messages. Outside, the mist has risen, and, lit up in white lights, the jagged tip of the Shard is a constellation. But if I shift focus, my reflection appears, ghostlike on the London skyline. It looks like I'm not really here. Perhaps I'm still staring at the plastic bag on the welcome mat? But if that's true, then I am also still standing on the tube platform last night, looking at the white threads in his jacket, wondering what to do. If universes sprout from moments of indecision, then I have created hundreds. Amy once told me that I need to learn how to end a story: *Babe, no offense, but I'm just not confident you'll get us where we need to go.*

IT WAS WEDNESDAY NIGHT. The day had bled from the room, but I hadn't turned the lights on. It was just after eight. Mum and Paul would be a bottle in. Cheese board littered with rinds, terra-cotta pot soaking in the sink, two glasses, one with a lipstick print around the rim. I had eaten a scotch egg and taken two painkillers with a glass of supermarket wine.

He was coming over at ten. He said he was at work, which meant that he was either at the bar or writing. He just said "work," and I didn't want to ask *which* work in case he accused me of being passive-aggressive.

Just before nine, the phone rang, and I let it vibrate three times before answering, like I was playing chicken.

Enola, is that you?

I . . . *What?* Mum, you called me.

Yes, she said tartly, but I'm calling you from a different number. I told her that if that were the case, she would still know who *I* was. She sighed and then spoke as if she were the bigger person.

How are you, Enola?

Okay. It's Amy's wedding this weekend.

Are you going?

Yes. How are you?

Oh, you know.

I did know. She grew vegetables. She painted. Paul's children visited with their children. But she got a weekly phone call with the daughter she never wanted. The detour she took on the way to France. The role she was miscast in: motherhood.

When Mum moved to France, she told me that I could come up during the holidays, and I stayed for a whole summer once before my A levels. I wanted to stay with Ruth in London, but my grandparents put me on a plane. I cycled down country lanes. Walked through fields. Everything existed in subtext, in the dark corners of the vineyard that Mum was painting in the corner of the living room where the light was best.

That's good, I replied, as if she had actually answered the question. And how is work?

She wouldn't say "writing," because she didn't view that as work. She wasn't wrong. No one was paying me to do it. After Amy's book launch, I had considered telling her about Diana, but I had imagined how that conversation would go: *You have a book deal? No, Mum, an agent isn't a book deal. But you have an agent? No, Mum, an agent just wants to read my book. And how much money will you get for that?* So I replied that work was fine and asked her about her garden. Mum liked to talk about her garden.

Well, the roses aren't looking great but they're so tricky and we've had bizarre weather. The green around the arch is looking good, though, and we just dug up a lovely lot of potatoes, she said.

I walked to the bedroom and took another painkiller.

I asked her to remind me what she grew, and she said: The usual. I paused, expecting her to clarify, but she didn't, so I suggested carrots. She repeated the word like it was offensive, so I chose another vegetable: Cabbages? She said yes; she grew cabbages and lettuce and some leeks. She also had a load of gooseberries and was going to make rhubarb crumble.

With gooseberries?

No, Enola. With rhubarb.

I checked the time. It had only been two minutes. I thought about him. If he was coming from the bar he would smell like muddled strawberries and whiskey and I would run him a shower. If he had been writing then he would be excitable or stressed and I would stroke his hair.

I went back to the living room and turned on the side lights.

How is Milton, Mum?

Milton? She repeated his name as if she had never heard it before.

Yes, Mum . . . Milton.

Milton died, Enola.

What? I exclaimed. When?

She made a noise and said: Oh, I don't know. A few weeks ago? I squeezed a sofa cushion and the sequins dug into my palm. Mum was always offended when I didn't have the information that she hadn't provided. I said that she had never told me about Milton. She told me to calm down: You never even met Milton, Enola. I returned that I *had* met Milton.

Well, now he's dead. Turtles don't live very long, Enola.

They do, Mum.

Mum never sugarcoated things. It's how she dealt with everything, like she was just finishing up paperwork. I heard a deep voice in the background: something about pears? Mum shouted to put the kettle on. Grey. Yes. Earl *Grey*. No, not that one. It's in the tub at the top of the cupboard. Yes, that's it, the one with the badger on it!

Mum?

Enola?

I wished she would stop saying my name like she was trying to remember it.

No, the *badger*, the others are gluten-free.

Mum?

She snapped that she was trying to do a million things at once, so I told her to hang up then. She made a long "ooooh" sound and suggested that I go for a jog. I replied that I hated jogging, and she told me to pick a different activity. Milton was just a turtle, Enola. There was a click as the phone was put down, then it was picked back up and Mum said that they were going to watch a film and she would speak to me next Wednesday.

I hated how she said that casually, like it was an arrangement that I had co-orchestrated. And fuck her for telling me to choose an activity. I couldn't grow vegetables in a high-rise. Before I could stop them, the words flew from my mouth: You never asked me where I went on holiday.

You went on another holiday?

No, the one back in March.

She asked me why I was bringing it up now. It's June, Enola. Was I supposed to have asked you? I told her that it would have been a logical thing to ask. Fine, she said. Where did you go on holiday?

Kenya.

She went very quiet and then said: You're an adult, Enola, you can go on holiday wherever you want. Then she hung up and left me with all the same questions: Why do you hate me? And why did you leave me? Although presumably the first question answered the second.

AFTER I PUT THE phone down, I waited for him. The doorbell went around eleven, and he was holding a bunch of pink tulips with a yellow reduced sticker. Since the fight he had been making more effort:

putting kisses at the end of more frequent messages; asking about my book; suggesting plans rather than responding to them. But he would have hated it if I made a fuss, so I thanked him like it was an everyday occurrence that he bought me flowers. He walked to the kitchen and turned on the strip light. I asked him how work was, and he said that he had written a new chapter. *So, he was writing this evening.*

That's great. How is it?

He shrugged, but I could tell that he was happy, which meant that we wouldn't argue. As he showered, I put the flowers in the vase on the kitchen table. If I had asked him earlier "which work," then he might not have bought me flowers. Did that mean that I was finally getting to know him or making the wrong compromises? Either way, the flowers were beautiful.

When he got into bed, I clung to his arm like I was going into space. He didn't try to have sex with me. He never wanted to have sex anymore. He had seen my ugly pieces: the mess, the tears, the violence. But he kissed the back of my neck, and I held my pain as if it were a balloon that might pop. His breathing changed, and I was left alone in the dark with my balloon. I just had to keep him happy. He would stay with me as long as I made him happy.

CHAPTER 17

I KNEW THAT WE WERE GOING TO FIGHT AS SOON AS WE MET AT Victoria station. Before he said hello, he ranted about an author who had been nominated for a prize, and something in my body signaled like an alarm. I hadn't seen him for a while because of our schedules, and I'd missed him at the weekend because of Amy's wedding. It had been hot for weeks, and the forecast kept promising rain; London was fat and overdue.

We went to a self-serve wine bar that Ruth suggested. Everything was good at first; he put his palm on my back, which was bare in a black halter top, and we tried samples of different wines and laughed at the "notes." But then his voice and movements became bigger; his energy like a cat's before it knocks something off a shelf. He noticed a couple with two full glasses of wine. The man was swilling the glass and wafting the scent toward his nose.

Marching to the Argentinian reds, he decanted wine from an expensive bottle, gargled it like mouthwash, and announced that it tasted like piss. The woman looked embarrassed. But I couldn't tell who she was embarrassed for.

We're ruining their date, I said lightly.

Fuck them. Who comes to a bar like this and has just *one* glass of *one* wine?

I looked at them: his hand was on her knee; they weren't laughing but they were talking, nodding, widening their eyes. They were sweet, actually.

He tried a Malbec and said that it tasted like tomato juice. I told him that Amy's dad got the wine for her wedding from France.

He moved to another bottle.

Oh, and I didn't tell you! In his speech, the best man made a joke about her feet—

He said that he preferred the lighter reds.

So, you know that basic best man's joke about a woman's feet being small so she can reach the kitchen sink? Well, he actually made that joke. Like he had googled what to say at a wedding!

He said that for someone who apparently didn't enjoy weddings I certainly enjoyed talking about them. I apologized, but he rolled his eyes and said that he was joking. Then he suggested the pub for a proper drink. I told him that I was getting a headache, but I knew that we shouldn't continue drinking; I could sense the argument, like the rain.

We waited at the bus stop. It was still hot, but the wind was stirring. He got out his phone, and I knew who he was texting because when it rang, he didn't answer. I told him that he could take the call, and he thanked me for the permission. Before the silence could sharpen, the sky burst. Water bounced off warm tarmac, and the smell was invigorating! It reminded me of rainstorms in Kenya. Something came over me and I grabbed his hand. Let's go! But he took his hand back.

What are you doing?

Don't you want to be in it?

No, I don't want to be in it. Are you fucking mental?

Suit yourself.

I ran from under the shelter and held my face up as lightning struck the sky. It was incredible, and I was the girl in my book running into the rain at school; that emancipating moment before her school shirt turned see-through.

Enola, come on, he said. You'll be hit by a bus. I held out my arms to him, hoping that he would shake off his mood, but he told me that my mascara was down my face.

I returned to the shelter and asked him why that bothered him, and he didn't answer. Then he said that he wasn't going to stay at mine anymore.

Why, because of the rain?

Don't be silly. Because I need to write.

I told him that there was no way he would write tonight, and he frowned. What's that supposed to mean?

Just that you're drunk, I said as casually as I could. A car splashed past. He grumbled that it was illegal to splash people. I held his collar, but he didn't take his hands from his pockets. I joked about how that couple ordered a cheese platter to go with their *one* glass of *one* wine, but he hummed like he had realized something.

I think you'd quite like that, wouldn't you, Enola?

I let go of his jacket. What?

A nine-to-five. A boyfriend in banking. Big fancy wedding. I think you'd be happier with someone like that rather than a failed middle-aged writer. And you could have a nice job in admin. You'd like being told what to do and where to have the office party. Or be a stay-at-home mum.

Excuse me?

I'm just saying, honey, you never actually want to write.

I am writing!

Why haven't you sent your manuscript to that agent yet?

I felt conflicted then, because I should have sent it off. I should have finished it. But every time I opened my laptop, I thought about him. He was working so hard. He had always wanted to be a writer. *He* should have this opportunity, but I did, and I knew how he felt about that. I wasn't meaning to hold myself back but I just kept thinking if he could only finish his book first so that I could finish that little bit behind him . . .

I will send it, I said.

When?

When will you send yours?

Don't do that.

Your book is brilliant and it's *ready*. Why not now?

You really don't fucking get it, do you?

That was it: the band that we had been stretching over the past few weeks snapped. I could no longer say that the last fight was the last fight; it was just another one and the next could be worse. I told him that he didn't need to swear at me.

Oh no, oh god, not *swearing*, he mocked.

I started to cry, and he half laughed, half shouted: Oh, here we go again, *poor Enola*! He lifted his arms, and I flinched. He looked confused, and then his eyes narrowed.

I'm sorry. I didn't mean—

You *actually* think that I would hit you?

Excuse me, are you okay?

I turned to see a woman with a red umbrella, looking at me with a concerned expression. He raised his hands then slapped them to his thighs. She repeated the question. I nodded that I was fine, but she gave me this *look* before she left.

Great, now I look like the bastard! he shouted after her.

I hushed him and said that she was just being nice.

She was *being* a cunt.

She wasn't. She really wasn't. Please just leave it!

Because every man is the villain, right? You could never be the problem. He lit a cigarette.

Don't, I said gently, because he had been trying to quit again.

But he told me to fuck off. *Just fuck off, Enola.* He walked away, flicking the unsmoked cigarette behind him.

I stood, numb, as he turned the corner, then started to walk home. The rain had lessened. It wasn't invigorating anymore; it was just wet and I was a joke. I thought about calling Ruth, but she would just hate him even more than she already did. Amy was on her minimoon. I obviously couldn't call Mum. Would Dad have been someone I could have called? Oh god, I missed my dad. He wasn't even a person anymore, he was just slices of grief. Cord slippers. Bottle opener. Reading glasses. I wanted to be in our old house in Nairobi.

I wanted to run into the ocean. I wanted to be a child again, but I also wanted *him* to be there. Bigger than my pride was my desire to keep trying.

I called him three times but he didn't pick up, so I sent a message telling him that I was sorry. I hadn't meant to ruin the evening. I hadn't meant to do anything wrong. He replied quicker than I was expecting:

> *Sorry. I'll be there in ten just had to deal with Enola . . . x*

I moved into the middle of the road.

When I was at school, I was in a toilet cubicle when two girls were at the sink. I heard one of them say that I was weird because I was a white girl from Africa. Then the other said that I was weird because my dad had died. *That's why she was kicked out of Africa.*

Third person stings.

The headlights from a bus.

But another message would follow.

The bus got closer.

That message would allow me to forgive him.

The driver beeped.

That message would buy us another few weeks.

My phone vibrated:

> *Fuck, Enola, that wasn't meant for you and it also wasn't meant the way that I know you're taking it. I'll have a quick drink then come over to yours? Sorry for being a drunk twat. I'm just struggling with things at the moment.*

That message was a lifeline.

I stepped back onto the pavement.

IT WAS HIS BIRTHDAY, and I was making him a card. I had drawn him as a superhero, and his superpower was his laptop. He said that he wasn't a birthday person, but I pushed, and so he said that I could meet him for a drink after his shift. I needed the card to be perfect. This was his first birthday since we had been together, and he had made me that beautiful CD for mine.

Ruth rang and asked how I was feeling. She did that a lot at the moment, and I kept saying the same thing: *I'm fine. Why?* She said that she was just checking. But if I told her the problems we were having she would try to fix them, and her solution was absolute: *End it.*

I laid my clothes out on the bed. A denim skirt, crop top, and Ruth's vintage leather jacket that she kept forgetting to collect. I would tell him that I had been out with a friend for dinner so that he didn't think I had made the effort just for him.

I checked the time: I had a hair appointment at four. I put my elastic band around my wrist, grabbed my bag, and headed out.

THE HAIRDRESSER WAS GLASWEGIAN with a platinum shag. I tried to look happier, because she was looking at me with pity. I told her that I just wanted a trim. You'd look great with a pixie cut, she said. It will lift everything and make you look younger.

Ruth was always changing her hair or getting a tattoo or a piercing, but I always looked the same. I wore the same neutral makeup, and my hair was always mid-length. I wanted to turn up to the bar tonight a different person. Someone stronger and sexier and funnier. Someone he had never seen cry or shout or run into the rain.

I told the hairdresser to do what she wanted, and she looked thrilled.

It's going to be great, she said.

I WAITED IN SOHO on the stoop of a townhouse with a black door. He was fifteen minutes late, which was unusual. I called, but he didn't answer. I held my phone out to look at myself in the camera. My hair was dramatically different. It was angular and tilted toward my chin, and the back looked like the back of a chicken (but when I said that to the hairdresser, she looked offended). I called him again, and this time he said, Hello? with an audible question mark. There was laughter in the background. I asked if he was on his way, and he said that he was having a quick drink with the guys from work.

Oh, okay. Shall I come to the bar, then?

Sure, if you like, or look, why don't I just meet you back at yours later on?

But I'm in Soho already.

I just don't want you to wait, honey.

An uncomfortable silence. I gripped my bag. Why can't I come there? I asked, uneasy. He said that I *could* come, but that it was just the team. I snapped my elastic band. He said that the guys were getting him drunk. I said that I had been sat here for fifteen minutes. He said that it was his birthday, like I didn't have a homemade card in my bag and a haircut like a chicken's arse. I felt angry and stupid, but I agreed to go home. I hung up the phone and that small rebellion made me feel good, but then it made me feel the opposite. Instead of calling him back to apologize, I called Ruth. She answered like she had been waiting by the phone: Enola, are you okay?

I told her that I wanted her advice on this one thing. Please don't say anything else though, Roo.

Okay, she said slowly.

I told her what had happened. I explained that I had a new hair-cut and had made him a birthday present—even though those details weren't necessary. Ruth asked if I was afraid of his reaction. I told her that I didn't want to talk about that. Fine, she said, he's canceled on you last-minute for no good reason, he doesn't get to have his cake and eat it. Birthday or not. That's shitty behavior. Go *home*, Enola, and look—

But that was all I needed to hear. I fluffed my chicken hair and headed to the bar.

I TOLD MYSELF THAT I wouldn't be me. I would be the woman with the new hair. I would be Steph. She wouldn't wait for him on a stoop, but she wouldn't go home either; she would demand fun.

He was alone at the bar with a half-drunk pint. I hadn't seen where he worked before, and it only occurred to me now that that was strange. It was a small square with neon on the walls and a jukebox. It was what I imagined the bars in Nashville or Austin to look like. A seventies pop song was playing, and the air smelled like hops and urinals. I felt sick, but it was too late to change my mind, so I walked up to him and flung my arms around his neck. Happy birthday, gorgeous man!

He looked shocked. Enola, what are you doing here?

I told him that I wouldn't let him celebrate his birthday without me. Come on, let's get shots!

Honey, I thought we agreed that I would come to yours later?

I know, but—

I told you that I was here with the guys.

I looked around to see where "the guys" were, and when I looked back, he was frowning. Jesus. What have you done to your hair? Someone came up behind me, and it was then that I noticed the second drink: a Guinness and whiskey chaser.

Enola! I didn't know you were joining us!

I knew that when I turned, I would see Steph, but I couldn't tear my eyes from him. His expression was uninterpretable; then he said: Don't start, Enola. She just came by for one. Steph laughed.

I turned around: Excuse me? She lifted her hands and said that she would leave us to it. Adrenaline flooded my body. How could you? I said. Where *are* the guys?

He told me to calm down. I don't need this on my birthday, Enola.

I told him that it was only *this* because he made it *this*. He said that I was the one making a scene, and he kept his voice low to ensure that was the case. I turned to wipe my nose and saw Steph pretending not to watch from outside. She thought I was as sensitive and jealous and crazy as Jessica. But Jessica didn't seem crazy. Jessica looked nice. Jessica knitted outfits for her sausage dog. *Fuck.* I should have gone home like Ruth suggested. But if I had, I wouldn't have known the real reason he canceled. I would have showered, perfumed, and made myself a concubine for him to come home to after he had fun with *her*. I picked up his pint glass, but he grabbed my arm.

What the fuck are you doing, Enola?

But I didn't know what I was doing. Or what I had been planning on doing with the glass. He downed the liquid and moved the glass down the bar. Then he told me to leave. I was sobbing now.

I don't understand, am I even your girlfriend anymore?

Sadly yes.

Yes, what a fucking *nightmare* I must be for you, how fucking *awful* it must be to be with me!

He led me outside. Steph gave his arm a squeeze.

And you can fuck off! I shouted.

Just go home, Enola. He went back inside, shaking his head. Steph stubbed out her cigarette and followed him. I stood on the street, watching through the streaky window as they sat back at the bar and picked up their drinks. Then I turned and left before I could see them laughing.

I ARRIVED AT RUTH'S warehouse with mascara on my cheeks. She gave me a T-shirt to sleep in and hid my phone. I asked her over and over again what I had done wrong.

Why doesn't he want me?

But she kept changing the question: Why do you want *him*? I couldn't think of anything specific; it was just an overwhelming desire: I wanted him. I needed him. I would die without him.

That's what love is, isn't it?

She shook her head and whispered that love should make you happy. I couldn't remember the last time that we'd been happy, without the threat of unhappiness following like a shadow. I thought about Amy's wedding; I had spent the day texting him details to show that I was cool and funny and "not like other girls." The linen napkins. The foliage. The vows. But there had been a moment, watching Amy and David dance to a song with a key change, happy and unselfconscious, when there was nothing to joke about. I wanted to call and tell him that I missed him. He had told me that he was writing, but I knew that he was out with Steph. And so I didn't call him because I didn't want to have the confronting conversation where I either chose not to care and be *that* woman or chose to care and be the other. One I hated and the other he did.

I let Ruth comfort me, and I cried until my stomach ached. As I drifted off, the last thing I heard her say as she stroked my back in warm circles was that she loved my hair. I loved it before, but I love it now. You look beautiful, Laa.

In the morning, I hoped that it had all been a dream, but when Ruth gave me back my phone there was a message asking me to breakfast, and I knew that it was over.

THE COFFEE MACHINE WHIRRED behind the counter, and a group were laughing down the table. He was calm, like someone had advised him how to handle me. He ordered chorizo and eggs, and I ordered avocado on toast that I felt too sick to eat.

Honey, I'm not saying that we should end things, but judging from last night, I'm not giving you what you feel you deserve.

His tone was sweet and his phrases sloped like mountains. He was breaking up with me but trying to make it sound like a compliment. Ruth had asked if there was a part of me that had gone to the bar to confront him. I wondered whether she was right, because this didn't feel like a surprise.

I'm really sorry, but when I saw Steph—

He told me that Steph had surprised him, and he thought that he could have a quick drink with her before meeting me. Enola, I can't have a night like that ever again.

Neither can I, I thought.

That wasn't how I should have handled it, I said.

It's okay, he replied, like I was admitting full responsibility. He took a bite of his food and a drop of chorizo oil landed on his chin. He didn't wipe it away but I was too nervous to tell him that it was there. I asked if what he was *really* asking for was a breakup. He said that he just needed space. I have to focus on my book and I don't want to resent our relationship, honey.

I'm really sorry that I ruined your birthday, I said.

Don't be.

He still hadn't said sorry for *his* actions. I thought about my own book. If that was the reason for the break, then shouldn't *I* be the one demanding it? Diana asked for my manuscript weeks ago, and I was ruining the best opportunity of my career. And for what? So that he could feel less like a failure? He would never do that for me. I would never ask him to. But then again, he hadn't asked me to do it. Or had he? His eyes were bloodshot. Maybe he was hungover, but maybe it was more. *If only Mum had been more patient with Dad.*

I told him to take all the time he needed, and he told me that he appreciated me understanding. He smiled, and my appetite returned.

He asked how my book was going. I lied and said that I should be able to send it off soon. He told me that he was proud of me. Thank you, I said, that means so much. He told me that he liked my hair. I said that the back looked like the back of a chicken, and he laughed. It was the best conversation we had had in weeks. But then he signaled for the bill because he had to meet a friend. Like breaking up with me was just the first task of the day. I wanted to snap: *You're not going to work on your book, then?* But I had to wait until I was home to crack; if I handled the breakup perfectly then he might realize it was a mistake.

We stood outside the café on the pavement, half in and half out of our relationship. I thought about that night when he almost told me that he loved me. I had based so many justifications on the fact that he loved me. Yes, he was difficult, yes, he could be mean, but he loved me. The reality, though, was that neither of us had said those words.

Can I ask you something?

He nodded, so, with his permission, I continued: That night in Kenya, when we had that fight in the bar, you started to say something outside the beach house—what was it?

He blew out air. Fuck knows, Enola. Anyway, we could go over and over this and it won't do us any good. He leaned down to kiss me, but I stepped back and asked what the rules were.

In what sense?

Can I call or text you?

He told me not to overthink things. We make the rules, Enola.

My throat was throbbing. Was I making the rules? It didn't feel like I was making any rules. He tried once more to kiss me, but I held up my hand. Wait. Not yet.

He folded his arms. Come on, honey, you know how I feel about keeping people waiting.

I know, I just . . . I made you this. Happy birthday.

I reached into my bag and handed him the card. I wanted him to realize that he was walking away from someone who bought the good paper and colored inside the lines, but he just said thank you, then looked inconvenienced that it was so large. Actually, honey, do you want to just give this to me next time, as I'm out all day? He handed it back, and it was instantly a child's drawing, strips of white where color should be and pencil markings that hadn't been rubbed out. So, with no tricks left, I walked away like I had on the first night we met, only this time he didn't summon me back.

CHAPTER 18

I PUT ON A SHORT MAROON DRESS, MY BROWN BOOTS, AND RED lipstick. I drank half a bottle of prosecco and looked at my body from every angle. *This is what being single and happy looks like*, I said to my reflection. Ruth and I joined Sasha and their friends in Hackney. At the bar, we downed tequila shots and held our beers.

Come on, I said.

We danced, but really I was hunting. I scanned the checked shirts and white T-shirts: tall men with brown hair and short, stocky blonds. I moved suggestively and wished that he was here to watch me.

Ruth touched my waist. Toilet?

I waited outside the cubicle, and she asked how I was doing. I told her I was doing really well. I feel so free! She said that was because he was a narcissist. I told her that I could see it now. I *really* can. Paper was pulled and torn; then the toilet flushed. Ruth washed her hands, and I leaned against the hand dryer.

I think I was just swept up in how attractive he was?

God, what is it about these ordinary-looking men and gorgeous women. It's the Judd Apatow effect, and I'm sick of it.

I'm not a gorgeous wom—

You are way hotter than he is!

You just didn't like him, Ruth.

I moved so that Ruth could dry her hands. Straining over the noise, I ranted about things he did that I now realized were manipulative.

But despite my words, there was a voice in my head countering: The first time we had sex and he ignored my doubts? *He's not a mind reader.* That time that he took over the risotto? *I hate cooking.* The times that he gaslit me about Steph? *I was paranoid.*

Ruth shook water from her hands. I'm so happy to hear that, she said. It's been killing me watching him do this to you.

We left the bathroom, and I asked if she thought that I should tell him it was over. She paused. Isn't it already over? I shook my head and said that we were just on a break.

Don't contact him, Laa.

Okay, but shouldn't I tell him that *I* don't want to be with *him* anymore?

Ruth stopped, and we leaned against the wall. The club was ahead, blue and moving. She said if I wanted to show him that it was over, silence was the only way to do that. Otherwise, you're still giving him the power! She said that by focusing on him, I made him responsible for my happiness. You need to look at your role in this, Laa.

I felt the blood drain from my face. You think it's my fault?

She held my face. No, not at all, not even slightly!

I asked her if she thought I should have been more laid-back. She said that he should have loved me unconditionally.

So, you *don't* think I'm laid-back?

Enola, you are laid-back in many ways but—

Not in others?

You, Enola, are perfect! Don't let his definition of a flaw be yours.

I asked what she meant about my role in the relationship. She said that, on more than one occasion, he had showed me who he was and I wanted him anyway. I mean, we've been talking about him forever and—

Okay, well, I'm sorry for talking too much.

That's not what I meant!

Ruth put her hands over her face. For a second, I saw the same despair in her eyes as I used to see in his. She tried again: Okay, so this is a really simplistic example but, like, you know when you get upset about the coffee grounds spilling and it's clearly about something else?

No. It's always about the coffee grounds.

Fine, that's a bad example.

Ruth said that she was worried I would get into this situation again if I didn't figure out why I liked him to begin with. I reassured her that I would never get back together with him, but she was still frustrated. I didn't mean *him* necessarily, Enola, I meant—Forget it, I'm not expressing myself well.

I put my arms around her and told her that I was sorry. She told me not to apologize. I said that she would never lose her mind over someone. She hummed. That's not true—remember a few years ago, my obsession with that yoga instructor? I told her that people were supposed to became calmer toward their thirties but that I seemed to be regressing. She said that I wasn't regressing, I was—

But the music was too loud to hear the last word.

At the bar, I ordered another tequila and a Jägerbomb. Ruth looked concerned, but we returned to the dance floor. Everything was fun until I caught sight of myself in the mirrored wall. My hair was flat, and my skin was pallid. There were black flecks under my eyes, and I could see the line from where my underwear cut into my waist. I was the ghost that appeared when a photo of a group of friends was developed—one of those images shared on social media with a message saying you would die in seven days if you didn't pass it on. But Ruth looked beautiful. She hadn't even wanted to come out tonight, but she was immaculate. There wasn't a pore on her face, and she had the figure of an "after" picture. I noticed then the men gathering around her, dancing with their friends but keeping one eye on her, edging closer, willing her to look at them.

God, yeah, it must be a nightmare going out with Ruth.

Ruth put her hand on my shoulder and asked if I was feeling

okay. I told her that I needed some water. She said that she would get it, but when she left, I took myself home.

My phone pinged with messages.

> *Where did you go?*
>
> *I'm with Sasha by the left speaker.*
>
> *Are you okay??*

I lied that I was in an Uber.

It was warm, and there was no breeze apart from the traffic. I put my headphones in and listened to music on shuffle. Being surrounded by songs made me feel like my pain was normal, beautiful even, until the opening chords of "Video Games" teleported me back to the beach. But I played the song over and over until, somewhere between Dalston and Shoreditch, it lost meaning.

After about fifteen minutes, I sensed someone following me.

I kept my headphones in but paused the music.

What would I do? Confront them? Run into the middle of the road? What would a feminist do? That was a stupid thought. A feminist would do what any woman would: try to survive.

I saw a broken bottle on the ground. I could plunge it into their neck? Argue self-defense? *But she was wearing a very short dress.* I worked up the courage to look behind me, but it was just another woman, jacket pulled up, phone gripped like a weapon.

WHEN I GOT HOME, I ran to the bathroom, crouched over the toilet, and vomited until alcohol stung my nose and throat. When there was nothing left inside me, I curled onto the tiles and sobbed. *This is what single and happy looks like.* God, I missed him. I missed him so much. I got my phone—ignoring the missed calls from Ruth— and rang him. It was one in the morning—he *had* to answer. If he didn't answer, was he with someone else? I wanted to smack my head against the tiles. The phone rang and rang but, at last, his voice: Enola?

I need to see you.

Oh, honey . . .

Please, *please*. I just need to see you, okay?

He said my name as if he were a parent warning a child, but I pleaded desperately. Why not, though? Why can't we see each other, just for tonight? I reminded him that we made the rules: That's what you said—that *we* make the rules? I held my breath until he spoke. He told me that he had friends over for poker but would be finished in an hour.

I SHOWERED AND DRESSED again like it was the beginning of the night. As I walked to his flat, I knew that this relief was temporary, but I didn't care, because in a few more steps it would be him.

Hey.

Hey, you.

His pupils were dilated, and there was a beer in his hand. He walked me into his bedroom, put his beer on the desk, and stood by the unmade bed. The sheets were the same. He said that this was breaking the rules. Definitely, I agreed, like they were my rules to break. I ran my fingers through his hair. He moaned to let me know that it felt good and the sadness left my body. But then he pushed my hand onto his crotch. Come on, then, is this what you wanted? Everything happened next as on a fairground ride: fast and unpredictable. I couldn't stop it. I couldn't keep up. His hand pushed up my skirt and pulled at my underwear. When he lifted his top, I could smell dried sweat. *He hasn't showered?* The main lights were on, and the curtains were open. Nothing was cozy; nothing was safe. This was wrong. I was trading my body for the hope of his heart, and he was saying yes to a cup of tea that he didn't really want because someone else was making it.

Quick and hard, he took several fistfuls of me until he shuddered into my neck. After he came and I didn't even pretend to, he put his clothes back on, and, for some reason, I began to shiver. I asked if he could lend me a jumper.

Oh no, honey, you can't stay . . .

Of course not, I didn't mean that, I . . .

He waited for me to finish the sentence even though it was clear that I couldn't. He reminded me that tonight was a one-time thing. We promised we would take space, remember? I told him that I was just cold, and he said that it was August. I said that he didn't need to make me feel like I was insane, and he looked at me like I had something stuck in my teeth and he was the only one willing to point it out.

Enola, did it ever occur to you that if you feel insane there might be a reason?

Are you calling me insane?

He told me not to put words in his mouth and then opened his laptop and started writing as if I wasn't there. I watched him and then gathered my clothes. I went for the bathroom, but he held out his arm. My flatmate is in there. Use these. He handed me a couple of sheets of paper torn from the skinny gray toilet roll on his desk. I held them awkwardly between my legs, then put them in the plastic bag over his door handle that he used as a bin.

I had wanted this so badly. His body. His hands. His smell. But what was it that I actually wanted? Because the sex was never *good*, was it? It was just a period of time where I had him. It was addictive. It was control. But he didn't want me and he wasn't even pretending to.

I got into my own bed after three. I kept the blinds and the windows open. The lights were stars, the traffic was lions, the footfall was wind rustling grass, and, as I closed my eyes, for the first time, I didn't miss him.

CHAPTER 19

IT WAS A DAY IN LATE SEPTEMBER, AN INDIAN SUMMER—WHATEVER
that meant—and Ruth and I lay on the grass in bikini bottoms. The
ladies' pond at Hampstead Heath was busy but not crowded. *It's
because it's just women*, Ruth had said when we arrived. All around,
limbs were draped over limbs and conversations drifted in the warm
air. The pop and hiss of a tin, then Ruth passed me a gin and tonic.
The condensation dripped onto my chest as I sipped the cool citrus.
She asked when I would hear back from Diana. I explained that it
could take three months.

Although it's been ages since the book launch. God, I can't believe
I might have ruined this.

Ruth scratched my head. Diana knows how long it takes to write
a book—don't worry. I'm just so proud of you! And I know it's been
hard, everything with, you know.

I honestly feel much better.

I know, I can tell.

I turned onto my stomach and rested my head on my forearms,
the marks faded and my wrists bare.

I asked Ruth how her job search was going. She said that she had
seen a life coach who told her to make a list of things that she enjoyed
and things that she didn't. I told her that she could do anything. Not
anymore, she said. We're approaching thirty. I might have been able
to do anything when I graduated, but now? I'm nearly middle-aged—

We are *not* middle—

—with a CV full of jobs that I didn't stay at for longer than a month.

I told her that anyone who interviewed her would see how brilliant she was. You're *you*, Roo. There isn't anyone that you can't talk to or any subject you can't talk about.

You always do that, she said, tipping her drink into her mouth as if testing how high she could pour it from.

Do what?

Think too highly of me. I'm just a good blagger.

Then, she propped herself up on her elbows and said that Catherine was driving her crazy: Emily is the textbook success story and my parents were both the exception in that they managed to actually earn a living off their art. But I got the most useless attributes from both of them. The personality of an artist without the talent of one.

But she was wrong. Ruth was good at everything. Sometimes it seemed like she refused to own up to that because if she did then she might have to see something through.

I asked Ruth which of my parents she thought I would end up like but she looked uncomfortable. I turned onto my back and imagined that I was on the ocean bed as a plane moved through the blue like a shark. Ruth asked if my breasts had got bigger.

No, sadly, it's just that time of the month.

She said that every month her left breast swelled to double the size. I told her that she had spectacular tits. She said that the life coach didn't think that would help with the job search.

Progress for feminism, I said. Did you know that as we get older our body produces two eggs at once as a way of telling us to hurry the fuck up?

Excellent. Our bodies aren't feminists then.

WE FINISHED OUR TINS, then went for a final swim. The pond was cold, and the smell of wildlife surrounded us. We floated in the sunlight until I decided to go home. Ruth said that she would stay for a bit.

Call you later.

Love you.

Love *you*.

As I crossed the Heath, I realized that I was completely alone; no dog walkers or picnics. And so I sat in the grass. I picked a dandelion and blew the seeds, but I didn't have anything to wish for. Perhaps for Diana to represent me? But I wanted her to choose me because I was good and not because I had picked the right flower. I decided to let Ruth know that I was still here, but when I opened my phone, there was a message from him.

The air was sucked from the sky. There he was: the letters of his name. Like seeing a teacher outside of school. Ruth wanted me to change his name to "DO NOT ANSWER," but I knew that I would never hear from him, and even if I did, after that night at his, I wouldn't be tempted to answer. Why was he texting now?

> *Hey, can we talk? I would really love to see you but I understand*
> *if you'd rather not xxx*

All summer, I wondered how this would feel. But his words didn't have the same meaning. I was happy. I had finished my book. I was spending time with my best friend. The impulse to jump when he told me to was gone. I didn't need to text him back. I didn't want to text him back.

So, what harm would it do if I did?

We met two weeks later at the Church Street entrance to Stoke Newington cemetery. Ruth hadn't hidden her thoughts, but after a long conversation she did her usual laconic summary: *It's like a nineties horror: the killer has to die twice.*

He was leaning against the stone wall, and my heart beat faster. I was unsure when to look up or what expression to have when I did. He was in faded blue jeans and a white T-shirt, with his clavicle visible. His skin was tanned, and the lines in his face were more deeply drawn. I was wearing a floral dress with a denim jacket (Sandra in *Practical Magic* rather than Nicole). He stood from the wall and held out a white takeaway cup. The first words he uttered were "white Americano" and then: I wasn't sure if you were going to chicken out.

His voice was exactly the same, and I felt a strum of pain.

Are you glad you didn't?

I'm not sure yet.

I took the coffee, but I didn't want to drink it because I didn't want it to affect my breath. He pulled me into a cautious hug. His after-shave was the same, and his skin was moist. Being close to him again was like opening the door to the beach house—as familiar as unfamiliar. Shall we? We walked into the tangled graveyard and the sun cut shapes through the trees. The paths were narrow, and the ground was uneven, but rather than walking ahead, his hip grazed mine, like he was trying to get as close as possible to me.

He told me that he had finished his book and was finally ready to query. I listened not because I owed it to him but because I owed it to the version of myself sobbing on the bathroom floor. He then thanked me for giving him space. And, honey—

He stopped walking and took my hands.

I *do* want to be with you.

I didn't know what to say. Shouldn't he have known at the time that he wanted to be with me? And when did he realize that the space he said he needed wasn't about his book but about me? Or had he always known? Because *I* had known. Even if he hadn't said the words, he had sat in that coffee shop and told me that he no longer wanted to see me or speak to me or sleep with me.

Did you hear me?

I nodded.

He smiled, eyes pale green in the sunshine, and told me that it was nearly a year since we met.

He seemed different. Or rather, how *I* seemed to *him* was different. He was looking at me like he used to and it was intoxicating.

Like smelling a perfume that I hadn't smelled for years or eating the first piece of chocolate after Lent. He used to *like* me. He used to *want* me. I wanted to scream at this forgotten feeling, this person back from the dead. My eyes fixed on a vein on his neck, vulnerable and hot in the sunshine. Last week, I'd imagined slashing his skin with a kitchen knife.

Honey, I'm not expecting us to go straight back to how we were, but maybe we could start slowly?

Really?

His lips curled into a half smile. Two truths and a lie, he said. One: I've quit smoking. Two: I have a king-sized bed. Three: I've really missed you, Enola.

There were two voices in my head. The first screamed at me to leave while I was still strong. Maybe that was what I *really* owed to the version of myself sobbing on the bathroom floor. But the second was curious, addicted to seeing what I could get him to feel next. At Amy's wedding, the best man talked about their "tumultuous start." This could be the *real* beginning of our love story.

I've missed you too.

He kissed me, and it was as easy as falling asleep. It wasn't earth-shattering; it was normal (like a couple who would go to a self-serve wine bar and order *one* glass of *one* wine). With a flurry of happiness, the version of myself from before peeled herself off the bathroom tiles and slipped her hand into his.

We continued strolling through the graveyard and, as I looked at the headstones, so permanent and romantic, I felt an old anger at Mum for not throwing Dad a funeral. I would have liked a grave to put flowers on.

Where did you go? his voice brought me back.

Nowhere.

He smiled at me and I felt like I had come home. He started telling me about a book that everyone had loved, but he had hated, and my eyes caught the gravestone of a couple who died two days apart. The wildflowers around it were dead. A shiver ran up my spine and I thought of a phrase we used to say at school: *Someone's walked over your grave.* I squeezed his hand to make sure that he was alive, and he squeezed mine back like he was having the same thought, then pointed to the name on the headstone, laughed, and said: Willy.

CHAPTER 20

I WOKE UP WITH MY EYES OPEN AND DIDN'T REMEMBER SLEEPING. He kissed the back of my neck. Happy birthday. How does it feel to be twenty-nine? I told him that it felt the same as yesterday, but that might have been a lie. I said that Ruth would be here in an hour. He said that he didn't want to be in the firing line. I told him there were no gunmen.

Ruth understands that things have changed.

He got up, walked to my side of the bed, and crouched. But do *you* understand that things have changed, Enola? I brushed his hair back from his face.

He showered, and I checked my phone for birthday messages. Louise had sent an e-card: an animated image of animals dancing in a forest. *Darling Girl.* Mum had posted a card, which arrived yesterday with some information about the vegetables. I wasn't expecting him to get me anything.

When we were both ready, I walked him to the door, and he said that he'd be over later. Are you sure that you don't want to do anything? I told him that I had no money. He said that it was his treat. I said that *he* had no money. But it wasn't just the money. I didn't want to celebrate. I wasn't unhappy, but I wasn't happy either. We had been back together for a month and it did feel different, but I was waiting for it to change, waiting to say or do the wrong thing. And now with my book waiting for Diana's verdict, everything in my life was about waiting. Even twenty-nine was just waiting to be thirty.

This time last year I was making your birthday cake, he said, squeezing my breast.

There was a knock at the door and he made "pew pew" gunshot noises. I reached behind him to open it, and Ruth stood there with balloons and prosecco. It was awkward while they registered each other and then he said: Well, have fun.

We will, Ruth said, closing the door behind him. She pinned a birthday badge on my shirt and said that she couldn't believe a whole year had passed. It's going to be 2016. Isn't that insane? She held up the prosecco. Breakfast cocktails?

I'm working, Roo!

Meh. The bankers won't notice if their coffee art is squiggly.

THE SHIFT MOVED PAINFULLY slowly. I drank three coffees and continually refreshed my inbox in the hopes of an email from Diana. Halfway through the afternoon, Virinder approached in a long gray coat and tartan scarf. He appeared almost every shift with a compliment, a bad joke, and a generous tip—regardless as to whether I made a coffee or just filled up his copper water bottle. (*Copper is amazing for you, Enola.*)

I could smell his clean scent as he placed a neatly wrapped present on the counter. His cheeks were blushed from cold, and his thick hair looked starched.

Happy birthday!

How did you know?

Ruth. But the badge gives it away, he said, nudging the present. I asked him what it was, and he said it was a surprise. I told him that I didn't like surprises, and he said that it wouldn't bite. I thanked him and asked if he wanted coffee. He held up a pink portable cup and said that he was doing his bit for the environment. Then he winked and said that he would see me later. I told him never to wink. He laughed. You love it, really.

The square present was wrapped in dark blue textured paper

with gold constellations. The sort of paper that costs three pounds for a slice. I wanted to keep it, but Steph wouldn't reuse paper; she would rip it and probably forget to recycle.

I peeled the paper, and the scent of someone's summer emerged, fresh and lovely. It was a candle, and on the back was printed: To LIGHT WHEN YOU'RE WRITING YOUR BESTSELLER.

THE DAY FINISHED, AND he returned to my flat at six in gym clothes. I had changed and taken off my makeup. He removed his headphones, and I could hear the music for a second before he stopped the track.

How was work? Best birthday ever?

The best, I replied, matching his dryness.

I went to hug him, but he said that he was sweaty. Let me get showered.

I took a blanket onto the balcony and waited for him. I thought about Dad. I had been thinking about him more and more recently. Perhaps it was because I was getting older and he was getting further away. It had been twenty years this month. Twenty years ago, Mum, Dad, and I went to a meat restaurant in Nairobi. We ate crocodile. Dad and Mum fought in the car on the way back. I had a stomachache. A few days later, Dad was dead. I couldn't see the stars tonight— you could rarely see them in London—but I knew they were there. The same ones from the grassy bank in Watamu. The same ones from the roof of the car in the Mara. Everywhere and all the time. Invisible but there, there but dead: the gravestone I couldn't put flowers on.

This is how I feel.

I am heartbroken, always. I am endlessly sad.

The door slid open, and he handed me a box of chocolates. Sorry it's not a cake. I told him that he couldn't have any.

(the "playful" piece)

He said that he wouldn't dare ask. He told me that I looked

pretty. Twenty-nine agrees with you. I told him that I wasn't wearing makeup. He said that he preferred me without it. I said that my makeup wasn't for his approval.

(the "sparky" piece)

He pulled me close to him and said that it was freezing. Shall we go in? I told him that I just wanted to sit here.

(the "independent" piece)

He got out his vape, and the mint wafted toward me. He told me that he was doing better at quitting this time. Who's the candle on the table from?

My mum.

(the "dishonest" piece)

He accepted the story, which meant that he didn't understand the damage between me and Mum. Which was my fault. But this truce between me and him lasted only as long as we kept everything sweet. Nothing real could survive.

He kissed my neck. So, anything else you'd like for your birthday?

I looked at the night sky and imagined all the comets and stars that existed above the layers of pollution.

RUTH, EMILY, AND I lay on the corner sofa. Ruth was nursing eggnog with the consistency of rice pudding that she had made herself. Emily was drinking tea, and I had one of each drink. A tree by the upright piano filled the room with the warm, spicy smell of pine.

I loved Christmas here: the cake Catherine made months ago that Jon complained never contained enough cherries; the pillowcase stockings; the card games when Ruth cheated and Emily stormed off. Growing up, Catherine hosted a holiday party during which Emily would wear something straight off the mannequin in the Oxford Street Topshop window and Ruth and I made cocktails from the dregs of drinks. My grandparents referred to Ruth's family as "bohemian," which they never had a real answer for, but it was clear what they meant.

How is the relationship going? Emily asked.

I answered that he was being lovely but that something felt off. Perhaps you're realizing that you don't love him, said Ruth.

How do *you* feel? asked Emily, as if to accuse Ruth of speaking for me. Which she wasn't, but my position as middle sister precluded me from taking sides. I said that I didn't know how to be without him, but I didn't know how to be with him anymore either. Emily laughed and said that our generation was so dramatic.

Ruth rolled her eyes. We are the same generation, Em.

Ruth, my two children are downstairs doing a jigsaw with my husband. You live in a warehouse with eight other people. We are *not* the same generation.

The door to the kitchen opened, and we could hear potatoes sizzling and smell the hot goose fat. I took a sip of eggnog, and Ruth nudged me. How is it?

Delicious. Is it *meant* to curdle? I said without swallowing. Ruth giggled.

Relationships take work, Emily continued. You have to persevere if you want something to last.

Ignore her, Enola. She's talking to me, said Ruth.

Excuse me? snapped Emily.

You've not met him, Em. He's not one of Samson's accountant friends. He's not *normal*.

Catherine shouted from the kitchen: Emily, Ruth, *Enola* . . . dinner's ready!

AFTER DINNER, I HELPED Catherine clear while everyone watched a film. I rinsed the plates, and she put them in the dishwasher. There, all done, she said, passing me the towel. I went to leave, but she told me to wait. I have something for you. She took a photo from the miscellany drawer and pressed it to her chest.

I didn't want to give you this in front of everyone in case it upset you, but . . . well, you never are upset, are you, sweetheart? You're always so strong.

She handed me a photo of my dad.

My dad.

My legs grew weak, and the lights appeared brighter.

We were standing under a tree in the garden. My body was bent to his, and my lips were curled under in a cheeky grin. Dad looked younger than I remembered him, in beige shorts and a beige shirt. Behind us the table was set for Christmas.

Catherine said that it was the Christmas we spent together with some friends. I doubt you'll remember them—Brian and Debbie, I think? They had a boy Emily's age.

I wish Mum had kept our photos, I said.

I hate her I hate her I hate her

I know, sweetheart. But it was all very hard on her and she had her reasons for handling the situation the way that she did.

The *situation*. Catherine had that look that grown-ups got when they spoke about Dad. I told her that it had been twenty years last month. Did you know? Catherine said that she wasn't sure on the day. I told her that I wasn't either. I just remember it was after my birthday. She looked at me in that way again. I told her that I was okay. Every day is the anniversary of something, right?

Twenty years since he died. Twenty-three years since he stubbed his toe on the sofa. Twenty-seven years since he burned the toast. It all hurts.

I wanted to tell her how much I appreciated the photo and how much I appreciated her calling my name when she called for dinner, but part of me worried that if I did she might stop doing it.

Just then Evie charged in and wrapped her arms around my legs. Nola, she said, come watch *Frozen*? We're doing Elsa makeup! Ruth entered with her face covered in glitter.

Yes, let's cover Aunty Nola in this shit too.

Catherine said Ruth's name sharply. Evie whispered, "Shit," in my ear. Ruth laughed, and Catherine shook her head. Evie wobbled out of the kitchen with Ruth following, arms stretched to catch her.

I asked Catherine if I could keep the photo, and her chin jutted.

Of course! It's for you! But just don't mention it to Jon—he didn't think I should give it to you.

She hugged me and said that she was proud of me. Her jumper was thick wool, and she smelled like the potpourri she put in the decorative Christmas boxes around the house, the ones that she'd let me fill with her when I was little, generously allowing me to correct her when a box contained too many cinnamon sticks or not enough orange segments.

When she pulled away, she moved my hair from my eyes and asked how my book was going. I replied that I still hadn't heard back from Diana. She said that it was probably a busy time of year. Keep the faith and please try to spread some of your passion to Ruth?

RUTH WAS WAITING IN the corridor. She grabbed my elbow and asked if she was being a shit friend. Do I listen enough? Her brown eyes were wide. For me, Christmases here were safety, but Ruth found them hard. She and Emily were very different. I liked to think of myself as the middle sister, but in actuality Ruth held the complex middle role.

Roo, you always listen.

Because Emily doesn't know the whole story. She doesn't know how hard it's been. She hasn't had to watch you cry over him again and again!

I indicated for her to keep her voice down, because Catherine was still in the kitchen.

Ruth said that she was worried that he hadn't changed. It's a short time for someone to change, you know? I told her that she was probably right, but I needed him. She told me that I didn't. You're enough by yourself, Enola. You've always been enough. I fingered the photograph in my pocket. I told her that even if she was right, I still *felt* like I needed him. Ruth lowered her gaze as if she were trying to protect her argument and said that there was a difference between needing someone and *feeling* like you need them. I told her that if a hypnotist told her that she was starving she would still eat a sandwich.

You've just described mind control.

The calories would be real.

But if you know that it's just mind con—

Nola! Come onnn! It's Ellssssa! Evie ran from the living room and stretched my cardigan. I detached her hand from the fabric and told her I would be there in a second. Ruth shuffled her feet. She was wearing the penguin slippers that Emily had bought her for Christmas. I told her not to worry because she was a great friend.

And you would tell me? Because you can be too generous with people, Enola.

I sighed. Fiiiine. Last week you came over with a croissant for yourself and not for me. That was shitty. Ruth grinned and took my hands. One sleeve of her Christmas jumper lifted to reveal her wrist, where delicate letters read: LOST AT SEA.

Later, Jon would get the port, and we would watch old Christmas specials with a box of chocolates. Then, when it was time for bed, Catherine would turn off the lights, and I would go to the spare room and study the photo of my father.

CHAPTER 21

TWENTY-FIVE MINUTES PAST SEVEN. I REFRESH MY EMAIL, AND seven new ones appear from skin care brands reminding me of my age. Then I go to the wardrobe and pull out a wooden box engraved with elephants. It's where I keep the pieces of Dad that Mum didn't burn. Inside is the photograph that Catherine gave me last Christmas. I don't feel anything when I look at it. We are both strangers. You have to work to keep the dead alive, but no one helped me with Dad. *That's enough of that*, *No point dwelling in the past*, and *None of that silly business* were commonly used.

I try to reconcile the man from my memory with the man from the image. Fragments come back like the middle pieces of a jigsaw: the sound of his laugh while watching television; the smell of his suit before work; how he rubbed his face when he was tired. He died twenty-one years ago. And it feels worse than last year because it's the start of another decade without him. I can't believe it's almost Christmas again.

I press on my bruise until my eyes water.

IT WAS JANUARY, BUT I kept my small plastic tree up. When I opened the door, he was grinning. Happy fake Christmas!

Happy fake Christmas.

We kissed, and he started removing layers. It's a fucking desert in here, Enola. He walked down the hall to the kitchen, and I noticed his T-shirt. It was gray cotton and clung to him; the curve of his biceps, the depression at the base of his neck. There was a tag hanging. I got the nail scissors and cut it off for him. He moaned that he couldn't return it now. Karen had bought it for him. All right, honey. Have you put the turkey in the oven?

It's a chicken, but yes.

What did you stuff it with?

What do you mean?

He laughed and told me to put my feet up. Have you got an onion? A lemon will be overpowering. He said that he would pour me some wine, and when he handed me the glass, he pretended to be annoyed but his eyes were gleaming. He put Christmas music on, and I stared at the tree, the colored lights blurring the green. I used to lie beneath the tree when I was a child and imagine a magical world; Mum and Dad argued more over the holidays.

After we ate, and the dishes were piled in the sink, we lay on the sofa; his heart was beating fast, always fast, beneath the soft gray cotton. The air smelled like roast chicken and my eyelids kept trying to close. But then, in the stillness, the late sun illuminated the dust in the air, and I had this sensation—like my brain was creating the memory alongside experiencing the moment—and, in that second, I understood the versions of us that existed like strings on a harp: where we met in the pub; where we watched the sunset; where we walked among the gravestones. I even understood the alternative ones: where Dad spoke at our wedding; where our child was born; where I never took the bus that night and we never met. But then the sensation vanished in the way that a dream did when you woke from it. I lifted up and studied his paper face, tried to hold it in my mind.

What?

Nothing, just . . . déjà vu.

That isn't real.

I rested back on his chest and circled the mole on his forearm. He asked me why I liked that mark so much. I told him that it looked like a planet. He said that all moles looked like planets, and I said that wasn't true. His was unnaturally cylindrical. He kissed the top of my head and said: Well, that's because it's not actually a mole.

I lifted up, and he laughed at my reaction. It's a pencil mark from school. A girl called Tracy stabbed me with an HB in English class.

No way! You've been lying this whole time!

You got me.

I told him the story of when I was bitten as a baby. Mum was looking at nurseries, she left for a second, and then wham! I moved his fingers to the ridge on my skull. See? He said that explained a lot. We fell silent. He hummed "White Christmas," and I listened to the vibrations in his chest. But then his breathing changed. I traced down his body. His fingers scrolled my thigh. We stood from the sofa and walked to the doorframe. I placed my palms on the wood. He lifted my skirt. His zipper dragged down. *Oh god, I want him. I will always want him.*

Fuck, honey . . .

His breath rattled in my ear.

Afterward, he kept his hands on mine. His mouth hot on my neck. I loved him more than I had ever loved anything. I wanted nothing but him. His smell covering my skin. His pulse under my hands. I wanted to swallow him, to drink him, to absorb him until I was more him than me. I wanted to make him happy. I wanted to reassure him. I wanted to please him. I wanted to serve him. I wanted to love him. I wanted to beg him to love me. But there was nothing else to do. No new depths. No new tricks. No new tool for worship. Before I could talk myself out of it, the words formed like mud.

I love you.

There was a kindness in the pause that followed that made me think he might tell me that he loved me too. But he wouldn't. Of course he wouldn't. And so, with the weight of my words between us, he gave his answer.

Don't be silly.

And just like that, the moment became the memory.

OKAY, HONEY. I UNDERSTAND.

I bet you do.

I hung up and threw my water glass against the bedroom wall. I drank the contents before throwing it, but the shards went everywhere—the floor, the bed, the corners of the room. I knew that I would be finding pieces weeks later: the damage.

Ruth ran in from the kitchen. Oh my god, are you okay? She looked at the smashed glass and then at my phone. Her pitch dropped. What did he say?

That he understood.

Of course he fucking did. She told me not to move and left the room, returning moments later with two cups of tea. She handed me mine the way she always did, with the handle first so that I wouldn't burn my hands. We sat for a moment among the ruin, and then she said: Maybe your first impression of him was the right one.

What do you mean?

You didn't like him.

I don't remember that.

We were figure drawing, and you said he was rude and unpleasant. And, Enola, the thing is, sometimes the good bits of people aren't the rule, they're the exception.

I looked at the mug in my hand. It was the one that I would make his tea in because he liked the size. Neon orange with black print: LOOK FORWARD NOT BACK. I told Ruth that I couldn't remember the bad bits. She squeezed my hand. I promise that you will, she said, smiling. She had a pale pink sheen on her lips.

But what if I ended it too early, Roo?

Were you happy?

I shook my head.

No, you weren't. You were terrified of breathing. And, Enola, let me tell you, when something is real, you can't ruin it. Like a van Gogh.

I told Ruth that I was pretty sure that I could ruin a van Gogh, and she looked relieved that I had made a joke.

My phone vibrated on the floor. I saw the name, and my hands went to my mouth. Ruth growled. Is it him? I nudged the phone toward her with my foot. She looked at it and then looked at me. She asked me if I was going to read it. I told her that I didn't feel strong enough. She inhaled, held the breath for a second, and then said: Why don't you rip off the Band-Aid and then tomorrow can be a new day? Remember, the universe doesn't give you anything you can't handle.

Will you read it?

If you want me to.

There was no one I wanted to hear bad news from more than Ruth, with that Scottish lilt from Catherine and Norwegian musicality from Jon. She was there the day I received the worst news of my life. We had eaten tacos while Jon took the phone call that confirmed what, in hindsight, everyone but me already knew.

I closed my eyes as she read silently. Then she told me to open my eyes. You need to read it for yourself. She put the phone in my hand. I read the email and burst into tears.

> I loved the book. Can we find a time for you to come to the office and chat further? Diana

Ruth stood, held out her hand, and told me to get the hoover.

CHAPTER 22

January moved dark and quick and erased December. February was still cold, but the sun cut through. I was refilling the marshmallow jar, and Stefan was telling me about his love life: I just don't see why that can't happen for me. I mean, she's sat on the plane with her dry Chardonnay, and he, like, just appears?

When my shift finished, I stepped through the glass doors and heard my name:

Enola! Oi oi!

Virinder hugged me, which felt strange, because we had always had a counter between us. His coat was the expensive wool that made your skin itch. His aftershave was strong, and, in the cold, it caught in my nostrils. I asked him why he wasn't at work. It's Fri-Yay! he said. I waited for the sarcasm, but it didn't come. He told me that I looked different. Have you changed your hair?

My hair had only half grown back, currently somewhere between short and long, and too frizzy to look deliberate. My hands went to my head in apology, but he told me that it was cool. I said that no one would describe me as cool.

You're ridiculously cool! You and your friend Ruth!

Ruth is cool. I'm just her sidekick.

He laughed and asked me what I was doing now. There was something about how unguarded he was. It wasn't unexpected that he might be interested; he had bought me that candle and Ruth had thought that he liked me. But I hadn't considered him like that. He was attractive and nice. His face was the sort that my grandma called "open." Why *hadn't* I considered him like that?

I started to tell him that I was going home, but then a breeze curled down the street and lifted the edges of my coat and I said instead: Nothing, fancy a drink?

Now?

Now.

Before I change my mind.

He said that his friend was having drinks on the King's Road. I don't suppose you fancy it? I wasn't dressed for a West London pub and I hadn't brought any makeup, but it was a new year and I was a new person. Why not? I said. It is Fri-Yay.

THE PUB LOOKED LIKE it belonged in Lincolnshire. Deep green walls and vintage sports prints in gold frames. Virinder led us to a formation of Chesterfield sofas, where he was greeted by a man who looked like a gnome. Spilly, this is Enola, he said as Spilly kissed me on both cheeks with damp lips. Spilly said something I didn't understand that made Virinder howl, then waved to ice buckets on a gilded table.

Virinder started to pour champagne, but I told him that I didn't like champagne. Who doesn't like champagne? he said, before adding that I was a cheap date. He said that he would go to the bar. What would you like instead? I told him a white wine. He asked me what kind, and I told him any kind. He seemed to find that amusing.

I sat down and a blond woman held out a manicured hand with a large diamond: I'm Jonesy's fiancée. I told her that I was with Virinder. She glanced over her shoulder and leaned into me. He is such an angel, she said. Honestly, I *can't* believe that man is still single.

Virinder returned and handed me a glass of wine. He said that it was a dry Chardonnay. Don't worry, he said. I tried it first and it was lovely. I imagined him swilling and gargling like the man in the self-serve wine bar. He introduced me to the table. Enola is a writer!

Fun! said a woman in a sheer pink dress. What do you write?

I'm working on my debut—a young adult book—with my agent.

Virinder's mouth dropped open. Enola! Amazeballs! I didn't know you had an agent. That's the big leagues. My mum met the woman who wrote—oh, what's that one with the fish on the cover? She met her in Waterstones. Oh, bloody hell, what was her name?

Virinder searched for the name, and I searched his face. His cheekbones were chiseled, his jaw square, and his dark eyes contained flecks of amber.

He put his hand over his face. What? Have I got a bogey?

I told him that I hadn't noticed his eyes before. He laughed and said that they matched his highlights. I told him that I liked his hair. Does it move in the wind? He put his hand on the sofa, and his thumb grazed my leg. He said that my eyes were the first thing he noticed about me. They're crazy! You look like a superhero!

We stayed in the pub for an hour, talking, laughing a little, and then after my second glass of the nicest wine I had ever tasted, a sixties melody from the speakers lifted me like the breeze had lifted my coat, and just as unexpectedly, I said: Do you want to come back to mine?

I DIDN'T CARE THAT my flat was messy or that I was wearing old bleached pants. Virinder told me that he had thought about this since the first time we spoke. He bit his lip and, holding my wrists, lifted my arms over my head. I didn't mean to but I laughed.

What? he said.

Nothing.

But I was thinking about how many men had read *Fifty Shades of Grey* thinking that because it was written by a woman it must be what every woman wanted.

What do you want? he said. Tell me what you want. I told him that I wanted him to fuck me, because I did; I wanted to be fucked the way that *he* used to fuck me. Virinder folded his clothes neatly: white shirt, chinos, golf socks. I threw mine haphazardly and pulled him onto me. His warm, dry body felt alien on mine. His muscles were sculpted, and his skin was a hairless, soft brown. I tried not to think about how different this man was to the other. But then something unexpected happened; he was moving so gently, so slowly, that in the middle of pretending to feel intense pleasure, I actually felt it. I started touching myself.

Yes, baby, he said. That's so sexy.

A sensation like elastic stretching started and started and started. He noticed a change in my breathing, and he started thrusting faster and deeper until—

Oh my god.

I STAND UP TOO quickly, and everything fades to black, reappearing pixel by pixel. But before it does, in that quiet, dark second, everything is clear.

I scoop up last night's clothes, take them to the kitchen, and shove them in the machine. In one hour and three minutes, my THIS IS WHAT A FEMINIST LOOKS LIKE T-shirt will be clean of last night.

Just a few things to say that I miss you and that I'm still quietly confident . . . —Virinder

When we broke up, Virinder said that he wouldn't wait for me. And yet here he is, leaving gifts on my welcome mat. At the time, I wasn't quite ready to be loved; I didn't have the daily agenda of getting someone to want me, and feeling settled wasn't something that I was used to. *Idle hands,* my grandma would say, like she was worried about something more serious than boredom. But maybe I'm ready now.

On our first official date, a poreless woman sat us in a booth by the window in a city bar where an app matched virtual surroundings to fifteen-pound cocktails. Virinder's face lit up when he talked about sunsets in Mumbai and his aunt's dal makhani, and I knew I wanted to see him again. The first morning at his, he led me up a spiral staircase to a roof terrace. *The pancakes are almond butter*, he said, pulling out a chair. At night, we sat up there under the stars. You could see the stars in Primrose Hill.

I go back to the bedroom and read the messages I've been ignoring:

I would love to talk to you. I'll pop over on my break. V xxx

Hey, babe, I dunno if you're getting these but I left you a surprise outside. V xxx

The last time I checked Virinder's profile picture, he was skiing in the Alps. Now his hands hold the wheel of a boat, yellow tank top clinging to his leonine frame. His status appears: "online." I write the words quickly, ripping off the Band-Aid.

Come over?

There are immediately two blue ticks and—

. . .

I'll be over in fifteen?? Just round the corner in the pub! xxx

I check the time: just after seven thirty. I feel a rush of energy quickly followed by panic. I sweep the room for trauma, closing drawers and smoothing bedding. I return the elephant box to the wardrobe. I brush my hair and spray perfume. I dust my cheeks. Fill in my eyebrows. Fix my lips. The buzzer in the hall goes. I press enter on the intercom. *What have I forgotten?* The cereal bowl! I begin scraping out the soggy contents, but there is a knock at the door. I drop the bowl into the bin.

I walk down the hall and imagine seeing Virinder in the doorway: he smiles and holds out his arms and everything falls into place. It's like what Ruth's dermatologist said: *When a person takes care of one problem area, the other problem areas take care of themselves.* Virinder listens to me. Virinder asks what I want. Virinder makes plans for our future. Virinder loves me. Virinder's only shortcoming is that he isn't someone else and that's not a problem anymore. Ruth once said that Virinder was the sort of man you would call to help you drag a body across the kitchen floor.

I open the door and there he is, smiling like he's won the lottery.

Shit. I've made a horrible mistake.

CHAPTER 23

THE DOOR OPENS, AND I REMEMBER ALL THE REASONS WHY I BROKE up with him.

"Hello? Enola?" he sings.

An irrepressible frustration emerges like it's been waiting all day, and I feel like I'm covered in mosquito bites.

"You're miles away!"

Virinder waves his hands in front of my face and expels air in something like a laugh. It's always the same sound: indistinguishable whether he's watching a funny video or being polite to a stranger or in this case just making a basic observation.

"Well, I'll go first, then. You got my presents?"

He attempts self-deprecation but fails.

"I did. Yes. Thank you."

I want to make him disappear, but he is hanging his Barbour jacket on the hook, putting down his leather bag, removing his heeled shoes.

"Oh, baby girl," he says. "I'm right here."

His eyes are wet with forgiveness that I don't want. He needs me to go to him, like a child who storms off only to return for dinner. I shuffle to him, and he sways me as if we're dancing. Is this nice? I'm not sure. He is still the same; the scent on his neck, the cool feel of his tie. It's okay. This isn't a mistake yet; it's just a hug.

His face inches closer.

Fuck.

He angles his jaw, then he kisses me.

I pull away. "Wait, this isn't . . . I mean, could we just sit for a moment, maybe?"

"Of course. Whatever you need."

I feel some air release. This is fine. I just need to explain my mistake. I sense him smile as he follows me to the bedroom. He always smiles with both rows of teeth. I sit on the bed as far from him as possible and leave the door open, but he closes it and sits next to me. He exhales to show that he is enjoying the moment; he assumes the awkwardness is something else.

I adopt a casual tone. "So, how's work?"

"Oh, the usual. Dull. Bleurgh," he says. "Have you had any book news yet?"

"Not yet."

Virinder loves that I'm a writer, yet despite his fetishization of my profession he never grasped the realities. Once, I told him that I couldn't afford to go out for dinner, so he said that he would pick a cheap restaurant. I assumed that meant a six-quid burrito, but we arrived at a tapas place in Marylebone, and when the bill came we went halves because he understood that I was a feminist.

"You sound like you don't really want to talk . . ." he says with that breathy laugh.

I look down at my bedsheets, but he reaches for my face.

"So, let's not."

He turns my face and kisses me again. His hands find the edge of my shirt.

"I guess you really have missed me," he murmurs. I pull away again. He asks me if I'm okay but leaves no space for my reply. He notices my bruise.

"Ouch, babe. How did you get that?"

"It's nothing."

"Seriously, are you all right?"

"Yes, I'm sorry. I—"

"No, don't say anything. It's okay. We got a bit overenthusiastic, didn't we?" He laughs again. "Come on." He sits us both up against the pillows and strokes my hair. It is almost nice until his fingers move down to my arm, the inside of my elbow, my waist, the side of my breast . . .

"No, stop. Just *stop it*, Virinder."

"What?"

"I'm sorry, I'm really sorry. But this was a mistake. I think you should go. Please, can you go?"

"Baby girl, you're trembling!" He moves closer. "Have I done something wrong?"

"No, not at all. It's me, it's all me. I'm sorry."

He nods his head like he understands. "Do you want to meet tomorrow and talk about—"

"No!"

"No?"

"I'm sorry."

"Can you stop apologizing?"

"Sorry."

Virinder stares down at his thighs, smoothing the fabric with his thumb. Then he speaks in little more than a breath. "It's him, right? God, I'm such a schmuck!"

"Don't say 'schmuck.'"

"What should I say then?"

"Nothing. I'm sorry."

He turns his lips under and nods repeatedly. "I wasn't sure whether I should tell you this, but I had plans for us." He waits for me to say something, but when I don't, he continues. "I wanted to take you back with me to Mumbai this summer. My cousin's getting married and I wanted you to be there. I almost bought the tickets." He looks at me without moving his head.

"Are you waiting for me to say thank you?"

He slaps his thighs. "No, I don't want you to say *thank you*, Enola."

I grit my teeth. "Don't you? Because whenever you do something nice for me you remind me that you've done it."

"Well, is it so bad to want someone to tell you that they appreciate you? Besides, I only told you about the wedding because I wanted you to know that I was all in, yeah? I'm *still* all in. So, if you're not, then you need to stop this."

"Stop what?"

"Leading me on!"

"Leading you . . . ?" I restart carefully. "Look, I'm genuinely sorry about tonight, and for ruining the plans I didn't know you had made for us, but I feel like you're rewriting things a little bit. This is the first time we've spoken since the breakup."

"That was barely two weeks ago!"

"I know but—"

"So, are you with him now?"

"I'm—"

"No, don't answer that."

He slumps and sweeps his hands through his hair, which bounces immediately back into place. When he emerges, his face is pink and his lips are pursed. "Why would you go back to someone who was shitty to you!"

"I didn't say that I was back with him!"

"But he *was* shitty to you, Ruth told me."

Fuck's sake, Ruth.

"Fine. But, Virinder, leveraging the shit I went through with my ex to benefit yourself is shitty too."

Virinder breathes slowly and loudly, like he's blowing up a balloon. I want to scream at him to say something. Finally, he speaks, but his sincerity makes me want to scream again.

"You know what I think?"

He waits for me to answer his rhetorical question.

"What do you think, Virinder?"

"I think I'm too nice for you and that's not what you want."

I want to laugh. It's the idea that there are just two types of men available to women: the Bad Boy and the Nice Guy. If we don't want the Nice Guy, it's because he is too nice. It's just a myth perpetuated by the opposite sex to soften the blow of being dumped. It's the compliment attached to rejection: *I was just too nice for her.* It's a clever weapon, really, because it's such an innocuous word: "nice." Nice guys deserve girlfriends. Nice guys are entitled to girlfriends. Nice guys earn girlfriends. Nice isn't a personality trait or a characteristic; it's an adjective for a tablecloth. It's the bare minimum. It's what women *have* to be or they'll be called a bitch.

She's not worth it, mate, leave her. Bitch.

"Virinder. I'm sorry but I never asked you over with any intention of things happening."

Virinder stands and moves to the bedroom door, folding his arms like punctuation. Mean doesn't suit him. He is a child learning emotions from a nursery chart: this is what anger looks like, this is what sadness looks like. This is what *nice* looks like.

"Why did you invite me over, then, Enola? You clearly knew how I felt!"

I put my head in my hands. "I don't know, okay? It was a mistake."

"I don't understand you. Why won't you give this a real chance?"

I look back up. "But we did give it a chance! We were together for nine months!"

"But you never let me in! Not really. I don't understand. Why don't you want to be happy?"

I remember *his* words to me: *Because you're happier being miserable.* Why is it that not being happy with them must mean that you're not capable of happiness? I'm not happier being miserable. No one is happy being miserable.

"I do want to be happy!"

"Fine, be treated well, then—why don't you want to be treated well?"

"I do! But I don't *just* want to be treated well. I'm a woman, not a dog! Other things are important."

"Such as?"

"Oh, I don't know—shared interests, chemistry, a common sense of humor?"

"We have the same sense of humor!"

"Do we?"

"Don't we? We laugh all the time! And chemistry, Enola? Come on, we have that!"

I pause to consider my response, and Virinder's brown eyes widen.

"You don't think we have chemistry?"

"Virinder, what good is this doing? We've been over this already!"

He shakes his head. "Well, apparently, you didn't do a good enough job tying up the loose ends. The loose ends meaning me, BTW, the rebound guy."

I want to scream at him to use the full words. He's not on the internet. God, I hate him. It's not right or fair or deserved, but I actually hate him. He is leaning against the door like he's off to work. His brown suit perfectly matches his tie, and his hair looks like Sonic the Hedgehog's. Why does he highlight it? His highlights are shit. They're like little squares of paint or refractions on carpet where sunlight hits. He lifts up his shirt to tuck it in, and I know that he has tensed his abs for that exact moment. To let me know what I'm missing. To let me know that I'm walking away from someone who takes care of themselves. Who makes me cum. Who buys the good paper and colors inside the lines? Okay. Breathe. Be kind. Be nice. Be a tablecloth.

"I could have been the love of your life, Enola. But you've fucked it."

Be. A. Tablecloth.

"Virinder." I say his name like I'm closing the argument. "We're not the loves of each other's lives. I don't think you love me. You love giving love and there's a difference."

His face lights up like he's finally realized my problem.

"So, *that* is the real issue! You don't believe that I love you, Enola?"

He shifts like he's about to move toward me, but I stop him.

"No! That's not the *real* issue. I'm just trying to say that I think you'll realize this is the right thing for both of us."

He retreats; his shoulders drop.

"God, Enola. You treat me like I'm this . . ." He searches for the word, but I'm not going to help him find it. "No one's ever treated me this badly," he says, shaking his head.

I think about how easy it must be to be a man sometimes.

"And it takes a *lot* to hurt me."

With that, he turns to go but stops and looks over his shoulder. There's a softness in his face that disarms me; I think about his clean shower, the anxiety medication he keeps in a small copper pot, how he kissed me on the forehead before leaving for work. Amy once said in the writing group, when Hugo became annoyed with a fictitious character, that the people who frustrate us the most are the people who remind us the most of ourselves.

"The thing is," Virinder starts in a new tone, "it's not even your fault. It's mine. I knew that you didn't love me. Sometimes I wondered if you even *liked* me. It always felt like everything I did . . . like I was never . . . And my friends warned me, but I thought, well, she's come out of a bad relationship and she just needs some time. So, mock me all you want but that does make me a *schmuck*."

With that, he leaves, swinging the door so hard that the handle hits the wall.

I listen to the actions of his exit: the clip-clopping of his heels, the swish of his jacket, the door being opened and closed. Then I go to the door and watch through the peephole. He is waiting for the lift. He is looking at his Rolex. He is opening the door to the stairwell, where he will take the stairs down two at a time. Confident that he isn't coming back, I return to the bedroom and take out my birthday CD. I trace the list of songs, where I still exist somewhere, in the curves and slants, the comets, the stars.

Well, this is going rather well, isn't it?

I scream into my pillow.

CHAPTER 24

Keep us close to your heart,
so if the skies turn dark,
we may live on in comets and stars.

WE CROUCHED IN SAND RIVER WITH THE SUN ON OUR SHOULDERS.
Dad put his finger on his lips. Elephants fire a warning signal. We
must back away slowly. Never run. I could smell the fry that Mum
was cooking up the bank. The matriarch flapped her ears.

Dad . . . ? Dad told me to freeze, but the elephant flicked her trunk.
Dad gestured like a marine, and we crept back through the water. But
then she trumpeted loudly.

Run! Dad yanked my hand. The reeds whipped our shins, and
my ankle turned on a rock. We shambled up to where Mum held a
plate of bacon.

You got too close, Kit.

Mum told me to go back to the tent.

But—

Now, Enola.

WE SAT ON CANVAS chairs around the fire. Everything was tinted,
giving the illusion of early morning. There was a loud roar followed
by another one. The lions were close tonight. A star darted through
the black like a firework. Ruth and I made a wish. There was a distinctive rustling, and we all held still. Mum raised her torch as an
impala splashed through the water to the other side of the bank.
Dad went to take his bath in the river, and Mum told us that it was
bedtime. Do you need the scoop? We shook our heads and grabbed

our toothbrushes, water bottles, and torches. We brushed our teeth, then went to our tent, where we lay facing each other in the dark. Ruth whispered that Emily had kissed a boy.

What was it like?

Weird and wet.

Ruth told me that when she was older, she wanted to kiss girls, and I told her that I didn't want to kiss anyone. Ruth said that she could hear my parents. I said that they were just arguing. Ruth turned onto her stomach and fell asleep, but I lay awake listening to the conversations of the lions reverberate like thunder across the plains.

DAD LEFT THE ENGINE on, and "Wichita Lineman" played across the savanna. We sat on the roof and watched herds of wildebeest and zebra grazing in the distance. As the sun drip-fed the horizon, my eyes adjusted. Dad drained the rest of his beer. You must always take time for a sundowner, Enola. I put the empty bottle in the cool box and handed him a new one. Your mum is always go go go, he said, punctuating each word with his fist. I wrapped my arms around myself; Mum would tell me off for not bringing a jumper. I told him that I had been given a gold star in school, and he asked if I had heard the story of when his childhood dog, Dodger, ate his homework. As he spoke, the remaining orange drained from the sky. The air turned cold, and the radio seemed too loud.

Should we go back now, Dad?

He pointed somewhere in the dark distance. Listen, hyenas!

Dinner might be ready now, Dad.

He sighed and said: Go go go.

I slid through the hatch onto the back seat, and Dad went to the front. Look, he said, poking his head out the window. That's the Big Dipper. And that one? That's the Plow. Some of them are dead, he said, turning on the engine.

DAD WAS DRIVING, MUM was in the front, and Ruth and I stood in the back with our bodies through the hatch. Lions had been spotted in No Man's Land. There was a small sign to Tanzania, and Mum said that we shouldn't go any farther, but Dad said that no one would care; we could drive to the other side of the Serengeti if we wanted.

Dad negotiated the car down a small valley, through patches of black sand that fixed to the wheels like tar until we made it to greenery on the other side of the stream. Ruth screamed. Mum told us to sit down. The roof was put back up, and the windows were closed. The car became hot and airless. We pressed our faces to the glass. A male and a female were lying beneath two acacia trees. The lion prowled toward the lioness and mounted her. Ruth pinched my arm. They growled, and the male bit the female's neck as she thrashed her head. Thirty seconds later, he returned to his spot, and the female rolled onto her back and let her legs hang upward.

WE WERE EATING BREAKFAST when the sky cracked and opened. We gathered up as much as we could and ran underneath the canvas where we kept the kitchen supplies, toiletries, and torches. I thought about all the animals running for shelter. The warthogs and zebras and buffalo. I wondered if they all huddled in a temporary truce under the same tree. Ruth said that her bacon was wet. I tried to bite my sandwich, but the bread fell apart. Ruth grabbed my hand and yanked me into the rain. Mum told us to come back, but we held our faces up and stuck out our tongues. We laughed hysterically, our clothes wet through, our shoes, our socks, our pants; the air was water. I shouted to Mum and Dad to join us. Mum told us to stop being silly but then Dad pulled her from under the tent, and they joined us, spinning and laughing and squinting in the rain. I wondered if any animals were doing the same thing, or perhaps *this* was how we were different.

WE HAD DRIVEN TO see the buffalo, but, on the way back to Sand River, we became lost. It had been a long, hot day; we had seen families of warthogs and cheetahs and zebras and wildebeest; we had stopped for mango juice and peanut butter cookies on a bridge and seen elephants and crocodiles and hippos. But now there were no herds, and the land was dead. Mum fanned us with her book. We noticed, then, hundreds of brown anthills spread equidistant like graves.

Look. Ruth pointed to a carcass.

Dad slowed the car, and we stared at the remains, burned to leather by the sun. The flesh torn away in ribbons. First by lions and then by hyenas and then—Dad pointed to the branches of a leafless tree where two vultures perched, weighty and hooded. Above, more circled in the sky. Dad turned the engine off and stepped out of the car. He lit a cigarette and looked through the binoculars.

It's like the elephant graveyard, whispered Ruth.

Kit, Mum said through the open window. How much gas is left?

Dad lowered the binoculars.

Kit?

He turned back, eyes dark.

CHAPTER 25

EIGHT THIRTY-FIVE. VIRINDER WILL BE SITTING ON HIS WHITE leather sofa, with a preprepared meal in the oven, ringing someone to tell him, just as Ruth told me, that he is lucky to be out of that abusive, toxic relationship.

A beeping from the kitchen: the washing is done.

I go to the machine. Wet, my THIS IS WHAT A FEMINIST LOOKS LIKE T-shirt is even more of a bad joke, but at least his aftershave is gone. I drape the items over the radiator and turn the thermostat up. I sit on the sofa and smell the flat as it warms: the dust on the metal. Ahead, on the bookshelf, Amy's debut, *The Dark Side of the Coin*, stands in bright yellow. The reviewers called it "gripping."

When we were working on my book, Diana asked questions like, Is this *really* what it is like? She helped me focus on telling a story as opposed to being a writer. She told me to save my first draft. *The more you edit, the more you stray from your original intention*, she said. It's the same in relationships. We form a connection with someone at a writers' event or in a hedge fund café, and over time that connection gets replaced by its memory, and so we edit and rewrite and delete in an effort to recapture what we felt. Maybe the many-worlds interpretation of quantum mechanics is just different drafts of the same story. Virinder was just tonight's mistake, that's all.

CLOSE YOUR EYES AND hold out your hands.

In my palms, Ruth placed a black T-shirt with gold writing that read: THIS IS WHAT A FEMINIST LOOKS LIKE. She was wearing the same one in pink and silver.

We were meeting Sasha and their friends in Soho for Pride, but the plan was to walk there along the river and stop in different pubs on the way. We got ready at mine, drinking dark rum and putting glitter on our faces. Ruth did us both, because the last time I did her face, she told me that she looked like a child's finger painting.

There, she said, finishing the last gold star on her blue cheekbones. What do you think? I told her that she was hot and politically relevant. Ruth said that she'd have to put that on her Tinder bio.

Didn't Virinder want to come today?

Nah, it's not really his thing.

Hates the gays?

Can't stand 'em.

She asked how long we had been dating now. I told her since February. Nearly five months. Ruth's eyes widened. That long? I smiled, thinking about how great things had been going.

It's just so *easy*, Roo. He actually cares about my needs. And he's such a grown-up! I told her that my favorite thing about staying over at Virinder's was falling asleep to the sound of the dishwasher and waking to the sound of the coffee machine.

So, you like that he's rich?

I *like* that he's organized.

I asked Ruth if there was anyone that she was interested in at the moment, and she shrugged and rummaged inside her bum bag for her lipstick. She applied a matte pink to her own lips and then offered it to me. Can you? She held my chin, and I closed my eyes.

Okay, she said, blot. We turned to the wardrobe mirror. Her: leather skirt, pink T-shirt, hair in caramel braids. Me, jeans, black T-shirt, and a checked shirt. We had stood so many times posing like this, like we were still eight-year-olds saying cheese for a disposable camera.

Do I look too emo?

Ruth laughed. Was that not what you were going for?

I told her that I loved her hair like that. She said that she wasn't sure. She had wanted the braids to be a cooler shade; it was too warm. Then she looked at her strawberry watch and said that we should leave. I turned her wrist. Roo, it says seven in the morning! She laughed, but then I looked at my phone and conceded that she was right. She put on her platforms, and I reminded her that I had plasters in my bag. She told me that going out with me was like going out with a girl guide. Then she summoned the lift while I checked the lights and the stove. Virinder did the same thing when he left his flat. Being with him made me feel normal. Better than normal: fun. Because he thought I *was* fun.

Outside, it was perfect June weather. Pale blue sky with cartoon clouds. I felt the same as I did last September when Ruth and I were floating in Hampstead ponds. Everything was fresh and exciting and *light*; like how I used to feel at the beginning of a school year with my new pencil case and shiny shoes. Diana and I had agreed to have my book ready to submit to publishers in the autumn, and so weeks of editing lay ahead. But first, Ruth and I headed to Soho.

THE NEXT DAY, I woke to the smell of toast. There was a pint of water by the bed with a Post-it that read DRINK ME and two painkillers with another that read EAT ME. I rolled off Ruth's mattress and followed piles of clothes, like stepping stones from the night before, to the kitchen, where Ruth was sat on the stained counter. Sasha was at the stove. They still had glitter on their faces.

You're awake! How do you feel?

Good!

Ruth said that she felt rough this morning but better now. She asked if I wanted to come to Catherine's later. I told her that I was going to Virinder's. She said he was texting a lot yesterday. I grinned. Yes, he does that.

Sasha grunted toward the French press. Ruth reached for a mug. I poured a cup. Ruth said the beans were from a new place in Hackney Wick. I jumped up next to her, and she leaned on my shoulder. She smelled like last night's perfume and secondhand smoke.

All right, Sasha said. Bacon's ready. Sorry, Enola, it's vegan. Toast's in the toaster. But there's no butter because *someone* forgot to buy it.

Ruth looked to me and said that *someone* was grumpy because *someone* didn't get any at Pride.

BEFORE HEADING TO VIRINDER'S, I stopped at mine for some clothes, but as soon as my keys hit the monstera tray, I heard: *Don't be silly.* Six months and the flat was still a graveyard.

When I got to Primrose Hill, Virinder was wearing a white tank top and tracksuit bottoms. Sweat glistened on his skin. He asked if I wanted dinner. I said that I had just eaten breakfast, and he laughed. How was Pride? You and Ruth sounded pretty hammered.

It was fun and, no, it was more sugar than anything else.

Ruth is a bad influence!

He said that he had set my writing desk up for tomorrow. I reminded him that I didn't have to work at his, but he said that he loved me being there. I told him that I didn't want to take advantage. He moved toward me. Oh, I see. Using me for my flat, is that it? I told him that I couldn't help it. Primrose Hill had the good pastries. Don't you dare work anywhere else, he said. We kissed, and he tasted like peppermint.

Summer sun flooded the skylight, and a candle made everything smell like mimosa. I felt tired, but it was nice, like I had taken a sleeping tablet and my muscles were relaxing. The shower clicked on, and I had an idea. I stripped and opened the bathroom door. He turned like a startled animal. What are you doing? I climbed into the bath. He said that he wasn't big on shower sex. That the function of a shower was to get clean. I told him that there could be another function, and he played along, but mostly he looked uncomfortable. I wasn't sure if this was something I actually wanted or something I would have done in my last relationship to prove that I was *that* girl. I went to climb out, but he held my waist. I didn't say I wanted you to leave, Enola. Then he washed my hair for me.

Later we curled on the couch, and I dozed to the sound of him laughing at a show about scientists. He nudged me awake when it was bedtime—which, as always, was at ten thirty—and we went to bed. He slept, and my brain activated with thoughts of my book. When it moved to other things, I took two painkillers and waited for the harder edges to soften.

CHAPTER 26

SEPTEMBER WAS COLDER THAN IT WAS LAST YEAR. I PULLED AT MY lilac jumper. When I'd dressed this morning, I thought about what Amy might wear, but the fabric scratched my skin and the color washed me out. Diana tapped her pen on the desk every time she articulated a thought.

Enola, I really think you need to introduce this character sooner.

Her perfume was light, but the whole room smelled like it. I couldn't tell what the scent was. Citrus and jasmine? It was probably from one of those independent Covent Garden shops.

Enola?

Yes, I'm listening. Sorry!

Diana smiled and said that it had been a long summer. But we're nearly there, I promise! She stood and went to the door. Let's get you a coffee. She came back in and said that her intern would bring them. I was an intern once.

You started here as an intern?

She looked proud as she told me that she did. Then her left hand met her right, and she played with her diamond in a way that told me it was still a novelty for her to wear it. I fingered a red bookmark on her desk. She explained that her friend had bought it for her after she did a quiz that told her she was a Gryffindor. I remembered how *he* said that those quizzes were data collection. I had called him a Slytherin and he had called me a Huffletrout.

I told Diana that I got Ravenclaw, and she smiled and said that made sense.

A scruffy-haired twentysomething who looked like he went to private school put two coffees on the desk. Thanks, Toby. He glanced at the hardbacks on her shelf before he left.

Did I belong in this world? Everyone knew what they wanted and what steps they needed to take to get there. There was a photo on Diana's desk of her parents looking happy and proud at her graduation. Last Wednesday, I had tried talking to Mum about my book, but all she wanted to talk about was how happy she was that I was dating a lawyer.

Diana sipped her coffee and shook her head in acknowledgment of a need for caffeine; then she asked if I had questions. There was really only one question: Would I be able to do this? For so long, all I'd wanted to do was to finish a book, and then it became about getting an agent, and now the goal posts had shifted. Now I wanted to get it published, but it seemed like that was something that happened to other people, like the ring on Diana's finger.

Diana looked puzzled at my question. You *are* doing this, Enola.

I exhaled. Okay. When do you want the final draft?

Diana clicked her tongue and said that she'd ideally like it in two weeks, ready for the book fair in October. I told her that I would do my best, and, like a Gryffindor, she told me that she believed in me.

WHEN I OPENED THE door with the key he gave me, Virinder was putting two preprepared training meals in the oven. I told him that I might skip dinner because I needed to write. He said that it was fine but proceeded to cite an article about working hours and animal types, concluding that I might find it easier to work in the morning. I told him that I had a shift at the café. He said that he was just trying to help, and then turned back to the oven. I put my hand on his back, but he stared at the hob. He mumbled that I had been writing for months, and he never saw me. You're at work most of the day, I said gently.

Yes, but that's *work*.

And writing is *my* work. I don't come to your office and tell you to spend more time with me.

But this is my flat, Enola, not your workplace!

I started to remind him that I had told him I didn't have to work at his, but he pulled me to him and pressed my head against his chest. His jacket smelled like a new car. I'm sorry. Look, there's something I—

I pulled back. What is it?

It's nothing, but . . .

He inhaled like he was about to announce an award winner and then said: It's just this new medication for my anxiety.

You're on anxiety medication?

He nodded that he was. I asked why he hadn't told me. He said that people treated him differently when they didn't think he was perfect. I asked him why he had told me then, and he laughed.

Because you already know that I'm not perfect, Enola!

Other people would never acknowledge their limitations, let alone seek help, but if Virinder strained a muscle he would go to the physiotherapist; if he needed vitamin D, he would go on a sunbed; if he made a mistake, he would apologize. I kissed him and said that he was perfect. He asked what was perfect about him. I told him not to fish.

I'll tell you what, he said. I'll draw you a bath. Are you at the café tomorrow?

From two.

So, if you get up at seven, you'll have six hours.

He made it sound like a compromise, and even though it wasn't, it was hard to say no to him. He put meditation music on and drew me a bath. He added bath oil, and in the notes of citrus I saw my mum with a glass of wine as the sun descended lazily over the vineyard. *Get in the bath, Enola. He's a lawyer.* I smuggled in my laptop and put it on the toilet seat. After thirty minutes, and a character moved from chapter five to chapter two, Virinder called dinner, and I jumped in and out of the bath. That's better, he said. You look much more relaxed!

VIRINDER KISSED ME ON the forehead, and I pretended to be asleep. When the door locked, I got out of bed. He had set up the French press next to my favorite mug (the only one he owned that wasn't white, a bumblebee-patterned one from Anthropologie that his mother bought him). There was a note on the desk that read:

Happy writing, love V xxx

I felt guilty for being annoyed with him yesterday. He had been feeling anxious, and yet what he chose to do with that feeling was to try to look after me. And he *did* look after me. Virinder had been a big part in helping me finish the book. His perfectly painted walls were a serene palette of eggshell, and it was like writing in a museum café. Here with him, I wrote like writing was work and not compulsion. I still changed the font obsessively, but I did it for a logical reason, to help me see the mistakes. The chaos over, now was my favorite part: order.

I made coffee and then edited for two hours until a message from Ruth snapped me out of my trance.

> Hey, not seen you in ages! Wanna go dancing? Trump might be president of the world soon so we should dance while we still have joy in our hearts.

I replied that I still needed to write, and so she suggested next weekend. Chris from the writing group was having a birthday karaoke thing, and I asked if she wanted to come. She said yes and proposed dinner first.

> Perfect. Can't wait. x

I closed my laptop and went for a shower. Maybe it was having a plan with Ruth to look forward to, or the fact that my book was nearly finished, but, under the water, I felt excited about my life. I fantasized about winning a literary award wearing that green silk dress from *Atonement*. I picked up Virinder's pepper-scented shower gel and held it like an Oscar.

Thank you so much, everyone! I couldn't have done it without you. Especially my girls!

Women, Ruth corrected me, *we are women, not girls!*

Virinder was in the front row in a designer suit, looking happy and proud, but then I noticed a tall figure at the back of the room. Denim jacket with a rip in the shoulder. Eyes burning with regret.

I detached the shower head and lowered it between my legs.

He dragged me to the toilets, wild and wolflike, and pushed me against the wall. He bit my neck and fucked me. *Is this what you want? Is this what you want, you cunt?*

I came hard but quick, so once the sensation faded it was like it had never happened. I replaced the shower head and picked back up my award.

I'd like to thank my best friend . . . I'd like to thank my agent . . . I'd like to thank my dad . . .

WHEN I TURNED THE corner into the courtyard, Ruth was on the swinging seat by the vegetable patch with a bottle of prosecco. She stood when she saw me. *You finished the book!* We hugged each other hard; I couldn't go this long without seeing her again.

Sasha made a stew, and we sat on the floor around the conjoined crates used as a table, tearing bread and drinking red wine. Sasha's friend Olivia, a petite girl with a mullet, was telling us about her friend who was becoming one of *those* brides. She doesn't get that not everybody is comfortable upholding archaic patriarchal structures, she said. Nodding in agreement, Ruth said that her sister had had a traditional wedding. I reminded Ruth that she had cried at Emily's wedding and she stuck out her tongue, purple from the wine. Olivia asked me if I wanted to get married, and I answered that I didn't know. That means *yes*, Olivia said, putting her bowl down. Society won't change unless we change it. Ruth said that society wouldn't matter if the world ended. I told Ruth that she couldn't invent an apocalypse to avoid commitment. She replied that I couldn't deny an apocalypse because I was excited about my career. Olivia huffed: Climate change is real, Enola.

I know that climate change is real, Olivia, I thought. And then: *Fuck it.*

I know that climate change is real, *Olivia.*

Ruth stifled a giggle.

Sasha contributed sagely: People will be extinguished but the planet will continue. Ruth said that Sasha might get lucky, and the planet might save the vegans. Sasha threw a napkin at her. Olivia said that Brexit was step one in our extinction. Sasha asked what step two was. I suggested Bowie, and everyone laughed apart from Olivia. Ruth gestured to ask whether it was okay for her to finish the bread. We nodded, and so she took the crust. I passed her my bowl to scrape. Well, Sasha said, whatever the order, we can all agree that Trump is stage three. I said that I didn't think Trump would win.

Olivia spoke to me but looked, smiling, at Sasha. So, you think that people don't hate women, Enola?

I think he'll be assassinated before we find out.

What, like shot in the chest at a Republican convention?

Or between the toes with a needle.

Everyone laughed again apart from Olivia, who said that I watched too much American television and not enough of the news. Ruth picked up her phone and started scrolling. Ah, she said. Bowie died first. Bowie died and then it all went to shit. Did anyone think to check between *his* toes?

AFTER DINNER, WE CHANGED our clothes and brushed our teeth. I wore a denim skirt and a burnt-orange cardigan, and Ruth was effortless in black jeans and a black T-shirt with a brown belt. We split an Uber with Olivia and Sasha, who went into Soho. I asked Ruth why Olivia had been funny with me, and she said that Olivia was intimidated by people like me.

Who are people like me?

Well, from an outsider perspective you're a professional writer who owns her flat and your boyfriend is a lawyer.

So, she thinks I'm the poster girl for cis heteronormative white female privilege, basically?

She just thinks that you have your shit together. Speaking of, how's it going with Mr. Perfect? You never speak about him.

I said that there wasn't much to say. Everything is fine.

Fine?

Great, everything's great.

It's been, what, seven, eight months now?

Erm, yes, I think about eight.

We arrived at the Korean barbeque karaoke. All around the restaurant, meat was sizzling on hot plates. Chris and his friends were having dinner. The table was dirty, and their faces were red. Enola, you came! he said in a way that made me feel like I shouldn't have. We're the reception guests, Ruth said under her breath. Chris said that the room was ready and that they were just paying the bill.

Downstairs in the booth, Mat was on his own looking glum. He asked if anyone else from the writing group was coming. I answered that Hugo was working and Amy had a phobia of karaoke. Mat told me that he saw an advert for her book on the tube. I replied that it was a great cover, and he told me not to judge. Ruth nudged my arm. He's funny, she whispered, emphasizing the pronoun.

One shot of tequila and half a beer later, Chris and his friends appeared in a cacophony. Chris kicked the night off with a corporeal performance of an eighties power ballad, and Mat and I talked over the music. He asked how my book was going, and I said that it was finished and that my agent wanted to submit next month. How's it going for you?

He replied that he had been longlisted for a competition. Then Mat asked the question that I was hoping to avoid: Have you heard from *him*? I shook my head and said that we weren't in contact. Mat's face didn't change, so presumably he still didn't know that we used to be a couple. But then he said: So, you probably haven't heard his news then.

What news?

He's just got signed with Simon Longman!

I choked on my beer.

Simon Longman was a renowned agent. He only signed people who he thought were going to be huge successes in literary fiction and then he made sure that he was right. Every day he tweeted something intimidating like: *Never query unless you're happy with every single word.*

I know, right? Mat continued. I bumped into him and his girlfriend the other day and he told me like he wasn't fussed. I could have punched him. Imagine being signed with Simon Longman and not giving a shit!

Girlfriend.

What did you say?

I could have punched—

Come on, it's us! Ruth placed a microphone in my hand. People were cheering. Someone shouted "Girl power!" I was dragged up. Was I singing? A girl was sharing my microphone. Her arm around me. Tugging the microphone closer to her mouth. *Girlfriend—he has a girlfriend?* I ducked under the arm and shimmied backward. The door shut like a vacuum. I followed signs to the toilets and pressed down on the sink.

Okay. Breathe and break it down.

Firstly: he would never have introduced someone as his girlfriend. Mat probably saw him with a woman and *assumed* she was his girlfriend. It might have just been Steph. *Fucking Steph.* Secondly: Why did I care? We broke up months ago! And Simon Longman . . . Oh my god. He was about to become huge. Like, literary-prize huge.

Why wasn't I happy for him? Was I jealous that I wouldn't be the one sharing in his success? No, I knew what the problem was. Ruth told me that *he* was the issue, that he struggled with commitment and intimacy and insecurity, and I had started to believe her. After all, I was the one with the agent and the new boyfriend and the new life. But if he was thriving then maybe she was wrong. Maybe I was the problem.

My heart started beating fast, and my hands felt numb. Fuck, I hadn't had a panic attack in months. I instinctively reached for my wrist, but I hadn't worn my band in months either. I splashed water on my face instead and swore at the mascara beneath my eyes. How the fuck did women in movies do this?

My jacket and bag were in the booth, so I ran in, snatched them, and left. With Chris attempting to rap, I didn't think anyone had noticed but halfway up the stairs I heard her voice: What are you doing? Ruth was on the bottom step looking confused and then hurt. I didn't know why, but I felt angry with her. I told her that I needed to go home. Okay, she said. Were you planning on saying anything? I told her what Mat had told me, and she pleaded with me not to get upset.

You've been happy, Enola. Your career is going well and I've not seen you cry in ages. Please don't let this derail you, okay?

I nodded because it was the reaction she wanted.

But you can't just run away, she continued. This is what he does. He makes you reckless. He makes you unsafe! I told her that I was always safe, and she scowled. Fine. You're *always safe*—whatever the fuck that means—but overlooking that, it's just rude! You can't push away the people who care about you!

I wanted to punch a hole in the wall. I wanted to rip my hair out. I wanted to run as fast as possible. I wanted to scream.

Look, Roo . . . I—

Fine, Enola. Just go.

What will you do?

Meet Sasha and Olivia, I guess.

Remembering they were in Soho, I felt better. Ruth would be

happier with them. But her face was fixed in an expression normally reserved for Emily. *Just text me when you get home this time, Enola.* I moved one step down to say goodbye, but she turned and went back to the booth.

I WALKED HOME AND stopped on London Bridge. Tower Bridge was green and glowing ahead, and the moon was bright. I could feel my skin turning pink in the cold. Virinder messaged asking what time I would be over. I lied that I was staying at Ruth's.

But I've put fresh sheets on the bed and bought stuff for breakfast?

Why was that my problem? I hadn't asked him to do that.

I'm sorry. I'll come over in the week. Is that okay?

He was "typing" for ages, so I sent another message saying that my battery was dying and put my phone on silent. I rested on the stone wall and stared into the black. Dad told me that drowning was the most peaceful way to die. The Thames looked calm but the undercurrent was dangerous. I lifted onto my toes and leaned over. I couldn't see the water, just flickers as light caught movement. It would be so easy to—

Hi, I'm so sorry but could you maybe take our picture? Our selfie stick has broken!

I turned to find a European couple, both tall and blond with shiny puffer jackets. She handed me a phone in a glittery case. He kissed her cheek. She made a peace sign. They pretended to laugh. I passed the phone back and twenty-five minutes later I was home.

Opening the door, the smell was familiar and comforting. I put on my *Mario Kart* T-shirt that was still under my pillow; then I held Otter and cried until I was breathless.

CHAPTER 27

I AM IN THE GARDEN IN NAIROBI, AND HE IS HERE. HIS VOICE shares a frequency with the low breeze in the grass. The table is set for Christmas, and music is playing. The warmth of the sun. The sound of the ocean. But we are six hours from the coast? Six hours against the sun-soaked window. Anthills appear all around. Vultures circle. I hear the crescendo of the train and—

SHH. IT WAS JUST a nightmare, baby girl. Virinder pressed my face against his chest and hushed me like I was resisting him. He nodded to the painkillers on the bedside table. Did you take these again, Enola? He said my name like I was an idiot. I told him they were painkillers, not crack. He said that I didn't need them. I reminded him that *he* took medication. He said that anxiety medicine was not the same as misusing painkillers.

You just need to relax, babe. You've been all over the place.

He was right. I hadn't been myself since karaoke. And it wasn't helping that my book was now finished and on submission to publishers. There was space to fill in my mind, and what was filling it wore a ripped denim jacket.

Virinder told me to close my eyes and go to a happy place, and so I went back to Kenya. I walked through the beach house until I saw *him* by the gate with the moon behind him. He opened his mouth to tell me that he loved me, but before he could say the words, Virinder interrupted, treacly-voiced: Where did you go, baby girl?

Lisbon with Ruth.

Maybe we could go away together? I have some holiday I've not used and—

Can we not talk right now?

Of course, he said. But he didn't mean it. He was insecure. I was *making* him insecure. He started to stroke my hair, lightly, like he was more focused on the appearance of the action than the purpose. But then his hands moved down my body, between my legs.

What are you doing?

He said that he wanted to help me relax. He was so good with his fingers that I didn't tell him to stop. Tell me if I'm going too fast? I nodded, breath thickening. I reached back, but he told me not to worry about him. I just want *you* to feel good.

Afterward, Virinder fell asleep, and I put on his dressing gown and walked up the spiral stairs to the terrace. The night sky was cloudless, and you could see the stars. *There is the one that looks like a cock. And over there is the other one that looks like a cock. And finally, there's one more that looks like—you guessed it—a cock.* I did something I never let myself do: checked his social media.

Because I'd deleted his profile, the only information available was old, so I searched for Steph instead. Careful not to send an accidental request, I scanned her timeline for clues of his new girlfriend, but Steph only had a few photos visible: one with him, one with Patrick, always laughing, always drunk. I opened our archived message chain. His picture was a selfie that he took on the beach in Watamu. I used to think it meant something that he had kept it but the reality was that he just liked the way he looked. Just then, his status changed to "online." *Fuck.* Could he see me? No, of course he couldn't see me. But I could see him. I watched the word like I was watching him from the shadows outside his house. I pictured him picturing me, each of us waiting for the other to move. Perhaps his new girlfriend was asleep next to him just as Virinder was asleep downstairs. Perhaps she understood him. Perhaps she made him happy. I scraped my thumb against the brick wall.

Back in bed, my skin tingled next to Virinder's warmth. I took another painkiller and hoped, as I had for a while now, to feel differently in the morning.

IN THE MORNING, THE clouds moved like water in the skylight. Virinder was stood at the door in his brown suit, and I was perched on the arm of the sofa in my *Mario Kart* T-shirt.

You're quiet this morning, honey.

I told him not to call me that. He laughed, an airy monosyllable. Sorry, baby girl.

I clenched my jaw.

Will you be here when I get back? he asked.

Not tonight.

I said that I had promised to help Ruth prepare for an interview. He joked that Ruth had a job interview every week. I told him that wasn't funny, and he apologized. He explained that he had a case that wasn't his area and he felt out of his depth. I was hoping to see you tonight. But if you need to be with Ruth, I totally understand, he said, looking at his shoes. I was about to protest, but he noticed a mark on the maroon leather, and I watched as he went to the kitchen, retrieved a shoe polish kit, cleaned the invisible stain, returned the kit, and then stood back by the door. He looked twice more at the shoe before looking to me.

Fine, I said. I'll cancel with Ruth.

He went to kiss me, but I warned him that he would be late. He hesitated at the door. You know, Enola, you can talk to me.

What do you mean?

Just, if anything isn't okay?

Virinder was looking at me with concern, but there was a smile in his eyes as if he wanted me to be upset so that he could comfort me. It was the opposite to how *he* was; he recoiled at emotion. I wasn't sure anymore which was worse.

I told Virinder that everything was fine, and he asked if I was sure. I wished that he would stop asking. How was I supposed to know? Was I supposed to tell him my doubts before I understood them myself? And it wasn't just the pressure to feel what he wanted me to feel; it was also his behavior. We always ended up doing what he wanted. But because the things that he wanted to do were nice, I couldn't complain.

Yes, I'm sure. Go, you're going to be late.

Okay, bye, *Enola*. He wanted me to laugh because he wasn't calling me honey. But it wasn't funny. I love you, he said.

See you later, I replied.

Virinder told me he loved me after two months, and I still hadn't returned the words. I knew it was awful. I knew that I was doing to him what had been done to me. I could feel myself chilling and growing scales, my eyes turning black. I was looking at Virinder the way that I used to be looked at. And still, it was Virinder that I blamed. I wanted to take his love and beat it out of him.

He chuckled like my lack of love was a challenge. It's okay. You're still not ready. But I'm quietly confident . . .

The door shut, and a persistent hum settled beneath my skin. I looked at the canvasses of convertibles and strangers in coffee shops. I picked up the Italian colognes and caffeine shampoos. Time moved around me like hoovering around furniture; I didn't even boil the kettle. Something was wrong, and it wasn't just my doubts about the relationship. My period? A full moon? Perhaps it was the threat of change. It was the end of October. I was nearly thirty. America nearly had a new president. Then I received an email and understood.

> Hi Enola,
>
> Sorry that the first bit of news isn't good, but we've had the first no. See below, but they said they didn't connect with the voice. Don't be disheartened. They are just one publisher. Onward!
> Diana x

CHAPTER 28

NOVEMBER ARRIVED BEFORE I WAS READY FOR IT, AND THIS MORN-
ing I was thirty. Mum left a voicemail saying that she had posted
something, but it hadn't arrived. Louise had sent an e-card with the
same design as last year. I rolled over and imagined that he was next
to me.

Happy birthday, honey.

I kissed my hand and pretended it was his mouth.

Did you get everything you wanted?

What did I want?

*Dad is living on the beach. Ruth and I have a joint birthday on
the grassy bank where the seaweed curls to black, bulbous mounds.*

Was it strange that Ruth hadn't pushed me for birthday plans? It
was my thirtieth. But she had been busy. She had a second interview.
She had just started seeing someone. Besides, I had told her that I
didn't want to do anything. I had no money, three more rejections,
and I didn't want to celebrate with Virinder. I had made a plan to see
him on Sunday, which gave me two days to decide what I wanted.

I got out of bed and went to the kitchen. The sky was white like it
might snow. I turned on the radio, filled the kettle and waited for it to
boil. I looked at my face, pale and warped, in the kettle. Every year it
would get worse. My jaw would drip to my neck until my face became
a skull like the ones that we saw in museums on school trips. I stood
wondering if other people found it this hard to understand themselves,
and then made a cup of tea.

*   *   *

AT WORK, STEFAN WAS training a Canadian girl called Amber. Amber had a tattoo of a wolf on her wrist, and at lunch, a banker howled. Nice ink, he said, handing her money for the coffee that I had made him. Keep the change, Amber.

Thanks, she said, putting the eighteen pence into the tip jar.

It did feel sad that I was here on my birthday again. Shift work was acceptable in my twenties, but I was thirty now and, according to Amy, should have special paint on my walls. And I still hadn't heard from Ruth. We always planned our birthdays together. For her thirtieth she had wanted to go to Vegas, but we couldn't afford it, so we went to the casino in Leicester Square.

At last, the shift ended, and I was hanging up my apron when Virinder charged through the doors. Surprise! I'm taking you for dinner! My stomach dropped. He was dressed in a textured blue suit, and his teeth looked newly whitened.

Amber elbowed me. Is he your boyfriend? she said, hitting the "your" unambiguously. I used to love when people commented on Virinder's appearance, but now it bothered me, his preplanned meals, the time spent in the bathroom, how he always kept his muscles tensed. I indicated my work clothes and said that I wasn't dressed for dinner, but he said that didn't matter.

See you later, girl, Stefan said.

VIRINDER TOOK ME TO a restaurant near Bank with dark walls and lobsters in glowing blue tanks. City couples surrounded us. Women in tight dresses with hair extensions. Men with short haircuts and strong aftershave. I took off my coat, and Virinder pointed out a coffee stain like it was adorable. I wondered how adorable he would think it was if I threw coffee on his shirt.

Happy thirtieth, he said. I've always wanted to date an older woman. I smiled, but I hated the joke. I thought about the short, dead, crispy strands of gray in my hair. The women in this restaurant didn't have gray hair.

Virinder ordered us champagne and said that he hoped that it was okay that he hadn't got me a present. The meal and the flowers will have to be enough, he said with a wink. Then he added that we had only just had a celebration dinner for my book, verbalizing the letters "LOL."

I've told you before that I don't like champagne, I said.

I've seen you drink champagne lots!

You've seen me drink prosecco and slowly *sip* the *occasional* glass of champagne.

Well, slowly sip this, then. It's a hundred a bottle.

When the food arrived, Virinder did most of the talking. He spoke about his brother, who had just had another baby, and reminded me that I had promised to give him some dates for us to visit. Then he talked about how much he wanted children and asked how many I wanted. I hated that. A man would be asked whether he wanted them at all.

I'm not sure I want them, I said.

He told me that his friend Kelly used to say that, but now she has four. *Four*, he repeated, and laughed. He talked about how he couldn't wait to propose. He said that he understood feminism, but, for him, he liked the tradition. That will be my surprise, he said. And her surprise will be when she tells me that she is pregnant. He was looking at me like he was talking about me, but he was using the third person. I wondered then if he actually loved me or whether he had just decided to. He told me once that he had broken up with a woman because she wasn't "the one."

Virinder, why do you like me?

He laughed. Baby, what?

I told him to tell me the truth. Why do you want to be with me? His smile flattened. He said that I was different from the other girls. That I made him laugh. He liked that I was a writer, and he liked taking care of me.

Then he asked me the same question, and I answered honestly: I loved hearing you talk about India and your family on our first date.

I loved how positive you were. I loved how dedicated you were to your career.

Why are you speaking about me like I'm dead?

I told him it was unintentional. He said that he was pleased that I had mentioned India because he hoped to take me there. I asked where he considered home, Mumbai or London. He didn't pause for breath. London, because I was born here, he answered, like a game show contestant thrilled to have been asked a question they knew the answer to. I moved food around my plate. He asked if the gnocchi was okay. I told him that it was just filling. How's your steak?

Amazeballs!

We chewed again until the waiter (whose name was Rish, because Virinder asked) cleared the plates. Virinder joked about the way that he was holding them. I'd drop them everywhere! The waiter smiled with blank eyes. Virinder told me that he would give him a generous tip. It's so important, he said. I screwed my hands into fists and told myself that I just had to get through dinner.

Did you speak to your mum today?

Just get through dinner.

No, Virinder, it's Friday.

Even on your birthday?

I didn't acknowledge the question, I just continued drinking champagne. He watched and refilled my water glass. In nine months, I had never seen Virinder drunk. I wanted to fly across the table, slam my knee into his chest, and shove the one-hundred-pound champagne bottle into his mouth.

We ordered dessert, and Virinder asked what I was going to do next with my writing. I told him that I couldn't think about what was next until I knew whether or not this book was dead. He hummed like he understood, then went into an unrelated anecdote about a guy at work who thought he was interested in corporate law but now works in pensions.

JUST GET THROUGH DINNER.

Virinder got an espresso, and I got a peppermint tea, and we talked about the American election. I told him that I was terrified Trump would win on Tuesday. Virinder hummed like he understood, and then his face lit up: Have I shown you this? He waited for me to respond even though there was no way I could know the answer, then played a video of a friend doing a bad impression of Trump talking about grabbing women by the pussy.

Finally, Virinder paid the bill. I picked up the lilies, and when he put my coat over my shoulders, he commented on the stain again. I told him that he should have let me get changed.

Baby girl, that stuff doesn't matter to me!

And then I realized: Not only did it not matter, but he *liked* it. I was his scruffy writer girlfriend who couldn't say "I love you." He wanted me the way that someone wanted a tattoo or a sports car. I was his fetish. And he was my fetish too. The fetish of being treated well. The kink of a different life. It was a magic eye, and now that I had seen it, I couldn't unsee it. There was nothing to be conflicted about; it was sad but inevitable: it was over.

OUTSIDE THE RESTAURANT, VIRINDER suggested that we stay at mine, but I couldn't spend another night with him. I told him that I wanted a night to myself, but knowing that I needed to break up with him in person, added that I'd still like to see him on Sunday. He puffed out his chest and moved like a boxer. I asked if he was all right, and he stuttered: I know that you prefer my flat, but sometimes it would be nice if you invited me over. I know that you have commitment issues but—

I don't have com—

I've made a huge effort this evening, and, well, I just think that . . . that . . .

His face was red, and there were beads of sweat on his hairline. I had never seen him panic before. He said he needed the toilet and ran back inside. After two minutes I got a message from Ruth:

FFS. Just come back to yours, Enola . . .

* * *

OPENING THE DOOR, I knew it was coming, but I still felt sick.

SURPRISE!

Because my entrance was small, I could only see Ruth and Amy and Sasha, but as I turned the corner there was Fiona and a girl I didn't recognize and then, oh god, was that Chris? And Stefan from the café. It was an awkward mix of people. Ruth shouted to Virinder to put the music on and dragged me to the bathroom. She shut the door and put her hands on my cheeks. Firstly, *don't worry*, I made the flat look great. And I know you hate surprises but Virinder was certain that it was what you wanted and I couldn't say no because, well, I didn't want to imply that he didn't know you like I know you, you know? And then I thought, well, we haven't spoken much lately so maybe a surprise party *is* what you want and—

Ruth, what?

Well, we've not seen each other as much recently, she said, looking down.

My pulse slowed, and I took her in. She had a thin layer of green glitter above her eyelashes and was wearing a silver mesh top over a black tube. Her hair was piled atop her head, and she smelled like coconuts. I put my hands on her shoulders and assured her that there would never be a man who knew me better than she did.

Even if there was, like, a weird sex thing?

Especially if there was a weird sex thing.

We laughed, and I said that I was sorry that we hadn't spent much time together, and she told me not to worry. In my mind, she had been the busy one, but I brushed it off. I also brushed off the fact that I hadn't heard from her all day. We looked at each other, and then I clamped my hand over my mouth. God, Roo, this is so weird, what am I going to do?

Ruth suggested putting on some makeup and a dress. Then fuck it, let's have a fun night? Sometimes these weird nights turn out excellent. Also, I brought a date . . .

Sally?

Ruth nodded.

Wow. I don't think I've ever known you to bring a date before. That's quick!

Not really. It's been a month.

There was a knock at the door. Then, saccharine, Virinder said that he had two glasses of prosecco for "the girls." I opened the door a sliver to take them and thanked him for my surprise. He mimed mopping his brow. Phew! I was so worried because you told me that you hated surprises. But then I thought, well, everyone *says* they hate surprises but no one *actually* does. Ruth nudged me and I nudged her back. I told Virinder that we would be out in a minute; then I put on some makeup and changed into my black dress.

RUTH WAS RIGHT. ONCE I got over my lack of control, the party was fun. We sat on the floor around the coffee table, and Ruth fed vodka jelly to people with a teaspoon. I spoke with Amy about the submissions process, and she encouraged me to start something new while I was waiting to hear from publishers. Sally spoke with a soft Huddersfield accent and asked me lots of questions. She was nervous, and Ruth kept putting her arm around me instead of her, which wasn't helping. Virinder was in the kitchen playing host. He makes everyone his best friend, Ruth said. Then she paused. Is that a bit annoying?

We put on nineties music, and Ruth pulled me up, and we did our favorite thing, but then Virinder grabbed my waist and I stopped dancing, and slinked back down by the coffee table. Oh, I forgot, no PDA! he declared with a compensatory laugh.

Don't worry, Virinder, said Amy, mispronouncing his name. Enola is like one of those creatures you have to pour water on.

Everyone looked at her.

You know, those squeaky ones that come to life, she clarified.

Gremlins? suggested Sally. Ruth burst out laughing and put her head on Sally's shoulder, and Sally looked thrilled. Virinder said that I *was* like a little gremlin. I asked him if he had seen the film, and he said, No, are they like Pokémon? I told Ruth to stop feeding Amy vodka jelly. Sasha whispered to Ruth who whispered to me that they had some coke? *Fuck it,* I thought. When in Rome. Virinder, who hadn't properly heard, declared that he *loved* Rome, and he and Amy began discussing the Vatican.

We went to the bathroom, where Sasha made some lines on the edge of the bath. Sally perched on the toilet. She was a tiny human, and with her knees pulled to her chin, she fit perfectly. Sasha stretched across the length of the floor, their long legs in flared pink denim. Ruth draped herself in the bath as if she were in a music video, and I crouched against the door. Sally asked me if I was having a nice birthday, and Ruth said that I hated surprises. Sally asked why she had planned me a surprise party then. Ruth said that it was what my boyfriend wanted.

Why did she say "boyfriend" like that?

Sally told me that Virinder was nice, and Ruth turned to me. Do you ever worry that when people constantly tell you how nice your boyfriend is, it means that they think you aren't?

Okay, Sasha said, sitting up. Sal?

She's Sal already?

Sasha handed Sally a rolled-up five-pound note, and she did the first line and then passed the note to Ruth, who did the fattest one in the middle. Sasha did the long one at the end, then handed me the note. I split the difference and did half of the remaining one. Instantly, I felt that numbing chemical drip. I had only done coke twice. The first time, I panicked that my throat was closing up and made Ruth search the warehouse for something we could use for a tracheotomy. But by the time we found scissors and a straw, the sensation had passed.

The door hit my back. Hello, is this where the party is? We beckoned Chris in. Ruth indicated for me to join her in the bath, so I slotted between her legs while Chris squatted by the door. Sasha handed him the note, and he finished my line. I whispered in Ruth's ear: Why did you invite Chris? She moved my hair off my cheek and whispered back that he had been surprisingly fun at karaoke. I told her that she thought everyone was surprisingly fun, and she replied in the manner she always did, that everyone *was* surprisingly fun. I smiled, but then I had a thought. Ruth took everybody as they came. She always found the fun in them. But she had never given *him* the benefit of the doubt. I shuffled up the bath away from her and rested my elbows where Sasha had presented the lines. Sally smiled over my head at Ruth. She had small, neat white teeth, and rosacea gave her cheeks a blush. Was Ruth smiling back?

Woooweee, Chris said, like an extra doing coke in a film.

PEOPLE LEFT FOR LAST trains, and Sasha turned the lights down. Amy told me that she had a hen in the morning. I would stay longer, but honestly, hon, we were waiting for an hour. She shouted: *Floo! Ahmed is one minute away.*

Ruth put on *Ceremonials* and smiled at me from across the room. We'd seen Florence and the Machine at Alexandra Palace four years ago. Before him. Before Brexit and Bowie and Trump. Before the apocalypse. We'd added MDMA to the rum, but it only hit after the gig, and so we ran barefoot across the grass under the full moon.

The album played and one by one people came up to me as in confession to tell me, unwarranted, what they thought of me. Sasha told me that when Ruth introduced us, they hadn't thought that we would be friends. You seemed a little cold? They kissed me on the lips and asked if I wanted more coke. I shook my head, and they rubbed their gums.

And the arms of the ocean are carrying me.

Something in the lyrics made me think of him.

Birthday girl! Birthday girl! Chris chanted like at a football match. He said that he didn't realize I was fun. You always seemed uptight. I told him that he always seemed like a cunt. But he didn't hear me. He jumped us up and down before flopping on the sofa, sniffing a drink in front of him and drinking it.

Ruth had her arms around Sally in the kitchen. The moonlight from the window connected them. Ruth said something and then left. Sally came over, and I pretended that I hadn't been staring. Sally said that she had been nervous to meet me. Her breath smelled sweet like rum and coke. You mean so much to Ruth, she said, playing with the small silver hoop in her lobe.

I know that, I said.

She laughed nervously and switched to the other ear. She said that Ruth was really excited about the new job. I asked her what new job, and Sally's face changed. Did you not know? I looked around the room. I hadn't seen Virinder in a while. I told Sally that I was going to find him.

I hope I haven't said—

No, not at all.

Ruth was in the bathroom. I could hear singing through the door. She was even a brilliant singer. Why did that annoy me? I checked the bedroom; Virinder wasn't there, but Amy had left her cashmere scarf on the bed. I knew it was cashmere because she told me. I went back into the living room and found him on the balcony facing the skyscrapers. The wind whipped the building, and the edges of his blue jacket were flapping. Like a movie villain, without turning, he asked if I had taken some.

Some what?

Don't play dumb, Enola. *Cocaine.*

Half a line. Why?

He said that he didn't take me as someone who did drugs. I replied that I *took* drugs; I didn't *do* drugs. He asked if there was a difference. I said that there was enough of one. He told me that my eyes were saucers. I told him that it was only half a line. He told me that it was hypocritical of my left-wing hipster friends to be okay with coke. It's upholding some of the world's worst regimes. Not to mention the trafficking. And you do know your doors are glass?

I looked behind me: inside people were dancing and hugging and kissing; it looked warm and safe.

And?

And you've barely spoken to me all evening. I'm not an idiot. I know something is wrong, Enola.

I quickly rehearsed what I was going to say but I stopped myself from saying it. It didn't matter if he was being unreasonable, because he was right, and I couldn't keep lying to him. I told him that I was sorry and he told me that he was going home. I said that I would call him tomorrow, and his face fell, as if he were hoping I might have said something different. He said that *he* would call *me* and then he left.

Ruth came out wearing her gray raincoat. She said that they were going to Bethnal Green. Are you coming? She was avoiding eye contact. I asked if she *wanted* me to come.

What does that mean?

It is *my* thirtieth, Roo.

I know it's *your* thirtieth. *You're* the one that didn't want us to celebrate together.

What does *that* mean? I said, borrowing her words. Who else would I want to celebrate with?

She looked at me like the answer was obvious. I told her that I never wanted to celebrate with Virinder and I certainly never wanted a surprise party. She said that Virinder insisted this was what I wanted. I reminded her that she knew me better than he did.

So, this is *my* fault? she said in a higher-than-normal pitch.

I reached for the creases in her coat. Look, Roo, I don't know what's happening with us but it's fucking freezing. Can we please go inside? But neither of us moved. I asked why she hadn't told me about the job. She said that she *wanted* to tell me. I shook my head. Don't. We don't play those games. She said it wasn't a game.

I didn't tell you, Enola, because you didn't ask! You were meant to help me for my interview, remember? But you were at Virinder's. Man. It's like you're disappearing again but in a totally different way this time.

Okay, but—

Do you know that you're the last of my friends to meet Sally? Do you know how weird that is?

Ruth looked like she was about to cry. I wanted to hug her, but Sasha poked their head out and asked if we were coming. I said that I had to work in the morning, and Sasha laughed: Why on earth did you have a party?

The plan formed without my input, until everyone was standing with their shoes on by the front door. Sally told me that it was lovely to meet me. Chris couldn't stand up straight. Sasha apologized for the mess. Ruth was swaying slightly. I told Sasha to make sure she drank a pint of water before bed. Ruth snapped that I wasn't a doctor.

I closed the door behind them and leaned against the wood, listening to their voices disappear. My eyes were stinging and my feet were aching. I was so frustrated, so *angry*. But then someone knocked. I opened the door, hoping to find Ruth laughing at how absurd we had been, but it was Virinder.

I thought you went home! What are you still doing here?

I looked at my wrist like there was a watch there.

He didn't say anything. I repeated the question. He still didn't say anything. I wanted to tap my foot. Then he spoke: Why didn't you follow me? I asked what he was talking about but he just said it louder: *Why didn't you follow me?* He looked up to the corner of the ceiling and inhaled like he was fighting for his life.

Look, Virinder. It's my birthday. I've been working all day. I just want to sit down and—

I've been working too.

Yes, but you planned this party, I thought.

I asked if we could please talk tomorrow. He told me that if I cared about him, I would have followed him when he left. He shook his head and told me that he deserved better. I wanted to tell him how absurd that was, but then he asked the question that had been burning a hole, the question that I had been too afraid to ask when I had been in his position: Do you love me?

What? I asked, to buy time.

It's always me trying.

If this is about the champagne and the meals then—

No! It's about *you,* Enola. I try and get you to open up—I thought perhaps when you were finished with the book—but you've actually become more distant! I keep thinking that you'll get there but . . . You know, most people would say that I'm a catch.

And just like that I was furious.

Virinder, where were you?

When?

Well, you left and reappeared twenty minutes later so—

He ran his hands through his hair.

—where were you?

He told me that he had been hiding by the rubbish chute. I took a breath and held it, partly to steady myself and partly to demonstrate that I needed steadying. Virinder, you tell me you're leaving; I assume you're leaving. I'm not chasing you down the fucking hall. He told me not to swear. I told him to grow up. We stood for a minute; then he said that he *was* leaving. I tapped my foot. He said that he had put the lilies in water and added the sachet. He waited for me to thank him. I didn't and he left.

The living room was strewn with glasses and teaspoons of half-eaten vodka jelly. And I had run out of bin bags. *Fuck.* I didn't know who I was angrier at: Virinder, Ruth, or myself. No, it was me. I had snapped at Sally. I had argued with Ruth. I had hurt Virinder in the same way that I had been hurt and I wasn't even sure I felt bad about it. I was a horrible person and this was a horrible birthday. Worse than my fourteenth, when I had mumps, and my eighteenth, when my mum forgot. I picked up my phone from the coffee table to text Ruth and found a message:

Happy birthday, Gay. Get everything you wanted? x

AMERICA WAS VOTING ON THEIR PRESIDENT. TRUMP WAS PROBABLY a rapist, but Hillary had sent an email from the wrong account. It had been four days since my party, and Ruth and I still hadn't spoken. I was sat with two gin and tonics when she arrived in an oversize sports jacket and red dungarees. Her expression was uninterpretable, but then she smiled. *Thank god.* Roo, I'm so sorry.

She shook her head. Don't be. I was drunk. I've just had stuff going on.

What stuff?

It doesn't matter.

It does matter. Please tell me. What stuff?

Ruth played with the button on her jacket. I just think sometimes everyone thinks that I'm flaky and shit. And I get it because I *am* flaky and shit. But maybe I want to change and I can't do that if everyone keeps telling me how flaky and shit I am.

You're not flaky or sh—

Virinder joked about it.

What?

We were planning the party and he joked about me not keeping a job. And, Enola, he said it in this way like you guys laugh about it all the time. I expect that stuff from Emily, and Mum, even, but not you.

I stretched out my hand. Ruth, no. I think that you're the most exceptional person and I'm so sorry that I didn't realize how much this job meant to you.

She said that she had been afraid that she was losing me to the pod people of Primrose Hill. I told her that she would never lose me to anyone, person or hill. She laughed, and her cheeks dimpled. I told her how sorry I was that Virinder made her plan my thirtieth. That must have been really weird. She replied that it had been, and she couldn't completely explain why. There was a moment between us; then we redirected our hands to our drinks.

I asked when she started her new job. She told me January, but there was a training thing in Bath next Thursday. Do you remember at school when we had to build bridges out of tape and straws? I reminded her that our bridge had been predominantly tape because she hadn't waited for me to come up with a plan. She retorted that in the time it was taking for me to come up with a plan, we could have constructed the Sistine Chapel. Then she leaned in like she was about to tell me a secret: I'm actually excited. It's a new company, so I'll be creating the role. And because of what the charity does, I get to travel. I might even be able to go to Colombia!

Ruth had never spoken about a job with enthusiasm before. I told her that I was sorry for not asking sooner. She circled the rim of her glass. I should have just told you, she said. I was being petty or jealous or something, I don't know.

We looked at each other and smiled. The clouds lifted, and I felt lighter.

I told Ruth that I liked Sally, and a dusky blush spread across her freckles. I said that I would love to meet her properly, when I wasn't ambushed in my own house. Ruth said that Virinder wasn't one to take no for an answer. What is it with you and these men?

Ruth didn't know yet, but I had gone to Virinder's on Sunday. He had opened the door and gestured to his dining table, where candles were lit. *My ex is back in the picture. I thought your ex was a dickhead? I'm sorry. You know, that's not as helpful as you think it is.* I had gathered my belongings while he stared into the sink like it held the answers I didn't. *I'm not waiting for you, Enola.*

I told Ruth that we broke up. I worried that she might be upset that I hadn't told her sooner, but she just said that she was sorry and she didn't think that he was right for me. You never seemed happy. I mean, you didn't seem *unhappy* but you didn't seem happy either. I told her that I wanted to want him because he was so perfect. Ruth said that he wasn't perfect. I asked her if she thought that I was a sociopath because I didn't feel bad, and she said that sociopaths didn't worry about being sociopaths.

Do you think this is how *he* felt when we broke up in January?

Oh, Laa, who can say what *actual* sociopaths feel?

She told me that Virinder may not have been perfect, but he was, at least, the kind of man you could call to help you drag a body across the kitchen floor.

I told her that I would call *her* for that.

She suggested that we get another drink. Then, baring her teeth, she asked how Virinder had taken the news. I replied that he had taken it surprisingly well.

I just told him that my ex was back in the picture.

Her head shot up. *Is he?*

Shit.

No, I just thought it would be easier to—

Lie?

This way he doesn't have to worry about what he did wrong?

Ruth looked away like she was bracing herself, then turned back. Enola, maybe he *should* worry about what he did wrong. Why can't women ever tell men that they don't want to be with them? Why do they need to make up an excuse? I played with the lime wedge in my drink and said that I didn't represent *all* women, I represented *me*. She said that it would be cool if my breakup passed the Bechdel test.

Roo, I was in a relationship with a man. It was impossible for my breakup to pass the Bechdel test.

But why are you even thinking about him? she asked, like even his pronoun was toxic. I told her that I wasn't and asked if she could cut me some slack. I'm sorry, she said, twirling her coaster. I'm just wound up because of the election. I said that we were lucky to live in England, and she told me not to be naïve. This is the beginning. *Roe versus Wade* won't last long. I asked if she was going to watch the coverage. She said that they were watching it in the warehouse. I waited for her to invite me, but she didn't, and so I said that I would probably just wake up to the results.

Like Christmas morning?

Ha. Yes.

For fifteen minutes while we finished our drinks, we passed the Bechdel test by talking about tweets we had seen, podcasts we were listening to, and shows we were watching. I asked Ruth if she still wanted another drink, but she said she had changed her mind.

AT HOME, I PUT on comfy clothes and settled on the sofa, but I was still addled by our conversation. I felt shamed, which is not something that I normally felt by Ruth. I considered the women in my life. My mum, who, on the one hand, told me that women wore matching underwear for themselves, yet, on the other, was pleased that I was dating a lawyer. Perhaps her feminism was just a criticism of my dad? Then there was Louise, jumping to follow any man who could give her a new life. My grandma might have been a feminist if she had been born at a different time, but one of my earliest memories was her telling me to smile because boys didn't like a sour face. Amy once said that she didn't think of herself as a feminist and yet all she did was champion other women. Ruth dated women, so that automatically made her a better feminist than me; I was sleeping with the enemy. But she was right. When we were teenagers, we would tell the men who groped us that we were gay or that the male friend with us was our boyfriend. We lied so that they didn't feel rejected. Sometimes we would even kiss each other to prove the point, but we knew deep down that we were winding them up. We liked the way that they were looking at us. We didn't realize that their gaze wasn't a compliment; it was the way that lions look at impalas before ripping their throats out.

I stood and made a coffee. I ground the beans in the grinder that Ruth bought me in part so she could use it when she stayed over. The smell of dark chocolate, figs, and raspberry diffused. When the kettle whistled, I filled the French press. Virinder once told me to let it stand for four minutes. I'm a barista, but I pretended that he was telling me something I didn't know.

Four minutes.

An anger grew where my stomach met my chest. Did men sit around wondering if they were *good* enough or *right* enough men?

Three minutes.

Millions of people with arms and brains and favorite television shows were going to vote for Trump. Millions of people didn't consider policies that repressed women bad enough to consider voting for one.

Two minutes.

I became aware suddenly of the helplessness, the hopelessness that existed in me.

One minute.

Fuck it. I poured the coffee, opened his "happy birthday" message, and replied:

Thank you . . .

I turned on the election coverage and watched the map turn red and blue; then I took three painkillers and went to sleep. In the morning, I woke to a text from Ruth:

Happy Fucking Christmas.

And to another from him:

Nice ellipsis. Drink . . . ?

CHAPTER 30

WE TEXTED LIGHTLY FOR A FEW DAYS; POLITICS, THE WEATHER, funny things we had seen, and then on Tuesday, I agreed to meet him. I settled on a loose dress beneath my winter coat and deliberately mismatching underwear.

I pushed the Art Deco doors, and he was at the bar with a pint. I looked at my feet, half in and half out the door. I knew that when I looked up, I could be lost to him again, but hadn't I felt his loss deeper than my own over these past ten months? Besides, it might be fine. We might just chat as friends. I prepared to look at him as at an eclipse.

One.

Two.

Three—

There he was, and I immediately existed in all the same ways as before.

I walked up to the bar, and he pulled out a stool. Well, this is a pleasant twist! He looked like a teenager being told not to laugh. I said hello, but my voice sounded like I was speaking in an accent. There were marks on my fake leather bag, like how my grandma's cat left nervous paw prints at the vet's. He asked me what I fancied. *Complicated question.*

A red wine, please. I slipped off my coat, and his eyes gleamed. There was more silver in his hair. He ordered a large, and I said that a small would have been fine.

Why, you have somewhere to be, Enola?

He edged his stool so that our knees were touching, and I remembered waking up with him in the beach house: white sheets, grains of sand, legs wrapped around legs. I reminded myself to stay alert. A drink with him was like crossing a busy road.

He took a fake sip of his cider for impact.

I heard about Simon Longman, I said, keeping my tone casual. I couldn't believe it when Mat told me!

He narrowed his eyes. Why? Because I was such a failure when we were together?

No! You were *never* a failure! Your writing is incredible. It's astute and funny and—

He grinned.

That's not funny!

He laughed, and it cut through me like it used to, like I had earned it. I called him a prick, and he said that nothing had changed there. I wondered if that was true, though, that nothing had changed. Did he have a girlfriend? He was looking at me like he was imagining me naked.

You must be over the moon, I said.

Simon is over the moon. He gets to spend his evenings drafting emails about the real function of a semicolon.

And what is the real function of a semicolon?

No one knows.

He asked about my book, and I told him that it was on submission. He said that he was proud of me, and I wanted to hibernate in his voice. I told him that he shouldn't be *too* proud because it didn't look like anyone wanted to publish me. Six rejections so far.

We stayed in the pub for two large glasses of wine and conversation concurrently razor-sharp and watercolor. I wanted to write it all down so that I could read it back. We shared a packet of cheese-and-onion crisps and discussed our work. I told him that when I was redrafting my book, I once woke to a note on my bedside table that read: People who can't ride horses should ride friendly centaurs. He said that he did the same thing with voice notes. I told him that I was worried Diana would drop me when the book didn't sell. He told me to focus on the writing. That's your only job. Leave the rest to Diana.

We traced the American political situation. He told me that people voting for Trump was less about misogyny and more about disillusionment. I told him that they weren't mutually exclusive. We chatted about the books that we had read since breaking up. When he said the word "breakup," I felt my cheeks warm. If we had broken up then we had also been together; we had seen each other naked. I could lean over and put my tongue in his ear. But I didn't. I told him that I still had his copy of *Catch-22*, and he said that he had been looking for that.

We asked about each other's families. How's the crazy aunt? I told him that Louise was fine. I asked about his parents and Karen, and he said that the doll collection had grown. He asked after Ruth, and there was a beat when we both remembered how much he had hurt me. I asked about Pat and felt stupid for using his nickname when we had never met. But then he said that Pat had mentioned me recently.

Pat was always rooting for this—for us. He liked you, Enola. Or maybe he just knew that I did.

You did? I thought but didn't say.

I looked at my glass and asked about Steph. He said that she was filming a pilot in LA. I lied that Mat said he had bumped into them. Was that before she left? It was a pathetic attempt to garner information, but I had to know if Mat had seen him with a girlfriend. I braced for the cauterization, but he nodded and subsequently affirmed that the woman he had been with was, in fact, just Steph.

Thank god.

Then he took my hands. His skin felt rougher, and his fingers seemed larger. He said that my hands still looked like a child had drawn them. A circle with five sticks. I slipped my hands away and took the last sip of my wine. Were we just friends or was this a reconciliation? Both thoughts made me sick. The former because seeing him made it impossible for me not to see him again. The latter because I would have to tell Ruth.

He placed his palms on the bar and asked if I wanted another drink. But I shook my head; the edges of the pub were smudging. Well, he said slowly. I suppose we should go home then? Unless there's something else you want to do? I nodded that we should go home, and I meant it, but then I floated to the ceiling and watched myself suggest that he come to mine so I could return his book.

THE COLD WOKE ME up, and so when we got to mine, I asked him to wait by the door, but he followed me to the bookshelf in the living room. I found the thick silver spine and gave it to him. He pulled out a turquoise Vonnegut and moved it into the orange section. I went to move it back, but he caught my arm and told me that losing control would be good for me. He said that he would lend me this new book he was reading when we saw each other next. Then he corrected himself. *If* we see each other. His hand was still on my arm. I had to take charge of the moment.

All right, I said definitively.

All right . . .

I walked back to the door, and he followed. I gave him the kind of hug that I would give a friend. It was so quick that I barely noticed his lips graze my hair or the smell of his neck. I reached for the door, but his hand lingered on my waist. Neither of us moved. He searched my eyes for the approval I didn't mean to give, and then he kissed me. I said his name, but my words melted on his tongue. His hand pressed the wall to steady us. I brought up a tsunami of concerns like swells of a tide, but his voice was in my mouth when he said: Wouldn't it be sexy to say that your ex-boyfriend came over and fucked you?

Those aren't the words I would use.

He was crude, but he delicately unbuttoned my dress.

I was being led to my bedroom like it was his.

Pushed onto the bed.

It wasn't like coming home. It wasn't beautiful. We both tasted like the cheese-and-onion crisps we ate at the bar, and when I removed him, heavy and hard, from his red boxers there was a sourness, but it was the most alive I had felt since the glass shattered against the bedroom wall.

AFTERWARD, I ASSUMED THAT he would leave, but he suggested a bath. He went to the shop and returned with a bottle of red and a chocolate egg. Don't say I never gave you anything. I wasn't sure if he remembered that he had given me one before.

We poured two glasses, and I waited in the water as he put some music on his phone. They were songs that he used to play, and it was like time travel. He climbed in, quipping: Sorry for the view. I unwrapped a bath bomb that Catherine had given me for my birthday. He dropped it in the water with a "kaboom," and it spewed pink glitter that caught in the bubbles like dirt in a corner of a lake. He leaned back and closed his eyes; then he opened them and it felt like I had been caught staring at a stranger on the tube. But he just shook his head and said: I just can't believe I'm here again.

Me neither.

Good surprise?

I'm not sure yet.

He asked if he had been a dick to me when we were together. I told him that I had been thinking about that recently. I was seeing someone, and the experience made me realize that I had been unreasonable. He shook his head. You weren't unreasonable. You were just sensitive and I felt—

Like you were responsible for my feelings all the time?

He nodded.

When we got back together—

You don't have to—

I know but—

I was the one who . . .

No, I was . . .

Our voices trailed off, and we just looked at each other. He said that maybe time was how we fixed things. I didn't agree or disagree, because the moment felt too unsteady. He asked if I remembered our holiday, like it was an episode of a show we watched once. He said that he regretted going away together so early. I said that it was four months in. Either way, he said. I think we should have gotten to know each other more. I told him that it never seemed like he wanted to get to know me. He said that I never seemed like I wanted to be known. I felt brave then and asked: So, what do you want *now*? His eyes sparked, and he lowered his hand under the water. He started writing letters on my thigh. The first word was "I," and the second started with a "w." He was writing "I want." I joked that this was like playing Scrabble. He moved his fingers up and asked where the triple word score was. He wrote the third word three times and then looked at me questioningly.

Yes, yes, I want you too, I said without speaking.

He adjusted so that he was on his knees and moved toward me. Water splashed over the side. I lifted one knee so he could push inside me. His hand reached around my back and pulled me closer. More water splashed over the side. Fuck, he said, fuck. Hands reached my neck and squeezed like he was trying to fold me up like paper. Pressure rose. My elbow caught the wineglass, which tipped and turned the water red. He caught it without removing his mouth from my neck. I reached into the water and touched myself until I came; then he pulled out and came on my chest.

Oh god. Oh my god.

That was the first time that had happened, and I had to fight to stop from crying. He said that was intense. I agreed but didn't tell him why. I felt stupid that I hadn't been able to do that before. He fell back by the taps, and the bath bomb shriveled to a raisin. He said that he had felt it fizzing and it wasn't unpleasant. We laughed, and I pointed out that the water was cold. There's not much of it left, he said with a double eyebrow raise. I bit my cheeks, and he asked me why I did that. I said that I thought it made me look like I had dimples. He said, dryly, that it didn't. Then, holding up one hand, palm facing me, he declared that he was a prune. I said that he was a prune before the bath, so it wasn't a fair experiment. He splashed me, and I remembered being in the ocean with him on the holiday we never should have taken.

CHAPTER 31

THE NEXT DAY, I WOKE UP FEELING SICK. IT WAS PARTLY THE USUAL apprehension at it being Wednesday and having to talk to my mother, but it was also because I needed to talk to Ruth.

I told her that I was in the neighborhood, but I wasn't. I was wearing the T-shirt that she had bought for me for Pride: THIS IS WHAT A FEMINIST LOOKS LIKE. We were really happy that day. I wanted her to remember that day when I told her.

As I turned the corner into the community, she was on the swinging seat wrapped in a blanket. She put her mug on the ground, and we went inside. She put the kettle on and waited for it to boil.

Go on then, she said.

I asked her how she knew, and she said that she could just sense it, like the seasons shifting.

God, is it that monumental?

I just know *you*, Enola.

I took a deep breath and explained that being with Virinder had made me think about things. She told me that she didn't know where to start. I asked her to please not judge me, and she said that she wasn't *judging*, she was *worrying*. I played with my hands. Roo, sometimes your worry can feel like judgment. She looked at me incredulously.

It's true, I said. I can tell what you're thinking.

Okay. What am I thinking?

That I'm a shit feminist who gets lost in my relationships.

That would make you a shit *friend*, not a shit feminist.

The kettle clicked, and it was only when she added milk that I realized she wasn't making two cups. Aren't you having one? She shook her head and left the tea on the side for me to pick up.

Ruth's room was a white rectangle with a white mattress on the floor. There was no other furniture apart from a metal clothes rail. The walls were covered in Polaroids, sketches, and clippings of things that she found interesting. She had plants by the window, and a hanging ivy reached her pillow. It looked more like the room of a writer than mine.

She sat on the bed, but I stayed by the door. My coat was still on because I had missed the moment to remove it. Ruth was looking at me, and so I started the conversation by saying that she saw the best in everyone apart from him. She responded that it wasn't about him. We don't have to like each other's partners as long as they make us happy. Does he make you happy, Enola? I thought about the way he had dropped the bath bomb with a childish "kaboom."

Yes, I answered. He does.

And the times when he doesn't?

I told her that she was just remembering the bits she wanted to remember, and she said that I was hardly one to talk. She rubbed her forehead. I can't have this fight again, Enola. Just tell me what you've come to tell me. I explained that I had been soul-searching and that, in hindsight, I realized I had been oversensitive. She shook her head and said that, if anything, I wasn't sensitive enough. He was abusive, Enola.

Abuse is subjective.

Someone's intentions aren't subjective. He made you feel like shit.

Or did *I* make *myself* feel like shit? Because when I was with Virinder, I felt suffocated and—

The world isn't made up of two men! It is possible for both of them not to be right for you! And, Enola, he is not right for you. Until he sorts his shit out, he isn't going to be right for anyone.

I left my tea on the floor—I hadn't really wanted it, I had just wanted things to feel relaxed—and sat next to her on the mattress. Ruth, I think perhaps I've been going through something these two years and maybe I projected that onto him?

She took my hand and said that she thought that was true. Kenya must have brought up a lot, and I know that your dad could be—

I snatched my hand back and returned to the door. Why would you bring up my dad?

I'm sorry, I thought that's what you were saying!

That's literally the opposite of what—

I took a steadying breath.

I was *saying* that the relationship *wasn't*—Look, my dad was incredible, okay?

Ruth ran her tongue over her gums the way that she did when she was uncomfortable. But I was uncomfortable too. Fine, Enola. I shouldn't have mentioned your dad, but stop lying to me. Going back there was hard. And you've admitted that much. You got back and fell apart. That can't have all been about him. I'm sorry, but it can't have been.

That's exactly what I'm saying—that he wasn't to blame.

No. That sounds like what I'm saying, but it's not.

So, what are you saying?

I'm saying that maybe you should try and think about yourself. You've literally gone from one relationship to another and now you're telling me that you're getting back with him. With *him*. The man who made you cry every day, who made you so anxious that you started hurting yourself—

I was not hurting myself! Don't be so dramatic!

She cried out in frustration and said that she was so sick of hiding her feelings about this. I laughed.

Come on. Ruth, when have you *ever* hidden your feelings?

She said that she hid her feelings all the time when it came to him. She said that he lied to me, manipulated me, played on my emotions, and then made me feel guilty for having them. She told me that deep down I knew it but that I loved him so much I didn't care. Then she inhaled sharply and said: Your dad—

No! Stop it!

I told her that I was sick of hiding my feelings too. I said that she made me feel like a shit friend for not talking about her life, but then whenever I tried to, she pushed me away. I said that she wasn't upset about *him*. She was scared because *her* life was changing. She looked hurt and said that it was unfair to use what she had told me last week against her. I said that she was using my childhood against me. She shouted that it wasn't *against* me, it was *for* me. I said that I didn't realize her latest career was in psychology.

Don't . . . she said, shaking her head.

Don't what?

Be a bitch.

Oh, can we use that word now?

Stop! Ruth shouted, her voice squeezed through a straw. She put her hands over her face, and the blood drained from my own. I rushed to her side and put my arms around her. She was hurt. I had hurt her. I'm so sorry, I repeated over and over. I'm so sorry. I didn't mean it. She wiped her nose on the back of her hand like a toddler.

Enola, she said, he breaks you, and I'm worried that I won't be able to put you back together again.

All the king's horses?

Don't joke.

Sorry.

Ruth ran her hands back through her hair. You won't listen to me, but will you please just do this one thing? Ask yourself what you really want and what makes you happy. Promise me that you will look inward and think about it, Laa. *Think about how he makes you feel.*

When the police dropped me off at Catherine's house, Jon was on the phone and Catherine was cleaning the cupboards. But Ruth was showing me what went first: lettuce and then beef and then cheese. I couldn't lose her but I loved him.

I asked what would happen if, when I looked inward, all I found was him, and she told me that what I felt wasn't love. I asked if she would still be my friend if she was wrong. She went silent and then, staring at her palms, asked: Is that all I am to you?

What do you—

Nothing.

She stood and went to the door. She said that she needed to get sorted for Bath tomorrow.

You need the whole day for that?

Yes, I'm leaving tonight and staying over, she said, like I should have known. Then she added, more generously, that she was giving a presentation in the morning. I asked what the presentation was about, but she said that she needed to get on now.

Ruth, I—

Forget it, okay?

IN THE COURTYARD, THE blanket was bodiless on the swinging seat, and there was a full cup of tea on the ground. My tea was still on the floor of her bedroom. I wondered if Sally knew how Ruth liked her tea, and then I wondered if he knew how I liked mine.

I called him, and he answered like my name hadn't appeared on his phone. I told him that I was just coming from Ruth's and wanted to see him. He said that he was packing because he was moving tomorrow.

You're moving?

I am.

I asked where he was moving to, and he just said, "North," like we were in *Game of Thrones*. I asked him if I could come to his. He paused and then said: Fine, but I don't have ages. Pat's having a birthday dinner later.

THE BUS WAS SEVEN minutes away, and so I went to the tube station. I took the Piccadilly line to King's Cross and then changed to the Hammersmith and City, where the next train was due in three minutes. I went to put in my headphones, but something felt off. People were moving down the platform. I followed the glances and saw a man meandering close to the yellow line, wearing cream tracksuit bottoms with brown suit shoes, no socks, and a T-shirt that didn't cover his belly. He was cumbersome and, as I watched, drunk.

I walked up to him and saw that he was crying. Excuse me, are you okay? He looked at me like he had previously thought himself the only person on the platform, then said something that I couldn't understand, but I heard the words "prison" and "son." I told him that he should move away from the tracks. He lifted one foot and hovered it. My stomach dropped. *No! Don't do that!* But he laughed and dangled the other.

I looked back, and the platform was empty apart from a man with a red beanie who gave me a look that knew how this ended: *London Underground apologizes for the delay to your journey. This is because of a person on the tracks at King's Cross.*

The train was now two minutes away.

I edged closer and held out my arm. The man mumbled something, and I thought about grabbing him, but he was a big man. If he decided to jump, he could grab my hand and pull me with him.

The train was one minute away.

I told him that everything would be okay. He looked at me like he knew that it wouldn't be. His brown eyes were stained red. *Oh god.* I heard the train, a low rumble that would become a rip. Please, I said, *please* just move away from the edge. My heart was racing. He laughed again. I opened my mouth but no sound came out. Our eyes connected.

Just then, two members of staff arrived with the man in the red beanie and they maneuvered him against the wall as the train arrived.

MY HEART WAS STILL hammering when I arrived at Whitechapel. I called him, and he answered the same way as he had before. I told him about the man on the platform, and he said: Do you just want to go home, then?

What? No, I want to see you.

Okay.

I said that I would be there in ten minutes. I wanted to call Ruth and tell her about the man, because she would understand. I even considered going back the warehouse, but that old switch had been activated and I couldn't go anywhere else.

HE GREETED ME WEARING the gray T-shirt that Karen gave him last Christmas. I wanted him to hold me, to erase what had happened with Ruth, to erase what had happened on the tube platform, but he continued throwing items into boxes. I took off my coat, and he laughed at my T-shirt: Congratulations, very woke. His room smelled the same. Damp. Coffee. Aftershave. I never returned after we broke up because there was never anything to collect.

I asked him why he was moving, and he replied that last month he had found his flatmate staring into the cutlery drawer in the middle of the night. I said that we wouldn't be neighbors anymore. No borrowing that cup of sugar.

Or having that quick shag?

Well . . .

He arched an eyebrow. There's no time for *that*, Enola.

I sat on his desk chair, swiveling counterclockwise. I wanted to talk about our relationship, but his body language suggested that it wasn't the right time. I skated my fingers over his laptop: he would pack that last.

And what were you and Ruth up to? he asked with his head in a box.

What you feel isn't love.

Nothing, I said, explaining that she was preparing for a team-building day for her new job. He said that he hated those. I asked when he had done one, and he said that it was for a marketing job but it was stupid because he was a freelancer. I smiled at the thought of him working in a team. He continued derisively: We had to draw road maps as a metaphor for where we wanted the company to go.

I said that we did that in primary school once but for a different reason. Dad told me that people would die on my roads. He once told me about this insane accident where someone's head came clean off!

He turned over his shoulder and grinned. Is that why you're so jumpy? You thought that drunk man's head was going to come clean off?

That's not funny.

He sighed. Yes, I'm sorry. I'm an insensitive prick.

No, *I'm* sorry. I didn't mean that.

His phone vibrated on the desk, and he opened and closed his fist to indicate that he wanted me to pass it, so I did, and as he read, his face darkened. Fuck, he breathed, before dropping the phone on the bed. I asked if he was okay, but he erupted. No. Enola, I'm not *fucking okay.* I've edited this chapter a thousand times and he's still not happy.

Simon?

He's insisting on opening with one of Charlie's columns, like a prologue. If I had known that getting an agent meant changing everything, I'd have self-published. Fuck. I want a fucking cigarette.

He sat down on the bed and lifted his hands to his forehead. I hesitated and then sat next to him. I circled his back and told him that he should trust his instincts but that he should trust Simon's too. He said that he wasn't looking for advice and left the room. My hand dropped onto the bed, warm from where he had been sitting.

I felt a pain as familiar as the joy I'd felt in the bath yesterday. It was like pressing on an old bruise: how hard it was to make him happy. And there would always be something, a prize that he wasn't shortlisted for or a book cover that he didn't like. I remembered Ruth's words when we broke up: *Sometimes the good bits of people aren't the rule, they're the exception.* But I had argued that it was different. And so it had to be. He was the rule *and* the exception. The flaws that made him short-tempered made him brilliant. Just then his phone lit up. I didn't mean to look.

B, please can we talk. I miss you . . . x

I stood and backed away from the bed. What did it mean? The words could be innocuous, but the ellipsis? Mat had seen him with Steph that day, but were he and Steph . . . ? I recalled the joy in her eyes when she told me the story of their meeting. *And even though we were a terrible couple, we stayed mates.*

The door handle hit my spine. Well, why were you right there? he said, cross. But then he saw my face and asked what was wrong. He looked at his phone and then back to me. He charged to the bed and read the message. You have to be fucking kidding me. Then he moved to the desk like I might open his laptop next. How dare you, he said. *How dare you.* I asked if something had happened with Steph. He said that he didn't appreciate being treated like a villain in his own bedroom. Everything in my body went on high alert, and it felt like I was back on the tube platform. *We have been here before.* I tried to be different, clearer, more assertive. Ruth wouldn't be afraid to ask for what she wanted. Amy wouldn't be afraid of saying how she felt. I told him that if we were going to be a couple again, then we needed to be honest with each other. His features settled into a smile. Who said we were a couple, Enola?

I just assumed because you said—

What did I say?

But I didn't know how to finish.

Go on, Enola. What did I say?

What *had* he said? No, it wasn't what he had *said* but what he had written: *I want you.* But was that all he had done? When he wrote those words on my leg, I imagined the pronoun stressed: I want *you.* But what if it was just that he had *wanted* me. Hadn't he then moved up the bath and taken what he wanted?

Oh my god.

My eyes filled with tears. I thought about Ruth's cold tea.

He told me that he wasn't interested in watching me cry. He had packing to finish and a chapter to reedit. Then he continued putting things in boxes to demonstrate how little he cared about the argument. *Fuck him. FUCK him.* I asked what this was if not a relationship, and he turned, Christmas jumper in hand, and snapped: Look at yourself, you're in tears because you read a fucking message! I told him to answer the *fucking* question. He looked startled, but then he waved the jumper and said that we had hooked up once. Yesterday! We're having fun. Or we were before you demanded to know the state of our relationship.

How can you even—

But I couldn't finish because tears were streaming. I hated that this was my body's response to pain. At a sleepover in Nairobi, a boy punched me in the stomach to demonstrate how strong he was, and all I could do was double over onto his superhero rug. But I had wanted to hurt that boy then the way that I wanted to hurt this one now. There was a stack of hardbacked books by the desk. I thought about hitting him over the head with the *Oxford English Dictionary* and watching the blood drip, the life drain. But then he threw the Christmas jumper across the room and sunk onto the bed like I had made him as stressed as Simon Longman had. That urge to comfort him kicked back in, and the dictionary remained on the floor. I asked why he found it so hard to let me in.

Me let *you* in, Enola? Ha. That's rich.

What does that mean?

He gave me a look.

No. Stop changing the subject. Did something happen between you and Steph?

He said that he didn't owe me that. You don't see me demanding to know who you hooked up with, Enola.

His name was Virinder. Please just tell me!

He looked at me like he was surprised that I had said that and then answered: No, okay? Nothing happened between me and Steph. *Christ.*

I closed my eyes and caught the lights speckling. Outside, the wind moved the branches of a tree. I heard his voice, soft yet grave: Maybe this is a bad idea.

I opened my eyes, and he was shaking his head. My stomach turned. What is?

This, he said, gesturing to me. Clearly nothing has changed. And I get it. I can't imagine how hard it was to lose your dad, and your mum sounds like a piece of work, and so you have issues with trust, I guess. I don't know. I'm not a therapist and—

I don't want a ther—

He put his hands up and said that it didn't matter because he just didn't have the time. He said that he had worked so hard to get to where he was with his book and he couldn't lose momentum now. He buried his face in his hands, and my own thoughts flew from my head, leaving only that paralyzing desire not to lose him. I rushed to him and pressed my face to his shoulder. The softness of his gray T-shirt and the warmth of the blood beneath. I'm sorry. I'm so sorry. I ran my fingers through his hair and said things that I wasn't sure I meant but they came as easy as breathing.

The Steph thing is just an old insecurity, but I'm not that person anymore. I promise. Let's just have fun and see where it goes, okay? That's what I want. I just want to have fun and see where it goes. Okay?

He listed all the things he had to do on his fingers and then said: The thought of going through all that drama again, honey . . .

I assured him that we wouldn't. I said that I was just worked up because of what happened on the way here. He looked confused, and I reminded him about the man on the tube. I mentioned it like it was nothing but recalled the man's bare ankles appearing from polished shoes.

He rolled his eyes. Oh that. Jesus, Enola, it was just a drunk man. When you called, I thought you were going to say something *actually* bad.

I felt a whisper of anger again; he'd used similar words in Kenya when I admitted that I was struggling. Why was his instinct to belittle? I told him that it was scary at the time. He said in that case I was stupid to have gotten involved. I told him that I overreacted. About everything. He smiled and I was a baby bird again, featherless and helpless. I rested on his shoulder until he scratched my head and said, in a babyish voice, that he really had to keep packing. But then he added that, if I wanted, I could come to Pat's later.

Really?

He nodded.

This was huge. If he was inviting me to meet Patrick, then he must be serious about us. But was this what he *actually* wanted? I refused to put myself in another situation like when I met Steph. I needed him to *want* me there.

Do you want me to come?

He breathed in and out sharply. Enola, I've just told you that you can come if you want.

Yes, but do *you*—

Enola, stop it!

He said that he would be there, Pat would be there, and if I wanted then *I* could be there too. Like a maths teacher trying to explain subtraction: if Abdul takes two and Martha takes three, how many bananas does Jonathan have? He said the party was at Baker Street and suggested we meet on the platform at Aldgate in an hour.

As we said goodbye and I left his flat for the last time, two feelings permeated: the first was happiness that he was inviting me to the party and the second was how much I wanted to kill him.

CHAPTER 32

I TURN THE CLOTHES OVER ON THE RADIATOR, THEN GO BACK TO the bedroom and check my phone. No new messages, no updates, just a smashed screen, and it's gone half nine. I am out of time. What am I going to do? What would the women I admire do? That was redundant; they wouldn't have met him on the tube platform last night.

Think about it, Laa. Think about how he makes you feel.

Okay, break it down. What have I learned? I love him; I keep going back to him; I'm a mess. But *am* I a mess, or does he just *tell* me that I'm a mess? If I behaved in the same way and he called me adorable, would I *be* adorable? Is his voice just louder in my head than my own? Ruth is right: he is awful to me. But sometimes. Only sometimes. After every slap is a kiss in the sunlight. But is that just relativity? What if it was never real happiness? Just the absence of unhappiness? Like those seconds between period cramps when you're elated about the respite.

I reach back for the indentation in my skull.

Ruth told me to stop thinking about him and start thinking about myself. And she's right. He is two years out of thirty. That's less than ten percent of me. He is not responsible for everything.

I feel angry now, but it's a deeper anger, the way that arterial blood is darker red. I'm not what *he* tells me; I'm what *she* made me. It doesn't take a therapist to understand why I am the way I am. Because he died and she left. Because she burned the photos. They say that if you want a different outcome, you have to make a different choice. So I'm going to do something that I've never done on a Thursday: I'm going to call my mother.

I don't have to search for her; she is my first missed call from last night. A row of numbers that I never saved to my contacts but can recite from memory.

The fizzing sensation in my body is the same as before I told him that I loved him; before the words left my mouth, before the silence and the *don't be silly*. But I don't know what else to do. Amy told me that I needed to learn how to end a story, and Diana told me that a problem with the ending is often a problem with the beginning.

I wait for her to answer, but she won't. She's probably making a crumble or painting a picture of Milton the turtle or—

"Hello?"

Shit. I wasn't expecting Paul.

"Bonjour?"

Shit shit shit.

"Paul, it's . . . Is my . . . Is Sarah there? My mum. Is my mum there? It's Enola." There is silence, then whispering. He is holding his hand over the phone. I imagine her face changing when he tells her who is calling. She puts down her wine and tries to think of an excuse but—

"Enola? Is everything all right?"

She sounds worried. That wasn't the reaction I was expecting. I open my mouth, but the words catch.

"Enola, can you answer me, please? I tried to call you last night but you didn't pick up. What's wrong?"

Why is she worried? Mum is never worried. Inconvenienced, but never worried.

"Are you hurt?"

I regain my composure. "I'm fine, Mum."

"Enola, what is it, what do you need?"

I can't hear background movement or the television. Is she actually listening?

"For the love of god, Enola, what is it?"

"I want to talk about . . ."

"Yes?"

For a moment, I'm not sure what I want to talk about or even why I called. It felt as much an impulse as when I hit that girl at school with my hockey stick. But then the reason comes to me and I know that I can't exist another minute without the answers.

"Dad."

There is a pause while my words hang in the air, and I feel like I've said something that I shouldn't have. Mum shuffles and then: "Gosh, Enola, you are catching me a little off guard."

"Well, we never talk about him, so it's always going to catch one of us off guard."

"And I suppose that's because of me, is it?"

"Well, you don't bring him up, Mum. Twenty years went by last year without a mention. We never commemorate him. There's no grave. I don't even know the actual day that he died."

She laughs a small titter, like birdsong. "Why on earth would you want to know something like that?"

"Because that's what people do, Mum!"

"We moved on, Enola. *That's* what people do."

"I haven't!"

"Don't be silly. Of course you have. You've got your writing and your relationships in London."

"My writing? Not that you care."

"I care, Enola."

"No, you think that I'm never going to make it as a writer, you keep telling me how hard it is to get published, that's why you like Virinder. You want me to be with someone who can take care of me."

Her tone turns sharp. "Oh, Enola, it *is* hard to get published. Paul found these statistics the other day about writers and, well, it's statistically very unlikely. But I think you're perfectly capable. And I prefer Virinder, as you put it, because quite frankly he seemed more stable than that other man you were seeing. Catherine told me that he was quite tricky."

Bloody hell, Catherine.

"Okay, fine. I don't even care about any of that. None of that matters. I'm just so sick of not talking about the elephant in the room."

"And what's the elephant in the room?"

"Dad, Mum. Dad is the elephant in the room."

"I hardly think he's an elephant in the room."

"No, you're right. He's not an elephant, he's a body. A dead body on the kitchen floor and I can't breathe or move or *think* while he's lying there."

"Christ, Enola. Do you have to be so maudlin?" She stops, but I hold my ground and force her to continue. "Why you're calling to talk about something that happened over twenty years ago is beyond me."

"Dad wasn't just something that *happened.*"

She inhales quickly and immediately exhales the same way. "I'm not going to go over this now."

"When then? We never go over anything!"

"Well, I don't like to upset you. You won't remember it, but you would get very upset."

I do remember.

"But I was a child, Mum. You can't claim that you don't talk about Dad because of how I was as a child."

She makes a series of small noises. "Enola, let's talk about this another time."

"No! It can't be another time. It has to be now! Please, Mum."

"Goodness, you're always so dramatic. That's something that you got from him."

"See? That's what I'm talking about! Tell me why you hated him."

I wonder if she's hung up because she is silent, but then she speaks like she's trying not to be heard: "Enola, I loved your father."

I wasn't expecting those words. Photographs were burned in a bin in the garden. I had watched from my bedroom window and she had told me off for crying.

"You hated him, you hated Kenya, and you hated being a mother."

Mum makes a noise like a whimper, or a laugh. Then I wonder if it was the squeak of a glass. "That's not true. I liked Kenya—"

"No, you didn't, you—"

She interrupts me brusquely. "You've asked me a question. Let me finish."

I wonder then, am I looking for answers or am I just a toddler throwing down in a supermarket, kicking my legs?

She continues: "I liked Kenya but the reality, as with most things, was different to the idea. Your dad was working all the time. And the truth was that I was very isolated there by myself with a baby."

"With a baby? You mean me. Because you never really wanted me."

"Not wanting a baby and not wanting you—my daughter—are different things. You'll understand that when you're older."

"No, Mum. That line won't work anymore. I'm thirty now. I am older!"

"Well, then, you're old enough to understand that your father was a difficult man. I know that you have him somewhat on a pedestal but he was—"

"You just didn't understand him. He needed you and you didn't understand him."

I walk up and down by the bed. I knew my dad. *I* knew him.

"I didn't understand him? Oh, I see." She hums like she is nodding. "*This* is why I didn't want you talking to Louise. You should never have seen her when you went to Kenya."

I stop by the wardrobe and catch my reflection. "How did you know that I saw her?"

"Because she told me, Enola."

"You're in contact with Louise?"

"Occasionally. Louise is someone who needs careful handling. She always has."

My skin heats up. *What else don't I know?*

"Or maybe she's just angry and hurt. Dad was all she had."

"Jesus, you sound just like her." Mum sighs loudly, covers the phone, and says something I can't make out, then restarts with vigor: "We were always going to leave Kenya, Enola. Even before he died."

"Yes, because you hated it—"

"*Because* it wasn't working out for him at work. I'm not sure of the ins and outs, but his days had been numbered for a while. And Louise? Jesus, no one forced her to come out and no one forced her to stay. She used our house like her own personal hotel and spent most of her recreation time berating me. I cannot and will not be responsible for that woman anymore. We left as quickly as we needed to. I didn't want to start you any later in a new school year and the house belonged to the office. In terms of what happened—look, your dad left us with loose ends and I had to tie them."

My brain races to process everything. *Dad was going to be fired?*

"Fine," I continue, like a barrister conceding a point to make a larger one, "we had to leave and you're not responsible for Louise. But what about me? Why did you leave me? What did I do wrong?" As soon as I articulate that, my lower lip trembles.

"Don't be histrionic, Enola, I didn't *leave* you."

"*I'm not being histrionic!* You got on a plane! I was fourteen. Dad died and you got on a plane! *That's* how much you hated being with me."

"Don't be silly. There was nothing for us in Nairobi after your father died and after a few years in England, back at my parents', and, quite frankly, scrambling to pick back up a career that I had thrown away four years prior, I realized that there wasn't anything there for me either."

"There was me."

I pick at the books on my little bookshelf. Like in the living room, I've ordered them by color. I've arranged them as perfectly as I can, but close up the colors are all different shades.

"Enola, school in England was always the plan. Even if your dad stayed for work, we were always going to send you to England— god knows that the education system in Nairobi wasn't up to much and it wasn't *home*..." She takes a deep breath. "Maybe I should have waited until you were at university to go to France, but . . . well, Paul was an old friend from drama school and, after your father . . . Look, I needed a new start . . . *I* needed it . . . for *me* . . . and I don't expect you to understand, but that's just the way that it was. And I know that you're thirty now, you're a woman, but you've always been such a young soul. I suppose that's a miracle really, all things considered."

"Okay," I say, "but then why didn't you want me to come with you to France?"

"I did!"

"You did?"

"Of course I did. But everyone told me not to uproot you again and they were right. You had Granny and Grandpa and Ruth not too far away. You were starting your first big exam year. You were finally starting to thrive academically—you were very behind when you started. I wasn't about to move you to another country where you didn't know the language. You were just starting to be happy again. Staying in England was what you needed."

"What I *needed* was my mother."

"Well, I'm sorry for that, but I did my best and that's really all I can say about that."

"Your best? Your best was a cursory phone call every Wednesday? Like I was a task you didn't want to do, like taking the bins out?"

"It was the advice that I was given at the time. Therapists, teachers, they all told me to give you some normality. God knows you had been through enough. Structure was important. The only things that seemed to be working for you at the time were timetables and boundaries."

I remember that. Strict mealtimes. Time for my homework. Time to watch television or call Ruth.

"But if that was the case, then why do we *still* speak every Wednesday?"

"We don't, actually," Mum snaps. "We speak on *some* Wednesdays, whenever you happen to feel like it. You're an adult now, Enola—as you're keen to remind me—which means that you share responsibility. And to be quite honest, if we didn't still have the timetable in place, I'm fairly certain I wouldn't hear from you at all."

Is that how she sees it? I'm the ungrateful, selfish daughter. Is that what Paul thinks? Do they all complain about me around the big table on holidays?

"Fine, Mum. I could be better at sticking to our routine, but this isn't the point."

"What's the point then, Enola?" she says, exhausted.

"The *point* is why have we never spoken about any of this?"

"We have, actually. But like I said, you got very upset and, in the end, it was easier to move forward. I'm sorry that you have unanswered questions, but to be fair to me, I didn't realize that you had them until this evening. At the time, you didn't want to hear the details. You just wanted your dad and that was something I couldn't give you."

"I did try, though. I did!"

"And I gave you the answers I had."

I close my eyes and picture his face, but it's nebulous. I listen for his voice, but it's static. I don't remember Dad anymore.

Mum continues, softer: "I do know that I'm not always the best at these things, Enola, but they weren't exactly handing out instructions for how to deal with what your father put us through."

I can't hear this. He isn't here to defend himself. Mum is still the problem. She is still the problem. He is still dead.

"I hate the way that you talk about him."

"Enola, if you want to talk about your father, then you have to actually talk about him."

"He was amazing."

"Yes, sometimes. But he also drank too much and didn't think anything through. He was like Louise in that way. And it's not his fault—heaven knows the stories about his own parents were ghastly. But there were some days when I was scared to leave you alone with him in case he took you for a drive without any water or a spare tire. And his temper? His temper was getting worse."

"No," I say, "that's not how I remember it. Dad was always . . . He was the one who did everything. He was the one who played with me, who cooked, who—"

She interrupts me. "Your dad didn't cook."

"Not all the time but on Sundays! He cooked!"

"I cooked on Sundays, Enola. You were barely nine when your father died. I'm pleased that you have happy memories but you're blaming me for things that were out of my control. They say that people always blame the parent who stays."

How dare she . . . how dare she! The blood rushes to my head, and I start ripping the books from the bookshelf. All the greens and reds and blacks and yellows.

"But you didn't stay, Mum, you left, just like he did!"

I call her a liar. I shout that she was selfish to move to France and that the price of prioritizing my education is that I am now broken and it's all her fault. I shout that she treated Dad the way she treated Milton the turtle and that's why both of them are dead.

"Are you quite finished, Enola?"

"Stop it! You're acting like you're the one who . . . Don't put this on . . . If you had been there for him . . ."

Something drips onto my lip.

"That's enough now, Enola. I'm not listening to this anymore. It's time to grow up and remember things as they happened."

Her tone is harsh, but there is a vibrato that betrays her, and I have a gust of a memory. *She is handing me a glass of water and placing a cool hand on my forehead.*

I wipe my nose on the back of my hand.

"I do remember things as they happened. Dad was the one who . . . He was the one who . . ."

But as soon as I say them, I realize my words are wrong. My body turns cold. Because I remember: the shades of truth that I buried. That the face behind my own in the mirror that day wasn't my mum's, it was my dad's. It was the last time he tended to my bites. The last time he looked after me like that. The last time she let him? I remember the beer on his breath. I remember how she looked when she asked how I got the bruise.

My hand is smeared with blood.

"Yes. Fine. Enola, you're right. Your dad loved you and I'm sorry that I wasn't the mother you needed me to be. Now, Paul has just finished making dinner and so I'll speak to you next Wednesday. Okay?"

Oh my god.

"Enola?"

"Yes."

"Goodbye."

She hangs up the phone.

What have I done?

CHAPTER 33

I RUN TO THE BATHROOM AND PRESS TOILET PAPER TO MY NOSE. Blood is smeared down my chin. I think I might be sick, but it passes. I hold on to the side of the bath. Are all my memories wrong? Dad watched the stars. Dad ran to the sea. Dad told stories. Those memories are still true. Mum was detached. Mum was cold. Mum's voice sailed above his in arguments. But was that because she was crying? No, Mum wouldn't cry. She didn't even cry when he died. Yes, he could be reckless, and yes, he occasionally drank too much, but he wasn't a bad person.

I replace the red tissue with fresh sheets.

And she's speaking to me like I'm this child, like I don't know anything, but I'm the one who was with him that day! I may have rewritten smaller details, but I never rewrote that. If anyone deserves to be angry . . .

The tissue soaks through. I replace it again.

And then she has the audacity to accuse me of putting him on a pedestal! I had no choice! There wasn't even a funeral! All those years of silence. I didn't have photos. My grandparents wouldn't talk about him. Catherine was always more interested in talking about Mum. No one spoke about my dad apart from Louise. And her voice was so loud.

But what does that mean? Did I kill my mother to save my father?

There will be a knock at the door.

Ask yourself what you really want.

I breathe low and deep as the darkness turns pink. Both realities can be true. The vase is red and so it can't be blue, but once it could have been blue and so it still exists somewhere, floating around a dead galaxy in perfect blueness. I open my eyes to my hands. The same hands that twenty-one years ago gripped the seat belt and wondered if he was going to come back and take me for ice cream.

It's time to grow up and remember things as they happened.

BY THE TIME I got home, I had decided to meet him for Patrick's birthday. It meant something that he was inviting me, and I needed to see this through. I touched up my makeup and ran a straightener through my hair. He would tease me again, but there was no time to change, so my THIS IS WHAT A FEMINIST LOOKS LIKE T-shirt would have to do. Mum rang on schedule as I was leaving, but I turned my phone to silent.

At Whitechapel, there were delays on the district line. The station was heaving, and there was a group of drunk men wearing football shirts and chanting. I passed through the barriers and looked for him. He was standing in the middle of the platform with his feet over the yellow line. He was wearing his denim jacket and his black jeans. I remembered seeing him outside my front door holding a birthday cake, but then I remembered how Steph had helped him to make it.

I weaved through the crowds and squeezed until I was standing just behind him, close enough to see the white threads in the rip in his jacket. I went to tap him on the back but stopped.

I considered how he might feel when he saw me. So much of my happiness depended on his expression. Would he frown or smile? If the former, I would dance on the eggshells of the evening and try to please him like there was a gun to my head. The latter, I would be happy but know that it wouldn't last, would clutch the happiness like it was a bird in my hands until it suffocated. And he would tell me that it was my fault, that I killed the bird, but he would have been the one who put it there, placed his hand over mine, and squeezed.

A rumbling began in the tunnel. The lights of the train became visible. A receipt blew across the tiles. The football men shouted. I thought about every cruel thing he had ever done or said, and yet without thinking, I put my hand on his back and pushed.

Oh my god.

First the sound of metal, like screaming, then a hard sound, like a slap, like life leading you down a child's road map over a bridge of Sellotape and drinking straws, like *London Underground apologizes for the delay to your journey.*

What have I done?

The platform drew a uniform breath as he was sucked beneath the train. All the pieces of him that I loved were destroyed. The mole on his forearm and the glint in his eye. The items in his pockets and the smell of his cooking. His favorite songs and the sound of his laughter. His reading glasses and the gray in his hair. His silver chain and his plans for his weekend. His unpublished book and his unspoken words.

Here you go, Mum, look what I made you.

The panic was contagious as everyone fled, and in the push, I tripped. My phone skidded, and the heel of a shoe kicked back against my collarbone. But I made it out under the stars just as the sirens came wailing, and I ran all the way home.

I removed my clothes and left them by the wardrobe. I should have destroyed them—they were evidence—but they still smelled like his hug from earlier. My phone screen was smashed. That was evidence too. Not that it mattered, because they would watch the security footage and see that he was pushed. By his girlfriend? By his ex-girlfriend. He always said that she was crazy. Patrick would be waiting for us at the party. *He always liked you, Enola. He was always rooting for us.* I couldn't think about that now. I wanted to call Ruth. She would know what to do. Go to the police? Turn myself in? What do you do when there is a body? What do you do when someone is dead? I needed her to comfort me. I needed her to tell me my school shoes were cool. I needed her to help me drag the body across the kitchen floor.

I put on my *Mario Kart* T-shirt and got into bed. I told myself that it would be better in the morning. I would have some time. When the police arrived, I would be ready.

MY NOSE HAS STOPPED bleeding! I wash the blood from my hands and return to the bedroom. The books are all over the floor, but I don't want to tidy them. I don't want to do anything. I am exhausted. My body is aching from falling at the station. My mind is aching from the truth. That he is dead. That I killed him. *That he asked for it.* I'll just rest my eyes for a moment. The pillow is cold, and Dad is driving, but he won't say where we are going. Can we go for ice cream after? They'll be here soon, they'll be here soon, they'll—

SHIT.

Someone is knocking at the door. Or did I imagine it? Then—two definite raps. Here we go. I'm ready.

CHAPTER 34

BY THE TIME I GOT HOME, I HAD DECIDED TO MEET HIM FOR PAT-
rick's birthday. It meant something that he was inviting me, and
I needed to see this through. I touched up my makeup and ran a
straightener through my hair. He would tease me again, but there
was no time to change, so my THIS IS WHAT A FEMINIST LOOKS LIKE
T-shirt would have to do. Mum rang on schedule as I was leaving,
but I turned my phone to silent.

At Whitechapel, there were delays on the district line. The station
was heaving, and there was group of drunk men wearing football
shirts and chanting. I passed through the barriers and looked for
him. He was standing in the middle of the platform with his feet over
the yellow line. He was wearing his denim jacket and his black jeans.
I remembered seeing him outside my front door holding a birthday
cake, but then I remembered how Steph had helped him to make it.

I weaved through the crowds and squeezed until I was standing
just behind him, close enough to see the white threads in the rip in
his jacket. I went to tap him on the back but stopped.

I considered then how he might feel when he saw me. So much of
my happiness depended on his expression. Would he frown or smile?
If the former, I would dance on the eggshells of the evening and try
to please him like there was a gun to my head. The latter, I would
be happy but know that it wouldn't last, would clutch the happiness
like it was a bird in my hand until it suffocated. And he would tell

me that it was my fault, that I killed the bird, but he would have been the one who put it there, placed his hand over mine, and squeezed.

A rumbling began in the tunnel. The lights of the train became visible. A receipt blew across the tiles. The football men shouted. I thought about every cruel thing he had ever done or said, but before I could decide what I wanted, I was pushed.

I fell to my knees, and my phone skidded from my pocket. I retrieved it, but the screen was smashed. Three men in football shirts were shoving to the front, oblivious of the damage they had caused. My anger was now for them. The same person, the same man, the same predator. Like the women of Thebes, I wanted to rip them to pieces. I shouted, and one turned, red-eyed. What did you say?

You pushed me. Aren't you going to say sorry?

What the fuck is your problem?

You smashed my phone, you fucking arsehole. You should say sorry.

He grabbed me by the shoulders, and his thumb dug in below my collarbone. The other two men tried to calm him down: She's not worth it, mate, leave her. Bitch. He said that I was asking for it. But before he could give me what I was apparently asking for, the train doors started beeping. One of the men prized them apart, and they pushed into the swollen carriage, somewhere in the middle of which, on his way to Patrick's birthday party, he was.

Two women approached from the other side of the platform. One had flower beading in her blond curls. Come with us. They led me through the barriers. They were going to a hen do in Spitalfields and walked me home first. They told me familiar stories. One, about a man who followed her home. The other, about a man who threw a stone at her head. I forgot to ask their names.

I took my clothes off and left them by the wardrobe.

THIS IS WHAT A FEMINIST LOOKS LIKE.

I crouched in the shower until the water ran cold.

I put on my *Mario Kart* T-shirt and got into bed. The next time my eyes opened, light was seeping through the blinds. I reached for my phone and saw the cracked screen. There were three missed calls and four messages. I sat upright.

> *You coming?*
>
> *We're going to that pub by the canal. Call me if you're coming*
>
> *You could have let me know, Enola*
>
> *Look, you should know that I had a long chat with Pat tonight . . . I'll be over tomorrow at about 10 p.m. after I've moved house. We should talk. x*

CHAPTER 35

HE IS STANDING ON THE WELCOME MAT WITH TULIPS IN HIS HAND. I gesture for him to come into the living room, and he walks past me to the sofa. I put the tulips on the counter and wonder which of us should speak first. It's him, of course.

"So . . . you never showed last night," he says, like a police officer.

Somewhere, I am in bed with him talking about how much fun Patrick's birthday was. Somewhere else, I am alone wondering how Patrick's birthday went so wrong. He thinks that I chose not to meet him last night. He doesn't know that the choice was taken from me. He also doesn't know that, in another draft, he is a dead body on the tracks.

"Why, Enola?"

There is a gentleness in how he says my name, and my throat tightens. There he is: a blood shadow stuffing a turkey with an onion because a lemon would be overpowering. *This is our first Christmas,* I say, wrapping my arms around the torn ligaments in his neck. *It's not actually Christmas, honey. We've got mistletoe,* I say. *That's sage,* he replies. We laugh until the turkey is golden, and his corpse is scraped from the tracks like gum.

I wonder what it felt like.

"Enola?"

"Okay, so look—" I start to speak, but he stands up and advances, cautiously, like he's asking for consent to be closer. I don't give it but I don't refuse it either and so now he is holding me. His breath is coffee, and his eyes are red. He is wearing the same gray T-shirt. He is hungover and tired from moving house. (Somewhere, I am flattered that he made it over tonight.)

"Honey, yesterday you said that if we were going to be a couple, then we had to be honest with each other and, well, Pat said the same thing."

Honey. It's jarring, like hearing it whispered in an empty room.

"So, here's the thing," he continues, looking down, "you asked me about Steph, and the truth is"—he pauses—"that something did happen."

I go to move, but he locks his hands behind my back.

"*But* it's not what I want."

I try to pull away again, but he holds fast. "Please listen, Enola. You owe me that much."

"I owe you nothing!"

"I think Steph got jealous because she knew that you were the first person in a long time who I was really into. And then when I saw on Instagram that you were seeing that guy, what's his name, Vinchester?"

"*Virinder.*"

"Whatever. Look, I got jealous and something happened when we were drunk. She wanted it to happen again but I didn't."

My face feels hot and my heart is racing.

"Did you hear me? But *I* didn't."

"You lied to me."

"I didn't lie to you."

"I asked you a direct question and you lied!"

"Because it didn't mean anything and I didn't want you to make it into a big deal!"

"A big deal . . . How can you even . . . ?" I try to wriggle free, but he holds my face. I try to remove his hands, but I can't, and so I hold them as they hold me. I tell him to stop it, but he says no. His eyes are burning. "I'm sorry, Enola. Okay?"

"It's not enough."

"I know, look, you're right. I lied last night. I don't know why I'm like that. I'm a cunt. I'm an arsehole. I didn't want to hurt you and I felt attacked and I lied and I'm sorry. I'm sorry, okay?"

He has never apologized like this before. I loosen my grip, and he loosens his. I move away from him and sit at the kitchen table. He sits in the seat opposite. I drop my head and speak into the wood. "When we were together, did anything . . . ?"

"No! Of course not."

"Is it over now?"

"Yes! Look, it was a huge mistake. She's very intense and she thought that it all meant something that it didn't. If anything, Enola, you're the one who put the idea in my head."

I think about how he speaks about the women in his life. His ex-girlfriend, Jessica. His stepmother, Karen. Now Steph? Everyone was intense, everyone was crazy, lunatics all.

"So it's my fault you hooked up with your ex and lied about it?"

He cocks his head. "Honey, I admit that I reacted badly. But to be fair, you had just read my message—"

"*I didn't mean to read your*—"

"Yes, fine, you didn't *mean* to read it." He lifts his hands to instruct me to lower my voice. "But then when you didn't show up last night, I realized that I had been a twat and I spoke to Pat and he made some really good points. I'm thirty-seven now and everything is finally working out with my book." He waits for me to respond, but I'm speechless. "Well. That's something . . . isn't it?"

"What is?"

"That I'm telling you I want to be with you."

He looks as though he's spent weeks finding me the perfect gift, and it hasn't occurred to him that I don't want it. Strangely, the end sequence of *The Matrix* comes to mind, where Neo sees everything as green coding. I always knew that he was selfish and narcissistic, but, for the first time, I can look past the effect it has and see the mechanics.

"Isn't this what you want?"

Think about it, Laa. Think about how he makes you feel.

"No," I say.

His eyes search mine. "But yesterday . . ."

"Yesterday was a mistake. I asked you about Steph and you manipulated me and that's what you always do when things don't go your way."

"I didn't manipulate you."

"You're doing it right now! You're saying that you lied because you didn't want me to make a big deal about it. You're trying to back me into a corner, so then when I react, you can say: 'See, that's what I was afraid of!' We both know what you're doing. I don't want to hear your excuses. I just want you to leave."

His face changes, and he leans back in his chair. "You only want me to leave because you know what's going to happen if I stay."

"You speak like we're inevitable."

"We keep ending up together," he replies with a slanted smile.

"That doesn't mean what you think it does."

Shifting forward, he clasps his hands. "You can't just turn off your feelings, Enola."

I move back on my chair. "No, but I can change my actions."

"You're just angry because of Steph," he says, shaking his head.

I stand and move into the living room. "Of course I'm angry about Steph! It makes me feel sick thinking about you together! You've lied to me countless times about her and—"

He turns in his chair to face me. "No, I didn't lie! Not really. Not when it counted. It's just complicated between her and me sometimes."

I hate hearing that. *It's complicated between me and you.*

Out the balcony window, red and green lights zip up and down the Shard like shooting stars. Or shooting pains.

"I know that you feel something for me, Enola."

I turn back, hands wide. "Yes, of course I do. I love you." This is only the second time that I've articulated it. The words feel powerful. "But it doesn't matter what I feel because it's not what I want."

"And what about what *I* want?"

"I've been compensating for what *you* want for two years. You don't love me."

"That's not true," he says.

I wipe a layer of dust off the orange spines on the bookshelf.

"It's *not*," he repeats emphatically. "Look at me, Enola."

The turquoise Vonnegut is still in the wrong place. I move it back to where it should be.

"Look at me," he says again, and so I do. He is resting his elbows on his knees, and his eyebrows are forcefully raised. "Enola, I"—my heart flips the way it did that night outside the beach house—"I do love you." But after he says the words I have waited to hear for two years, he swallows and puts his fist to his mouth, grimacing in a way that implies it was last night's alcohol he just regurgitated.

I turn back to the books.

"Did you hear me?" he says, voice croakier from the stomach acid.

It's strange, but I always assumed it would feel like a victory when he said those words to me, like his love was a trophy I could win by running faster than everyone else. But now that he has said them, they sound unnatural, and I'm angry that he would be so reckless with my heart that he would fight to change my feelings knowing that his own might have changed by morning.

"You don't love me," I say.

He slams his hand on the table. "How *dare* you tell me how I feel? *That's* your problem, Enola. You always assume that you know how I feel. Fuck me. You're acting like you're perfect. Well, let me tell you, you're not fucking perfect. You're selfish. Self-obsessed. Self-centered."

I face him and shout: "*All of those mean the same thing.*"

"*Yes, well, that's how fucking self-absorbed you are.*"

"What else?" I ask. He is the band around my wrist.

"You're the victim of your own story. You apologize all the time and you think that makes you nice but it makes you manipulative.

You never say what you mean. You're passive-aggressive. You never give me the benefit of the doubt. You accuse me of things that you do yourself. You don't talk about your feelings; you don't talk about what you're afraid of; you don't talk about your issues. You're a hypocrite."

"Are you finished?"

"Do you want me to be? Because you're enjoying this, I think."

I laugh, and his tone softens; we are like waves in the ocean moving back and forth.

"Look, last night I was just stressed and—"

"You're always stressed."

He stands and walks toward me, but I hold out my palm and halt him by the coffee table.

"Fine. I'm a big stressy nightmare. I'll do better," he says with a sigh.

"No."

"No?"

"No."

"We're not even going to try?"

"We have tried."

"*I* haven't tried!"

"That's not my problem."

He lifts his arms then drops them. "Fuck, why are you being such a—"

"Such a what?"

He doesn't answer; he just looks to the ceiling like he needs a moment to recharge. But I don't give it to him. I don't need to do anything for him anymore. I don't need to be *cool* or *funny* or *nice*. I move past him into the kitchen and continue: "This is *your* problem. You only care about people when they're useful to you."

"What the fuck does that mean?"

"It means that you love me until you don't. You've just come in here and told me that you're happy with your book and you're thirty-seven and all that shit and *now* you want me. People are people. They're not things you can pick up and put down. You want me *right now* but tomorrow I'll say or do something that doesn't serve you and you'll lose your temper again!"

"People fight, Enola. It's not a big deal. And yes, thanks for pointing it out, I can be selfish sometimes, but you're the one who got insecure and sensitive and stopped being able to laugh at anything."

"I didn't stop laughing, you just stopped being funny. And I was right to be insecure because you *did* hook up with Steph!"

I face the stove, thinking about his hands in her black hair, her thin lips on his neck, the words he said to her in the dark. *You're the only one who understands me, Steph.* I hear him inhale on his vape pen like it's his inhaler. I turn back and notice how red his face is and the thickness around his waist.

He rubs his mouth. "Steph and I happened when you were with someone else, so it shouldn't really concern you. I didn't even need to tell you and I'm really wishing that I hadn't, to be frank."

"Don't do that. Don't backtrack."

"No, I *am* sorry that I lied. But you *are* insecure, Enola."

"If you think someone's insecure, then you reassure them! You don't double down!"

"I'm not going to pander to people," he says, matter-of-fact, the same tone he used when he told me that his dad advised him to prioritize himself in a relationship.

"It's not pandering, it's kindness, and I've spent years feeling like I wasn't good enough or loved enough, so why would I put myself through more of that just so you can feel like you don't have to pander to anyone?"

"Don't be dramatic. *Obviously* I've never wanted you to feel like that," he says lightly, flicking his eyes over his shoulder like there's someone there to agree with him.

I think about the way it feels when he smiles at me, like I'm in on the joke. I wonder if I've ever really been in on the joke. I remember what Ruth said at my party two years ago: *It seems to me like the jokes are his.*

"It's not *obvious*, though. You're a lion. You pounce. You wait for weak moments and then you pounce."

"You pounce too, Enola."

"You think getting emotional is an attack?"

"It is!"

"It's not!"

"Stop acting like you're innocent."

"That's not what I'm saying."

"You literally just compared yourself to a gazelle."

"That wasn't the point of the metaphor."

"It's not all my fault when we fight, Enola."

"But I never *want* to hurt you. You are actively unkind, and I've come to realize that is one of the worst things someone can be."

He begins pacing. "Great, so now I'm the *worst thing* that someone can be? Last night you wanted us to be together and now I'm the *worst thing* that someone can be?"

I pour myself a glass of water. He stops pacing and stares while I drink, challenging me to respond, which I do, calmly: "Yes, and I've been acting like I don't have a choice and I do have a choice. We always have a choice."

He scoffs. "Come on. This is just Ruth's shit."

I slam the glass down on the counter. "This has got nothing to do with Ruth. All Ruth has ever done is ask me what *I* want. When have you ever asked that? When have you ever cared about what I want or feel or think, even?"

He approaches me, and I back against the fridge.

"That's not fair, Enola. You can't accuse me of not being there for you when you never tell me anything."

"Because you don't want to know! You like to feel needed but you don't actually want to *be* needed."

"No, you're the one pushing *me* away. And it's not the first time. You broke up with me, remember? You're so quick to forget the things that don't support your argument."

"I broke up with you because I told you that I loved you and you told me not to be silly."

His mouth opens and closes as if he's thinking of what to say; then he sits at the kitchen table. "Fine, okay, I shouldn't have said that, and maybe I wasn't ready at the time, but we were just finding our feet again."

"You were relieved. Your exact words were: 'I understand.'"

"And then you moved on to that guy instantly."

"That was two months later and . . ." I put my hands over my face. "*This* is why I didn't want to talk."

He smiles and says: "Because you know that I'm right."

"*Because* it's pointless. It doesn't matter. What you're saying doesn't matter. This isn't about you. It's about me. I'm at the stage of my life where I know what I want and—"

"Aha! This is what it's really about," he says, nodding. "Houses and marriage and babies."

I slam my head back against the fridge. "*Shut up!*"

"'Shut up'?" he says, amused, angry. He folds his arms and looks at me like I'm a painting in a gallery he is studying.

"Firstly, there's nothing wrong with wanting that stuff and, secondly, stop telling me what I'm thinking and start listening to what I'm saying! God, why do you feel the need to dominate everything? You take up all the room! What I *want* is to be a person. A whole fucking person. And I'm never going to be that if I'm with you!"

He is silent, and then he exhales. "Look, Enola. I know I'm shit at the emotional stuff and I can be a short-tempered cunt but we do make each other happy."

"Feeling happy and being happy are different things."

His face contorts. "What the fuck would you know about being happy? You've just told me you've spent years feeling not good enough and not loved enough."

"Fuck you."

His eyes flash. He stands and moves to me. He presses his palm on the fridge and leans so our faces are close. "What makes you happy, then?" he says in a near whisper. "That guy with the hair? Does he make you happy?"

I maintain eye contact even though my heart is pounding. His black waffle jumper has a toothpaste stain, and I want to lick my finger and clean it for him.

"Normal things make me happy. Not existing from one fight to another, not wondering how you feel about me every second of every day, not spending those days thinking about you instead of myself. Not being in constant fight-or-flight."

"Okay, well then, just listen. I spent all night talking to Pat and—"

"No. There is nothing you can say. The last two years have been about you. The things you've said and the things you haven't. Even when I was with someone else, it was still about you—which makes me a really shitty person, by the way. But I'm done. I don't want my good days to be days that you decide are good and my bad ones to be ones that you decide are bad."

He tucks my hair behind my ear and his hand lingers on my neck. "Sorry to break it to you, honey, but that's a relationship. Maybe you're not ready for one."

He tilts his head like he's about to kiss me, and it would be so easy to let him. But instead, I say: "Or maybe you *are* just a cunt."

He drops his hand.

"Please go now."

He waits for me to say something else, but I slide away from him and walk down the hall to the front door. He doesn't follow imme-

diately, but when he does, he looks bemused. I hold the door open
for him to leave.

"Fine, Enola, if that's what you want, then. I'll go."

He moves to the door, and our faces are close again. I want to
run my fingers through the silver in his hair. He searches my face and
then says: "Goodbye, then?"

He's added a question mark because he thinks that we've been
here before. But this isn't another twist in the plot. This is the end.
Or rather, the revision. I'm rewinding the story until I'm back in the
pub in Broadway Market listening to Amy pontificate about paint
colors and he's putting his feet up and calling Chris a cunt and I'm
thinking about taking the bus home but deciding to walk because I
love the rain.

"Goodbye," I say with a forceful full stop.

I was never scared of living without him. I was scared of him
leaving. Like wanting a tumor removed but being terrified of dying
on the table.

"Wait." His hand stretches before I can close the door. "I'm sorry."

"I don't need that."

"I know, but I mean it. There is just something about us that
brings out the worst in me, but that has never been your fault."

He keeps his palm on the door as if he's afraid that I will close it
before he's finished speaking, then smiles—a burnt end of a smile—
and removes his hand. I think about the perfectly cylindrical mole on
his forearm that looks like a planet, how it's not actually a mole, it's
a pencil mark from school. Then I close the door and I am still alive.

AFTER HE LEAVES, I go to the bathroom, turn on the shower, and
undress. There is the comforting hum of the water pump as the room
heats with steam.

but that has never been your fault

I feel the water in my bones. It's like the first shower after camping. My skin is hot and cold at the same time. I imagine the hairs on
my arms like trees in a forest, myself as a universe.

but that has never been your fault
I turn off the water and wrap myself in a towel.
but that has never been your fault
I put on a new T-shirt, tuck myself into bed, and disappear.

CHAPTER 36

THERE IS A BREEZE THROUGH THE OPEN WINDOW, FLOATING THE curtains. There is calamine lotion on my bedside table. Mum is at the door with a glass of water. How is the itching today, sweetheart? She places the back of her hand on my forehead and—

"I KNOCKED BUT YOU didn't hear me, so I used my key." Ruth is on the edge of the bed, playing with her hands.

"Oh my god." I plunge across the bed. "Roo!!!"

"I bought croissants. *Two* this time, before you kick off."

She is here. She is here and she still loves me.

I inhale the morning in her curls. The books on the floor have been placed back in the bookshelf.

"What are you doing here?"

"One of the girls was driving back last night, so I jumped in with her. I felt weird about yesterday and you didn't message . . ."

"I didn't know if you wanted to hear from me."

"Of course I did!"

"You need to know that I thought about everything and I'm so sorry."

Ruth twirls the mood ring on her finger. The stone is a bright green. "No, don't be. I was just scared of losing you. But if you tell me that he's changed, then"—she tenses like a cat before it vomits—"then I'll support you."

"You don't need to. It's over, for real this time. The killer has to die twice, right? Or three times, in this case."

She stops twirling the ring and studies my face. "Don't say it if it's not what you want."

"It is. I promise."

"Okay, well, if it happens again, just know that I'll be here for you."

"That won't be necessary, Roo. It's over."

She tilts her head and smiles. "Laa, I know that you like to have everything tied up in a bow, but life is messy."

"I know life is messy."

"Yes, but you don't *like* that it is."

"No one *likes* that it is."

"I do."

"Then we're talking about different things."

Ruth suggests tea and leads me to the kitchen, where the light is pouring through the windows. The tulips that were left on the side have been trimmed and placed in the vase on the table. I feel something when I see them, but it's not unpleasant; it's more that I'm glad someone has taken care of them. Ruth gets two mugs out of the cupboard. One is the enormous Sports Direct mug. That will be hers. She will squeeze the tea bag and add a thimbleful of milk. The other is slimmer with a flower pattern. That will be mine. She will lightly dunk the bag and then pour milk until the liquid resembles pond water.

"So, how was yesterday?" I ask, leaning against the fridge, which he pressed me against last night.

She says that it was lame. "But I'm looking forward to starting properly. My presentation went well and I like the people. But if I hate it and decide to leave, then that has to be okay too."

"It will be, if that's what you want."

"I do have a hilarious story to tell you about the training exercises, though."

"Tell me."

"Later. You're not ready yet."

She tells me to sit while she makes the tea. I move to the sofa and pull the blanket over me. She puts her hair up in a bun with the leopard-print scrunchie from around her wrist and fills the kettle. "How was yesterday for *you*?"

The washing is still on the radiator behind the sofa. I touch my feminist T-shirt, and the fabric is dry.

"Ruth, honestly, it's been the strangest twenty-four hours. So, the night before last, after I saw you, I got into a fight with this guy at the station and—"

"A fight? *What?*" Ruth switches off the stove and sits with me.

"Not a *fight* fight, but I was pushed and then sort of pushed again."

"That sounds like a fight. Are you okay?"

"Yeah, I'm fine."

"Are you sure?"

"Yes. I mean, I lost the fight. But I should have handled it differently."

"Why, what would you have done?"

"I don't know. Maybe not confronted him? But he knocked into me and smashed my phone and I didn't want him to get away with it. But then he shoved me and got away with it anyway. So there's no winning."

"No, there's no winning. Well, no, that's not true. You're winning by being you. These guys are going to be the losers ultimately. Even if they don't know it yet."

Ruth tucks the loose strands of her hair into the newly constructed nest on top of her head. She always looks effortlessly beautiful, like an art student from a movie who's always got paint on her jeans and carries an armful of books and a portable coffee that she never spills even though she runs everywhere.

"Anyway, to cut a longer story short, I called my mum last night."

"You did? Wait, on a Thursday? What did you talk about?"

"Dad."

"Oh."

"She told me I put him on a pedestal and that he wasn't perfect. Did you know?"

"That you put him on a pedestal?"

"That he wasn't perfect."

"I mean . . . well, yeah. But, Enola, didn't *you*?"

"I don't know," I say, understanding now the capacity I have for both knowing and not knowing something at the same time. "But what does that mean? Am I supposed to just forgive her for everything?"

Ruth's chest drops with a breath. "I don't know, Laa. She isn't perfect either. She handled it badly. But she does love you."

I pull my knees up. "I have all these memories of my dad being fun and . . . now it's like I don't know either of my parents."

"How well do any of us know our parents? Think of my dad—he doesn't even know who his parents are."

"Has he ever tried?"

"I think he did once but there weren't great records. Lots of unwanted babies. Mum looked up her ancestry once, though."

"Oh yeah?"

"Yeah. My Scottish ancestors were rat catchers."

"Excellent."

"Ambition is in my genes."

The clouds move, and the room darkens for a second.

"Ruth, you don't have to answer, but what do *you* remember of my dad?"

She adjusts her bun. "I remember that holiday in the Mara."

"Were there good bits?"

"Of course! Look, I know you, Enola. You're going to be eager to organize your thoughts. But it's not about deleting the good; it's just about making room for the bad. Likewise with your mum. You must have some happy memories?"

I think about Mum at the door with a glass of water, and my eyes fill with tears. Ruth leans to hug me. "Don't," I tell her. "I'll just cry. Just tell me what else you remember, Roo. Please?"

"Honestly, mainly I just remember seeing you after," she says.

"Catherine made tacos."

"She did." Ruth smiles.

"I hadn't had tacos before."

"Enola, what do you remember of that day?" she asks softly, carefully, because she has never asked me that before.

I look at my hands.

The way a child draws hands.

"I remember the noise of the train. People telling me in Swahili that they would be here soon, and I thought the 'they' meant Mum and Dad. I remember the sirens and this pervading feeling that I had done something wrong. Everyone was so odd with me, especially Mum. I remember asking him if we could go for ice cream afterward. *Afterward.* Like he was going into the post office or filling up the car or something."

Ruth takes my hand and circles my palm like she's reciting that rhyme about the teddy bear in her head.

"Those train stations in England—you know the ones in the countryside?"

She nods.

"I still can't use those. They're nothing like where he . . . but I tried once, for a festival, do you remember? You were meeting me there, I think. Anyway, I had to leave the platform and catch the bus. It's weird. I don't remember the details but I remember the feeling."

"Enola, there was nothing you could have done."

"And, like, I keep thinking how far we must have driven—there are so many tracks in Kenya, but to find a working part, with that train to the coast, arriving at that time? And I would have just been sitting on the seat next to him, waiting to find the right spot, for hours, oblivious, just happy to be with my dad."

Ruth grips my hands. "It wasn't your fault. Okay? Your dad killed himself."

She looks at me like she has been waiting to say those words.

"I do know that. I do." I smile so that she knows I'm being honest. "It's strange. I used to have this place in my head, like *home*, and it's not home, it never was. And it's the same with Dad."

"You can't go home again—that's the saying, isn't it?"

"And it's especially true if you lose a parent."

The more that Ruth and I talk, the more I think that home isn't anything real, not a place or a building or a person; it's just a sense of something, an inaccessible realm of playing in the grass and being called in for tea, of a towel held out after a bath and ice cream dripping on bare toes.

"Fuck! I was making tea." Ruth slaps her forehead and goes to the kitchen. The stove clicks on. "You know, when I tell people that I lived in Kenya, they always assume I'm Kenyan. I mean, I was there for four years, the same as you. It's all very 'Africa is a country,' you know?"

I turn to the kitchen. "Where do you think of as home, Roo?"

"I don't know. But I've lived in London longer than anywhere else," she says, opening the fridge and sniffing the milk. "I'm really proud of you, Enola."

"Because the milk's in date?"

"Yes," she says with a grin.

Ruth gets the tea bags from the cupboard and puts them in the mugs. I turn to the bookshelf where all the books are in the right place.

"Roo, do you think that was why the relationship with him didn't work? Because I kept him at a distance?"

"That's ridiculous. He knew how much you loved him."

"But did he know *me*?"

"Did he try to?"

"Maybe not. But I don't think that I really wanted him to. He was never going to push, and so it was safe. I never even told him what really happened with Dad. If he had lied about something like that, I would have accused him of not letting me in."

The kettle begins to whistle.

"He *didn't* let you in."

"But you know what I mean."

Ruth scoops my tea bag out—

"Enola. I think you gave it everything. And I think you didn't give him that information about your dad because you knew, on some level, that it wasn't safe to."

—and presses hers on the side of the mug.

"I'm glad that I met him, though, Roo. Maybe these two years have been necessary. Like how a summer storm clears the air?"

But as I say it, I know that's the wrong metaphor; it's more accurate to say that something was disturbed, like how a change in weather can reveal a body.

"Save that for the next book," Ruth says, smiling.

I feel love thick as honey for her, my best friend, my partner, my family. She pours the milk with her tea bag still in the mug. She won't remove it until there is a residue like skin on custard.

"Roo, you told me yesterday that what I felt wasn't love."

"I'm sorry," she says, cringing visibly at hearing her words back. "I shouldn't have said that. It's not for me to say what you feel."

"No, you were right. But I don't think that love is one thing. We pretend that the word means the same thing for everyone, but it doesn't. I've been pushing you away and I'm so sorry. I promise I won't do it again. Because the way I love you is every definition, every dictionary, every translation."

We look at each other for a moment until we are interrupted by my phone in the bedroom.

"Go and get that. I'll put the oven on for the croissants."

In the bedroom, I get to my phone just as it stops ringing. There is a missed call from Diana. My heart instinctively races, the way it has every time I've seen Diana's name on my phone over the past few months and wondered if that email would be the one to change my life. But then my heart calms. I know why she is calling. This will be the final word, the *We'll have better luck with book two.* It's strange, but it doesn't feel like a failure. Writing my book was the best thing to come from the past two years, the thing that I will remember long after *his* name has faded from my lips. It's okay if no one wants to publish this book. I'm only thirty. I will write another one.

My phone vibrates. Diana has left a voicemail.

I look at the notification, appreciating how different I feel, and then press play. First, the sounds of the office, then my name, and then Diana gives the news. Everything slows and then accelerates until I am back in the kitchen, where Ruth is eating Virinder's peanut butter with a spoon.

"Can I eat this?" she says, mouth full. Then: "Enola, what is it?"

"That was Diana."

My voice is high and shaky, and Ruth puts the jar down.

"... and ... ?"

"... and we have an offer ..."

"... an offer ..."

"... to publish my book ..."

"Oh my god."

"It's an independent publisher. A small place. But Diana wants me to come to the office after lunch to talk about it. The editor wants to meet, apparently."

"*Oh my god!*" Ruth screams and runs to me. She lifts me up and spins me until we are both screaming and laughing. "*You're going to be a published author!*"

"*I'm going to be a published author!*"

My whole body is shaking. I hold my arms out to show Ruth, and she steadies them.

"Roo, I really wasn't expecting that."

"I was," she says with a wide smile. And she means it. *God,* I think, *I am so lucky.*

Less than a minute ago I had accepted that it was a no, but now that it's a yes I already know that everything has changed. What I'm willing to fight for. What I'm willing to accept. This *excitement*. It's like my body can't hold me, like I'm bigger than my bones. I'm on the top of a roller coaster. I'm dancing in the rain. I'm running into the waves.

"Does this make you want to call you-know-who? It's all right if it does. I would understand. He is a writer too."

I catch my breath.

"No. It's the opposite."

Ruth hugs me again. I tell her that I'm going to go to the bathroom to get ready. "But I'll come back and we can have breakfast. Do you want to come into town with me?"

"Yes! Croissants will be ready in five."

IN THE BATHROOM, I look in the mirror and try to process the last two minutes and the last two years. Someone wants to publish my book, my thoughts, my words. *My* words.

I weaved through the crowds and squeezed until I was standing just behind him, close enough to see the white threads in the rip in his jacket.

I put my hands to my cheeks and stretch the skin like clay. There are thin lines around my mouth and larger ones on my forehead; beads of moisture in the pores of my nose and half-moon shadows beneath my eyes.

A rumbling began in the tunnel. The lights of the train became visible. A receipt blew across the tiles.

I have my mother's eyes and my father's face, but the flaws are mine. Soon, the thumbprint on my collarbone will vanish like a leaf or a butterfly.

I thought about every cruel thing he had ever done or said, and yet without thinking, I put my hand on his back and pushed.

This is what it is like

But then she looked up, and he was pulling her with him down the path and across the burning sand to the ocean, the cool waves smacking them with the full force of happiness as their bones broke.

I am thirty years old
crouched in the river with
beach-burned soles and a cigarette breeze
rippling the air like rain like a
cool hand on my forehead and I'm
giddy drunk beneath the corpse stars.
Close your eyes and count to three and
I am the view from your face
I'm trying to make you perfume, Mum.
It's Wednesday
And I am waiting in the dust for you.

"Enola, they're ready! Are you coming?"
"Coming!"

or, at least, what it is like in words.

WE SIT ON THE sofa with tea and croissants, and I am the sort of tired you feel after going on a long walk. I stare at my tea, and in the second that it takes me to contemplate a sip, I miss him, but in the second that it takes me to have the sip, the feeling passes. I know it will be like that for a while, but not forever.

"I forgot, but Mum wants to know if you're coming for Christmas," says Ruth.

"Oh yes, she called me yesterday. And I want to but . . . I had another idea. And it might be a bad one. But would you mind if I missed this Christmas?"

"Why? What were you thinking of doing?"

"I was thinking about . . . France."

Ruth's eyes scan mine. "Enola, I think that's a *great* idea."

"You do?"

"I do."

"It's just a start."

"Do you want me to come with you?"

"I think maybe I should do this on my own?"

Ruth hums. "Like in the bad movies."

We look at each other and almost laugh. Then I break the moment. "Okay, Roo. It's your turn. Tell me about the training day. I want to hear the full story. Leave no stone unturned. No detail left out. Leave no . . . ? No, I can't think of another one."

Ruth tuts. "And you call yourself a *writer*?"

"Stop procrastinating."

"Okay, but are you sure you're ready?"

"I'm ready."

And with the winter sun pouring through the window, together as we've always been, as we will always be, Ruth and I drag the body across the kitchen floor and burn the remains.

ACKNOWLEDGMENTS

THANK YOU, BEYOND WORDS, TO MY AGENT, MILLIE HOSKINS AT United Agents, for lifting *What It's Like in Words* from the slush pile and pioneering it into existence. Thank you to my editor, Micaela Carr, for believing in the book, for gifting it with your intelligence, humor, and passion, and for making my first experience of a new industry a warm and wonderful one. Thank you to Hannah Campbell and the entire team at Henry Holt for turning these words into a book, to Emily Mahar for the perfect cover design and Young Park for the beautiful artwork that speaks to the soul of the story. Thank you to the team at Curtis Brown Creative, and to my tutor Suzannah for showing me that this was possible. Thank you to my writing group, and especially Kath for her incisive speed-reads. Thank you to my early readers and to those that offered—in particular Rose, whose early guidance helped me to find my voice. Thank you to the "*Madhouse* Theatre Book Club," who gathered in the bowels of the West End and gave me the push I needed to query. Thank you to Kim and her family for lending Enola your beautiful home. For me, this book starts and ends with friendship, and I want to thank my friends. There are too many of you to name, but you know who you are: those who understand me, inspire me, support me, commiserate and celebrate with me, listen to my inexcusably long voice notes; those I have toured with, rehearsed and performed with, and laughed with. You are all in the bones of this book. Thank you to my cat, Lord Nelson, the dual-wielding threat of Camberwell and

Peckham, for providing constant challenges to my concentration; every book needs a nemesis. Thank you to Paulette and Odvar for being the best parents-in-law that anyone could wish for. Thank you to Leah, my alpha-reader, my friend; writing is a solitary activity and having you as my partner in this adventure has made it less lonely and more fun. Thank you to my sisters for reading early drafts, offering invaluable advice, and being my best cheerleaders, always. Thank you to my parents for Christmases and Easters, for a childhood abroad, for family dinners and family holidays, and for your unwavering support. And finally, thank you to my husband, Derek, who claims not to know how I like my tea, but who loves me for exactly who I am.

ABOUT THE AUTHOR

Eliza Moss is the pseudonym of Sarah Moss, a London-based actor and singer. She double majored at the University of Manchester, graduating with First-Class honors in English literature, and studied method acting at the Lee Strasberg Theatre & Film Institute in New York. In 2021 she completed the Curtis Brown Creative three-month novel-writing course. *What It's Like in Words* is her first novel.